TWIN FLAMES

RACHEL HENKE

DEDICATION

This book is for all the courageous souls caught in the eye of the Twin Flame storm.

CHAPTER 1

"*According to Greek mythology, humans were originally created with four arms, four legs and a head with two faces. Fearing their power, Zeus split them into two separate parts, condemning them to spend their lives in search of their other halves.*" *Plato*

York, present day

Cara Bailey arrived at the entrance of *The Olde York Bookstore*, her favourite antiquarian bookshop in York. The shop, situated in an elegant Georgian building, meandered across three floors. It could do with a new coat of paint, yet despite the peeling exterior, the shop emitted a welcoming glow.

Cara stepped inside, out of the bright morning sunshine and the chime of a ceremonious bell announced her arrival.

'Hello Cara,' called the proprietor with a big smile.

There weren't many traditional bookshops around

anymore, and she'd been a loyal customer since her student days. Cara had come to collect a copy of a rare textbook she'd ordered for her latest project.

'Good morning John. How are you?'

'Very well, thank you. I believe we have something for you.'

'Yes. That's right. I'll have a wander upstairs first.'

'Right you are.'

'It's such a treasure trove in here; there'll be something I can't resist.'

She turned towards the spiral staircase and scanned the glossy shelves looking for something special to jump out at her. There was typically at least one book in the history section she was compelled to buy, and she fancied a new historical novel too. Cara took care not to confuse fact with fiction in her work because the lines could so easily blur. There was always an intriguing thread to follow; a detail or an idea she'd not come across before. Widely recognised as a pre-eminent authority on the Tudor period, Cara loved her job.

A quiet contentment washed over her, and she exhaled slowly, enjoying the moment. If there was such a thing as a happy place, this bookshop was hers. She had poignant childhood memories of trailing from bookcase to bookcase, after her father.

It was unusual to meet anyone in the history section at this time of day. She spotted a dark-haired man in the far corner who was engrossed in a book. She didn't give him any further thought; he appeared lost in his own world.

Cara studied the shelves. A glossy gold and rich burgundy tome on the top shelf caught her eye. She stretched on tiptoe to try to extract it. It was no good. Her height wasn't suffi-cient to hook the edge of the book with her fingertips. She scanned the area and noticed a thick wooden stepladder, which she dragged across the carpet. Cara rushed up the steps, and her fingers touched the book as the toe of her shoe snagged the hem of her skirt. Losing her balance, she cried out. Unable to regain her footing, she tumbled off the steps. She landed in a heap on the thick red pile carpet and banged her head on the bottom of the stepladder. Cara lay still, temporarily oblivious to her fate.

A moment passed before she opened her eyes to see the dark-haired man hovering over her.

'What happened?' she said, as she searched his face.

She pulled herself up on to her elbows and winced at the sharp pain which pumped through her skull.

'I don't know. One minute you were on the ladder, and the next, boom—I heard you cry out and saw you lose your footing, but I couldn't make it over in time to catch you. Are you okay? You hit the ground with such a thump. You gave me quite a fright,' he said.

Lines of concern creased the delicate skin around his liquid brown eyes, and for no apparent reason, Cara's heart lurched. Why was his face familiar?

Although fuzzy-headed, she experienced a flash of recognition, as if she knew him. She'd known something similar before, but only with places, not people. Perhaps she was concussed.

Then came a whooshing sound; at first soft, but gradually building into a piercing crescendo. It was an eerie high-pitched noise which haunted her ears. The man's face grew hazy and then disappeared. The floor tilted, she had a sensation of falling and reached out to try and grab something.

Was it an earthquake? She dismissed the notion. She tried to steady herself and clutched at a pillar as books fell off the shelves all around her.

What the. . .

She stared into a misty vortex as chilled air strangled her throat. She coughed and gasped for breath.

And then she was gone.

Newgate Prison, London, 1536

Cara saw two candles glowing on a wooden chest in the corner of the dingy room. She was surprised to find herself sitting on a hard, cold floor. Her last memory was of bookshelves collapsing and a handsome face. She stared about her in dismay.

A grubby, angry, short man with unkempt grey hair, called out in a rasping voice, 'Now, now ladies and gents, keep the noise down, please. We've had quite enough rabbiting for one day. We'll see what his majesty's service has planned for you tomorrow shall we, on your day in court? You'd better get yourselves a good night's sleep because it might be your last before your necks meet the noose.'

His sinister laugh echoed around the freezing cell as the door slammed and his keys jangled in the lock. Cara shivered and ran her hands up her bare arms in an attempt to warm her chilled skin.

Her eyes adjusted to the meagre light and she was surprised to find the man from the bookshop sitting alongside her on the floor. Her hand lay casually across his thigh. It was an intimate gesture, and he seemed at ease as if it was the most normal arrangement. The disconcerting thing was that it felt normal to her too.

'Don't worry my darling wife. We'll figure this out. It's simply an unfortunate misunderstanding. At least the children will be fine at Willow Manor with my parents, and they won't know any different.'

I'm in prison. Wife, children, Willow Manor!

He turned and pulled her slim body into his and stroked her tangled hair. Her eyelids grew heavy, and a wave of exhaustion hit her as she slumped against his shoulder and took solace in his embrace.

George savoured the comforting tickle of his wife's breath on his neck as she dozed. He didn't want to move for fear of disturbing her. They'd been apart for too long; he'd yearned to have her close and had been terrified he would never see her again after the recent tumultuous days at King Henry's court.

Unlike most marriages between nobles, theirs was a love match. Cara had been Anne Boleyn's favourite lady-in-waiting right up until the end. How could they have known the threat of the executioner would be the outcome of Cara's royal appointment to the queen? And even if they had known when Cara received the summons to join George at court, they had no choice but to obey the royal edict.

George grew weary and lost track of time; it could have been five or forty minutes later. He removed his jacket, taking care not to wake Cara. She stirred as he folded the material into a makeshift pillow and eased her head down on to it so she could sleep undisturbed. He had work to do, and he wanted her to gather her strength. She had endured a terrible few days, not knowing what had become of him after he was arrested. He must find a way to get them out of here before the trial tomorrow. They were accused of treason and Cara faced an additional charge of witchcraft. If they went before Henry VIII's court, the odds would be stacked against them, and they would have little chance of escaping the hangman.

George wouldn't permit anything to happen to Cara. What would become of their boy, Thomas, and their daughter, May, if they were both executed? Besides, he'd rather die than lose her. Life would be unbearable without Cara in his world.

Failure was not an option. He must find a way to save his family, and he must act now, or it would be too late.

'May I serve you, my lord?' asked an impish looking lad emerging from the shadows. He was scrawny, but George guessed he must be at least nine years of age. He had wise eyes which belied his years.

George was startled. 'How do you know who I am?'

'My eldest brother is in your service in York, sir: he's a stable boy. Never seen him so content. He sings your praises. He said you run a fine household and treat your servants fair.'

The boy doffed his cap and inclined his head towards him.

Possible plans flitted about George's tired brain, but options were limited with the trial due to take place early tomorrow morning.

'That's very kind of you. I may need your help. What's your name boy?'

'Everyone calls me Swifty on account of my being so quick.'

'I see,' said George, smiling at the boy and instantly liking him.

He sensed he could trust him.

'I can help you to escape, my lord. I've been locked in here before and escaped through the secret cellar. The night guard is a drunk and sleeps like the dead once he's down. I'm planning to make a run for it tonight.'

'If you truly can help us to escape before the trial, we'll take you with us, and you will be well rewarded for your efforts. Now tell me, how on earth do we get out of this hellhole?'

Swifty held up one grubby finger and pressed it tightly

against his lips, urging George to be quiet. He turned and beckoned George to follow him and then darted towards the other side of the long, dimly lit cell.

'Here, my lord, do you see over there?' the boy pointed to the bottom section of the filthy wall. 'If it's the same as last time I was in the clink, we can squeeze through. It's stinky and dangerous though, my lord. I don't know if my lady will be able to get down there. It ain't no place for a lady.'

'Don't worry about that. She's no ordinary lady. Show me exactly what you mean.'

They knelt next to the wall, and George saw what the boy meant. He could hear a gurgle below and the stench accosted his nostrils as he lowered his head. It was a long shot, but he believed they could squeeze through the narrow opening and enter the putrid underworld of Newgate. From there, Swifty assured him, they would be able to make a dash for it before daylight.

'There's something I haven't told you though, my lord.'

'Oh dear, I thought it sounded too simple. What may that be then?'

'Others have tried to escape this way and been ambushed by prison guards as they came out. It all depends who's on duty at the exit.'

George ran his hand through his hair and shot a rueful look at the boy. 'We take the risk of being slaughtered by crossbow or being hauled before the court with a high probability of facing the hangman by dusk tomorrow. I fancy our chances against the crossbow.'

George and Swifty huddled in the corner and began planning the details of their escape from Newgate Prison.

Cara appeared, rubbing her eyes. 'What's going on?' she said.

York, present day

Cara opened her eyes and realised she was back in the book-shop. She didn't understand what had just happened. One thing was for sure; the prison had seemed so real that she could still smell the damp cell. The vision must have been caused by blacking out. She tried to recall the details, but they were fading fast.

Get a grip, Cara.

She gawped at the man who towered above her.

Confusion engulfed her normally rational mind as their eyes locked. A jolt ran through her like a current of electricity.

'I'm George Cavendish.'

She accepted his outstretched hand, and he helped her up. Cara's heart pounded, and she feared he must surely hear it.

'May I get you something? Let me see if I can bring you a glass of water. Perhaps you're dehydrated; it's a hot morning.'

He dashed off before she could reply. Cara stared after him and patted her messy hair.

I must look a right state.

She stood in the same spot, feeling awkward, uncertain what to do. She contemplated dashing downstairs, but it would be rude to leave without saying thank you, and she would probably bump into him on the way out, anyway. A few minutes later, he reappeared, smiling as he walked towards her.

As she sipped the water, she attempted to come up with something sensible to say.

'I wish I'd been able to catch you,' he said, 'I just missed you as you toppled off the stepladder.'

'Oh no, really, it was all my fault. I was clumsy.'

Her cheeks flushed, and she shuffled from one foot to the other.

'How's your head?'

He seemed truly concerned and in no hurry to leave.

'It's fine. I must get going. Thanks for the water. I'm so sorry for the inconvenience.'

Cara was reluctant to tear herself away, but she couldn't think of a good reason to stay. She tried to not stare at him, but she was mesmerised. A force beyond her had taken over her senses, and she was compelled to be near him.

'Oh, yes, of course. Are you sure your head's okay? May I call someone for you, or drop you home? I could get my car.'

His smile caused her heart to flutter.

'No really, thank you, I'm absolutely fine. I was only out for a second. I can drive home, no problem.'

Cara looked towards the stairs, torn between making a quick exit and an ominous foreboding that she might never see him again.

'Well, it was lovely to meet you,' he said, looking into her eyes.

She stared back at him: neither of them broke eye contact.

'How about I take your number? That way, I can check in to make sure you're okay. It's the least I can do if you won't let me drive you home.'

His charm was irresistible. She rummaged through her handbag for a business card but couldn't find one, so she scribbled her number on to the back of a crumpled receipt and passed it to him. As he held out his hand, their fingers brushed. His skin was smooth and warm. Cara's hand tingled, and a fierce sensation surged through her. She had trouble breathing and maintaining an appearance of normalcy. Her lips moved in an unsuccessful attempt at a smile, she croaked a quick goodbye, rushed towards the stairs and then turned to give him a quick wave.

To her relief, the proprietor was nowhere in sight, and she spotted her textbook on the counter. An assistant took her payment and didn't try to engage her in conversation other than a brief, perfunctory exchange.

Smooth Cara, smooth.

She made her way along the cobbled street towards the car park. She couldn't have handled herself with less grace.

Oh well, what's done is done.

She pulled a face as she turned the key in the ignition and joined the lane of heavy traffic moving in the direction of her cottage in the suburbs of York.

She drove straight home; she'd suffered enough turmoil for one day and had lost her enthusiasm to go to the office and tackle her project. Her head was still spinning from the encounter with the enigmatic man in the bookshop. She needed some time alone to make sense of events.

Still reeling, Cara pushed the cottage door open, relieved to be home. How could an ordinary visit to the bookshop have such a monumental effect? Nothing much had happened. She'd banged her head, briefly lost consciousness, and then met Mr Hottie. What was the big deal? The thought that her life had been turned upside down and would never be the same again flashed through her mind.

She sipped her tea and tapped her nails rhythmically on the pale china cup. Physically she was present at the oak table in her favourite room; a cosy kitchen in the old Tudor cottage. Mentally she was miles away. Anxious thoughts collided into one another and jostled for her attention. Cara's brain yearned for a logical explanation for the morning's events so that she could move on. It seemed like nonsense, but she knew in her bones she'd experienced something pivotal. She flipped open her laptop and typed 'love at first sight' into the search engine. A long thread of results appeared. She clicked on one at random and scanned the article.

"Love at first sight is a rare experience of instantly recognising someone on a soul level. You feel as though you already know this person, even though you've never met them before in this lifetime. It's a feeling of Deja-vu: like coming home."

Cara scrolled down, trying to make sense of the words. Irritated and tired, she pushed her cup across the table.

Dr Cara Bailey PhD, award-winning Tudor expert, researching love at first sight. Whatever next?

The phone rang and interrupted her reverie. She recounted a severely edited version of the morning to her fiancée, Daniel, carefully avoiding any mention of George. Daniel would think she'd lost her mind if she told him what had happened.

'Are you sure you're ok, darling? I don't like the sound of you blacking out. How about I give Doctor Fitzgerald a call to see if he can fit you in for a quick check-up this afternoon?'

'No, really. Thank you. I'm absolutely fine. I was probably dehydrated. I'll stay at home and take it easy for the rest of the day.'

'Well, if you're certain. I know better than to try to push you, so I'll give you a call later to check-in. Promise you'll call me if you need anything or you feel unwell. I'm worried about you.'

The phone rang again almost immediately. It was an unknown number.

'Cara? This is George, from the bookshop,' she heard the warmth in his voice.

'Oh, hello. How are you?'

'You've been on my mind, the way you blacked out like

that. I couldn't stop thinking about you. . .' His words trailed off.

Cara melted. There was something magnetic about their connection.

After a moment, she replied, 'I'm fine. Thank you. I don't know what came over me. I'm sorry for causing such a fuss.'

'I'm so relieved to hear you're feeling better.'

'It's thoughtful of you to call to check up on me.'

'Perhaps we'll bump into each other again in the city without such dramatic consequences,' said George.

'Yes, that would be nice.' Cara paused but couldn't think of anything to say to prolong the conversation.

'Bye for now then.'

'Bye, Cara. It was lovely meeting you.'

Violent feelings of loss flooded through her and snatched at her breath.

She stood for a moment, as she clutched her phone, surprised at the intense emotions that gripped her.

Cara didn't move for several minutes. Then she rose abruptly, shook her head and resolved to put George out of her mind. Hoping for a good night's sleep, she muted her phone and went upstairs to bed.

At three in the morning, she awoke. Her heart beat fast and a sob caught in her throat. Her nightshirt clung to her sweat-drenched body. It had been an awful dream; as vivid as the vision in the bookshop. She was with George. Again. This time he'd been arrested. In the dream, she had looked on as one of the soldiers charged him with treason, by order of King Henry VIII.

Who is he, and what are these terrifying visions?

One thought crashed into the next until her head throbbed.

Cara walked into the kitchen and poured herself a glass of water. Her hand shook. She plucked a fresh t-shirt from a pile of neatly folded clothes in the airing cupboard and threw the drenched one into the wicker laundry basket. Her pale face stared back at her in the mirror; she looked as if she'd seen Anne Boleyn herself.

She sank down on to her bed and within moments, sleep mercifully transported her far away.

CHAPTER 2

Y ork, present day

Daniel Wetmore, Cara's fiancée, booked a table for two at
The Royal Oak on Goodramgate. Like much of York, The
Royal Oak could have been transported back to the fifteenth
century and wouldn't look out of place. They ate in one of
the quaint dining rooms towards the back of the pub.

Daniel's law firm had opened an office in York ten years
earlier, and he'd relocated from Manchester. He liked York
but didn't share Cara's devotion to the city. For Daniel, Cara
was the main attraction, and although he hadn't mentioned
his plan to her yet, he intended to persuade her to move to
Manchester. He knew he would face an uphill struggle to
prise her away from her beloved York but was counting on
her understanding his desire to be near his children.

Oh shit!

Cara thought she glimpsed George through the alcove.

Hold on; was it really him, or was she imagining it? She couldn't be sure. But yes, there he was, near the bar. He was animated, and his hands cut through the air in bold strokes as he talked. She couldn't see who was with him. Here he was, twice in three days. How odd.

Cara's first thought was to pretend she hadn't seen him. He may not spot her through the alcove; their table was tucked away from the main dining area. After all, it would be less awkward. Nothing had happened between them, but she felt irrationally guilty as if they were somehow intimate. But then again, they were intimate in her visions. Five hundred years ago, they were married, with two children. This was no schoolgirl crush. He was her husband! It was too much to take in. Cara avoided looking in his direction, trying to give Daniel her full attention but she struggled to register his words. She sank lower into the chair, praying George wouldn't spot her.

A few minutes later, unable to resist, she shot a glance at the alcove. He was staring intently at her, a bemused look on his face. As he caught her eye, he smiled and waved before disappearing from view. She waited, like a mouse snagged in a trap, mouth dry, senses reeling.

George bounded into the small dining area, and their eyes met. An instant rush of happiness flooded through her, and she hoped it didn't show on her face.

'Hello, Cara, what a coincidence to see you again.' He stood over their table, smiling, looking down at her.

Daniel, who was still explaining the intricacies of his somewhat dull day in court, toyed with his large glass of brandy. He looked up in surprise, unable to hide his irritation at the unexpected intrusion.

'Daniel, this is George. George was kind enough to assist me the other day when I fell off the stepladder at the bookshop.'

Cara attempted a casual tone, but her chest beat faster than a tap dancer's shoes. George stared at her quizzically as a light blush stung her cheeks. She turned her attention back to Daniel, tearing her eyes away from George.

'George, this is Daniel.' Then she added, 'My fiancée,' almost as an afterthought.

George raised his eyebrow, smiled and offered his hand to Daniel.

Daniel arranged his thin lips into a lukewarm response and shook George's hand. The introduction lacked enthusiasm on both sides.

'Great to see you, George. How strange we should run into each other again so soon,' said Cara.

They exchanged a few more words before George made his excuses and left.

Cara's favourite cheesecake tasted bland, and Daniel's conversation flew over her head. Her eyes kept returning to the alcove in search of George, but she knew he had gone.

It was as if he'd never been there. She was hollow. What was usually a pleasant evening with her fiancée, was suddenly pointless. Would she ever see George again? The thought slipped into her mind as she tried to act normal.

Nothing would ever be the same. At that moment, she knew it was over for her and Daniel. It was only a question of when—the sudden realisation terrified her.

Daniel paid the bill and pulled out Cara's chair as they prepared to leave.

'He seemed like an interesting chap. You didn't mention anything about meeting him.'

A slight frown furrowed his brow as he spoke.

'We only met for a couple of minutes.'

They wandered outside into the cool night air.

'How about you stay at mine tonight? It's been ages,' said Daniel.

Cara couldn't muster the enthusiasm; she craved being alone and quashed Daniel's suggestion.

'I'm exhausted. I slept badly last night; the fall must have unsettled me. I have a morning meeting so I'd prefer to sleep at home and get an early one. You know I sleep best at my place.'

'How about some company?'

'That's very sweet of you, but I wouldn't be any fun tonight with this thumping headache. My eyes feel as though they're about to shut any minute. I can't wait to go to sleep.'

Cara laughed in an attempt to lighten the rejection. It was unkind, but she couldn't face a night with Daniel amongst the jumbled chaos circulating in her mind.

She needed to be alone.

Cara had met Daniel when she'd attended a court hearing five years earlier, and he had pursued her. The initial friendship had grown into a steady relationship, championed by Daniel. Cara had been hesitant to get involved after a bad break-up, but Daniel was determined. He sent flowers every day. He wooed her with gifts and took her on a romantic trip to Paris. Cara was flattered by the attention, and she began to spend more time with him.

He was determined to marry her, but she was resistant and tried to keep things casual for as long as possible.

She was deeply fond of Daniel in a quiet, steady fashion, but she had no passionate urge to become his wife, and so was in no rush to reach the altar. They hadn't yet set a date for the wedding. She'd agreed to marry him only because she didn't want to lose what they had, and she had run out of acceptable reasons to delay. He was a difficult man to say no to. It was a good match on paper; they got on well and had similar values.

Daniel had three grown children from his previous marriage which suited Cara perfectly, although she wasn't sure why. All she knew was that she lacked the motivation to have children which featured so prevalently in many of her female friends' lives.

Daniel was successful, solid and set in his ways. He knew what he wanted, and he wanted Cara. Sometimes she suspected he viewed her as another sensible purchase, much like his investment portfolio. It didn't trouble her. She appreciated him and was settled into their predictable life together. Until now.

The following morning her phone rang.

'Hello?' Cara intuitively knew it was George.

'This is Cara.'

She pretended she had no idea who was calling. Her pulse raced, but you'd never have guessed from her tone. She was determined to be smoother in her exchange with him this time.

'Hi. It's George. It was quite the surprise to see you last night.'

'Yes, it was.'

'It seems we're destined to keep bumping into one other. I was meaning to give you another quick call to see how you're doing, after, what shall we call it: the bookshop blackout?'

He was delightful. She loved the rich, deep timbre of his voice. She found him incredibly sexy.

'I'm embarrassed just at the thought. I still can't believe I actually blacked out.'

George cleared his throat, 'I was wondering whether you might fancy joining me for a spot of lunch today. I'm intrigued to hear more about your work. I thought that perhaps we might collaborate as there's a definite synergy with what we do.'

A smile spread across Cara's wide mouth. Then Daniel's stern expression popped into her mind as she contemplated this dangerous but compelling invitation. She should decline; going out to lunch with a man to whom she was deeply attracted didn't seem like a sensible move. Daniel had already been frosty about their previous meeting. There was no need to poke the bear and complicate matters.

'I'd love to. What time and where shall we meet?' The words rushed out before she could moderate them. The pull was irresistible. She was drawn to him. She couldn't shake the mysterious visions of them together in another time and place. She must find out more about him, then and now.

'How about The Star Inn on the river, as it's such a beautiful day?' said George.

'Sounds perfect. I've not been there for years, but I remember it well.'

He said he would make reservations for a table overlooking the river and they agreed to meet outside.

Oh lord, I'm in trouble.

At the office, Cara oscillated between apprehension and excitement at the prospect of having lunch with him in a few hours. Anticipation bubbled within her, and she couldn't concentrate.

The traffic was heavy, and her car hummed slowly through the narrow streets towards the river. She tapped her fingers on the leather steering wheel and looked at the crowds of tourists, chatting and taking photos. Her stomach had knitted itself into tight knots.

Cara pulled into the car park, a couple of minutes after one o'clock. She approached the restaurant. There he was, standing to one side of the entrance looking at his phone. He wore smart beige trousers and a crisp white shirt which set off his dark eyes perfectly. He looked up, smiling.

'Sorry I'm a bit late,' she said. 'The traffic was awful. The tourist season has officially begun.'

'No problem,' he leaned towards her and planted a quick

kiss on her warm cheek. He was freshly shaved and smelled divine. She wondered which aftershave he used.

'They don't make reservations for the terrace so we'll have to take our chances,' he beckoned her to go ahead as they entered the air-conditioned restaurant and joined the queue to be seated.

The warm afternoon sun bathed them in a comforting glow as they settled on the pretty, flowered terrace, near the historic Lendal Bridge. A canal boat was moored below, rocking gently to the rhythm of the river.

Cara scanned the menu. She was far too nervous to eat. She ordered a salad and a bottle of sparkling water.

'Is that all you're having? I'm absolutely ravenous.'

He ordered cod and chips.

'I'm a vegetarian,' she said.

'Goodness, how thoughtless of me. I didn't think to ask.'

'No problem. I only want something light, anyway.'

'Do you fancy a glass of wine?' he said.

I fancy you.

She said, 'Um… are you having one?'

'Yes. I'll have a glass of chardonnay. Will you join me?'

'Thank you, that sounds perfect. I'm driving, so only a small one please.'

A few minutes later they sipped the chilled wine and Cara experienced a shot of adrenalin. She assessed George, her smoky grey eyes discreetly appraising his face as he selected a piece of wholegrain bread from the basket.

The dishes arrived, and Cara noticed George's beautiful hands. She was beginning to suspect everything about him was beautiful.

Lunch passed in a blur. They laughed at the slightest little remark, and there was no awkwardness between them as was so often the case with new acquaintances. Cara glanced at the clock and was shocked to see it was already half-past two. It was as though they'd only just sat down. She felt at ease in his company; almost as if they ate lunch together like this every day. She could tell instinctively it was the same for him. There was a warmth between them which needed no words.

Her mind flashed back to the prison scene. Perhaps this wasn't the first time they had eaten together.

'How did you come to be in the manuscript business?' she asked, between mouthfuls of salad.

'The business has been in the family in one form or another, dating all the way back to Tudor times when it was established by order of King Henry VIII.'

'It must be wonderful to have such a fascinating lineage,' she said.

'My ancestor, also called George Oliver Cavendish, was special advisor to the king. He and his team would track down and restore important manuscripts for the government's political and religious initiatives. We still have a particularly impressive manuscript from that period on display here in our York workshop. The Queen honoured us with a visit not long ago.'

'How fabulous. I'd like to see it one day.'

'Yes, of course, come over to the workshop anytime. I'm proud of my family's heritage as you can probably tell.'

George beamed, and Cara saw he had a dimple. How had she not noticed it before? She tried not to stare.

'That's lovely. It's rare to find someone who is truly passionate about their work. I love my work too. I can't imagine being in a world without history and books. How dull life would be.'

Their eyes locked for what seemed minutes but was no more than a couple of seconds. A tangible current passed between them. Cara's phone rang from the depths of her handbag, and the trance was severed.

Daniel's name flashed up on her phone screen.

'I don't know where the time's gone. Do you need to get that?' he said, his eyes probed hers.

'No, it's okay. It's not urgent.'

Cara shoved her phone back into her handbag. She wouldn't tell Daniel she was having lunch with George; partly because she didn't understand what was going on, and partly because she was certain he would disapprove. And she wouldn't blame him. No, best keep it to herself.

She didn't want to miss a minute with George. This marvellous serendipity would be over soon enough, and she'd return to her busy yet rather mundane social life.

'I'm off to Seville next week. I'm speaking at a conference,' she said.

'Really? What a coincidence! We have an office there, and I have a house in the city. It's an amazing place.'

'I've travelled to Spain a lot but have only been to Seville a couple of times. I'd love to see more of the city if I get a chance. You know how it is with these events; you end up travelling all over the world and only see the inside of hotel conference rooms.'

He knew exactly how it was. They discovered they had much in common through their work and had travelled to many of the same important cultural centres on the trail of historical research.

'Isn't it odd that we've never run into each other before?' said Cara.

'Yes, it's strange, especially since we seem to know many of the same people.'

The conversation took a more personal turn, and Cara told him how her father had rescued her from a children's home, and later adopted her.

'What an incredible twist of fate. To think, you would have had an entirely different life but for the events of that one day. I sometimes wonder where I'd be now if I'd made different choices. I have a daughter. She can be a bit of a handful, like most teenagers, I suppose. But she's quite wonderful. My wife assures me she'll calm down soon enough.'

George's innocent account of an everyday exchange with his wife twisted her gut. She felt as though she'd been knifed. His fingers were bare: he wore no wedding ring. She'd just assumed he was single.

Why did I think that? Because in my visions he's married to me!

It was all wrong that he was married to someone else.

Cara took a slice of bread from the basket and poured too much olive oil on to it. The excess dripped off the surface and splashed on to the table.

George grabbed a napkin and mopped up the mess.

She hoped he wouldn't notice her gutted expression. She knew she wore her feelings on her face.

'We were married in our early twenties,' he continued, seemingly unaware of the effect his revelations were having on her.

'Our parents were, in fact, still are close friends. They planned our marriage really. We were just kids. Joanna was my first proper girlfriend. It all happened so fast. We thought we knew it all back then.'

Cara tried to look nonchalant.

What the hell!

Why hadn't she considered the possibility he was married?

Well, you're engaged, she berated herself.

It didn't stop her having intense feelings for George. She didn't want to volunteer any information about Daniel, but George asked how long they'd been engaged and she felt obliged to reply. She thought she saw a shadow cross his face but couldn't be sure. Perhaps he was only interested in her in a professional capacity; he was married after all. It was immediately obvious they could collaborate to enhance their careers. They enjoyed each other's company, and it seemed as though they would work harmoniously together. But Cara couldn't shake the visions of them in another life. She briefly considered mentioning it to him but dismissed the notion. He'd think her insane. She glanced at the clock again. It was almost three. George noticed and signalled for the bill.

He touched her arm as they exited the restaurant. Her mouth was dry. She struggled to swallow.

'Thanks so much for a lovely lunch,' she said, trying to sound casual.

George escorted her to the door of her black SUV.

They stood together for a moment in the car park, neither knowing what to say but enjoying their proximity.

Cara forced herself to move away, and she slid into her car.

George closed the door after her and then poked his tousled head through the window. She was joyful in his presence. There was something about him that made her feel alive. The discovery that he was married hadn't dimmed her desire.

Don't be a fool, Cara.

'May I call you?' He sounded vulnerable.

Cara's breath caught in her throat and before she could stop herself, her tongue betrayed reason, 'Yes, absolutely. I'd love that.'

George leaned in to kiss her on the cheek for the second time in a few hours. The closeness of him and the touch of his lips on her skin sparked a primal yearning in her, which she hadn't experienced in years. She didn't want to say goodbye and suspected he didn't either, but maybe she was imagining it. He would need to get back to work. He would need to get back to his wife and daughter.

He slipped his business card into her hand, and she saw the Seville office address in thick gold lettering. She pulled out of the car park after a final wave and smile in his direction.

Cara felt as though she'd boarded a runaway train and was hanging on to the sides in a desperate attempt to stay standing.

CHAPTER 3

Y ork, present day

It had been ten years since Cara attended a hen party when the girls organised a surprise Tarot reading. When the others were hesitant, Cara volunteered to go first.

Several minutes in, Sylvia, the psychic, said, 'I see a deep bond of intense love followed by great turmoil. You share a karmic connection with a man who is yet to appear in your life. You have known him before.'

The psychic continued with her unsettling revelations as she reshuffled the card deck and instructed Cara to tell her when to stop.

'You'd have been burned at the stake just a few hundred years ago, my love,' she said as she looked into Cara's almond-shaped eyes.

'You have a rare time-related gift. It may be some years before it reveals itself.'

Cara had been relieved the girls were preoccupied, chatting and drinking. No one else heard the bizarre reading.

An icy chill crawled over Cara's skin at the memory. Were the predictions coming true? Were the visions something to do with what the psychic had called the time-related gift?

She had wanted to ask questions, but the reading was supposed to be light entertainment, and at the end, the others had gathered around. Cara was too self-conscious to continue and hurriedly thanked Sylvia before someone else took her place.

She had considered booking an appointment to find out more but had later dismissed it as a load of nonsense.

That was before George. Everything had flipped on its head since that day in the bookshop.

Soon after the psychic reading, ten years ago, James had come into her life, and turmoil had followed an intense love affair. Now she marvelled how she had once believed him to be the great love of her life. Anyway, that chapter of her life was over. Cara vowed she wouldn't go through any more heartache. She had been crushed when James had turned up at her cottage one day and ended it. Just like that. He said they were too young to be tied down. That was six years ago.

James moved to Australia and the last she'd heard; he had married. The memory of the rejection still carried a slight sting, but her feelings had dimmed to the point where she couldn't recall loving him. Hearing about his marriage meant nothing to her. It was like hearing news of a stranger.

A couple of years later, when Cara met Daniel, she began to cautiously embrace a personal life. Prior to meeting Daniel, she buried herself in work and had only been on a few stilted dates, mostly to shut her friends up but also to stop herself from becoming a social outcast.

She decided she would never again risk falling in love.

The price was too high. Being out of control in the love department was off-limits for Cara.

And now the red warning flag flapped violently in the wind. She had crossed into the danger zone, and despite her best intentions, she knew she was already in too deep with George to turn back. What was she going to do?

Daniel adored her. Her feelings had taken some time to thaw. She had put her heart on ice after James. It would never be romantic love with Daniel, but she enjoyed his company. The arrangement matched her needs, and he had fitted the bill perfectly. It sounded cold and business-like, but Cara had no intention of lowering her defences again.

The age gap was big: twenty years. But it worked in his favour because his maturity made her feel safe. Daniel had already lived a full life, and he didn't need much from her. All he asked was for some of her time, which until meeting George, had been easy enough to give.

Cara was grateful that Daniel was a dedicated professional who didn't interfere with her day to day activities. She wouldn't have been able to get along with him if he got in the way of her busy career.

They each had their own offices and homes, and secretly Cara still wondered why they must marry at all, but Daniel was traditional, and ultimately, he wanted her as his wife. When she agreed to the engagement, it had seemed a small concession for the price of a secure and settled life.

As an adopted child, she had painful memories of her early years. Cara valued Daniel's solid dependability. There were no surprises. So far with Daniel, she had received exactly what she had signed up for. And she appreciated that. Her work was the love of her life. She didn't need anything more. The relationship had served them well; they both got nearly everything they wanted.

She sensed, given the opportunity, Daniel would have

liked them to have a sexual relationship, but he seemed to accept she wasn't attracted to him in that way. She was grateful he didn't press or probe.

Their relationship was functional rather than passionate. There was no chemistry between them, but there was mutual respect and friendship. This was his concession, and he made it without complaint.

When they were about to get engaged, he had asked whether she was certain that what they shared would be enough for her. She was a woman in her prime; he expressed concern that her needs would grow. He worried she would change her mind about wanting children.

She delicately dissolved his concerns and assured him that she loved things just as they were. Daniel was relieved and said no more on the subject.

After James, she'd shut down that part of herself and wasn't willing to open Pandora's box. Cara was sexually charged, but she had made a conscious decision to curb her sensual nature, and it had been firmly under control, until now. Until George.

The morning after the hen night, Cara put the strange revelations down to an excess of white wine and high spirits. Psychics loved to create drama. It didn't mean what she said was true.

Now, shaking her head to break the spell, she called her friend, Alice, for a quick catch up and asked if she remembered the name of the psychic. Fortunately, she did. Cara called Sylvia's number, and after a brief enquiry, she booked a reading for that afternoon. Her stomach churned at the thought, and she reflected on her impulsive behaviour. It wasn't like her at all, but she felt a strong urge to talk to Sylvia.

You fool. You know damn well what prompted this urge.

Yes, well, fool or not, I need to talk to someone about these visions, or I'm going to lose my mind.

She headed to her office to prepare for the Seville trip before the appointment with Sylvia. It wasn't long until her attention wandered and she found herself holding George's business card, fighting an irresistible desire to call him. She shook her head and called her father instead.

'Hi, Cari. How are you, my darling?'

'I'm good Dad, thanks. I just wanted to see how you're doing.'

His voice dropped an octave, and she heard his concern. 'Is everything okay? You don't sound like your usual bubbly self.'

How did he know? I only said a few words.

She reassured him all was well and didn't mention her fall or the appointment with the psychic. He would worry, and there was no point giving him something else to worry about, all alone in that big, rambling house. Since he sold his blue-chip company and retired, he had a lot of time on his hands. Her adoptive father was a kind-hearted man, but she doubted he would understand what she was going through now.

He was relieved she had settled down with Daniel although he had initially been disappointed to hear she was marrying a man so much her senior. He wanted grandchildren. Cara was his only child, and she would inherit his fortune. He had been Cara's anchor ever since he'd rescued her from the children's home. She called him as often as she could, just for a chat and to hear his voice.

She loved her father and had never known another parent. She tried to not think about what would have become of her in that dismal children's home if he hadn't shown up that day. She doubted the other kids were as fortunate.

Thanks to her father, Cara had enjoyed a stable upbringing; albeit not traditional with a mother, father and siblings, but she had grown up with an abundant source of love and support.

Several hours later, nerves clawed at her empty stomach as she took a seat outside Sylvia's office. She'd pictured a dark and dingy setting with a crystal ball, but the waiting area was clean, bright and modern. An exquisitely dressed, professional-looking woman with designer sunglasses perched on her head emerged from the office. Perhaps coming here for guidance wasn't crazy.

Breathe Cara, breathe.

The psychic ushered Cara in with a charming smile. Cara took a seat opposite Sylvia, on a shabby chic green chair and pasted a smile on to her face.

'How can I help you, my dear?' asked Sylvia. She had cat-like, all-knowing eyes; the bright green pupils were flecked with threads of vibrant gold.

'Thanks for seeing me at such short notice. I met you years ago at a hen party, and you predicted some pretty fantastic things. I have to admit I promptly put them out of my mind. Until recently...'

'I see. Well, why don't you tell me what's going on and let's see how I can help.'

'I met someone, and everything's become dreadfully confusing,' said Cara.

'Ah, yes. That can happen,' Sylvia nodded and waited for Cara to continue, her green eyes curious.

Cara had planned to not share much detail; she wanted to see what Sylvia sensed, without feeding her clues. Cara was sceptical but felt desperate to understand what was going on between her and George.

'I'd love to know what you see in the cards for me.'

Sylvia shuffled the decks. 'Tell me when to stop.'

Cara waited. One card jumped out, mid-shuffle. She took it as her cue and called, 'Stop.'

'Let's begin with the wild card as it so obviously wanted to be read.' said Sylvia.

Cara's heart pounded, her throat was tight.

'Your career forecast is smooth, but there's major turbulence ahead in your personal life. You're going to be required to carve out time to allow love in. You need to balance the professional and personal because there's a lot of passion coming your way this year. I see that you invest most of your energy into your career. Your soul won't permit this one-dimensional living anymore; it's going to make sure it attracts your attention. This man is the beginning of a new chapter for you.'

'I'd like to know more about this mysterious man. What else do you see?' said Cara.

Sylvia turned the next card over on to the glossy wooden surface of the desk. It was from the Tarot deck.

'The death card,' Cara gasped.

Sylvia reached across and touched her arm. 'Don't worry; it's not as bad as it looks. In this spread, the death card indicates the end of your old life. I see it clearly. The high walls of your strategically constructed life are now tumbling down. This is a good thing. You've been fulfilling a tiny percentage of your potential. It could mean the end of another relationship to make way for this new man. Is there a long-term partner in your life?'

'Yes,' replied Cara.

'This new man is more significant in your life than any other,' Sylvia continued.

They went through more cards, and Sylvia saw a time-related gift, with no prompt or reminder.

'This is interesting.'

'What is?' said Cara. She was on the edge of the chair

now, legs jammed against the desk. Such was the suspense; she didn't notice her physical discomfort.

'You have the ability to see into the past and future. I'm not sure how this will play out for you. It's truly fascinating.' she continued.

'I don't know what to make of it,' said Cara. 'It all seems so farfetched.'

Sylvia flipped another card over. 'Ah. Now it makes sense! This is the Twin Flames' card from the Angel deck.'

'What does it mean?' Cara admired the beauty of the artwork; two lovers mirrored one another.

'It's not often I see this card in readings because it's rare to have your Twin Flame counterpart on earth. Most Twin Flames operate purely as spirit guides to assist their other half in navigating their journey with a soul mate. A soul mate is someone from the same soul group, unlike a Twin Flame who is 'the one,' said Sylvia, looking up to meet Cara's eyes.

Cara stared back at her, trying to take it all in.

'What are the man's name and his date of birth?'

'His name is George, George Cavendish. Um...I don't know his date of birth.' Cara was self-conscious. The irony of having a reading about a man whose date of birth she didn't know, now seemed ridiculous.

'George is indeed your Twin Flame,' said Sylvia, her eyes clamped shut. 'You've been together before, and it's time for you to reunite. You have lived many lives together, and your destiny now calls you into action. Do you know anything about Twin Flames?'

'No, I've never heard the term before,' said Cara.

'They incarnate together for their final life cycle on earth. By this time their karma has been balanced, and they are in the final stages of awakening. 'Ascension' is what the mystics call this journey.

She continued to stare at Sylvia, not knowing what to say.

'This is challenging, but you and George are called to do great things. There's no need to be afraid. Only souls who have volunteered for the Twin Flame experience are given this opportunity. The good news is that you are both fully equipped for the mission. Spirit never puts anything in front of us, which we're not able to handle. This is your life purpose.'

Sylvia had slipped into a trance, and her speech was now staccato-like.

'There will be heartache, misunderstanding and obstacles before you are fully united. This is the nature of the Twin Flame journey. It's the most intense experience of love. You are being called to love yourselves, as well as each other, unconditionally. It's typically the most testing piece. It requires a complete stripping away of ego for you both. There will be a rollercoaster of love and hate before you both understand you are one half of the same soul. You complete one another.'

Cara stared at Sylvia as waves of fear engulfed her. None of this made any sense, and yet, she heard the truth in the words.

Sylvia continued, 'There's no escaping this connection: you are bound to one another for eternity. The connection is so intense that one or both of the twins may run. It can feel unbearably vulnerable, and they fear the consequences of being together. It's a karmic dance; they run and return to each other repeatedly before understanding they are only running from themselves. Twin Flames mirror their counterpart's behaviour in different ways so one may accuse the other of doing something which in fact they do themselves. All that's ever going on is a rising up of old wounds and insecurities from relationships in past and present lives. It's an expunging of ego, a burning down of the old way. To come together fully, you must both reach the point of accepting your connection is inevitable. No amount of resisting or controlling your feelings can dissolve the bond. It's a waste of time and energy, but most go through this cycle before they accept it.'

'It's incredible.' said Cara.

'I'm telling you all of this to save you pain, but it's a lot to grasp, and you must find your own way to navigate.'

'I don't know what to say. I only met George the other day!'

'And it feels as though you've known each other forever.' said Sylvia.

She wasn't wrong. Cara tapped her nails on the desk.

'Have you any questions?' asked Sylvia.

'Yes. How is this Twin Flame thing different from other relationships?'

'This bond is unbreakable. I'm on my own Twin Flame journey. My husband and I are now at peace and no longer battle and spin in the old cycle. We had to overcome our own demons before we were able to live together in harmony. We each had emotional scars and baggage to release before we were free. No matter what you do to escape the cycle, the love doesn't diminish. The Twin Flame dynamic is chameleon-like. You think you've understood and then it changes again because it pushes you to your outer limits of self-realisation. Unlike other relationships where you over-come heartbreak, lose interest and move on, the Twin Flame connection cannot be extinguished. You are irresistibly drawn to one another. Forever.'

Sylvia asked to see Cara's hand. Cara placed it gently in hers and waited. Sylvia's eyes narrowed as she examined Cara's palm. 'Your lifeline is fragmented, which is highly irregular, it's as if you are simultaneously living more than one life. I've only ever seen something similar when I was a young girl under apprenticeship. A woman came to see my teacher and claimed to have the gift of time travel. She had the ability to live in different timelines.'

Cara's mouth dropped open.

A time traveller? Now that's taking all of this a little too far...

Sylvia released her hand and restored the cards to a neat pile. 'We're at the end of our session today.'

'Oh yes, of course,' said Cara, glancing at the clock on the wall. She couldn't believe an hour had passed.

'If you still want to know more, I suggest booking in for another session in a week or two. It's a lot to take in. That will give events time to unfold and allow you to gain insight into what you've learned today. In the meantime, I suggest you try to stay calm. Surrender to what is. Trust that you will be guided through this stormy period. Take it one step at a time and follow your intuition.'

'Okay. Thank you,' said Cara.

'Goodbye, my dear. Take care. I'm here if you need me.'

Cara left the office.

What now?

CHAPTER 4

Y ork, present day

Cara headed back to her office, barely registering where she was going. She couldn't get her head around Sylvia's prediction. Could it be possible she had glimpsed her past life, and she was some kind of time traveller?

This is crazy shit!

The idea seemed incomprehensible, but what other explanation was there for her vivid flashbacks and the Deja-vu she kept experiencing around George?

She was compelled to solve the puzzle and couldn't concentrate on anything else. George's gold embossed business card rested in her hand, and she pondered the situation. She yearned to see him again. The more she tried to evict him from her thoughts, the more he featured in the starring role. His dark eyes floated like a mirage before her.

She gulped the remnants of her coffee, grabbed her jacket

and dashed out of the office, shouting to her assistant as she ran towards the door, 'I'll be back later if anyone needs me.'

Cara set out in the direction of George's workshop. She knew the area. The Shambles was in the medieval centre of York, near the old market, about twenty minutes on foot. Her high heeled sandals pinched her feet as she ran, then walked, then ran. She didn't notice the discomfort because she was too busy turning over in her mind what to say when she arrived at his workshop.

I was passing by and wondered whether George is around?

She shook her head, irritably.

No. That sounded contrived and wouldn't do.

How about:

George invited me to see the Tudor Kings' manuscript and said I could pop in anytime. Is he around by any chance?

The more Cara rehearsed what to say, the more nervous she grew. She decided to take her chances. She was only making herself more uptight. Her heart did a fast canter as she played out the potential scenarios.

It was likely he wouldn't be there anyway. Wasn't it?

She was behaving like a naive young girl going on her first date. But she couldn't help it; she was at the mercy of a tidal wave of emotion.

It would have been better to call and arrange a time with him. This was a bad idea; maybe she should give it a miss.

Despite her doubts, curiosity outweighed her foggy thinking and spurred her on across the rambling, cobbled streets.

Cara cut through one of the famous snickleways and arrived in The Shambles. A few steps along the old Tudor style street and number twenty stood before her. She took a deep breath and pushed the shiny, black door inwards. Before she could compose herself, George's face appeared in the doorway.

She gulped. 'Oh, hello. I hope you don't mind. I came to see the Manuscript. At the conference in Seville, I'll be leading a break-out session about Tudor politics and the impact of Henry VIII, so I thought it would be helpful to study the manuscript before I go.'

Cara's words gushed out in a torrent, before drying up, as her eyes rose slowly to meet his. She did her best to appear cool and to hide her embarrassment.

Stop talking, Cara.

Damn, it was a challenge to be cool. He undid her with his eyes.

His face lit up. She released a measured sigh of relief. It was obvious he was delighted to see her. Perhaps dashing over impulsively hadn't been a huge mistake.

Smiling, he took her hand and drew her through the foyer and into a smart-looking visitor's area which looked as though it was once the front room of the old Tudor residence.

Gold framed portraits of British monarchs adorned the walls and a giant oak bookcase lined one wall, from the bottom all the way up to the thick wooden beamed ceiling. Cara stared about her in awe.

'What a fabulous room,' she said. It was regal yet comfortable. There was a sense of continuity and stability. History enveloped her, and the effect was calming on her skittish soul.

'This is a wonderful surprise! How lovely you came over. It's lucky I'm still here. I was just about to leave for the market. Another couple of minutes and I'd have been gone,' he said.

'Is it a terribly busy time? I could come back.'

'No, not at all. It wasn't anything urgent; I can take care of it later.'

He was still holding her hand as if it was completely

natural. His grasp was warm and firm on Cara's smooth skin.

She drew her hand away, even though she loved the feel of it nestling in his. He didn't seem concerned someone would see them.

Her face was slightly flushed. She'd never experienced such a tangle of emotions over someone she barely knew.

'Would you like tea or coffee?'

Cara was grateful to latch on to normality in an attempt to regain her composure. George bounded over towards an espresso machine in the corner and beckoned for her to follow. She watched him prepare a latte for her and an espresso for himself. His hands were large and beautiful; like those of a sculptor or painter. An artist's hands. She was mesmerised as she watched him perform the coffee ritual with precise movements.

Sipping her coffee a few minutes later, she stared into his dark eyes, drinking him up. He was even more attractive than she remembered, not classically good looking, but striking; with a roman nose and full lips. She was amazed once again to notice he had such an impact on her just by his proximity.

It was his presence which left her reeling each time they met. His face was like that of a dear, beloved friend but paradoxically also exotic and alluring. Her skin tingled at the thought of his large, beautiful hands moving over her body.

'Cara?'

She blinked.

'Sorry, yes I was miles away! It's been a hectic morning at the office. The coffee is excellent by the way. Thanks so much. I keep meaning to buy one of these machines,' she garbled.

George guided her through to the back of the building to

a neat, spacious workshop. They stopped before an impressive gold-rimmed display cabinet.

'This is the home of the Tudor Kings' Manuscript. Let's put some gloves on, and I'll pull it out for you to examine more closely.'

He extracted two packets of plastic gloves from a tiny drawer built into the maple wood counter.

In spite of the butterflies catapulting around her stomach, she was thrilled at the prospect of seeing the five-hundred-year-old manuscript.

George carefully removed the manuscript from the cabinet and lay it across the worktop. A cloud of dust shimmered in the air above them, and Cara sneezed. The sudden, loud noise seemed to spur them into a buzz of professional chit chat.

'Look at the handwriting. It's a work of art all of its own,' said George.

Cara leaned in towards his shoulder and peered at the manuscript. His masculine smell rushed at her senses. She tried to centre herself and to pay attention to his words.

What she suspected may have once been rich black lettering was now engraved onto the dull yellow parchment in muted, brown tones.

'It's a beauty,' she said, her eyes widened in wonder, and her dark eyelashes fluttered against her pale cheeks.

George stared at her face before tearing his gaze away to focus on the Tudor work of art.

'It's a collector's item; last time we had it valued it was estimated at £200,000.'

'Wow. I hope you've got insurance,' giggled Cara, hoping he couldn't tell how nervous she was.

As they pored over the parchment, their heads lightly touched, and their appreciation of both the manuscript and each other was tangible. A wonderful warm feeling enveloped them. It was the same feeling they'd shared at lunch.

Cara was bewitched by his eloquence and intrigued by their mutual fascination with the Tudor period.

They dragged out their time together, talking about every possible aspect of the manuscript they could each think of until George reluctantly popped it back into the cabinet and turned towards her.

'What are your plans for the rest of the day?'

'I have to get back to the office shortly to prepare my presentation for the conference. I shouldn't really have taken the time out to come here as I've got so much to do, but I wanted to see the manuscript,' said Cara.

And I had to see you again.

A stray lock of rich, auburn hair escaped her barrette and obscured one eye as she spoke. She moved to brush it aside, but George got their first, his fingers tucked the hair behind one of her ears. The gesture was assured: as if he'd done it a thousand times before.

She paused and smiled up at him. 'I'm glad I did come though,' she said, a note of shyness in her voice. Cara looked away, desperately searching for something to say to alleviate the tension.

Before she could come up with anything, George moved towards her; his hand caressed her cheek, he lowered his head and then his lips brushed hers. He gently pulled her into his arms as the kiss grew more urgent, and their bodies moulded into one. The sandalwood notes of his aftershave washed over her again, and she was consumed by lust.

They stood locked together, gently swaying. For the first time, Cara understood what people meant by the expression, 'Made for one another.'

And then just as suddenly as they'd been drawn together,

she snapped out of the trance, extracted herself from his arms and drew away.

'Sorry, this was a terrible mistake. I must go.' She turned and stumbled slightly as she dashed across the room, bolting for the door.

'Cara, wait,' said George, his voice low.

'No, I can't. I must go. I shouldn't have come. I'm sorry for the misunderstanding. This is all wrong. I'm engaged. You're married. This is too complicated. We can't do this.'

George thumped his hand down on the counter as he heard the shiny black door swing closed, and she disappeared from his life. Again.

Is that it?

He'd never felt so desolate. There was a throbbing ache in his chest. He leaned against the wall in an effort to steady himself and catch his breath.

What the hell was going on?

Seville, present day

The following afternoon Cara's flight touched down in Seville. She waited to deplane and sent a quick text to Daniel to let him know she'd landed. He worried about her; in some ways, he treated her like one of his children. She was hoping the text would buy her some time without needing to speak to him. Cara had been in a state of turmoil since she'd kissed George the previous day. She felt guilty and confused. Some time away on her own seemed like a perfect opportunity to clear her head and think things through. She exhaled deeply and made a conscious effort to relax; without success.

Seville was a stunning, vibrant city and ordinarily she'd be bubbling with excitement. Now she was conflicted. She couldn't stop thinking about George, and a sense of foreboding gripped the pit of her stomach. Every time his face popped into her mind, she couldn't think clearly.

Cara flagged a taxi, and the car sped through the busy streets towards her hotel on the edge of the old town. As the receptionist checked her in, she heard the familiar ping of a text. It was probably Daniel. She went up in the elevator to find her room. It was bright and spacious with vibrant coloured rugs strewn across the varnished wooden floor. The last rays of afternoon sunshine bathed the room in a soft glow, and she caught a glimpse of the Cathedral's spire from the balcony. She would wander over there once she'd unpacked her case and had a much-needed cup of tea.

Cara flopped on to the king-size bed and enjoyed the brief respite. She hadn't slept well in ages, but last night she'd found it impossible. Even when she slept, she wasn't fully relaxed and kept waking up. Her thoughts flitted from George to Daniel and back again, leaving her drained. She'd finally managed to drift off into a deep sleep but awoke feeling anxious again, just after seven o'clock. The phone rang. She eased her weary frame off the bed and scrabbled about in her bag.

It was George. She stared at his name on the screen, but couldn't rally her spirits to answer. She didn't know what to say after the kiss and run of the previous day. The phone continued to ring. It was loud and seemed to go on forever.

Finally, the noise ceased, and she saw there were two texts: an earlier one from Daniel and a recent one from George.

Two minutes later George called again. He was insistent; she would give him that. She felt unkind, not answering. And the pull was too intense. She pressed the button and just like that he was back in her world.

'Hello? Cara. It's George.'

'Yes, I know,' she said with a smile in her voice. 'This is starting to become a habit. . .so I added your number.'

'Oh, I like that. It seems only wise.'

She heard his deep, melodic laugh, and despite her intentions to pull away, she knew she was powerless to resist him. She was swept away on the giant wave of loveliness that was George. She couldn't get back to shore even if she wanted. She didn't.

'You won't believe it,' he said.

'Try me,' she said in a low, seductive voice which took her by surprise.

'I will be in Seville soon. This evening, in fact.'

'Really? Wow. You're right; I don't believe it! How come?'

'I'm as amazed as you, but sometimes these things just fall into place. There's some urgent business come up which I must attend to tomorrow. I told you I spend quite a bit of time there.'

'Are you free for dinner this evening by any chance?' said George.

Her heart performed a sharp salsa move.

Here was another opportunity to make a sensible choice.

I should say I already have dinner plans.

She gulped. 'Yes, I am.'

'Do you fancy joining me for a bite to eat in the old town and then we could take a walk to the Cathedral. It's quite marvellous.'

'Yes, I'd love to.'

'Great. I'll pick you up from your hotel at eight o'clock. Will that work?'

Cara nodded in a happy daze.

'Yes,' she whispered, remembering he couldn't see her. 'Yes, perfect,' she said.

They chatted a while longer, their spirits bolstered by the thought of seeing each other again so soon. George made her laugh like no one else. He had a wicked sense of fun. Daniel was a good man, but he took himself so seriously. George made her giggle like a schoolgirl. Being with him was no effort at all, but being without him was becoming increasingly difficult.

Sitting on the roof terrace of the bustling restaurant, Cara couldn't quite believe her luck. Here they were, alone yet together in the romantic city of Seville.

'Paella,' announced the waiter as he ceremoniously placed the hot dishes in the centre of the table.

'Gracias,' said Cara, smiling up at him.

Her naturally healthy appetite would usually take care of the paella, but with George's dark eyes resting upon her from across the table, she was too nervous to eat. She toyed with the rice, moving her fork around the colourful dish and managing only a few mouthfuls. She sipped her wine. It tasted good and hit the spot to dull her nerves.

Their hands brushed as Cara passed George the salt, and a shiver ran through her body. He ate heartily, in-between pausing to regale her with amusing stories of his Sevillian adventures. Cara watched him quickly dispose of the Paella and marvelled at how he was so at ease.

They shared a bottle of white wine and Cara was light-headed after a couple of glasses and not much food.

'Let's go for a walk,' he suggested when their table had been cleared. His hand touched her bare arm as he steered her out of the restaurant. Goose pimples coated her skin. His fingers seared her flesh, and she shivered. She found everything about him erotic.

They admired the majestic Gothic Cathedral and wandered around the old town, chatting and laughing about their travels. Cara stumbled on one of the uneven cobbles.

'Here,' George offered her his arm and smiled.

Cara melted. She slipped her arm through the loop. Da-dum. Da-dum. Her heart began to race. This was torture.

'Hold on tight. Let's not have a repeat of the bookshop blackout. I was terrified! I thought you were committing suicide by stepladder.'

Cara threw her head back and laughed as they conspired in the way only lovers do, talking and giggling as if no one else existed. They meandered through the tiny lanes of the old town until the streets began to clear and the hour grew late. Then in one sudden shift, the atmosphere between them switched from one of light camaraderie to a charged, pregnant silence.

Cara sought to kick-start the flow of banter but could find no words. Her brain was devoid of even one comment to guide them back to safe ground. George remained quiet. He looked sombre.

Conscious that her arm was still looped through his, Cara contemplated removing it. She didn't want to.

She longed to reach out and touch his face. She wanted to move into his arms and kiss him again. A physical throb of desire shook her. But her hands remained locked in place. She couldn't risk it. The fear of rejection was too great.

It's a terrible idea. Don't do it. I shouldn't have agreed to meet him tonight. I knew I would only yearn for him even more.

There was smouldering chemistry between them which was impossible to ignore.

She heard the ping of a text, extracted her arm and retrieved her phone from her bag.

'I have an early pre-conference meeting. I'd better get back to the hotel, or I'll be no good for anything tomorrow.'

The excuse sprang from her lips, but her heart sank as she listened to her own words. She didn't want to leave him. She wanted to hold him all night and be close to him. She wanted to lay in his arms. There was no doubt in her mind that making love with him would be incredible.

It would also be dangerous and irresponsible.

George walked her back to the hotel. The awkward moment passed, and the easy banter resumed. In spite of her disappointment, Cara laughed aloud at his witty observations. She could listen to him all day.

But you can't, can you? It's not an option. Don't be so stupid.

'Have a great conference tomorrow. I'll be in touch to see how it's going. What time are you speaking?' he asked.

Neither of them wanted the delicious evening to end. George leaned over to kiss her and said, 'I'd love for you to see my house. I think you'll adore the stucco architecture. It's only about fifteen minutes by car, and there's a wonderful view of the city. Perhaps we can do that tomorrow if you have time. Would you like that?'

Cara smiled, looked into his dark eyes and nodded. She all but fled towards the hotel and then turned to wave to him before she darted inside. 'Goodnight,' she called. 'Thank you for a wonderful evening.'

George stood, bemused, watching intently as she disappeared through the revolving doors. He was becoming accustomed to her sudden departures. But he didn't like them one bit.

He walked towards his car; hands thrust deep in his pockets, Cara's face in his mind. He wished she was still at his side. How he wanted her.

CHAPTER 5

S eville, present day

Cara propped herself up in the vast bed and leaned against the fluffy pillow. She was grateful for a few quiet moments. It had been a tough night. Sleep hadn't come for hours, and when it finally did, it was fitful and unsatisfying. George was always on her mind even when she was asleep. She ran her hand through her messy hair, checked the bedside table and then patted the other side of the bed. Where had she put her phone? There was a text from Daniel from the previous night.

'Hope you're settled into the hotel. Sleep well, my love. xx'

She replied, 'Good morning. Sorry I missed you. I fell asleep. Running a bit late for conference. I'll be in touch later. xx'

She craved more sleep. Shards of bright light seeped through the blinds making her eyes squint.

What if she and George really were Twin Flames? And stranger still, if possible, what if she really was a time traveller? The psychic's words whirled around her head as she scanned her emails on her phone.

If what Sylvia said was true, it would explain why she and George were repeatedly drawn back to one another.

Could any of this be true?

She rubbed her eyes and stretched. Every muscle ached, but she must get dressed. She pushed herself to get ready for the day, competing thoughts of George, Sylvia and the conference all battling for attention.

After a hasty breakfast of scrambled eggs, toast, orange juice and tea, she rushed downstairs to the conference centre.

The coordinator escorted her to the back of the room, and she was fitted with a microphone and did a quick sound test.

She could really have done without this today. Her head wasn't in the game.

When her turn came, she went through the motions in a slightly robotic fashion. People didn't seem to notice, and it was soon over.

'Thank you,' said Cara, she smiled and left the stage to an enthusiastic blast of applause.

Thank goodness, I'm done.

She'd not been her best, but she'd managed to pull it off.

She signed copies of her new book, *The Rise and Fall of The Tudor Dynasty*, for a line of delegates and then excused herself. Her head ached. She took a few gulps of water and then checked her phone. There was a message from George. Her heart did a little jig.

'Good morning. How did it go?'

She debated whether to resist responding immediately

and to instead focus on the next speaker or to reply and risk being carried away on an inevitable riptide of emotion.

Ten minutes passed, then twenty and then thirty. Each minute seemed like an hour, and Cara wasn't able to concentrate on what was being said. Her fingers twitched with the urge to respond. Finally, her resolve exhausted, she typed a short message to George. It was rude not to reply, she reasoned, and then she put her phone away.

After the dullest hour, they broke for lunch, and she fished her phone out of her bag.

There was one missed call from George. The phone rang almost immediately. 'How are you doing?'

It was him. He didn't give up easily.

'Very well thank you, how are you?'

The sound of his deep voice was all it took. She wanted him.

'I finished my talk.'

'How did it go?'

'I wasn't my best, but it seemed to go alright.'

'How fabulous. I bet they love your book. You're a superstar author now.'

'Um, not quite,' she said, embarrassed.

'What are you up to for the rest of the day?'

'We've just stopped for a two-hour break and then I'm due back for the afternoon session. How's your unexpected business going?'

'I took care of it earlier. Wasn't as complicated as we thought.'

'That's good,' said Cara. Her heart tolled louder than the cathedral bells.

'I wondered if you'd like to come for lunch. Valeria, my fantastic housekeeper, is preparing a huge salad and delicious home-baked bread as we speak, and apple pie to follow.

You'd truly be doing me a great service by joining me, or I'll probably scoff the lot.'

Cara giggled. 'It would be cruel to ignore such an urgent plea for help.'

'Exactly. You mustn't! It's settled then: I'll send my car for you now. I'll ask Alejandro to wait for you at the front of the hotel. Keep your eyes peeled for a black Mercedes and a friendly smile.'

Cara rushed out of the conference room and into the elevator. She reapplied a pale lip gloss with precision and checked her appearance. Not too bad. The earlier weariness had miraculously dissolved, and her eyes sparkled. She looked a little feverish.

It must be lack of sleep.

She smoothed her hands over her skirt. It was creased, but there was no time to change now, which was probably just as well because she had nothing better to wear. She was jittery at the idea of meeting George at his villa, and she had no appetite. Again.

Alejandro steered the black Mercedes up the steep bends of the winding hillside whilst Cara tried to calm herself. It was futile. She was nervous as hell. She was so agitated she began to regret accepting the invitation.

What am I doing? Well, it's too late now.

Her phone rang just as the car turned into a wide regal driveway lined with crème coloured stone pillars which were adorned with a brightly coloured crest.

Goodness. A family crest. What was that all about?

Daniel's name flashed up on the screen, and she hastily put her phone away. She couldn't talk to him now. She'd have to deal with the consequences of her impulsive behaviour later. She was in enough of a spin already.

George stood waiting in the bright entrance hall. The terracotta floor and varnished wooden beams set off to perfection by the white-washed walls.

It was happening again.

I've been here before. I know I have.

She did her best to appear calm.

'Here you are,' he said as he looked into her eyes. 'I'm so pleased you came. Welcome to Casa Cavendish.'

Her heart performed a double backflip at the sight of his mischievous smile. He looked so gorgeous she could eat him up. His lips were shapely; if as in high definition. She imagined tracing them with her tongue. She stared at his mouth and was consumed by desire.

'Have I got something on my face?' asked George, pretending to wipe his mouth, then smiling.

Cara blushed. *Oh God, he knows I'm lusting after him. How embarrassing. I've never been as hot as this for anyone. Not even Ben, my first big crush at university.*

'Hey,' he said, drawing her closer and giving her a quick hug.

'Hey yourself,' said Cara, she feared she might melt in a pool of desire. He smelled gorgeous as usual: today it was an alluring blend of aftershave and soap.

Lunch was served by his housekeeper, Valeria, on the top terrace of the stucco-style, red-roofed villa. They stood shoulder to shoulder, admiring the views of the city from the hilltop, enjoying each other's presence. Valeria left for the day, and they were alone.

George turned to face her, gently traced his finger across her cheekbone as if wiping away a tear and then pulled her to him. His lips brushed hers: gentle at first and then with a growing fever. Cara didn't hesitate. She entwined her fingers in his dark hair and returned his kiss with equal passion. Their tongues probed each other's, and they clung together.

All of the complications vanished; she'd never been clearer. He took her hand and led her along the sunny hallway, up the majestic stone steps to the next floor. The moment had finally come.

What a beautiful room,' said Cara, her hand cocooned inside his, as she admired the white textured walls, Spanish rugs and gleaming dark wooden furniture. Everything about the room was elegant and very George, she decided.

He released her hand as he stretched to close one of the heavy shutters. The light instantly receded. With a couple of steps, he was back at her side, raising her hand to his mouth.

'I'm so pleased you love the villa,' he said, smiling at her as if he couldn't drink in enough of her face.

Cara slid into his welcoming embrace. It was like coming home. For a second, she recalled that she had resolved not to do this, but it was inevitable. They had crossed into new territory. There was no going back now.

Sometimes things which make no logical sense and should feel wrong, feel right.

She tasted his warm lips. The electric current between her and George was unlike any she'd known. The energy between them was heated. He stood about an inch behind her and dropped light kisses on to the back of her neck as he held her hair in one hand and her waist with the other. She felt the dampness between her legs. Every cell of her being longed to join with him. He closed the tantalising gap and pressed his erection against her. They were ready to explode before they'd begun. The prospect of being with him intimately aroused Cara to a feverish state. He turned her around to face him.

He raised her top gently over her head, as though unveiling a precious manuscript. Her skirt was next and fell to the ground with a shimmer. She stepped out of the crumpled material, still wearing her heels, her lightly tanned skin, bare, but for her black silk underwear. She shivered with anticipation; goose pimples covered her skin, and her eyes searched his face seeking reassurance.

'You are even more lovely than I imagined,' he said. 'Come here.'

She helped him pull off his shirt, and he scrambled to remove his trousers. They were both impatient. His masculine hardness pressed against her soft thigh flesh and she ran her hands up his chest, over his biceps and across his wide shoulders. She burned with desire and yearned for the moment he would take her. It was as if he was her: his pleasure would be hers too. She ached to please him. They fell on to the bed, kissing and caressing, stroking and licking as they explored each other's bodies. Then she steered him inside her. His eyes widened as he entered her. They clung to one another as their passion built. He groaned.

'Oooooh,' she said. His reaction turned her on even more. She watched the ecstasy play across his face as her hips moved.

It was as if they'd always been lovers. All shyness and hesitation had vanished. His body fitted into hers like a missing puzzle piece. She could wait no longer. Waves of pleasure ripped through them, gripping them in a rhythmic sway until they simultaneously erupted in a long burst of searing pleasure. They collapsed together, damp skin on damp skin.

It was just as incredible as she had known it would be.

Cara's heart burst with joy as though lit from within like a beacon. She kissed his lips and then his beautiful hands, wishing they could stay locked together like this forever.

If only her time-related gift would allow her to make, time stand still. He held her in his arms until they dozed off, basking in the afterglow of passion.

'Are you hungry? George asked a while later.

'I am. But I don't want this to end. Let's stay like this forever.'

'Um. I have a better idea. And I think you'll like it.'

'What is it?' she said, searching his dark eyes.

He flipped her on to her back and said, 'Let's do it this way now, to be sure we have covered our bases.'

'You're right. I do like it,' she said. 'Food is so overrated.'

And they were lost in each other once more.

'Okay. Now I am starving. Let's go and eat!' he said.

Cara's head rested on his shoulder and her hand on his chest. She was at peace for the first time since the day they'd collided in the bookshop.

She withdrew her hand and sighed. 'Yes, I'm starving too. And I'll need to get back soon. I agreed to be on the panel.'

'Of course, no problem. We'll get you back on time.'

She picked up her skirt and slipped back into it. George's fingers recaptured hers as he led her down the winding staircase and back outside. Dishes of colourful food awaited them on the terrace. 'Want some bread?'

She nodded. 'Ooh, yes, please.'

He popped pieces of Pan Rustico, dipped in olive oil into Cara's mouth.

'Yum,' she said, licking her lips and trying to stop oily crumbs falling on to her top.

He served them both a huge pile of salad and tucked into his as if he hadn't eaten for days.

'Wow. You are hungry,' she said.

He paused mid-fork, smiled, rolled his eyes and then continued eating at the same furious pace. She laughed until tears rolled down her cheeks, and she bent over and clutched her sides.

'What's so funny? What did I do?' said George. He laughed too. Her laughter was contagious.

Surely, I must have been happy like this in the past.

But she couldn't locate a memory to match the elation she felt right now. She loved him.

Her phone rang. She picked it up from the table and looked at the screen. It was Daniel. Damn. She'd forgotten to mute the volume.

Newgate Prison, London, May 1536

'Cara, Cara, wake up darling,' George tapped her shoulder several times.

Finally, she stirred.

'What? What is it? Where are we?' Cara looked around the gloomy cell. Her eyes took a few seconds to focus in the dim light.

Oh shit. We're back in that bloody prison. Only a moment ago we were laughing on the terrace in Seville. What the hell is going on?

Memories of their lovemaking flooded into her mind. She glowed with tenderness as she gazed up at George. If this strange sequence of events wasn't happening to her, she wouldn't believe it. She was somehow living two simultaneous lives. Cara didn't understand how this was happening, but she was certain of one thing. She adored this man. He was her husband here in whatever year it was, but he was somebody else's husband in present day. As scary as being in prison was, she was grateful to be with him in any circumstances. Pictures of them together in the inner sanctum of King Henry VIII and Anne Boleyn flashed through her head.

Poor Queen Anne had been good to her no matter what evil gossip the propagandists had spread in order to precipitate her downfall.

'You're awake!' said George. 'You must have been sleeping deeply. You were miles away.'

He looked as if he hadn't slept for days. His lustrous dark hair was peppered with grey, and his dark eyes were weary and framed by deep grooves. He didn't look as debonair as the George she'd just left behind.

Living in Tudor times is brutal.

She reached up and touched his face as he leaned over her.

'How long have we been in this dreadful place now?' she asked.

'You talk as though you just arrived, my darling. I've been counting the hours. This is my sixth day and your fourth.'

'Oh, my God. What a nightmare,' she said.

It already seems an age since Queen Anne was beheaded, but it's barely a week. I can't believe so much has happened in such a short period. One minute I was on an urgent mission with the king, as one of his most trusted advisers and the next I was arrested for treason. The whole court's gone mad,' said George.

'The days blur one into the other. Why do you think I wasn't arrested at the same time as you?' said Cara.

'I don't know. I've not been able to get any word from the outside from our kinfolk. My guess is the council thought to spare you for the sake of the children but then decided to persecute everyone who was connected to Anne. The new queen's advisors will want to make a clean sweep of anything connected to the old order. It's a tragic business. I overheard the guard saying the royal wedding will be in a few days.'

He clasped her hand in his and pulled her to her feet.

'You'll be happy to know we've hatched a plan to get us out of here,' he whispered.

'What is it? And who is we?' asked Cara.

There's a lad in here called Swifty who's going to help us escape. We can trust him. His brother is a stable boy at Willow Manor.'

'What a wonderful coincidence,' said Cara. 'But how dangerous is it to attempt to escape from here?'

'We have little choice with the way things stand. Everything is dangerous but nothing more so than waiting here for the hangman to claim our necks.'

'Yes, that's true. I'd rather die trying to escape than sit here doing nothing, fearing the worst. I'm so worried they've already taken Thomas and May. If so, they will be terrified.'

'The plan is for us to reach the children before the king's men do, and then we'll find a way to smuggle them out of Willow Manor to safety.'

George signalled for Swifty to join them. Swifty approached. 'Here's the lad now.'

'Hello Swifty,' said Cara.

'Pleased to meet you, my lady,' Swifty nodded his head.

'I'm ready when you two are. Let's go. Another moment in this foul stench is one too many,' said Cara, scrunching up her nose and pulling a face.

Swifty shot a conspiratorial look at George who shrugged his shoulders.

'I'm afraid the stench is going to get considerably worse before it's improved.'

'Why, what do you mean?'

George took Cara by the hand and led her towards the end of the cell next to the wall. The prison was still and silent except for the occasional cough or moan from the inmates; some wouldn't make it through the night in these dismal conditions. It was around three o'clock in the morning, and many of the prisoners were new arrivals, sleeping off the effects of heavy liquor.

The far end of the cell was rarely used; it stank even more than the remainder of the prison, due to its proximity to the hole. In the dim light of a candle, he pointed to the opening, 'We're going to squeeze through the hole and make a run for it through the cellars below. We shouldn't have too far to go before we reach the exit - all going to plan. Swifty will lead the way because he's escaped from Newgate before.'

'Newgate? This is the infamous Newgate?'

'Yes. Of course, this is Newgate. What do you mean? You knew that!'

'Oh, ignore my ramblings. I'm still half asleep,' she said, squeezing his arm. She must be more careful.

Rats scurried around in the dank corners and Cara shuddered at the thought of the foul underworld below, but they had no choice. It was make a run for it or face almost certain death of one or both of them tomorrow. Thomas and May's sweet, innocent faces spurred her on. She wouldn't let them down. She wouldn't let George down. They were in this together.

There was one thought that terrified her more than all others. What would it mean for the future George and Cara who met in the bookshop, in modern-day York, if he was executed now? Would their whole lineage and the five hundred years between the timelines be completely obliterated? She didn't know. But she wasn't going to take any chances. However, she realised that there was little point trying to figure it out when she understood so little.

Swifty performed some speedy chicanery as if he escaped from prison every day. George beckoned for her to follow Swifty as the boy's head disappeared. Cara eased herself down into the narrow black hole, her heart hammering so fast she thought the inmates must hear it on the other side of the prison. But no, all was silent. She dropped into the dark emptiness below, trying to not think about the potential horrors that awaited.

'Here, my lady—take my hand. Let me help you,' whispered Swifty.

The soles of her dainty shoes hit the slimy bottom of the cellar before her ankles were submerged. The sludge coated her skin, and she winced as she tried not to think about what was in the water. She had tied the skirt of her dress into a knot so her movement wouldn't be hampered and to keep it dry. They would need to make their way through the streets of London if they were to have any chance of being on the road to Willow Manor before the guards informed the authorities and the king learned of their escape.

George jumped down after her, and she grabbed his hand to help him to keep his balance as he lowered himself into the dark, slippery waters. Swifty inched back up the wall like a black widow spider to check all was still clear above. He didn't want to alert the guard unnecessarily. If they were fortunate, it could be hours before anyone realised they were gone. They broke into a laboured trot through the secret cellar. The stench accosted Cara's nostrils again and she pinched her nose in an effort to block it out. It was impossible. She gagged. The urge to vomit was intense, but she must keep on moving. Their lives depended upon it.

All the years of studying the Tudors hadn't prepared her for the reality of these dreadful, lung wrenching conditions.

The cellar was long and winding with a network of poorly formed tunnels which made it easy to take a wrong turn. Cara prayed Swifty had a good sense of direction or they would be lost in seconds. They pushed forward as fast as they could for what seemed like hours. Her heart beat fast, and her breathing was shallow. She feared she would faint as the warm stench overpowered her senses. Progress was slow until she glimpsed a crack of light ahead. She was close to retching all of the way. None of them had said a word.

Swifty whispered, 'Now let's go very slow and quiet, so the guards don't hear us or we've ad it.'

Cara let out a strangled gasp as she tripped. George reached out to steady her.

'Are you okay?' He asked.

'Ew. Something ran over my foot. I think it was a bloody rat.'

'Lord, it is intolerable in here. It's so bad it's even got you swearing. Are we nearly at the exit, Swifty?'

They continued on until they reached a light-filled crevice which was partly covered by a piece of wood. They could see the dark brown sludge clearly now. Swifty lifted the wood carefully with George's help and one by one, they squeezed through and crawled out to the street above. They gulped the fresh air into their lungs and caught their breath.

There was one guard, slumped on a chair, fast asleep, to the far side. They were in luck: no one else was in sight. The alleys were deserted, and the half-moon shone yellow in the sky like a glowing chunk of cheese.

'Let's make a run for it and get as far away from here as we possibly can,' whispered George.

Cara removed her now heavy, sodden shoes and clutched them in one hand.

'I wish I could dump these,' she said.

'Hold on to them for now, my love. If we can get you a fresh pair, we will. You can't go all the way to York barefoot.'

'I can't wait to breathe in the fresh York air and see the children's faces.' Cara was desperate to get back to Willow Manor to be reunited with Thomas and May. She was surprised to experience this new maternal instinct. She'd certainly never felt anything like it in her present-day life.

'Hey! Wait there!' boomed an officious voice.

'Let's go,' shouted George and off they sprinted, narrowly missing a barrage of arrows which hit the mud and clay wall near to where their heads had been just a few seconds earlier.

'Which way to York?' whispered Cara.

CHAPTER 6

Hampton Court Palace, 1535

Cara sat on a window seat as she embroidered exquisite jewels on to the border of a rich silk curtain commissioned for the queen's bed-chamber. Anne Boleyn paced back and forth across the parlour like a prowling cat. The restless movement grated on Cara's nerves, but she was careful to maintain a pleasant expression. Miserable faces were not welcome at the palace.

All was not well at court. King Henry VIII was due back later in the day, and Anne had received word from one of her informants that the king was displeased with her and had been seized by another fit of foul temper. Again. What had begun as a fairy tale romance had quickly morphed into a bad dream. All those in the royal couple's inner sanctum suffered. Henry and Anne argued frequently, and the queen was distraught much of the time. She'd lost her influence and was under suspicion no matter how much she tried to appease the king.

Lady Cara Cavendish had become Anne's most favoured lady-in-waiting after being summoned to serve at court, alongside her husband, Lord George Cavendish. George was a long-standing loyal advisor and beloved companion to King Henry. Both Cara and George preferred to be with their children at Willow Manor, the family residence in York. But refusing to serve the king and queen was tantamount to treason. Cara had joined George at the palace two years earlier. Nobles did not get to come and go as they pleased but rather must fit in with the court. Cara was only occasionally given leave of absence to visit dearest little Thomas and May, in York.

Anne quizzed Cara, her black eyes darting from side to side in her pale face. 'When do you think the king will be here?' Cara could see the queen was tormenting herself again.

'I don't know, your grace. By nightfall, I imagine. Is there anything I can do? Should I prepare a tisane? You are fraught; it's not good for your nerves.'

'Before the king left, he was like a bull with a sore head.' The queen sank onto the window seat beside Cara and lowered her voice to a whisper. 'I'm beginning to fear for my life and for the safety of my household. Do I imagine the plotting and the intrigue? It's as if I'm in a living hell. I swear I must be in Dante's Inferno. The king has become impossible to live with since his accident. I can barely look at him without him losing his temper. He is simply irascible.'

Cara had to think quickly. She had sworn to be a loyal confidante to the queen, and she too feared for their positions at court; for their lives. She was also aware that one wrong word overheard by a vengeful pair of ears was as good as signing her own death warrant and that of her family.

'Is your dear husband accompanying the king on this trip? Please do tell me what you've heard. I don't trust Cromwell: he seeks to stir up only trouble between us. He serves his own interests purely,' continued Anne.

'I will enquire for you tomorrow, your grace,' replied Cara. 'I haven't heard anything of import. You know how the servants hesitate to tell us anything which may cast them in a poor light. I've received only a short note from George assuring me he is well and asking after my health and that of the children.'

The queen questioned her no further, and Cara was thankful she'd managed to buy herself a little time to think things through. She would try and have a private word with George upon his return so they could decide on the best course of action. He was a master in matters of diplomacy. He would know what to do.

Anne and Henry's court which had once been renowned around the world as a sensuous delight of feasting and merriment was now as poisonous as a viper's nest. Cara focused on her handiwork, but she was overcome with a dreadful sense of foreboding. The future had never looked so dark. As she sewed, she silently prayed George would return soon with King Henry at his side, in good spirits, and they would all be restored to their former state of contentment.

London, 1536

Cara, George and Swifty ran as fast as they could once they exited Newgate Street. They darted in and out of narrow alleys in an attempt to put as much distance between them and the prison as possible. After about ten minutes, Cara could barely breathe, and she glanced at George to see whether they might rest a moment. He had slowed down, and his steps faltered.

'George, are you okay?' She turned back and retraced her path. She noticed bright red blood pooling on his hand and spilling through his fingers as he clutched at his neck. The blood dripped onto his shirt. 'Oh, my God. You are wounded. Why didn't you say?'

'It's nothing; just a surface graze from one of those damned arrows, although these wounds do bleed like the devil. We must get away from here fast; there's no time for dawdling.'

'But darling, your neck: it looks bad. Let me see.'

Cara touched George's shoulder as she waited for him to lower his head for her to examine the wound. It was a bloody mess, but the gash was small.

'I think you're right. Let's hope it's only a flesh wound. Thank God. Swifty we need water to cleanse Lord Cavendish's neck, or we'll be in trouble. I fear it will become infected.'

The lad looked at her with a puzzled expression. 'Infected?'

Cara clicked her tongue, impatient as she realised she might as well be speaking Chinese.

People drank ale. The water in the Thames was putrid and you'd be liable to get very sick if you drank it.

'What does your mother do when you or your brother cut yourself?'

'She wipes the blood away with a cloth and then wraps it around the wound to stop the bleeding,' said Swifty.

'So, she wouldn't try to clean it?'

Swifty moved his head to one side as if seriously considering this proposition. 'No, she don't do no cleaning,' he said.

If Cara wasn't so worried about George's condition, she'd have laughed at Swifty's befuddled expression. She tore a piece of fabric from the lining of her long skirt. Tying it up had been a good move. The material was clean and dry. This would have to do for a bandage. She had no water or ale.

'Let me tie this around your neck to stem the blood flow. It looks like quite a gash, but I think if we can just stop the flow, it will soon congeal and you should be fine. We can tend to it better when we stop for the night.'

George obediently knelt down on to the dusty ground, bowed his head, and she secured the cloth around his wound with a tidy knot. Girl guiding came in handy in Tudor England.

'You look pale. We'd better try and get some ale and bread to restore your blood sugars. We won't get far if you're weak.'

'Blood sugars? You do come out with some strange things lately.'

'I've been reading some new books from the continent,' she said. 'They are way ahead of us in medicine, you know.'

'I see.'

'Well, I don't know about blood sugars, but we have miles to go along the Great North Road. We're almost at Smithfield now, and from there we can join the road. If we get lucky, we'll be able to ride with someone by carriage, or failing that we'll need a couple of horses.'

'We must disguise ourselves,' said Cara. 'We have a good few hours yet to get a head start but once they summon us for the trial and realise we're gone, no doubt they'll begin searching for us. That's if the guard didn't realise we were escaped prisoners and already sound the alarm.'

'I suspect it's likely he thought we were suspicious characters and took a pot shot at me for the hell of it. We probably look more like common thieves than nobles, after our stint in Newgate,' said George.

'I worry we're very predictable, heading to Willow Manor. I wonder if we might be better to try and get word to your parents and ask someone to bring the children to us rather than going all the way there. As much as I'd love to see home again, we're not going to be able to stay long, and we may only put them all in danger.'

'Yes, good point. We'll put the servants in jeopardy by showing ourselves. The authorities will question them at some point and who knows what trouble will befall them for trying to protect us.'

'What shall we do then?' asked Cara.

'Let's figure it out when we're on the road. I've got an idea, but we'll have to see how quickly we can move and whether anyone's looking for us.'

'Ew,' said Cara.

Rotting corpses were piled in a hideous heap at the edge of the street, and the stench turned her already queasy stomach. Cara slowed down to observe the real-life history lesson. This really was almost too much to take in.

'We must not linger,' said George. 'There has been another onslaught of the sweating sickness. Every second counts, and it's too late for these poor souls. Let's not join them, but instead, make haste.'

Swifty lived up to his name and was ahead of them the entire time.

'We've recruited a good lad,' said George. 'I've got a feeling we're going to be grateful we've brought him along. Here we are. This is the road to York. Let's stay off the highway and run along the hedgerows out of sight of any travellers so as not to attract unnecessary attention. When you spot a horse or carriage, signal me, and we'll spin them a yarn, and endeavour to prevail upon their hospitality.'

They picked up the pace. As the morning sun shone high in the sky, Cara noticed George losing ground again.

'How are you feeling?' she called.

'Let me rest awhile. I'll be fine in a few moments,' he said.

He sat down on the grassy bank away from the road, Cara ran back, but before she could reach him, he keeled over on to his side.

'Swifty, Swifty,' called Cara. 'Pray, come. All is not well with my lord.'

'George, George, wake up. Can you hear me? Please wake up.'

Cara touched his forehead, a sheen of sweat coated his face, and his skin was the colour of clotted crème, not its usual healthy glow.

'Yes, my lady?' said Swifty, running towards them.

'My lord is weak from the neck wound. He's hot and clammy; I fear he's lost consciousness. We need to get him something to eat and drink, and we must get him to York as soon as possible, or he'll die without the hangman. He can't even walk in this state, never mind run.'

'The Black Eagle is over the road. I'll go and see what I can beg there for the master,' said Swifty over his shoulder as he dashed off.

George stirred and attempted to sit up but fell back down again, groaning, hand on head.

'You don't look too good. You need water to drink. You're dehydrated.'

George stared at Cara. 'Drink water? Have you lost your senses, my love? Are you delirious like me? Come and rest here awhile. Don't go drinking water; you'd be better to drink your own piss. We drink wine when we can get it and failing that we partake of ale. I could do with a mug of wine right now; it would revive me somewhat, I'm sure.'

'Swifty has gone to the inn across the way to try and procure some food and drink.'

They didn't have to wait long before he appeared, beckoning for them to make haste. Cara helped George to his feet. They moved as fast as they could and followed Swifty down the embankment into a cluster of oak trees. He held the reins of two gleaming horses, one chestnut and one jet black.

'What the heck?' said George. 'Where did these beauties come from?'

'I borrowed them from the innkeeper's stable yard. We'd better get going before he notices,' said Swifty. He shuffled his feet and didn't meet George's eyes. He looked a little shamefaced, but there was a hint of defiance in his eyes once he raised his pointed chin.

'Stealing is a hanging offence Swifty, but as we were fortunate enough to make your acquaintance in Newgate Prison, I suppose I'd better not judge you too harshly. Well done for your cunning, my lad. You are a loyal and wise servant, indeed.'

'Thank you, my lord.' Swifty looked pleased. 'I know it's wrong, but we're not going to reach York without horses, and I was worried you would die from your wound.'

'That's true enough lad, no need to fret, although I thank you all the same.'

Swifty produced a bottle of ale and a couple of hunks of dry bread from his pockets, which he passed to George and Cara.

'Thank you.' they echoed in unison.

They tore into the bread and downed the ale. 'I don't remember ever being so thirsty,' said Cara, wiping her mouth. The colour has returned to your cheeks, George. Thank goodness. I was worried for your life there for a while.'

George mounted the jet-black horse and Cara jumped up behind him with Swifty's assistance. Swifty rode the chestnut, and they set off at a fast trot down the track.

They would be in with a chance of making it to York if no one from the inn spotted them after they realised the horses had been stolen.

'Stop, thief!' A loud voice shouted.

George dug his legs into the mare's sides.

'Hold on tight,' he said.

The horse lurched forward. She inched closer and moulded her body to George's back. Her long hair flew out behind her in the northern winds like a waving flag. Her heartbeat pummelled against her chest.

Please, God, don't let them catch us.

'Come on, Swifty,' she shouted. 'Let's go. If they catch us now, we are all dead.'

CHAPTER 7

The Great North Road, 1536

Cara, George and Swifty had been on horseback for hours, riding hard and fast through the clammy heat of the afternoon. Cara's body ached, and she longed to stop, but the fear of capture was greater than the ache of her tired muscles.

She had swapped places with Swifty when it became evident he was liable to fall off and break his neck.

'My brother loves horses, but I've never ridden one,' he said. 'I thought it would be easier.'

Cara handled the beautiful chestnut with quiet confidence, surprised that she was so comfortable on a horse. She had no memory of riding, apart from a few obligatory lessons as a child. She was thrilled to find herself quite the seasoned horse rider.

Cara decided she would visit Sylvia, the psychic, again, as soon as she was back in the present. She wanted to find out more about how time travel worked, and Sylvia was the only person who might be able to help.

How do I get home?

She felt a pang of terror at the thought of being stranded indefinitely in 1536. She was accused of treason and witchcraft, under threat of execution by order of King Henry VIII. Was the real purpose of her arrival here, to save George? Or had she fallen prey to an accident in the grand scheme of time, and shouldn't be here at all?

She looked over at George. Either way, she was thankful to be near him, but their lives were at stake. Questions darted about her mind. She didn't know much, but she did know for certain that it was 1536. Queen Anne's death proved it. A chill ran down her spine as she remembered the queen's execution; it was a vivid picture of the dreadful event. She wondered whether she'd ever remember more of her Tudor life. Her memory was so unreliable. It was frustrating.

Cara had prayed with fervour for the king to pardon Anne, right up to the second before the queen's head was severed from her pale neck. Cara and George had wanted to believe that their king would be merciful. At one time, he had desired Anne so deeply he had defied the Pope, to establish a new church in England so they could marry. Alas, it had all been for nothing.

Cara witnessed the sword slice through the air as it moved to enact its bloody deed. She could still see the queen's black eyes. They were shining pools of desperation as she beseeched the king and made her final statement. She was courageous to the end. The only blessing was that dear Anne hadn't suffered the indignity of a brutal axe beheading. King Henry must have pitied her sufficiently to arrange the special execution. She was thankful that her queen had died instantly, not at the hands of a fumbling axe wielder.

By some unorthodox twist of time, Cara now found

herself living in an era which was her foremost area of expertise.

Was this her ultimate destiny?

'Look,' said George, startling her. 'There are wanted posters nailed to the trees.' He rode closer and pulled on the reigns of the jet-black steed so he could read the headline. Poor Swifty almost slid off the horse.

WANTED! EARL AND COUNTESS CAVENDISH. Accused of Treason and Witchcraft. £1000 Reward (Preferred Alive.)

'Oh my God,' said Cara. There were crude sketches of their faces on the dusty posters which bore a mild resemblance to them. 'At least they don't know you're with us, Swifty. They're not after you, so that's something to be grateful for.' Cara reached over and ruffled his hair. She couldn't imagine what hardships he had endured on the streets of London.

'I'm just another boy with no name in Newgate,' Swifty said, displaying remarkable maturity for his years. There was no self-pity in his voice; just clarity about his place in the natural order of things. 'They won't notice I'm gone.'

'When we're through this nightmare, they'll be a place for you at Willow Manor with your brother,' said Cara.

George turned and smiled at his wife. They looked at each other. No words were necessary. He adored her generosity.

Swifty's blue eyes welled up, and tears glistened on his long eyelashes. He wiped his filthy sleeve across his face and cleared his throat.

'Thank you, my lady. You and my lord are the most kind and generous folk. My brother was right when he spoke of you. I would love to be with Bertie again.'

'He'll need to teach you a thing or two about horses.'

George laughed. 'Come on. We'd better get off this road. We're far too visible, and we need to stop and rest awhile.'

They cantered on the grassy track for a few more minutes before Cara guided the chestnut down the bank and on to a narrow track. George and Swifty followed.

Five miles back along the road, King Henry's soldiers rode in vigorous pursuit of the escaped prisoners. They had firm orders to deliver the Earl and Countess to The Tower of London, preferably alive, but dead if necessary. Their escape was an embarrassment to the council, and the king was livid. He had declared that no one must escape from Newgate Prison again.

At the Black Eagle Inn, two men huddled around a table in a dim corner, waiting for their chance to continue their conversation with the busy innkeeper. They drank their ale and waited. They were keen to know more about his stolen horses.

York, present day

Cara opened the front door to her cottage and entered the bright hallway, which immediately raised her spirits. She loved her home. It had been an exhausting day. She dropped her suitcase on to the shiny wooden floor and sighed. The return journey had been difficult because images of Daniel pecked at her conscience at every turn. She caught herself grinning like a love-struck teen when she thought of George, but her happiness was soured by guilt. She had decided she would tell him their engagement was off as soon as she had a chance. There was no real choice: she could fight her feelings, but she was certain she would lose. After what had occurred in Seville, she couldn't keep up the charade any longer. She knew the truth in her soul. The partnership she had talked herself into, was dead. Her relationship with Daniel was built on a bedrock of self-deception. It was no one's fault but her own. She'd been lying to herself all along, and now the bubble had abruptly burst. She was drowning in conflicting emotions.

She had pretended to herself, and to him, that what they had would be enough. She had wanted to believe she could be fulfilled in a life with Daniel because it was the sensible choice. Cara liked order and good sense. Messy, unpredictable emotions made her feel dangerously out of control. She'd lost any illusion of being in control since meeting George.

Being thrown into another time, without any say over when she came or went, was a leveller of epic proportions. She was too preoccupied with her feelings for George to battle anything else. She couldn't now settle for an ordinary relationship. It wasn't fair on any of them.

But that won't make it any easier to tell him.

A heavy mass of emotion clogged in her chest, and the task which lay ahead looked ominous. She pulled her cardigan tighter around her shoulders and went to make tea. She was tired and cold. As she poured the boiling water on to the teabag, she pondered the kindest way to break the news to Daniel. Her stomach churned at the thought of hurting him. He was a good man; this wasn't fair to him at all, but ultimately, staying with him when she didn't love him, would be even worse. He deserved better. He would find somebody more suited once word got out that he was back on the market. She frequently heard women in York complain about the shortage of eligible men. They were apparently all, either married or too screwed up to marry.

Cara wished she could be happy with what she had. It would be so much simpler. From the minute, she'd collided with George in the bookshop, the old life she had so carefully constructed had begun to disintegrate. It was no longer hers to live. There was no going back to the way it was; to the way she had been. There hadn't been an earthquake in York that day, but there had been a monumental shift.

She sat at the wooden table, cradling her mug of tea, pondering how she'd got herself into this crazy mess.

Seville, the previous day

Cara had never felt so close to anyone as she did to George. Alejandro drove her to the conference and waited to take her back to the villa. George had asked if she would stay the night with him. She'd expressed concern about his staff. He had assured her that Valeria had the following day off, and Alejandro was discreet and had been loyal to him for years.

Cara lay in George's arms, prosecco like bubbles of joy fizzed in her belly. They had just made exquisite love again, and she felt emboldened. She trailed her fingers across his chest.

'Have you ever had anything like this happen to you before? I've read stories about couples who've met and fallen instantly in love. One of my friends met a guy in Canada, and they were married within two weeks. It seemed crazy to me at the time, but now I think I get it.' Cara blushed. 'I mean. . .I didn't mean we should get married, obviously,' she trailed off, wishing she hadn't spoken.

He's already married, you fool.

They were married in the Tudor timeline, but that didn't change the reality of their present-day life.

I know what you mean. I've never experienced anything like it before, either.' He stroked her shoulder and dropped a kiss on her collarbone. She shivered. She couldn't get enough of him.

'Apart from the French dancer and the Swedish librarian,' he said.

Her heart missed a beat. 'What?' she said, her voice high pitched and squeaky. Then she saw his smile. 'Ah, you are teasing me.'

They laughed and joked as they nibbled on Spanish delicacies, made more love and then fell into a blissful sleep just after midnight. It was the perfect evening. Cara awoke in the early hours to go to the bathroom and caught sight of her pink cheeks in the mirror. Her skin was flushed from George's stubble, and she glowed from within. She'd not known contentment like this existed.

I'm going to enjoy each moment and not worry about tomorrow.

She returned to the giant bed and nestled into the cocoon of his arms. He stirred and planted a trail of kisses on her neck. The sensation of his naked body touching hers aroused her. His kisses torched her senses like touch-paper. Her lust for him was unquenchable. His lips sought hers with increasing urgency. In seconds, they were tasting and devouring each other's bodies again. He entered her gently from behind, and she gasped with delight. She could feel his urgent desire throbbing as he thrust deeper into her, claiming her as his own. Her passion surged, and once again she lost all inhibitions. They undulated together to their own tempo as shards of dawn splayed through the wooden shutters.

First light cast a golden glow across the white linen sheets and illuminated the sleeping pair as they lay locked together. Cara had fallen into a deep slumber and dreamt of perfect days at Willow Manor with George, Thomas and May.

Seville, that afternoon

George drove Cara to the airport.

'I'm going to tell Daniel I'm calling off the engagement. It's only right,' she said.

George glanced at her and touched her hand. His other hand rested casually on the steering wheel as the powerful vehicle effortlessly hoovered up the miles to the airport. There was a heavy silence as her words hung in the air between them.

'Are you certain you want to do that?' he said, after a while.

His question knocked her off balance. She was suddenly reeling.

Did he not want her to do it? Had she misunderstood his feelings? Ouch.

'Don't worry. I don't expect anything from you. But I can't continue with him after this. It's not fair. You stay as you are if that's what you want.'

'I didn't say that.'

Cara could tell she'd upset him. Would this be their first proper disagreement?

'No, you didn't. You didn't have to.'

'I only asked if you're sure that's what you want. I was thinking about you, not myself.'

'That makes it worse,' she said. 'It sounds as though you don't care, as though it doesn't affect you, at all.'

'Cara, that's not fair. You're jumping to conclusions. Of course, I care.'

Tears welled in her eyes, and she looked away from George, out of the window. She didn't want him to see her cry.

He sighed. 'It's complicated. I can't tell Joanna just like that. I will need to take it slower.'

His words sliced into her heart like sharp blades. Did he really intend to continue on with business as usual, as if Seville hadn't happened? She must have misread him completely. What an idiot. Just because she was in love with him, didn't mean he felt the same.

'Cara look at me.'

'No,' she said. 'I can't. If that's how you feel, then it's all been a huge mistake. I won't get in the way of your perfect marriage. Forgive me for misunderstanding your feelings.'

'You haven't misunderstood my feelings,' he said.

She turned to him, tears spilling out of her eyes even as she willed herself to keep it together.

'What's unfair is you acting as though nothing has happened.'

'I'm not. I'm sorry if that's how it sounded.'

Cara turned away once again. The humiliation was too much to bear. She wondered whether him telling his wife would be as big a shock as he thought. She nibbled her bottom lip.

'Don't worry. I won't mention anything about you to Daniel. It would only complicate matters. Anyway, it's not really the point. Us getting together is a wakeup call. It's not the reason we're not fulfilled with our partners. If we were, we wouldn't keep seeking each other out like this.'

'Yes, but I doubt Daniel would see it that way,' he said.

'Does Joanna have any reason to doubt you?'

'I suppose she does, but not because I've been unfaithful. I haven't. . .until now. But our marriage was never really more than a friendship. Of course, I didn't realise it at first. I thought we were compatible on every level, but as we matured, it became evident we were more suited as friends than lovers. I suppose I believed it was true love because I wanted to.'

'Would she agree?'

'Probably not. She's in love with the idea of being in love. She's a romantic like most women. Our friends think we're the perfect couple and that's important to her.'

'Yes, well, girls are raised on fairy tales and get lost in the fantasy of being saved by the perfect man.'

'True. Although living up to an image of the perfect man isn't much fun. After a while, Joanna was so disinterested in sex; I stopped initiating. I grew tired of the rejection. I don't think we're much different from many couples; we started off with good intentions only to discover the initial attraction rapidly died. We were left poking and prodding the embers in a desperate attempt to reignite the feeble fire.'

'I see,' said Cara. Perhaps she hadn't misunderstood his feelings after all.

'We never experienced the spark you and I share, not even in the early days,' he said, touching her hand and looking into her eyes.

And just like that, the pain dissolved. Once again, Cara was overcome with a deep tenderness for him. They halted at a zebra crossing on the outskirts of the airport complex. His revelation soothed her tortured soul. There was hope. He too felt the depth of their connection.

They kissed goodbye in the car. Cara held him close as if trying to capture a piece of him to sustain her until they would be together again. He squeezed her tight for a couple of seconds before releasing her. She managed to stop herself from tearing up again. They walked to the terminal, hands brushing casually at their sides. The flight was due to leave on schedule, so it was almost time for them to say goodbye.

At the security gate, they hugged; it was a quick modest hug, much like good friends or family members might share. They both kept their emotions in check as if by agreement. They instinctively sensed what the other required. Cara turned to wave and blow him a kiss.

He watched her leave, sadness choking him. And then she was gone; lost in the throng of people rushing to their next destination.

Cara walked through the gate, curious what George would say if she told him about Sylvia's strange predictions. And she couldn't even begin to imagine what he'd make of their Tudor life together five hundred years earlier. He'd probably think her insane, and she wouldn't blame him.

No, I'd better continue to keep it all a secret for now.

CHAPTER 8

York, present day

'Darling, is that you?' called Joanna from upstairs.

George heard his wife's voice as soon as he entered the three-storey townhouse. He'd hoped she wouldn't be home yet and he would have some time alone.

Bloody hell. I'm not ready to face her yet.

'Yes! It's me. I'm home,' he called in as cheerful a tone as he could muster. He closed the door and let his leather travel bag fall to the floor as he bent down to stroke Blue, his beloved Russian Blue cat. 'First thing's first,' he said. 'Have you missed me, my girl?' Blue favoured George above all others; she nuzzled her head against his leg, purring her approval like a finely tuned motor. The cat preened and stretched, before laying down on her side in blissful abandon as her doting master stroked her soft belly. George stood in the kitchen, wondering what the hell he was going to do. He wished he were back in Seville with Cara. He had never felt so lost.

Cara missed George. It had only been an hour since she heard his voice, but it didn't stop her from wanting him. She missed him every minute she wasn't with him. It was a bittersweet longing she'd never before experienced. This must be what Sylvia meant about Twin Flames. She said Twin Flames share the same energy field and are connected even when apart.

'I'm fine, thanks,' said Cara, the next morning when Daniel called. 'I need to talk to you, though. It's important. I've got something to tell you.' Cara clutched her phone.

'You're very mysterious. Will you give me a clue?'

'I'll be there in about thirty minutes. I'll tell you then. You weren't planning to go out, were you?'

'No. Sally's going to pop in later.'

Sally, oh, God. She's the last thing I need today.

'Okay, I'll see you soon,' she said, ending the call.

Cara rushed to get ready. She must be gone before Sally showed up, or it would be intolerable.

It was Saturday. The spider's web of streets was thick with traffic, and the pavements were lined with shoppers as Cara drove across the city to Daniel's house on the river. The house she was supposed to move to when they got married. She was uptight, and couldn't wait any longer to tell him. She pulled into his driveway, and a few seconds later, he opened the front door with a smile and gave her a warm hug. It was a Daniel special; he oozed charm.

He knows it's bad news and is preparing to get his own way.

'It seems ages since I've seen you. I want to hear all about your trip. How was the conference? Come and sit down and tell me all about it. He patted the sofa for her to sit down next to him in his cosy den, where he liked to relax. I'll make some coffee in a minute, oh and I bought your favourite cheesecake too.' Daniel paused. 'You look a little pale. Are you alright?'

'I've got a headache. I think there's thunder in the air.'

'Did I tell you Sally is going to pop over this afternoon? She's been up on business all week and wants to see me before she goes back to Manchester. I was so busy in court this week we didn't have a chance to get together.' The steady wave of Daniel's chatter barely registered amidst her own frantic thoughts.

Daniel was aware that his daughter made little effort to conceal her disapproval of their relationship, but he preferred to ignore it. Cara looked at the clock.

'Yes, you mentioned it on the phone. What time is she coming?'

'I'm not sure. I think it'll be a while yet.'

Daniel and Cara had barely spoken during her time away. She sat down wishing she was anywhere but in this room with her about to be former fiancée.

'The talk seems to have been a success; several key people reached out to make enquiries about hiring me, so that's promising. I think I may have a contract about to come through.'

'Wonderful. And what did you do in the evening? You seemed pretty busy,' Daniel probed as he searched her face. 'I assumed you must be preoccupied with the group because I couldn't catch you on the phone.'

'Yes. I'm sorry I wasn't very responsive. It was all a bit hectic. Daniel. . .

'Yes?'

'I've got something important I need to tell you and. . .I'm sorry, but I don't think you're going to like it. I'm just going to come out and say it.' Cara stuttered a little, a habit which had bothered her as a child, which occasionally resurfaced when she was nervous.

'Let me guess. You want us to move to Seville?' he said with a wry smile.

'No, of course not. Please be serious—this is hard enough as it is.' His attempt to lighten her mood only irritated her.

He picked up her hand, pressed it to his lips and then held it in his. 'Okay, sorry, my love, go ahead. There's nothing you can tell me which we can't handle together.' He paused, 'You're not sick, are you?' He sounded shaken.

'No, I'm fine. It's not that kind of thing. It's, it's—I'm afraid I can't marry you. I'm calling off the engagement. We've rushed into this, and I can't go through with it. I'm sorry, Daniel. The last thing I want to do is hurt you, but there's no other way.' The words spewed out of her mouth.

'What? Why?' he said. And then a few seconds later, 'I see.'

She looked at his stunned expression and saw he didn't see at all. He was trying to piece the puzzle together.

'What happened in Seville? We were fine before you went. I don't see you for a few days, and suddenly you're calling off our engagement! It makes no sense. Calling off our future, as I understand it. Correct?'

He'd become cold and officious with the sudden shock. His tone was formal and clipped; he was now committed to gathering data. If there was one thing he was good at after years in court, it was asking questions and making people squirm. Cara could see he'd slipped into his barrister persona and expected the worst. She chose her words with care. 'I've been having second thoughts for some time. You know I was never keen to get married. It's nothing to do with you; I've never wanted to be married. I thought we were okay as we were, but you were so keen to formalise things. I didn't want to disappoint you.' Sentences tumbled from her lips, but her explanation sounded feeble to her own ears, and she abruptly ceased talking.

'Okay. So, let's not get married then. Let's be together as we were before the engagement. It's not my preference, but I can live with it if that's what you want. Marriage isn't the be-all and end-all. I know you aren't particularly conventional. I've always admired that; actually, it's one of the qualities I love most about you.'

Tears glistened on her lashes as she saw the hurt in his eyes. She put her head in her hands; looking at him was too difficult. She couldn't stay with him any longer, but telling him was excruciating. She wished she was back with George on the road to York. They were married and free to love each other without these complications.

Except for being hunted down for execution!

She pulled herself back to the present with an effort. 'I can't, Daniel.'

'Why not? Why can't you? What's happened? Something has happened, and you're not telling me what's going on. None of this makes any sense.' He was angry, and his words sliced through the air. 'You're not telling me everything. You at least owe me the truth,' he snapped.

He's right. I do owe him the truth, but the truth is too incredible. Well, you see Daniel, I met a man called George who I've been in love with for at least five hundred years, and I don't want to live without him. Um, he wouldn't believe me even if I told him the truth!

Instead, she said, 'I understand why you're angry, and I'm so sorry. It's not something I planned or expected. All I can say is that when I was in Seville, I had time to think about things from a different perspective. I think it's better we make a clean break of it. It's not fair on you for me to stay in the relationship when it's not the way you want it.'

'Please don't decide for me what I want and what's fair on me. What's fair on me is that you don't throw it all away with no logical reason.' His tone was severe. Cara felt reprimanded like a wayward child in the headmaster's office.

She drew a deep breath and calmed herself. 'Sometimes, there isn't a logical reason; not everything can be analysed and proven. It's just a feeling. I can't carry on as we are. I'm being as honest as I can with you even though I knew you'd be angry and you wouldn't like it.'

'Well, thank you very much. Am I supposed to be grateful that you've bothered to drive over here to rip my heart out of my chest? Is that it? You seem to think you're doing me some kind of favour!' He burned with anger and paced about the den from one side to the other. 'Can you really say you don't love me?' He dropped onto his knees in front of her, and he gripped her shoulders as his eyes beseeched hers. His stance softened as she looked back at him. 'Cara, my love. Please don't do this. We're supposed to be getting married next year. You've got cold feet, that's all. Don't turn it into a drama.'

'I'm sorry, Daniel. My mind is made up. It's not going to change. I wish it were different, but that's how I feel. You'll find someone who wants the same things you do; someone who'll be thrilled to marry you. Perhaps you'll marry someone from Manchester, so you can move near your kids again. You've tried to hide it, but I know that's what you want. It's what you deserve, and I can't give you that. York will always be my home.'

He sank onto the sofa with a sigh. The anger had left him, and he looked crumpled. Cara's heart expanded, and she reached out to him. 'I'm sorry Daniel. I'm grateful for the wonderful times we've had but staying together isn't the right thing for us. I know that now. You'll see it too once you get over the shock.' She released him and rose from the sofa.

'Please forgive me. I never meant to hurt you. It's the last thing I ever wanted to do.' She picked up her handbag and headed for the front door.

'Cara. Wait.'

She stopped and turned, 'Yes?'

He ran his fingers through his usually immaculate silver hair, it was dishevelled, and his eyes looked haunted, 'Is there someone else?'

Cara hesitated for a second, her chest tight. She struggled to breathe. She opened the door, looked at Daniel whose face was drained of colour, tried to say something meaningful, but all that came out was, 'I'm sorry.'

She slipped out of the door and into her car. An intense sadness gripped her, and she let herself sob for several minutes, her head resting on the steering wheel, before wiping her eyes with a tissue and turning the key in the ignition. Once on her way, a flood of relief swept over her as the car moved to the gentle rhythm of the road.

I told him. Thank goodness, it's done now.

It was as if the lid had been removed from a pressure cooker. All the build-up of steam was released. She was sad but free.

Back at the cottage, Cara sat in the kitchen for a while, doing nothing but staring out of the window at the dark clouds in the grey sky. Then she got her phone out of her bag and typed a message to George:

'Hi. I told Daniel. I feel awful, but it's done. How are you?'

A reply came within a few minutes:

'Doing alright. Tired. I hope you're okay. Will try and call later. x'

At ten o'clock that night she'd had no further word from George. She climbed into her big empty bed, pulled the soft cotton sheet up to her chin and drifted off into a deep sleep. It was after midnight when she awoke. There was still nothing from George, and she grew more anxious. She managed to sleep again, waking shortly after seven in the morning to the bright light streaming through the blinds. She checked her phone. Still nothing. Her heart throbbed. What was the point? This was all too painful.

There was a message from Daniel, 'Can't sleep. I need to see you. Did you really mean it?'

Cara felt fragile and small.

What am I doing? I've broken Daniel's heart for a man who can't even call me once he gets home.

And then a memory of them together at Willow Manor flooded her consciousness. It was as vivid as watching a movie at the cinema. Because of the frequent memories she'd been experiencing since meeting George, she knew they'd enjoyed wonderful years together before they were summoned to court in 1534 and lost their independence to the Crown. Now she saw a dashing young George; he must have been in his late twenties, holding her close as they swayed to the music. He whispered in her ear in the beautiful library, which was their favourite room at Willow Manor. A sharp longing to be back in his arms in those joyous days filled her. She was his wife then, not bloody Joanna.

Panic stirred in her chest as she rose from the bed and entered the bathroom. Then she heard the unmistakeable whooshing sound like in the bookshop when she travelled to her incarceration in the notorious Newgate Prison. Chilled air filled her lungs in time to realise she was about to time travel again.

Oh no! I don't want to go after all! I want to stay here and figure things out with George, not be on the run again.

She could remember their prison escape clearly, and the reality of fleeing to York in 1536 suddenly didn't seem as attractive as it had earlier. She tried to focus on staying in her bathroom, but she feared this mysterious force. She knew instinctively that she couldn't prevent herself from slipping away. And she possessed no recollection of when or how she had returned to the present day.

Do I flit back and forth between the timelines or are there two of me; Dr Cara Bailey and Countess Cara Cavendish, who are always present? Am I experiencing two different lives simultaneously?

She suspected this might be the truth of her bizarre situation but couldn't be sure.

I need to find a way back to Sylvia.

And then she was gone. She had no say in when she travelled.

Outskirts of York, 1536

Cara sat at a table with George in a sumptuous parlour. Red velvet curtains trimmed with gold silk covered the windows, and the walls were lined with solid oak panels adorned with tapestries. The light was dim, and the room smelled of musk and alcohol. Shapely, exotic looking women served drinks, swinging their hips and pouting at the drunken men.

Looks like I'm back! Where the heck are we now? I think I may be the only woman customer here.

She inched closer to George on the wooden bench and touched his upper arm to get his attention. He turned to her and smiled, glass of wine in hand, and said, 'It's quite an eye-opener, isn't it? This is the last place I'd expect to be spending the night with you! Hopefully, if we lay low here for the night, we'll lose the soldiers on our tail. I don't imagine they'll think to look for us in a brothel.'

Cara paused as his words sunk in.

A brothel!

She placed her finger to his lips to pause his chatter, raised her mouth to his and gave him a long, passionate kiss.

George looked a little stunned. He felt her kiss in his groin. 'Have mercy upon me. Do you want to give a man a bulging codpiece in public?'

Perhaps I'm too demonstrative for 1536? I am in a brothel, though!

Cara laughed with abandon, revelling in her new-found freedom to show her passion for George in public.

'Are you suggesting I escort your codpiece upstairs, my Lord?' Cara fluttered her long eyelashes and flashed him a coy smile. 'When in Rome and all that.'

'When in Rome? I've no idea what you're talking about, but my codpiece definitely wants more attention. Let's make haste upstairs. Madame Alicia has kindly arranged a room in her private wing for us so we should be comfortable.'

They left the parlour, hand in hand, glowing as only lovers do. No one would suspect they had King Henry's army seeking their heads except perhaps the two bounty hunters who sat at the opposite side of the parlour watching their every move.

CHAPTER 9

York, present day

Cara opened the front door.

'Wow. This is a surprise.'

'A pleasant one, I hope.' George flashed Cara a self-depre-cating smile. 'I'm sorry. I should have called first.'

Cara blinked. 'No, it's okay. I didn't expect you, that's all. You've been very quiet.'

'I had to see you,' he said.

'How did you know where I live?' She'd begun to think it must be over. Three whole days had passed since Seville. She assumed he must be confused so had decided to back off and leave it to him. His silence had been painful, but what else could she do? And yet suddenly he was here. Her heart stirred and began to clatter as their eyes met.

Here we go again.

'You mentioned your street and cottage name so I

thought it would be easy enough to find you if I drove over here.'

'I'm pleased you came.' She gulped and looked away, not knowing what else to say.

'How have you been?' said George.

'Oh, you know—okay. Up and down.'

'I'm sorry I've not been in touch. It's been mad at work. The York Gallery contacted us and asked to commission The Tudor Kings' Manuscript for a special exhibition.'

'How fabulous.' Her reticence dissolved, and she smiled.

'That's better' he said. 'Do you think you might invite me in or are we going to stand here all night?'

'Oh, God. Sorry. Come in.' Cara stood aside and gestured for him to enter the hallway. 'Go through to the kitchen, and I'll make us some tea.'

George admired the Tudor style beams in the kitchen, looked around and said, 'There's something about this room. I feel as if I've been here before. It's weird. Do you know what I mean?'

'Funnily enough, I do. I had that sensation in the book-shop the first time we met. I thought I knew you. It was like deja-vu. I didn't mention it...I was worried you would think me crazy!'

George laughed and shook his head, an expression of mock denial crossing his features, as he raised his palms upwards.

'What a beautiful kitchen.' He looked about with obvious appreciation.

'Joking aside, I keep having this feeling that I've known you forever. I can't quite explain it.'

She motioned for him to take a seat and then she put the kettle on and busied herself making tea. It was something to do besides look at him. She was so nervous she thought she might spontaneously combust at any moment.

I wonder if that's what causes me to time travel.

Sometimes, the feeling between them was so intense that it made her jumpy. She searched for something to say to lighten the mood. 'Time is such an unpredictable quantity. I've never thought much about it before, but over the past few days, I've been reading some of Einstein's work.'

Nice job, Cara. Quantum Physics. Light indeed. . .

'Einstein believed that time is an illusion. It certainly seems like it sometimes, doesn't it? The past three days have been long,' she continued.

George nodded and ran his hand through his hair. He was quiet whilst she pottered about making tea. She brought the teapot to the wooden table, sat down and poured them both a cup. She pushed a cup towards him and waited to see if he noticed anything strange about this simple interaction.

'Thank you. This is perfect.' He raised his eyebrow before looking at her curiously. 'How did you know how I like my tea?'

'I guessed,' she said, smiling as she sipped hers. She had remembered how he liked his tea. She had no idea how she knew, but she did. She followed an inner prompting and it had guided her correctly. He liked black tea with just a quick dip of the teabag.

'Why do I feel like there's an inside joke I'm missing?'

Cara smiled a sweet smile and said, 'I can't imagine.'

There was another silence, and George cleared his throat. 'I'm glad I came. I didn't know what to do. It's not that I didn't want to call. I wanted to see you. I've thought about little else, but, it's difficult.'

'I was upset you weren't in touch, but I realised it must be hard for you.'

'You said you'd ended it with Daniel. How did he take it?'

'Not well. He was shocked and angry. No worse than you'd expect I suppose, given the way I sprung it on him, but

it was horrible. I couldn't keep up the pretence after. . .'
Cara's words froze in her throat.

'After?'

She took a deep breath. 'After you and I were together. Pretending to be invested in the relationship when I'm thinking about you wouldn't work for me. It felt wrong to lie.'

Cara looked away. If he was going to reject her, then let him get on with it.

'Sometimes, I wish I could follow my heart more, instead of trying to please others.'

'As in Joanna, you mean?' She tilted her head to one side as she looked at him. There was no point being coy. They were either on or off. He either wanted her or he didn't.

George reached across and covered her hand with his. He raised it to his lips and planted a row of kisses across her knuckles. Her hand tingled. Her whole body tingled. His hands were beautiful. She remembered how they touched her body in the villa in Seville.

Why do I feel safe with him when nothing about this situation is safe?

'I can't stay long, but I wanted to see your face. I'd better get back to work soon as there's so much going on.' He withdrew his hand and sipped his tea.

'You've only just arrived. Can't you stay a bit longer?'

'Okay then, yes, a little while. Actually, I wasn't sure if you'd want to see me at all.' His dark eyes met hers again. 'I sat outside in the car for ages trying to decide whether to come in.'

'How could you possibly think I wouldn't want to see you after Seville?'

Their eyes locked in a silent loving exchange. There was no need for words.

Cara rose from her chair, heart-pounding, and moved

towards him. She was embarrassed by the depth of her desire, but she didn't want to let the moment pass without showing him how she felt. Better to risk looking like a fool than to feel foolish later. He withdrew his legs from beneath the table as she moved towards him. She ran her hand through his hair, touched his cheekbone with her fingers and then traced his lips.

Anyone might wonder what she found so mesmerising about them; they were, after all, just shapely lips. But as anyone who's been in love knows, other people's preferences have little to do with attraction.

The familiar fire ignited between them. He pulled her down on to his knees, and she sat facing him as he held her. Their lips touched and the spark flared with the ferocity of a new flame. They needed no warm-up.

'I've missed you terribly,' he said, before devouring her lips with hungry kisses.

'You said you haven't got long so we'd better make the most it,' she said, a coy expression on her lovely face.

They both knew the inevitable was about to happen. Cara unbuttoned his shirt and rubbed her fingers across his lightly muscled chest, revelling in the pure delight of touching him. Her desire for him made it simple to please him. No effort was required. It was just right. She wanted him, and he wanted her. It was a basic, primal instinct, and both of them responded to it. There was no hesitation on either side. She pressed against the hard, growing mound in his trousers and his hips moved against hers, his arms holding her close. He never wanted to be parted from her again. They weren't naked yet, but they smouldered with a burning heat. He unbuttoned her flimsy silk shirt and let out a low whistle as he saw her nipples standing to attention inside her lacy black bra. He unhooked the bra without ceremony and flung it across the chair. Her cherry pink nipples were set free, and he took each one into his mouth.

'Take me now; don't wait any longer,' she whispered.

He picked her up and eased her on to the edge of the large table. He made love to her in a way neither of them had ever experienced. It was fierce yet tender; waves of passion overtook them, and they came undone. For a few moments, George forgot he was in a Tudor style kitchen on the outskirts of York, madly in love with a woman he'd only known for a few weeks.

For a short while, Cara forgot she was making love to her Twin Flame who would soon return home to his twenty-first-century wife.

Willow Manor, York, 1525

Cara wrapped her arm through George's as they rambled around Willow Manor's immaculate gardens. It was a warm spring day, and the comforting scent of apple and cherry blossom wafted up their nostrils as they entered the orchard. To see them you'd know immediately they were in love. They were lost in each other and had no interest in anyone else. The bounce to their step and the attentive tilt of George's head as he looked into Cara's sparkling eyes, would make it impossible for any onlooker to miss.

George's mother watched them enchanting each other from her window in the upstairs parlour. 'I've never seen a pair so enraptured. We're fortunate Cara isn't a terrible match for him, or we'd have a rebellion on our hands. Our boy is headstrong; he doesn't like being reigned in. My concern is that they both have such high expectations of marriage, they're going to be sorely disappointed with the reality.'

'That's not a very complimentary observation to share with your husband of thirty years,' said George Cavendish Senior, as he thumbed through estate papers. He was accustomed to his wife's acerbic candour and had learned to manage her outbursts while maintaining his sense of humour.

'Well, you know what I mean. It's precisely because we've been married thirty years that I may say it,' she replied, rolling her eyes.

'Most nobles don't marry for love, so surely we should rejoice in their fortunate coupling and wish them well, my dear.'

'I don't know. Romantic love of that nature gives me a queasy feeling in my gut. It's not practical. He'd have been better to marry one of those solid, dependable Lovell girls,' she grumbled, a sour expression on what was once a pretty face.

'Possibly so, but it's all too advanced now to stop it, so fret not my love. All will be well. George will be married. He will have his wedded bliss and soon enough, God willing, we'll have another round of Cavendish children running about the orchard to keep their adoring parents out of mischief.

George pulled Cara off the path and beneath an apple tree out of sight of the house. He was familiar with his mother's overbearing ways.

'Come here, so we're out of sight of my mother's lookout tower.'

'What are you doing?' laughed Cara, a look of playful disapproval on her face. It's entirely improper for us to be alone like this, my Lord, you know. She lowered her eyes in false modesty.

'Come here, you little vixen. You have bewitched me, and I can't wait a second more for another kiss of your soft lips.'

'We'll be married soon, and then we'll be able to kiss whenever we want,' she said, her voice full of innocent wonder. 'I can't even imagine how incredible it will be to wake up with you every day and fall asleep by your side every night with no one to interfere and no chaperones frowning about our every move.'

They had met a little over a year ago, and they'd fallen in love that night. Cara's parents had all but promised her to another man, but fortunately, the betrothal wasn't yet formal. Cara was mature enough to know what she wanted but young enough to follow her heart and not listen to anyone else's advice about who she should marry. Her parents were disappointed but were consoled by the allure of George's lavish estate, plentiful lands and family title. They quickly readjusted their expectations, and the result was that Cara and George would be married this summer.

George planted kisses on the side of Cara's neck, and she shivered and clung to him. They were never allowed to be alone for more than a few minutes so they had only shared stolen moments of passion. They were both impatient with longing and could barely keep their hands off one another. There was a magnetic attraction between them which had been apparent the first time George took her in his arms. Cara thanked God every day that she had met George in time to stop the impending nuptials with her first suitor. She had liked him well enough as an acquaintance but had felt no attraction to him whatsoever.

She gazed at George, and her heart danced at the prospect of the years ahead when they would build a life together.

They heard a whimpering noise from the direction of the bushes. 'What's that?' said Cara.

'It's a dog!' John, the estate manager, said his greyhound had given birth to puppies; one of them must be roaming about.'

'Oh, I do love dogs. Do you think we might take a look?' said Cara. She darted off before he could reply and a couple of seconds later he found her holding a greyhound pup in her arms. 'This fellow with the long nose has won my heart almost as quickly as you did. May we keep him and take him up to the house? You could take care of him for now, and he can be our dog when we're married.'

'Well, he's a hunting dog, my love. They're usually kept in the stables, but you're right, he is an adorable fellow indeed. Let's play with him a while here and see if he manages to hold your interest.'

They turned back into the manicured gardens, and Cara held the puppy close to her chest, stroking his silky ears. He nestled in her arms, and his long pink tongue shot out of his mouth to lick her cheek.

George laughed at the startled expression on her face. 'He has impeccable timing; I'll give him that. He's managed to kiss you even quicker than I did! If I'm going to have male competition for your affections, then I'd rather it be from a dog. I say he's a keeper.'

'He looks to be the most faithful creature. I declare he's a talisman of our true love,' said Cara, happy high notes chiming in her voice. George loved to see her joyful. She was quite the most enthusiastic person he'd ever met; her joy was contagious.

'What shall we name him?' asked Cara. 'We must name him and make him officially part of our family.'

'How about Cornelius? He has wise, old eyes as though he's been alive for centuries.'

'I love it! He shall share the initials CC with me upon our wedding.'

'That's perfect, my love. Cornelius Cavendish, he shall be.'

They kissed again before emerging from the trees and turning towards the lodge in search of the estate manager so they could check he wouldn't mind them adopting Cornelius.

York, present day

George's wife, Joanna, exited the penthouse of the luxury apartment building which overlooked the river. She reached the elevator, pressed the button and then turned to blow a kiss to the handsome man in the doorway.

CHAPTER 10

Outskirts of York, 1536

Madame Alicia was sympathetic to George and Cara's predicament and keen to offer them her hospitality.

'So, you mean the soldiers are searching for you all over the city?'

'Yes, we believe so,' said George. Posters declare there is one thousand pounds on our heads, dead or alive. Who knows who else has the reward in their sights, and is in hot pursuit. I would like to assure you, Madame; we are innocent of the charges brought against us by the council. We, like so many in these dangerous days, are victims of political intrigue and have fallen from favour following the beheading of Anne Boleyn.

We find ourselves unexpectedly on the wrong side of the king. The quicker we get out of your home, the better it will be for all of us. We have no wish to endanger you and your household. I have high hopes we will be restored to our former position in the good graces of the king, as soon as he examines the evidence. I fear he was misinformed, and we have been misrepresented by the enemies of the queen, God rest her soul.

Madame Alicia fashioned herself in an exotic style but was an indigenous product of the Yorkshire dales. She was born during the reign of Henry Tudor and raised on camp-fire tales of the Wars of the Roses, and came from a family of enthusiastic House of York supporters.

'Whatever you need; simply ask. My humble home and resources are at your disposal, my lord. We never know what evil tidings the king's soldiers will wreak upon us next. I have no loyalty to them. Some are decent enough individuals who frequent my ladies, but as an army, they are cold-hearted rogues. And I'm tired of the endless taxes and the constant disagreements between the northern lords and the king.'

They stood clustered together in the sitting room of her private wing, and she spoke in a loud whisper. Everyone knew, speaking ill of the king and his government was to endanger one's life. A few misplaced words were sufficient to be charged with treason, so by collaborating with Cara and George, the risk was considerable. Even here in her establishment, miles from London, one couldn't be sure who was a Tudor informer. 'The walls have ears,' was a sensible tenet to live by in Tudor England if you wished to increase your odds of survival.

'Could you possibly lend us a carriage? I'll endeavour to have it returned to you as soon as we've reached our destination. It's safer for us all if I don't tell you where we're going, but if you trust my word, I swear I'll see you are reimbursed with interest. If we can't get the carriage back to you in the condition we take it; I'll have one of my men purchase a replacement and see that you are well rewarded for your generosity.'

'Think nothing of it. I'm honoured to help, and I accept your kind offer, my lord. I have a carriage in the stable below which you can take. If anyone notices it's missing or reports a sighting of it on the way into the city, I'll say it must have been stolen.'

'Brilliant idea. Thank you. We're most grateful,' said George.

'Madame Alicia,' said Cara, 'I think we'd be wise to disguise ourselves, or I fear we'll be recognised in an instant. Our faces line the trees on the road to the city. What could you offer us in terms of clothing and wigs?'

Madame Alicia pursed her lips as she pondered, 'Yes, I concur. I do believe I have just the costume for you, my lady. It will be a bit more challenging to disguise my lord, but I have a blonde wig which I think will be perfect for you. We can disguise you as a Parisian noblewoman, and if you are questioned, you can say you've come from King Francis' court. The French are unpopular in these parts, but you'll be safer than travelling without a disguise.' She bustled off to peruse the delights of her wardrobe, excited at the prospect of a good dress up.

George, Cara and Swifty sped along the last portion of the Great North Road and prepared to enter the city in the newly acquired carriage.

'Let's hope being conspicuous serves our cause in that we're so obvious; they will think we must surely be innocent! It's such an elegant carriage, there's no chance of us passing undetected,' said George.

'Swifty?'

'Yes, my lord?'

'If anyone speaks to you, act dumb. We'll say you're a mute from birth if necessary.'

'If you say so, my lord, but why do you wish me to be silent?'

'Because, after hearing your terrible attempt at impersonating a French lad, we'll have more chance of saving our necks that way. If they hear you, they'll know us immediately for the imposters we are.'

Swifty looked dejected, and his small shoulders slumped.

Cara smiled. 'Never mind, Swifty; think of silence as a gift. . . you'll have it easier than us. We'll have to put on a ludicrous French accent and pretend we've come from the Valois court.' Her blonde wig bounced upon her head as she talked. The colour suited her; the golden curls accentuated her high cheekbones, and the contrast with her sparkling, grey eyes was striking. Madame Alicia had painted a sizeable brown beauty spot above Cara's lip, and she looked every bit the chic Parisian. She suspected Madame might have taken it a little further than required, but Cara hadn't wanted to spoil her fun.

George cut a flamboyant figure in a burgundy and gold tunic, lavish lace undershirt, pointed beard and a full moustache. They'd styled his hair in the latest Parisian fashion, and the coiffed effect was ostentatious. Compared to his usual understated elegance, he looked quite the dandy. Madame Alicia had said she'd heard this fashion was all the rage in France. Cara caught his eye and winked, struggling to hide her giggles at his obvious discomfort.

'I feel quite ridiculous,' he complained. 'You may well laugh. You, of course, look stunning, while I look like a first-class fool with all of this pomp. My face itches as though an entire army of ants marched across it and back again continuously throughout the night.'

His nature was typically so amiable that Cara was amused

when he was grumpy, and found his outburst particularly adorable.

'Uh-oh, we have company,' said George, craning his neck out of the side of the carriage as they hurtled along the bumpy road towards the entrance to the city. 'Soldiers ahead. There's a checkpoint. Let the games begin. Pray, we may fool them with our sheer ridiculousness.' His tone was playful—he saw no need to increase the tension.

'Bonjour,' George addressed the soldier who poked his head inside the carriage. 'How may we help you?' He said in his most exaggerated French accent.

Hampton Court Palace, 1536

Cara and George's fortunes plummeted on the night the soldiers burst into their apartment at Hampton Court and dragged him from their bed. Cara hadn't slept all night, terrified of George's fate, but she had made sure to arrive, as usual, to assist the queen in dressing. She knew what George would advise her to do. He would tell her to continue in this unfortunate masquerade as if he wasn't in disgrace.

'Do you have any word of George?' asked the queen, dropping the usual formalities.

'I'm afraid not, your grace. I've heard nothing since they arrested him in the middle of the night.' Despite Cara's efforts at stoicism, she couldn't hide the tremor in her voice, and tears clouded her eyes.

I mustn't crack. I must stay strong.

The queen touched her shoulder. 'Try to be calm, my dear, I pray the king will awaken from this madness soon, and restore us all to the peace and tranquillity of bygone days. Earlier this morning I prayed for the good health of the earl and your family as well as a full pardon so he may be restored to you forthwith. I will do my best to influence my husband, the king, in my next audience with him. My influence is greatly diminished as we both know, but perhaps I can reason with him by reminding him of the loyalty your husband has shown us. It's little more than a year since he created him an earl, in recognition of his esteemed service to the crown. His work on the Tudor Kings' Manuscript was outstanding. The king was delighted with the commission, but I fear it has temporarily slipped his mind.'

'I am grateful, your grace. Your words bring me hope in these dark days, although I must confess to feeling quite despondent, thinking of my husband locked up, I know not where.'

'It's dreadful. I will make enquiries as to where he is being held and see to it that he receives additional supplies at the first opportunity. I still have loyal servants throughout the city.'

'Thank you, your grace. You are very kind.'

'I can't imagine what the king is thinking by accusing him of treason when he has been such a loyal advisor and trusted confidant. No doubt Cromwell has a hand in it. He is a master at planting false evidence to embroil those who rival him. Your husband has risen too high, too fast. Cromwell's ambition will be the death of us all if we underestimate him.'

Cara didn't attend the May Day Tournament at Greenwich Palace; she made her excuses to the queen, saying she felt unwell. She wished to remain quietly in her apartment at Hampton Court. George's arrest had taken its toll; she could not bear to face the king. Queen Anne was sensitive to Cara's precarious situation and thought it wise that she not draw attention to herself.

'Through my network of spies, I've learned that George is

in Newgate Prison,' said the queen. 'I don't have any details at this point but will endeavour to ascertain more.'

Cara's skin was pallid, and she feared she might throw up upon hearing the queen's words. She had yearned for news but receiving it was a bitter blow. 'I'd hoped there had been some mistake. I prayed our worst fears wouldn't be confirmed,' she said.

'I know. I'm sorry, my dear. I was on my knees in the chapel at dawn, but it would seem that God has not answered my prayers. I will do my best to have someone get word to him. Newgate is shocking by all accounts. Why the king hasn't put him under house arrest or in a solitary cell in the Tower, I can't imagine.'

Cara bid her beloved mistress farewell, not suspecting the next time she would see her would be to witness the queen's execution. Several days later she received a letter from one of George's men, which read:

'The queen has been arrested. She is being transported by barge to the Tower of London to await trial. Leave the palace immediately. Go into hiding for your safety. I am doing my best for G.'

Cara burned the note, gathered some of her belongings and prepared to leave, under cover of night. There were several people in the palace she could trust, and they would figure out a plan for a quick getaway.

'Please open up my lady.' There was a banging on the door before the handle turned. Her maid tumbled into the room and fell at her feet; such was her distress. 'I'm sorry,' Mary gasped for breath. 'I ran as quickly as I could,' she clutched her side.

Cara helped her maid to her feet and gripped her shoulders to steady her, 'What is it? Make haste, please tell me now. Do you have news of the earl, my lord Cavendish?' She felt like shaking the maid; such was her impatience.

'No, my lady.' She lowered her eyes and whispered, 'They are coming for you. I heard the soldiers talking. They're coming to arrest you next. I ran as fast as I could to tell you.'

Cara's blood rushed from her head, and she thought she would faint. She sat on the bed for a few seconds, trying to calm and organise her thoughts.

What can I do? How must I get away to rescue the children?

She tried to form a plan but couldn't think what to do if the soldiers were already on their way to her rooms. There was nowhere to hide. She grabbed more of her jewellery and hastily adorned herself with as much as she could. Her hands shook as she slid gold rings set with precious stones on to her fingers. She thrust a hefty purse of coins into her bodice and dashed for the door.

'Say as little as possible, Mary. If they question you, don't say you've seen me. Say you came to serve me, but I was nowhere to be found.'

'I will, my lady.' Mary began to sob.

'Please calm down. You must stay calm for your own safety. Say nothing, and you will be safe.'

Three soldiers burst through the door and grabbed Cara roughly by the arm. 'You're under arrest for treason and witchcraft, by order of King Henry VIII.' One of them held up a notice as he read the charges.

York, present day

Cara tried to settle back into her old life. She went to the office each day and attempted to immerse herself in her work. Where once she would light up at the idea of a new project, her work had now lost its appeal. Reasonably, she knew it was crazy to think about a man so much, even one with whom she shared such an affinity. But reason played no role in her feelings for George.

I'm like a lovesick girl who can't think about anything or anyone else. Ugh.

She'd thought women weak who behaved in this way. She would never be like that, or so she had believed. Now she had a new compassion for the poor souls whose hearts had been enslaved to the point where they couldn't eat, sleep or think about anything or anyone else.

She'd been infatuated with James, her first love, and had been sure he was *the one*. Now it was evident that what they had shared had been nothing compared to this all-consuming desire to be with George. Sometimes it was like a curse, and she wished they had never met. Her life had been dull and bland before that day in the bookshop, but at least she wasn't heartsick.

She picked up her phone and called Sylvia, who scheduled her in for the next available appointment. At least she would be able to talk to someone about her travels to Tudorville, and her feelings for George. Sylvia was the only person she could trust in this madness. The time travel was wacky. She knew it was happening, even though it was surreal to think of it, but the intensity of the pain in her heart about George was unbearable. She was despondent. Conflicting thoughts cycled round her head, competing for her attention, day and night. She had given up trying to justify her state of mind. Their last conversation replayed itself in her head throughout each day, ever since George told her he was leaving. She wished she could somehow turn that conversation off.

He had phoned late one night a few days earlier, and after a bit of light banter, he said, 'I'm not used to feeling this way. I've never felt the way I do about you. I don't know what to do.'

A rush of intense love flooded her being, and the relief was palpable after a stressful day of doubt and indecision.

It's going to be okay.

He continued, 'I can't tell Joanna. I don't know how.' His voice faltered. 'Jane is in her final year at school and has exams soon. It doesn't seem right to leave now.'

'I see,' said Cara. 'Yes, of course.' Disappointment crushed her short-lived elation. Bile rose in her throat, her stomach flipped over and she felt sick.

'I'm going to the London office in a couple of days. There's so much going on as a result of *The Tudor Kings' Manuscript* publicity. The media is going bonkers about all things Tudor, and people who wouldn't usually consider it, are commissioning manuscripts like crazy. The BBC has asked to interview me at Hampton Court Palace.'

'How wonderful,' said Cara. She fell silent, reeling at the implication of him not leaving Joanna and instead leaving for London.

'The publicity will be great for your work too,' he said.

'Yes, yes, I suppose it will.' She didn't care; it was little consolation. Knowing he was nearby had given her hope.

After a pause, she asked, 'How long will you be away?'

'I don't know. It depends how it all goes.'

'Will you be going alone?' Her heart pounded as she awaited his reply.

'Yes. We have a small team permanently based at the London branch, although I may ask my assistant to accompany me.'

Cara's mood turned darker at the thought of a glamorous assistant working side by side with him in London. She'd never been the jealous type, but recently she saw a new edge to her nature which both surprised and alarmed her.

Is he going to London to put distance between us?

CHAPTER 11

Y ork, present day

Cara sat at her desk, trying to focus on a client proposal. She was agitated and still couldn't get George's words out of her mind. He was going to London today. He hadn't told Joanna he was leaving her, and he didn't seem to have any intention of doing so, any time soon.

He'd sensed Cara was upset the previous evening and said, 'Don't be sad. We'll talk every day. I'll phone you tomorrow.'

She tried to be positive but was tempted to rip the plaster off and just end the relationship. What was the point? She sat for hours, unable to motivate herself to move as she stared into space, filled with dread. Then she rose from her chair, picked up her phone and sent George a message.

'I don't think we should stay in touch if you're not going

to tell Joanna. It makes no sense. I can't do it. I hope London goes well. I'm sorry. x'

Barely two minutes passed before her phone rang.

'Hello,' she said.

'I'm on my way to London. What are you talking about? Why would you say that?'

He's upset.

It wasn't his fault they were in this mess. It had come at them from nowhere. But his lack of action to get them out of it was.

'I don't see the point of us talking every day if we're not going to be together. It will only make it harder on us both. If you want to stay with Joanna, then I think it's best all-round if we call it a day.'

It's not really over. I'll see you in Tudorville.

She was comforted by the thought that she wouldn't lose him completely. Never had she experienced such a range of conflicting emotions as in the past several weeks since they met. One minute she was a beaming ray of pure ecstasy, the next, an ominous thunder cloud about to burst. The emotional rollercoaster was a nightmare. If he wouldn't fight for her, it was over.

'Didn't you think we might talk about this? Sending a message like that wasn't very nice.'

His tone was high-pitched, and he sounded frantic.

Cara's throat tightened. She was overwhelmed with sorrow, and she swallowed her tears. Hurting him, hurt her. 'I didn't know what to do. I'm sorry. I don't want to be the reason your marriage ends, but I can't be with you if it doesn't. If you're happy as you are, then I should leave you to it.'

'It doesn't work like that,' he said. 'My feelings for you have nothing to do with my marriage.'

'Perhaps not, but to me and the rest of the world, it looks

like they do. You're happy enough. If you weren't, you would leave her. It's that simple when it comes down to it.'

'I don't care about the rest of the world. I'm pleased it's so simple for you. You can just end it like that,' he said. He was angry, and his sarcasm stung. 'From here, it doesn't look simple at all,' he added.

'I said it's simple, not easy. Your choice to pretend everything is fine is not fair on any of us. None of us are getting what we want. Joanna can't be satisfied sharing her life with a ghost, for Christ's sake.' Cara only swore when she was furious. 'You're kidding yourself if you think you can continue to pull this off. On some level, she knows. She has to unless she's asleep or just doesn't bloody care what you do.'

There was a long silence which George finally broke, 'Please. . .don't do this Car, give me some time to figure things out. I know it's difficult for you.' His voice cracked.

Cara shut her eyes. She was shaking.

Hearing him use his pet name for her, made her want to cry.

A chill shot down George's spine. He was miserable at the prospect of even one day without her.

I can't lose her now I've found her.

'Cara,' he said.

She heard the pain in his voice and couldn't bear for him to be so desolate.

'I don't know what to say,' she said, barely able to push the words out.

I love you; you know that, but this has all happened so fast,' he appealed.

'Are you going to London to put distance between us?'

'No, of course not. I have to go on business. I hadn't planned it. I only found out I was going just before I told you.'

'You make it sound as though it's out of your hands.'

'I often have to go to work at the other branches.' He sounded miffed, like a sulky schoolboy being reprimanded.

Cara melted despite her resolution. There was something about him she could not resist. But it was no good. That's why she was in this crazy mess. She mustn't go soft now.

'What does Joanna think about you going away indefinitely?'

He was quiet for a second. 'I'm not sure. She's used to it, I suppose. I go away a lot. We don't spend much time together. Maybe she'll come to the London flat at some point.'

'Aha,' said Cara.

'Now you sound annoyed again.' His tone was careful, his words measured.

'No, I'm fine. Take your time and have a safe trip. I've got to go now. Client's coming in a minute. Bye.' She pressed the button to end the call. She couldn't take anymore and was about to lose her composure. Tears flooded her eyes and spilt on to her hot cheeks. Her heart ached, and she longed to wail with grief. If her assistant weren't next door, she would give in to the urge. She hadn't wanted George to hear her that way. It wasn't fair on him. He had enough to deal with.

I'm a wreck. This has got to stop. I have to get a handle on my emotions.

She'd been tearful ever since he had told her he was leaving York. Any little reminder set her off—she had seen a man who resembled him, laughing and holding a woman's hand. It was becoming clear to her; she and George would never share carefree moments like that. At least not in this lifetime. It wasn't on the cards for them.

To complicate matters she had two timelines of memories to juggle and sometimes the two merged and became confused.

Maybe I should tell him the truth. Could he handle it if I told him we're married in another life? She shook her head.

No, I'll wait until I understand it all better.

She didn't feel guilty about being with him. Ordinarily, she thought she would. But everything about their connection was different to how she would have imagined such a love affair. It was as though he was already hers. It didn't feel wrong.

It feels so right. Why would we be thrown together like this after five hundred years, if we're not supposed to be together?

In rare moments when she was calm, the day to day reality of his marriage seemed insignificant. It was as though their union was inescapable. They were Twin Flames; being together was their destiny, so why fight it? Yet, the second she lost touch with the magic of their love, she panicked. Other people were involved. She'd already ended it with Daniel. Of course, she wished she could have avoided hurting him, but she knew it was for the best. George's scenario was more complicated.

How does he handle it? Even if he can reconcile being involved with two women, I can't reconcile being one of them for much longer.

She'd ended her relationship with Daniel because she couldn't bear to live in the grey. George was all hers in 1536, but the contrast only made it harder when he wasn't. It had only been a short time since their lives collided in the bookshop, but it seemed like forever. Cara considered herself open-minded; not judgmental of others' lifestyles. Still, she was shocked she was wedged in this moral dilemma.

And yet a deeper part of her knew they were supposed to be together. Perhaps they'd been together in other lives too. It seemed likely, given what Sylvia had told her about Twin Flames. Even so, if her experience of 1536 wasn't so vivid, she was sure she'd wonder if she'd imagined the whole thing.

She heard the ping of a notification. It was George. She knew it was him without checking. Since he had come into her life, she didn't doubt telepathy.

York, present day

'I have a problem, and I need your help again,' said Cara.

'Only one? Well that's good,' said Sylvia, smiling.

'Have you any idea how I can expedite my travel? I have to get back to my old life in Tudorville to save my children. I know it sounds crazy, but we're on the run to York in 1536 and if we don't get to our children, Henry's army will. It won't be long before they think of using them to blackmail us if they haven't already taken them. I'm hoping they don't realise Thomas and May are at Willow Manor.'

'Tudorville, that's funny. It's great you've maintained a sense of humour,' remarked Sylvia. 'I must say I'm a little envious of your adventure. If I hadn't seen your gift in the cards with my own eyes, I would doubt the truth of it. It's as fantastical as a fairy tale.'

'Yes, I know it sounds mad. It's such a relief to be able to talk about it with you. Thank you,' said Cara. 'You've been amazing.'

'What's going on?' said Sylvia.

'Well, I've only ever travelled involuntarily, but I want to learn to go back on demand. I want to go now, actually. It's hell being here. George is married to someone called Joanna. I've no idea what her role is in the grand scheme of things. And I can't stop crying. I'm starting to hate my life which isn't like me at all. I'm usually quite a happy person. At least if I go back, I can be of use and take my mind off this nightmare.'

Sylvia reached out to touch Cara's hand. 'Slow down, my dear. It's all going to be okay.'

Cara was grateful for the compassion she saw in Sylvia's shining eyes.

'I will try to help, but please remember that there's no escaping the Twin Flame cycle. It's relentless. The sooner you accept it, the sooner you will be united with George,' said Sylvia.

1536 looked increasingly more attractive to Cara each day.

Cara nodded but wondered how the hell she was supposed to accept this crazy love.

'I'm also unsure as to whether I've messed up the future by going back, so I need to do all I can to make things right, just in case. If we don't get our children away from the soldiers, who knows what it means for future generations. We may be wiped out altogether. If I don't sort it out, the present-day may never happen! I know it sounds wild because we're experiencing the present, now, but do you see what I mean?'

'I think so. But you're right; it's mind-boggling. I do see the need for urgency. Tell me what happens when you travel.'

Cara described the whooshing noise, the chilled air, and how she felt herself slip into a vortex just before she went.

'I suspect I'm more vulnerable to going when I get stressed. But then I'm stressed nearly all the time these days, so I'm not sure if it's really the case.'

'What we need is someone on your team who has a deeper understanding of how time works. I guess that you have this incredible superpower at your disposal, but at this point, you have no idea how to use it to its full potential. From what I know of magic, your skills will develop through practice. But I do know a man who may be able to help speed up the process. I haven't been in touch with him for a while. I'll have to see if I can get hold of the professor now.'

'A professor of time? Wow, that's impressive.'

Sylvia picked up her phone and pressed his name. 'May I speak with Professor Eddie Makepeace, please? Oh okay, thank you, yes I'll wait.'

She covered the phone with her hand and whispered, 'They're trying to locate him now. This is a number he said I'll always be able to reach him on. They're transferring me to Royal Holloway. He must be working there now. Oh, here we go.'

'Eddie? How lovely to hear your voice. This is Sylvia. Sylvia Skye. How are you?'

'Hello, Sylvia. It's been ages. I'm well, thank you; very well. I must say, I'm surprised to hear from you out of the blue. What a wonderful surprise. Is everything okay?'

'Yes, thank you. I know you'd said this number was good even in an emergency. I have a rather unusual assignment for you. I don't want to say more on the phone. Could my client possibly come and see you?'

'I'm teaching at Royal Holloway. I should be around for the next week or so and, of course, anything to help. I'd be happy to see her. I'll give her a call later, and we'll see what we can do.'

Sylvia gave the professor Cara's details.

'Cara Bailey,' he said, rolling the name on his tongue. 'Ah yes, I've been waiting for Cara. She's certainly taken her sweet old time.' Sylvia was familiar with the professor's strange outbursts and let him have his moment.

'He's a quantum physics geek and specialises in time-related phenomena,' she explained to Cara after the call ended. 'If anyone can help you, he can. The only thing is, he has, how can I say? A loose relationship with time, so don't be surprised if he calls at an unsociable hour. He's a good soul and is quite brilliant. You can trust him.'

'Wonderful, thank you. I'm so grateful. I can't tell you what a relief it is to discuss all of this with you. I'll wait for the professor's call and will let you know what happens.'

'I should warn you; he says he knows you. Mentioned something about waiting for you. He can be a trifle eccentric.'

Cara smiled at the irony and thanked Sylvia once more.

The psychic tarot card reader thinks the quantum physics professor is eccentric. I couldn't make this stuff up.

Cara left Sylvia's office with a renewed bounce to her step. She felt lighter at the thought of the mysterious professor who understood time.

Royal Holloway University, London, present day

'I've been waiting for you, Cara.' The professor bounced out from behind his desk, grasped her hand and gave her a hearty smile and handshake.

Cara felt a flash of recognition, similar to when she met George, minus the fuzzy emotions. She knew the professor - she didn't know how. It was like meeting an old friend after years of being apart.

'It's coming back to you, isn't it? I can tell. The minute Sylvia said your name, I knew it was you. Cara Bailey. I knew you must be my dear friend, Countess Cara Cavendish. It's so good to see you.' He embraced her in a warm bear-like hug.

We must know each other from Tudorville; it's unbelievable.

'Gosh, my mind is blown. I feel like I know you, but I can't quite remember how. I do have a sense that you weren't a professor back then. You were, you were. . .Thomas and May's tutor! I can't believe it. You are the very person I need to get back to in 1536. The children are in your care at Willow Manor.' The words tumbled out.

'Come and sit down my lady, let's catch up. I've missed you. I hope you're not in a rush. It's been about five hundred years,' he said, a smile playing on his lips.

Her phone rang; it was George. She would call him later. It was probably better she didn't mention she was with their children's tutor from five hundred years earlier.

'Was that the earl?'

'Yes, indeed. How did you know?'

'You'll see soon enough. Or perhaps you've already noticed. We know things that other people don't.'

'Sylvia said you might be able to help me learn more about how time travel works. I can't believe I'm saying those words to a professor on the campus of Royal Holloway, but there you have it.'

'Yes, we need to formulate a plan. I've been having vivid dreams. That usually happens when I'm about to be assigned a mission. As I said, I've been expecting you. But then that could mean you'd come today or in ten years. Time is a capricious mistress; unrelenting in her march and unpredictable by nature.'

'I need to get back to 1536, Professor.'

'Please, let's drop the formalities. Call me Eddie. In 1536, you were my employer. We became great allies and dear friends in the dangerous days of Henry VIII. I would do anything for you and his grace.'

'I'm frightened to ask, but do you know what became of us? Do you know if we got away safely? Were we able to save Thomas and May?'

'Honestly, I don't know. But rather than sitting here talking about it, shall we go back there now to find out?'

He took her hand. 'Just relax. Think about 1536; think about Thomas and May.'

A few seconds later, Edward's office on the Royal Holloway campus, grew cold and a whooshing sound enveloped them both. Cara looked at Eddie in alarm. She'd wanted to go, but this was sudden. She was nervous about what awaited her in Tudorville. And then they were gone.

If anyone had entered the room, they'd have seen Dr Cara Bailey and Professor Eddie Makepeace, chatting like old friends.

CHAPTER 12

W illow Manor, York, 1536

Edward Makepeace's schoolroom at Willow Manor faced south and the afternoon sun cast a luminous sheen over Thomas and May's bowed heads. Thomas was a studious child who applied himself to each lesson, while his younger sister, May, received frequent reminders from their tutor, to pay attention. She spent much of her time daydreaming about her beloved mare. There was nothing in the world more thrilling to May, than Nutmeg related activity. At six years old, she was already a skilled horse rider and jumped higher fences than her brother. Thomas, aged nine was more the scholar, and Edward Makepeace declared him advanced in mathematics for his years.

There was a sharp rap at the door. Edward thanked the kitchen maid for delivering the letter and unfolded a thick yellow sheet of paper under the curious gaze of two sets of brown eyes. It wasn't often mail was delivered directly to the schoolroom, especially during lesson time.

'Something must be up,' whispered Thomas, poking May in the ribs.

'Ouch,' she cried, giving Thomas a hard shove in his side.

'Now, now, children, settle down please,' said Edward in a kind, firm tone, peering at them over the paper. He pushed his spectacles up his large nose and resumed reading.

'Is it from mother and father, sir?' asked May. 'Are they coming home soon? I miss them so much.'

'No, I'm afraid they're not coming home just yet.'

May's tiny frame slumped, and tears welled in her dark eyes. Thomas, sensitive to his sister's volatile nature, reached out to pat her arm. 'Don't cry, May. If they're not able to come home, it's because they are on important business for the crown. Mother has explained this to us, remember?'

'May's bottom lip trembled as she stared up at him, but she visibly held herself together. The children had grown used to not having their parents at home, but occasionally May became melancholy.

'I have good news. Can I trust you both to keep a secret?' asked Edward.

May perked up immediately at the promise of intrigue. 'Yes, of course,' the children chimed in unison.

'What do our parents say, sir?' asked Thomas. 'Are they well?'

'They wish you to come to them, but it must remain an absolute secret. No one but us must know. Your father says our lives depend upon it, so children, I'm deadly serious when I say we must keep this between us. Do you understand?'

They nodded, the solemnity of his words hitting them both simultaneously.

This must be serious, indeed, thought Edward.

His hand shook slightly as he contemplated the bold black instructions on the letter. 'You know how your father goes on secret missions for the king to locate important manuscripts? He didn't pause for a response but continued, 'Well, we shall be embarking on a mission of equal importance, so I'm going to need you both to have your wits about you and to be on your best behaviour.'

They nodded again. May couldn't sit still.

'Are we to go to them today, sir?' she enquired. 'May I ride Nutmeg? She will help us on our secret mission.'

I want you both to go and get changed into the warmest, old clothing you can find. May, borrow some of Thomas's clothes. You are finally going to get your wish to dress like a boy. For this mission, you shall be as if you are Thomas's little brother. And blacken your faces too. You need to look grubby; like stable boys or kitchen hands.'

May gulped and sped out of the room as fast as her wiry little legs could move.

Thomas tidied up his equipment, looked intently at his tutor, and said, 'Sir, are my parents in very grave danger?'

Edward tousled the boy's hair; he was fond of Thomas. 'I won't lie to you, dear boy. We are in dangerous times, and it sounds as though your parents have had to go into hiding. Best to keep it between us men for now. No need to alarm May any further. Do I have your word?'

'Yes, sir, you can count on me.' Thomas hurried from the classroom and went in pursuit of his sister and some suitable clothes to prepare for their secret mission.

Thomas was steady and mature for his age. Children of noble birth were in many ways privileged, but George and Cara had schooled Thomas in the realities of courtly life. He was aware of the perils of their position. Edward, who was named after Edward of York, King Edward IV, had taught the children the history of The Wars of The Roses. They knew courtiers could fall from favour in a blink of the king's eye. Since their parents were summoned to court, the children had led a quiet life at Willow Park, under the guardianship of their Cavendish grandparents and tutor.

Edward looked at the letter once more.

'Please don't tell my parents. For all concerned they shouldn't know. I trust you to follow my instructions regarding the children.'

George had signed the letter with a rich flourish and the ink was slightly smudged.

Our peaceful life is about to change.

He hurried out of the schoolroom and up the back stairs to his quarters, to prepare for the journey ahead. His pulse quickened at the thought of the dangers involved in smuggling the children to their parents, who were now on the run from the king's army.

Twenty minutes later, Edward led the children quietly down the servant's stairs. They looked like a couple of ragamuffins with their frayed clothes and blackened faces. 'You did a great job. Now we just need to get you to your parents, and all will be well.'

'What will you do, sir?' asked Thomas.

'I'll do the bidding of your parents whatever that may be. I'm their loyal servant. I'll do my best to provide whatever they need of me.'

'I hope you can stay with us,' said Thomas.

'Yes, me too,' whispered May. 'Please don't leave us, sir.'

Edward squeezed one shoulder of each of his wards, to comfort them. 'I hope I can stay with you, but whatever happens, you'll be with your parents, so there's no need to fret.'

They arrived at the stables and Edward jumped into the shabby carriage used by the household's staff for errands. He signalled to the children to follow, giving them a hand up. He'd sent word earlier to Swifty's brother, Bertie, as per

George's request, asking him to prepare the carriage, explaining the need for urgency and secrecy.

He nodded to Bertie, to indicate they were ready to depart and the horses' hooves clicked immediately into action. The less they lingered, the safer for all concerned. Edward planned to exit the grounds of the manor quickly as if he was going about his regular routine. There was nothing out of the ordinary in having two servant boys in the carriage to assist him.

Purchasing school supplies was heavy, tiresome work.

He planned their potential alibi, in case soldiers stopped them as they crossed the city.

London, present day

Cara sat nursing the remains of a latte in a coffee shop on the Royal Holloway campus.

What's going on?

She'd time travelled back to Tudorville with the amazing professor, but here she was already back in present-day London as if it had never happened. There was one significant difference to previous trips; this time, she could recall the details. Eddie had assured her that her recollection of the previous timeline would be readily accessible the more she travelled. He had discovered his ability to time travel ten years ago and was intimate with the process. He had been travelling back and forth between present-day and Tudorville ever since. He explained that the information from her past life must have been stored in her memory since the moment her gift was activated when she met George in the bookshop.

Thanks to her fortuitous introduction to Eddie, she was

beginning to understand how time travel worked. She'd just witnessed several days of her previous life in 1536, but in this timeline, it was as if nothing had changed. She found it disconcerting. It reminded her of when she'd travelled abroad for a gap year. Upon her return to York, everything seemed oddly different but also much the same, as though she'd never been away.

It's the most incredible thing. How will I ever tell George about our past life?

Cara ran through what she'd recently witnessed in Tudorville, trying to piece together how events had unfolded. She and George had made it into the heart of York, undetected, fooling the soldiers with George's foppery and her Parisian finery. George's childhood friend, Sir John Locke, suggested they hide in his basement. He was sympathetic to their plight and shuffled them into the safe haven upon arrival. Understanding the need for discretion after seeing the posters in the city, he didn't ask questions. The Yorkists stuck together so although soldiers were searching for them, being in the heart of York was the safest place they could hide.

Cara played back the scenes as if watching a technicolour movie.

Sir John Locke's Basement, York, 1536

'Do you think Edward will be able to get the children to us?' Cara asked George. She was tormented by the possibility of the children being captured since the despatch of their letter to Willow Manor.

'I have a good feeling about it. Edward is smart and trustworthy. We've counted on him for years. He'll do his best, and if anyone can get them to us, it's him.'

After a torturous couple of hours, they heard horses' hooves and the sound of a carriage hurtling into the circular driveway. Cara rushed in the direction of the tiny window, leapt onto a stool and craned her neck to try to peer out.

'It's no good. By our lady, I can't see a thing,' she cried and stepped down, throwing her hands up in despair. 'George, I pray you come over here, and see if it's the children. I can't wait another second, or I will explode.'

George balanced on the stool and peered out with ease through the grille of the high basement window. 'Good news, my love. Here they are! Edward has arrived, and if my eyes don't play dastard tricks on me, he brings with him two children whom I believe to be our very own. They look more like grimy chimney sweeps, but I suspect Thomas and May will be revealed beneath those filthy faces.'

'Thank the good lord,' said Cara. She rushed into George's arms, and he held her tight.

A few moments later they heard high pitched, chattering voices on the stairs, followed by admonishments from Sir John to keep the noise down. The children burst into the basement, and May ran to Cara, wrapping her thin arms around her mother's waist. Thomas was more restrained when he greeted his father, but he couldn't hold the tears back for long, and he clung to George. Then they all hugged, and Cara was overcome with emotion. The basement conditions were dark and damp, but their love was palpable. They settled on to a blanket on the hard floor and feasted on a supper of bread, cheese and ale. Despite the rudimentary nature of the food, none of them had enjoyed a meal so much in ages. They were together again, and that was all that mattered. A chill ran through Cara as she wondered how long it would be before she was swept back to her complicated life in present-day London.

'Where's Eddie?' asked Cara, looking at Thomas and then at May. 'How awful of me. In the excitement of seeing you both, I forgot all about him. How clever he is to have brought you here so quickly. We must thank him.'

'Eddie,' said George. 'Who's Eddie?'

'Oh, silly me, I mean Edward, of course.'

The children giggled and nudged each other at the ridiculous notion of their tutor being called Eddie.

'How quaint,' George chuckled. 'What brought that on? But yes, indeed, you're right, we must thank him and decide what he should do next. I'll ask him to join us shortly. I imagine he's dining in the servant's hall along with Swifty. It will be good to see Edward and to hear the latest news from Willow Manor. It seems like forever since I saw my parents.'

London, present day

Cara's phone rang and jolted her out of her daydream and back to the dregs of her cold latte. She couldn't avoid speaking to George any longer. 'Hi, how's it going?'

George filled her in on the details of his business in London and then asked how she'd got on with her meeting.

'Did you make the progress you wanted?' He probed.

When she'd texted him, Cara had been deliberately vague about the purpose of her trip. She didn't want to lie but also didn't want to tell him the real reason for her meeting with quantum time traveller, Eddie Makepeace.

'Yes, he's a brilliant fellow. I think he'll be a good contact, so it was worth the effort.' She could sense his curiosity, and purposely changed the conversation.

'It sounds as though you're very busy. I think I'll head back to York shortly.'

'Oh, okay. I thought I might see you,' he said, after a short pause, sounding disappointed.

'It's been a long day. I left York so early to make the appointment with the professor.'

Cara yearned to see him, but it was all so awkward, and she didn't want to get in the way of his work commitments.

'How about you join me for the visit to Hampton Court? Would you come for the interview? I could do with a quick consult with the pre-eminent expert in Tudor affairs. I'm a bit nervous, Dr Bailey.'

'Don't be silly. You know everything there is to know about that manuscript,' she laughed.

She knew from previous discussions that he was a pro at dealing with the media, but she felt a warm glow at his persistence. His charm was impossible for her to resist. She would love to be with him at Hampton Court.

I'd love to be anywhere with him.

He continued, 'I'm at the company apartment in Knightsbridge. Why don't you come over and stay here tonight? We can grab something to eat, and if you're free, we'll drive to Hampton Court together in the morning.'

Cara was silent for a few seconds before saying, 'How could I resist the temptation of Hampton Court? It's such a wonderful place. I did the research for my doctorate there.'

He let out a low whistle, 'I'm relieved to hear it, although I confess my ego is a little wounded that it's only Hampton Court you can't resist.'

Cara laughed again, 'Don't push it, Cavendish.'

'Fair enough, after our last call I thought you might not pick up the phone today, never mind accept an invitation, so this is promising.

'By the way,' he smoothly changed the subject, 'I meant to

tell you, I was reading some archive papers and discovered something quite bizarre.'

'Oh, really, what?' Cara's heart thumped as she wondered whether he could possibly have found out about their past life together.

'Well, it's strange, but it seems as though George Oliver Cavendish, you know, the one who was in charge of the Tudor Kings' Manuscript for the king. . .'

'Yes, yes,' said Cara, unable to stop herself cutting in, what did you find out?'

'His wife was called Cara: Countess Cara Cavendish! I nearly choked on my tea when I read it. I couldn't believe it. Isn't it a weird coincidence? It's not as though Cara is a particularly common name. It seems delightfully serendipitous.'

'Gosh, that is incredible!' She laughed, ping-ponging between being nervous and ecstatic that he was beginning to see their connection went deeper than anything he had previously imagined.

'My ancestor's work was acknowledged by King Henry VIII, and that's why he was made Earl of Gloucester. I wanted to call you immediately to tell you about Countess Cavendish, but you were so angry with me, I didn't.'

This was dangerous territory, so Cara steered the conversation away from Tudorville. She wanted some time to think through how to handle this revelation.

'I'm never angry with you for long. Don't you know that by now?'

'Great, so now we've established you're never going to be pissed off with me again, and you're always going to accept my invitations, when will you get here?'

'Do you know which tube line I need to take from Royal Holloway to Knightsbridge?'

'Let me think. . .um, no. You must have me confused with a man who knows every route in London!'

'Ah, yes, true. Okay, well I'll look it up and get to you as soon as I can.'

'Come to Russell Square, I think that's the nearest, and I'll be there to meet you.'

'Ah, wonderful, yay.'

'Cara?'

'Yes?'

'I've missed you. Hurry up.'

CHAPTER 13

Hampton Court Palace, present day

At nine the following morning Cara sat next to George on the worn leather seat of his sports car and watched him steer the olive-green Porsche 911 through the palace gates, along the stately drive and into the car park. She loved his quiet confidence and found it difficult to take her eyes off his profile. She was turned on by his beautiful hands and wanted to touch them; or better still, for them to touch her, again.

Sensual images of the previous night flashed through her mind. They'd predictably been unable to keep their hands off each other during dinner. The minute they entered his flat, he raised her skirt up to her thighs, gently pushed her into the kitchen, lifted her on to the smooth cold surface of the marble island, removed her black silk knickers and took her right there. She moaned then screamed out as her desire mounted; never had she been so sexually compatible with a man. No warm-up was required. After ten days apart they were erotically charged to boiling point.

The classic Porsche complemented him perfectly; they both had an understated glamour and effortless charisma. She found George enigmatic and yet delightfully innocent in his enthusiasm. He was a puzzle; she thought she understood him, and then he unwittingly revealed another piece of his character which she couldn't slot into place. It was like a dichotomous riddle, and she suspected she would never weary of stripping away the layers which revealed the hidden corners of his mind. Doctor Cara Bailey couldn't resist an unsolved riddle, and her sharp intuition invariably found the answers she sought.

It must be the novelty of being with him.

Cara considered her predicament for what seemed like the thousandth time. Not being able to see him as much as she would like, only seemed to serve to intensify her longing. She found him irresistible, and he seemed to reciprocate her feelings, despite the complexities of the situation.

But then it hit her; they'd been together on and off for at least five hundred years, so how could it possibly be a novelty? She forced herself back to the present moment.

He turned to look at her with a smile and said, 'Everything okay? If you keep staring at me like that, I'll be paranoid before the interview even begins.'

'Sorry.' She laughed and rested her hand on his thigh, 'It's just so lovely to be with you for more than a few hours.'

He squeezed her hand as Hampton Court Palace rose up before them in all of its red-bricked majesty. The decorative rouge and black patterned chimneys glinted in the bright, spring sunshine.

'This place never fails to take my breath away,' she said.

'Yes, it's beautiful, isn't it? I used to come here a lot, years ago. It feels good to be back after so long.'

You have no idea.

Cara was tempted to say the words out loud but stopped herself. Now wasn't the time. She wasn't sure when the right moment to reveal the details of their shared past would be, but she had a feeling she would know when it came. Now she wanted to enjoy every minute with George, in the palace, where they'd lived together as husband and wife when it was one of the favourite residences of Queen Anne and King Henry VIII.

'I get goose pimples just thinking about what went on within these walls,' she said.

'That's because you're a little history geek.' He captured her hand in his and dropped a light kiss on to her palm.

'Good morning,' beamed a ticket collector standing at the main entrance. George displayed his guest pass. 'I won't wish you a wonderful day because I can see you two are already having one.' He winked conspiratorially at George. 'It's good to see such happy, smiling faces. Some people turn up looking so miserable; it makes me wonder why they bother coming at all.' He shook his head in disapproval as he pointed in the direction of the crew who milled about as they prepared for the interview.

'Ok, as I suspected, we've got a while to wander about before they need me for makeup,' said George. He rolled his eyes as he returned to her side.

Cara giggled. 'One always benefits from a touch of highlighter on the cheekbones. Wow, you're actually going to be a T.V star.'

He grimaced, shook his head and swore under his breath.

'Come on. I'm here for moral support,' she said.

George offered her his arm, and the intimate gesture made her heart swell. She was overcome with love for him and had to work hard to contain her emotion.

'It's not that bad. Let's start in Henry VIII's apartments; that will set the scene nicely for the interview.'

'Thank you, good idea, perhaps the Tudor ambience will work its magic,' he said, grateful that he wouldn't need to face the interview alone.

They walked through the ancient Base Court, up the stairs, and entered the apartments via the Great Hall, eerily familiar to Cara from her recent visits to the past. She weaved slowly between the long wooden tables and glanced at the tablecloths imprinted with facts about Tudor life. She remembered the lavish banquets with hundreds of courtiers in attendance, where she occasionally sat next to George but more frequently her presence was required at the queen's table. It seemed so real as if Queen Anne would appear at any moment. Looking up at the intricately carved ceiling, she spotted the eavesdropper statue; the constant reminder that walls have ears. She wandered back towards the entrance, in search of the initials which were carved into the wall, by order of Henry VIII. The Great Hall was built and decorated in honour of Queen Anne Boleyn who the king, at that time, had called his one true love. Cara had seen the initials on previous visits, but after her time in Tudorville, she now had a burning thirst to re-examine the details. Her long-standing fascination with the period made perfect sense. She stared at the last remaining set of entwined Henry and Anne initials which the king's craftsmen infamously missed as they scoured the palace clean of any trace of poor Anne, following her execution.

'Shall we visit Clock Court where the most trusted courtiers had their accommodation? I love those apartments.' Cara and George meandered through the network of long corridors and into the apartment which Cara guessed had been theirs between 1535 and 1536.

'It looks so different,' she blurted out.

'Different?

'Oh, you know, I'd forgotten what it's like, it's been years since I came into this part of the palace,' her words trailed off.

The energy shifted in the room, and she glanced at George to see if he'd noticed. She could see he was absorbed in reading the placards with historical references about the rooms.

He doesn't know anything weird is going on.

She let out a ragged sigh of relief. She didn't want to try and make sense of any of this now. It was too much for her to get her head around, never mind explain to him.

'It's lovely in here,' he turned, a warm smile crossed his features, his dark eyes shone. 'You're right; these rooms have such a wonderful atmosphere; I feel at home. Hard to explain. Do you know what I mean?'

Cara nodded, touched almost to tears.

He leaned over to kiss her; a thoughtful, tender brush of his lips on hers.

So, he does feel it.

They were both conscious of their ever-deepening connection, but neither understood fully how it had occurred.

She tried to look casual, but her heart pounded. She was torn. She felt duplicitous in not telling him what was going on, but where would she even begin?

We've got enough to deal with right now without me laying another complicated life on top of the complexity of this one.

She took in the sumptuous decor of the rooms, but in her mind, the apartment looked as it was when it was theirs; the room where she'd been arrested on one of her recent trips to Tudorville, the bedroom where they'd shared some of their most intimate moments. Her heart raced at such a pace; she struggled to say his name.

'George,' she called out. 'George. . .' He turned and sauntered towards her, palace map in hand.

Cara saw his lips moving but couldn't hear his words. In that instant, she was pushed back into the time traveller's vortex. She was going, and there was nothing she could do to prevent it. She yearned to stay with him and experienced a flash of anguish as the cold air rushed into her lungs and caused her to gasp. She gulped as she tried to catch her breath and clutched the corner of one of the tables to steady herself.

But it was too late. She was on her way. George had no idea what had happened as he enthusiastically regaled her with the story of his legendary ancestor, George Oliver Cavendish.

'He was an interesting fellow; very close to the king by all accounts, until he was accused of treason and fell abruptly from favour. Being a member of the king's inner circle was a dangerous business. He's the one who was married to Cara. Remember I told you about them?'

'Yes,' Cara nodded. She observed her other self, engaged in conversation with George before she silently slipped away to Tudorville.

Two timelines; two of me living simultaneously but only occasionally conscious of the other.

Who would believe this?

Well, Sylvia for one. . .and Eddie, the quantum physics professor; my friend from five hundred years ago. If it wasn't for them, I'd think I was hallucinating.

George continued, 'I still can't believe the coincidence of your name. Our records say the Tudor Kings' Manuscript was commissioned as a special surprise gift to the king.'

He draped his arm around Cara's shoulders with an easy familiarity, as if he'd done it thousands of times. They exited Clock Court and headed back to locate the film crew.

Hampton Court Palace, 1536

Cara looked around and found herself sat at a long wooden table; mid Tudor banquet. Her stomach lurched as a stuffed baby partridge landed on her gold plate with the compliments of the queen. The sight of it made her want to heave. She hadn't eaten meat for years in her other life and couldn't face it now, even at the risk of incurring her mistress's displeasure.

Imagine the scandal if I declared myself a vegetarian.

Wealthy Tudors typically ate between one and two kilos of meat per day. The freaky thing was that Cara could recall eating meat at the banquets. She didn't know when or how it happened, but Professor Eddie Makepeace's prediction had come true; the knowledge bank of her own personal memories from Tudorville had been unlocked. Each day memories of her past experiences here in what seemed a foreign land dribbled into her mind. It was England, but the way of life was alien to her. Cara had been raised by her wealthy philanthropist adoptive father, so she wasn't unfamiliar with luxury, although her father wasn't particularly extravagant, preferring to channel his wealth into investments and charities. Nevertheless, Henry's court was flamboyant beyond anything she could have imagined and ostentatious beyond what she considered good taste.

Cara raised her hand to the servant in a polite gesture for him to desist from piling more animal flesh on to her plate.

'Please bring me a dish of pottage.'

'My stomach is a little queasy,' she whispered to the inquisitive lady next to her. Cara couldn't see the traditional dish on the buffet tables.

She would live on pottage, she decided. In addition to meat, the wealthy ate a lavish recipe of vegetable soup so she would try to be inconspicuous. She would pretend she suspected herself with child and of delicate constitution. She caught sight of King Henry VIII and watched his double chin wobble as his teeth ripped the dark red Venison meat off the bones with the help of his fat and greasy fingers.

Ew.

He guffawed at the frantic attempts of his court jester to entertain him. Cara stared at the king; this was a Tudor historian's dream.

The dashing good looks he was renowned for as a young man had already faded and been replaced by a portly middle-aged demeanour. It was thought that Anne, a seductive young woman with haunting eyes which glinted alluringly like black diamonds, hadn't married him for his charms.

Cara caught her husband's eye as he chatted with the king at the top table.

Thank goodness George hadn't run to seed.

He winked at her and an intense feeling of gratitude flooded through her.

I get to be with him today, and we're not on the run yet.

The king called for silence as the dishes were cleared from the tables, and satiated diners gathered to watch one of Queen Anne's ladies-in-waiting, Jane Seymour, perform for him at his special request. Later that evening, Cara whirled around the dance floor, elated to be in George's arms. She always took infinite care not to draw the king's attention. She was aware that any attractive woman in his sphere couldn't be too cautious.

As they danced, George dropped a row of light kisses on to the delicate skin at the side of her neck. She shivered. He had a mischievous glimmer in his eyes but continued to make light conversation.

'We unveiled the manuscript for the king this morning, and he was delighted. He is naming it *The Tudor Kings' Manuscript,* in anticipation of his prosperous male bloodline.'

'That's wonderful, my darling. Well done. It was a truly inspired idea of yours. The king seems in good cheer tonight indeed.'

'Let's hope the queen soon produces a son.' He spoke in a furtive tone as his deep, musical voice dropped an octave.

She whispered in his ear, 'I think we've danced enough to fulfil our courtly duty for one evening. Shall we retire now?' She flashed him a seductive smile, knowing he wouldn't be able to resist her.

George nodded, and he went to bid the king goodnight before returning to escort Cara to bed. They glided hand in hand through Clock Court and into their luxurious apartment.

Exhausted from a hectic day, they climbed into the four-poster bed and snuggled beneath the heavy bedding to keep warm against the cool night air. Cara's head sank into the pillow, her shiny chestnut mane draped around her shoulders like a silky curtain, as George pulled her close and tucked in behind her. She drifted off to sleep, safe in the cocoon of his arms.

Cara became aware of the gentle hubbub made by the army of servants who rushed quietly about their duties beneath her window. As the dawn haze of another glorious London day lit up the palace courtyard, Cara, who was a light sleeper, lay on her side in a contented doze. She relished the peaceful interlude before the night stole away to be replaced by a bright new London morning. She felt George stir behind her and shivered with delight as he nestled into her, and began to stroke her skin with a strong, firm touch. She couldn't suppress a giggle at his insistency, and she teased him by pulling her elaborate nightdress down in a show of pretend modesty.

'It's a little late for that don't you think, my lady?' said George, as he pressed his hard manliness against her soft thigh flesh until, impatient with her games, he pushed the bed cover aside in one sharp movement. He jerked her nightdress upwards, so nothing prevented their feverish skin from touching. He was fast but assured. His smooth hands touched her in the intimate ways only he knew drove her mad with lust and before long Cara whimpered and cried out as the waves washed over them, and he claimed her. She relinquished herself fully to him; mind, body and soul.

Hampton Court Palace, present day

'Thanks for watching,' said the presenter as he brought the interview to a close, smiling at the camera after shaking George's hand.

George's eyes scanned the room for Cara.

Where had she gone?

He'd seen her leave the room a few minutes earlier; he'd almost lost his flow mid-sentence. It wasn't like her; she was usually so attentive. Something must have happened; she hadn't returned to her seat. He checked his phone and saw a message.

'You were great! I'm so sorry. I had to dash. Terrible news from Daniel's daughter. He's had a heart attack.'

George called, but her phone didn't ring.

She must be in a poor signal zone.

'Oh, no. Serious?' he texted.

'They're not sure yet, but his daughter's in a state.'

'Where are you?'

'I'm in a taxi on my way to the station.'

George wished he could be more sympathetic, but he was crushed at her sudden departure. The interview had been a success, and he was on a high. He wanted to discuss it with her and celebrate over dinner. Given the broken engagement, he couldn't see why she needed to rush off to Daniel, but he restrained himself and replied, 'Right, I see.'

He has his family. He isn't alone.

'I feel as though I must go to be with him,' typed Cara. She sensed his disappointment and wanted him to understand.

'No problem,' he texted back, feeling like he'd been punched in the gut.

'Your interview went brilliantly. I loved it. Well done! I'll call you later. xx,' she responded.

And she was gone. Again.

Right then, Cara.

George headed out to the car park, fired up the engine of his beloved 911 and drove back to Knightsbridge, alone with his conflicted thoughts.

CHAPTER 14

L ondon to York, present day

Cara was only semi-conscious of the lush green fields rolling by as the train sped en route from King's Cross to York. She stared out of the window in a daze, her thoughts hijacked.

She longed to stay with George, but her guilty conscience needled her to be at Daniel's side. What if his heart attack was brought on by the stress of her leaving? He'd been in great shape at his last medical, or so he had let her believe.

Had he hidden the news of his poor health because he didn't want her to worry? It seemed unlikely; he wasn't typically the secretive type.

Who knows what's really going on in people's heads? They seem to so frequently say one thing but think another.

Cara nibbled her thumbnail, pondering the quirks of human nature, as the first-class carriage rumbled on through the open countryside. She should arrive in an hour. Daniel's daughter had surprised her by offering to meet her at the station and take her to the hospital.

Cara disembarked from the train and scanned the platform. Sally appeared, waving and smiling.

'Hi, how kind of you to pick me up. I'm so sorry about your father. You must have been through hell,' said Cara.

'It's been awful.' Sally's cheerful facade crumpled and she leaned against her shoulder and began to sob. Tears streamed down her face and dripped on to the lapel of her navy-blue jacket. She made an obvious effort to stem the flow but only grew more agitated as she tried to contain her emotions. Usually cold and distant with Cara, today her composure disintegrated.

'It's okay; it's okay,' said Cara, wrapping her arms around Sally. 'Your dad will be just fine. He's a fighter and has everything to live for.'

Sally pulled away, wiped her damp, red eyes, and said, 'I don't know. Since you guys split up, he's not been himself. I've never heard him sound so low. I've made an effort to call him more often, but it doesn't seem to help. Your leaving hit him hard.'

A fresh wave of guilt clutched at Cara. She'd hoped she'd managed to cut her ties to Daniel and was free. Now she feared she was about to be sucked back into his life in this emotional whirlpool.

When did everything get so complicated?

I want George.

Daniel wants me.

Who does George want?

Cara doubted whether even he knew and she was tired of trying to understand.

Cara entered the private room in the hospital ward and saw Daniel, his head thrown back on the pillow as he snored. The low hum comforted Cara. His snoring used to irritate her, but now it was a reassuring sign of life. He looked frail as he slept. His vulnerable pose plucked at her heart.

She sat by the bed and waited. He wasn't a physically unattractive man, at one time she'd believed herself to be in love with him. But then she realised she was trying to persuade herself to be in love because she was in love with the idea of love.

Once she realised this, the relationship flourished, and she accepted it for what it was. She didn't explain her feelings to Daniel. And he didn't have a need to explain his feelings to her. He seemed content with the situation as it was and so she let it be.

One night when he was tipsy on one too many measures of whiskey, he had confided in her that the last time his wife had tried to make love to him, they had both known it was over. Soon after, she filed for divorce.

Cara became good friends with Daniel, and they eventually called it an engagement. Cara wasn't bothered one way or the other, so she had chosen to please him. She talked herself into thinking their platonic love and the lack of passion, would be enough.

It was enough until it wasn't. Until she met George. From the day he disrupted her life like a force of nature in the bookshop; she knew the way she had been living would never satisfy her soul again. Whatever happened in the future, she was positive that not a day would go by without her pining for him. It was one of those things.

When you know, you know.

She had thought the depth of love she felt for George was only the stuff of romantic novels. She hadn't expected to fall in love like this, to fall in so deep that it made her previous love affair seem like a pale ghost of the real thing.

Cara lightly thumped her fist against her forehead. Why

couldn't she want the man who wanted her? Then they could all be content with what or who they already had.

She was startled by the melodious ring tone of her phone. It was George. She turned the sound down. It seemed wrong to speak to him in Daniel's presence even while he slept. Besides, she didn't want Daniel to know about George. The less he knew, the better. He couldn't possibly understand the feelings which had erupted between them so instantly.

Daniel stirred, opened his eyes and smiled.

'Here you are. I knew you would come.' His voice was cracked, his throat dry.

'Of course,' she said. 'Here, have a sip of water,' She raised the glass to his lips and supported his head.

'The Lady with the Lamp, my very own Florence Nightingale,' he croaked. He shifted position and after a few seconds drifted back to sleep, satisfied Cara was at his side.

Cara messaged George to let him know she'd arrived and then dropped her phone into her bag. She was here now and would try to focus on Daniel even though she didn't want to spend the rest of her life with him.

George would be fine. He'd probably return home to his wife shortly. Cara pushed her bleak thoughts aside and busied herself with Daniel's chart. She couldn't understand it and decided to speak to his doctor at the first opportunity.

Daniel slept on, drugged with heavy medication. Cara grew restless. She wandered into the cafeteria, ordered a coffee and then picked up a dog-eared copy of her favourite classic from the waiting room bookshelf.

She settled into the armchair in Daniel's room. She used to plough effortlessly through books, though recently she'd lost her ability to concentrate. It troubled her. She was so distracted that fictional worlds no longer held her attention.

She turned the pages of *Pride and Prejudice*, conscious that even now her mind was preoccupied with thoughts of George.

Perhaps there was a spark of hope despite the circumstances.

She read Mr Darcy's passionate confession.

"In vain, I have struggled. It will not do. My feelings will not be repressed. You must allow me to tell you how ardently I admire and love you."

She scanned the text for a few minutes and then, with a heavy sigh, closed the book. George wasn't Mr Darcy. She must stop romanticising him and face up to the reality of the futile situation. Cara fished her phone out of her bag and saw three missed call notifications. Her spirits lifted, a smile shone on her pale, tired face and her feelings overpowered her dark thoughts.

How could she end it with George when he was present in every thought and in everything she did? He was with her every moment of the day. And what about Tudorville? Whatever happened, she'd see him there, so how would she be able to move on?

It was a conundrum with which she continuously struggled. She knew she should end their love affair. It made no sense not to. But she couldn't bear the idea of losing him. Six hours without him was like a week in the desert; a lifetime would be like being cast into an inferno.

Not religious, she prayed for the resolve to end it. None came. She read George's message.

'How are you doing? I hope Daniel's okay. Give me a call when you can.'

She'd call him on the way home.

Sally appeared in the doorway. 'Hello. How is he?'

'Oh, hi, Sally. You look refreshed. Did you get some sleep?'

'Yes, thanks. It was the first time I slept in two days. I could relax knowing you were here. Thanks for coming.'

'No problem, we may have ended our engagement, but I still care for him.'

Sally twisted her hands and looked down at her feet, 'I'm sorry I was so awful to you when you were with my dad. It was horrid of me. I resented you. You see, I always had this idea that my parents would get back together. I realise now that's never going to happen.'

Cara smiled. 'I can't imagine how tough it must be to see a parent with a different partner.'

'Please accept my apologies. Can we turn over a new leaf and be friends?' said Sally.

'Yes, of course.' Cara squeezed Sally's shoulder. She felt a surge of compassion for the poor girl. Daniel's heart attack had obviously shaken her. At least something positive had come of it. Daniel would be pleased to see they were at peace with each other.

It was late. Sally continued the vigil by her father's bed. The two women chatted a bit and then Cara decided to head home.

She called George from the taxi.

'Ah, there you are. How was it?' he said.

'It's been a long day. Daniel's stable but the doctor said they're keeping him in and are still uncertain as to whether he'll need surgery. It's touch and go whether he'll make a full recovery, apparently.'

'I'm sorry to hear that. You been there all day?'

'Yes, since I arrived back from London. He slept for most of the day, but I wanted to be there in case he woke up. And for the first time, his daughter was pleased to see me.'

'Oh nice,' She heard George's voice tighten. 'And did he wake up?'

'Yes, but just for a few minutes. He was pleased I was there.'

'I bet.'

'How was your day? Tell me about the interview. What happened after I left?'

'Not much really, except they said it went well and they'll be in touch with more details.'

'Wow, that's fantastic. You must be thrilled.'

'Yes, I suppose I am. It all feels a bit surreal. Would have been better if you'd stayed.'

'I'm sorry I had to dash off like that. The news came as a bit of a shock.'

'I'm returning to York soon,' he said.

'Great. So you're not needed in the London office as long as you thought?'

'They can manage. Joanna asked me to come home to be there for Jane while she takes a trip for work.'

'Oh, right. I don't think you ever mentioned what she does. I sort of got the idea she didn't work.'

'Oh no, she's pretty much always worked. She's an art dealer. Loves it actually. Does most of it in the UK but occasionally she needs to travel. She's off to the South of France next week.'

'I see. Good,' said Cara.

Oops. I said that out loud.

'Um, I mean good that she has work she enjoys.'

'Yes, quite,' said George. 'I know what you mean.' He laughed.

The Great North Road, 1536

George took a risk by throwing himself upon the mercy of King James V, but he didn't know what else to do. His family were as good as imprisoned in Sir John Locke's basement for the past two weeks, and he could stand hanging about on the whim of fate no more.

He saddled up one of the horses with Sir John's blessing and set off once again on The Great North Road in the driving rain.

Cara was terrified he'd be captured and thrown in the Tower. As he rode through the bitter winds, he saw her sweet face before him. She was his lucky charm, urging him on and keeping him safe on his mission. She'd initially been against his Scottish plan, to seek asylum from James V, because she thought it too perilous. But she knew it was fruitless to try to stop him when he'd made up his mind. And so, she swept her misgivings aside, and together they devised a plan.

United, they were a formidable force. He knew he could count on Cara to have his back even when she didn't agree with his actions.

He missed her when she wasn't by his side, but he felt her presence. They were constantly in each other's thoughts, and they could often sense each other's feelings, especially when together, but even over great distances. Words were of little importance to their eerily telepathic connection. If there was such a thing as a soul mate, then George was certain Cara was his.

She said they were the ultimate soul mates. They were Twin Flames, something she'd learned about when reading Plato's, *The Symposium*. She explained it to him, saying they were like mirrors, and that Twin Flames were two halves of the same soul, split apart. Their purpose was to heal each other, and in so doing, they shined the light of unconditional love on the world.

They shared an unbreakable bond since the first night they met. It was love at first sight. Many of his friends barely spoke to their wives beyond social and family expectations, but he and Cara were different. He couldn't bear to think of a life without her.

He pushed his horse hard through the cold nights and rested in the forest or travelled on back roads during daylight. He nibbled on the dwindling supplies in his saddle-bag, as he edged closer to the Scottish border. Sir John Locke had managed to arrange a meeting between George and King James V's special envoy.

King James V was King Henry VIII's nephew and under normal circumstances, appealing to the young Scottish king would be as good as signing his own death warrant. However, there was a long-standing feud between the two kings.

George was counting on King James's distrust of his uncle to work in his favour. He planned to ask for asylum, and if the king was agreeable, he'd send immediately for Cara and the children to join him at Stirling Castle or wherever the king would extend his hospitality. King James had supported the Irish Rebels and had a soft spot for the Northern Lords.

George lost count of the nights he'd been riding. By the time he reached Berwick-upon-Tweed, his hands were raw and chapped from the bitter winds, and he nearly fell from his horse, such was his exhaustion. He was to meet James V's envoy, and at the same time, he would send a note to Cara. He knew she would be anxious for word that he had arrived safely.

'It's courageous of you to come here, my lord, under the circumstances. How did you know King James wouldn't have you immediately arrested and delivered to King Henry for the handsome price on your head?'

'I confess I didn't,' said George. 'But I counted on King

James's honourable character.' George sipped his wine and warmed his cold body in front of the fireplace.

'There's a bed for you here, please stay a few days to recover from your long journey whilst we await word from King James. He'll know what to do, and we'll reconvene as soon as I hear from him.'

George quickly wrote to Cara and paid a lad to arrange for the note to be despatched, slipping him an extra coin for urgency and confidentiality. Later that evening George crawled under the bed covers and fell into a blissful sleep, content he'd completed the first part of his mission.

CHAPTER 15

York, present day

George missed Cara. The days were long and dull without her. Ever since she'd dashed off to Daniel, they'd barely talked. He wanted to be understanding, but as far as he could tell, she'd been at Daniel's bedside all week. It rattled him.

He paced around the Tudor Kings' Manuscript, phone in hand. It went to voicemail. Again. The more he tried to stop thinking about what she was up to, the more he worried she was slipping away. Perhaps he'd already lost her.

What if she decides to go back to him?

He didn't know what to do. He was damned whatever he did. If he left Joanna, he'd be the guy who turned his back on his wife and daughter. But if he didn't, he'd lose the love of his life. There was little to hold Cara as things stood. She wouldn't wait around forever.

He made a cup of tea, took a sip, and swore as the hot

liquid burned his tongue. His head hurt. He hadn't slept well in days.

Joanna was away on a business trip, and his daughter was in and out with friends at all hours. He wished he'd stayed in London out of the way. The previous night he'd laid his head on the pillow, exhausted and ready to sleep, only to find his mind raced. He couldn't settle. He worried about Cara, was nervous about his work, and in the dark, silent hours of the night, he dreaded the future. The incessant noise in his head whirred like a fan which gave him no respite. He finally managed a restless sleep at dawn where he dreamed he was a member of Henry VIII's court.

For the first time, he almost wished Cara hadn't come into his life. It would be less painful than this constant tug on his emotions. You didn't miss what you'd never tasted. He tried to recall what life was like before she appeared in the bookshop. He couldn't visualise it.

His phone rang, rousing him from his groggy state.

'Morning. How are you?'

'Ah, morning. There you are. Where did you go? I've been calling and calling.' He tried to make light of it but was tired and on edge. His voice sounded sullen even to his own ears.

'I'm sorry. I was talking to Daniel's doctor. They're in the process of deciding whether to go ahead and do the surgery or whether to wait and see how he does without it for a while. It's complicated. It's tricky to know what would be best.'

'Okay,' he said, polite but bordering on cold. He was fed up of hearing about Daniel but didn't wish to seem uncaring.

'What do his children say? They're his next of kin, so I suppose it's up to them to decide, isn't it?'

'Well, yes but. . .'

A heavy silence hung between them until George prompted Cara in a gentler tone, 'But?'

'It's odd, but now he's in this condition, they're being really lovely to me and keep asking for my input and wanting me to make the decisions.'

'Okay, but it's not your decision to make, is it? Unless you want it to be, of course.' He checked himself. He'd said enough.

He felt exposed; more vulnerable than he'd ever been. He detested feeling insecure like this. Logically he knew that what she did regarding Daniel wasn't any of his business. Given his position, he didn't think he had the right to question her relationship with him. But it didn't stop him feeling jealous. Alarm bells were ringing, and he didn't want to be caught with his trousers down when he should be making a quick exit. He took a deep breath and consciously drew back from the fire.

'No, you're right. It's for them to decide, but I suppose I feel a bit guilty,' Cara said.

'It's not your fault. It could have happened any time. You weren't to know.' He wanted to be supportive, but he was in a panic. None of this was in his control. He wanted her too much. The urge to protect his heart and pull up his emotional drawbridge kicked in.

Tears welled in her eyes, and her throat constricted as the love she felt for him threatened to overwhelm her. She wasn't prepared for the emotion in his voice. She knew he studiously kept up his bravado and took care not to lower his barriers, so in the odd moments he was vulnerable, it was all the more touching.

She yearned to go to him. She wished he would wrap his arms around her and she could sink into him as they shut out the world.

How could it be wrong for them to be together when they loved each other like this?

It was one of life's cruellest tricks; send you someone who

is your perfect counterpart and who fulfils you in ways you never imagined. But make them unavailable. Push you to the limits of your own good character so that you doubt your integrity and everything you thought you stood for. Their relationship pushed buttons neither of them had known they had.

'I'm in town if you want to stop by the workshop for a coffee.'

'I'd love to, but I'm not sure what time I'll be able to leave the hospital because they're running tests. I promised Sally I'd be here this afternoon. She was hinting for me to stay the night so she can go home, but I hope I won't have to.'

'Remind me who Sally is?' George had switched into sounding disconnected and business-like.

'Daniel's eldest daughter. She met me at the station, remember? Her husband brought the kids into town today. It's tough with them all living in Manchester. She hasn't seen them all week.'

'Ah, yes. I knew that.' He laughed, but the sound was hollow.

Cara knew he was annoyed. There was a steely edge to his voice which others may not recognise. She could sense his moods and often guessed what he thought before he could put it into words. This was how it had been between them since the beginning. It was the same for him. He could pick up on her thoughts and feelings. It was as though they were tuned in to the same antenna. It was unnerving at times to be so finely attuned to one another. Sometimes Cara feigned ignorance and let it be. It was simpler than trying to constantly analyse the intense frequency which connected them like an electric current.

'Are you going back to work soon?' George asked.

'I've got my laptop and been doing a bit of work here.' Cara sounded defensive.

'Sounds like you've moved in there!' He immediately wished the words hadn't slipped out.

There was an awkward pause.

You idiot.

He cursed himself.

'Try to understand. He doesn't have anyone but his kids, and they've fallen apart. I feel responsible. He's not been awake for more than short periods since I arrived.'

'Yes, I get it. Oh, Cara, Jane's trying to call. Let me speak to her. I'll catch you back in a bit.'

'Yes, of course. Okay. Bye. Have a good day.' Cara was still talking, but he'd gone.

She looked out of the window at the sunless landscape. The sky was as bleak as her heart. He was angry, and now she was wretched. She hated when he was angry with her. It was endearing that he was a bit jealous of Daniel, but she couldn't bear him being upset. Her heart throbbed, and a dark veil of gloom descended upon her.

In the brief time since they met in this life, they'd only had awkward exchanges about the elephant in the room: his marriage. Or more to the point, his limited availability. Now Daniel was back in the mix, George was getting a taste of what it was like to not have her waiting by the phone for when he could fit her in. He didn't like it any more than she did. That much was obvious. But what could she do? She couldn't abandon Daniel in this state.

Well, now he knows what it's like. Maybe he'll be more understanding when she was waiting for him for hours, sometimes days, whilst he disappeared into his life in which she had no place.

'Are you ok?' she messaged him, then stared into space as she tried to steady herself. She wanted to cry, but that wouldn't do here. She'd wait until she got home later. Sometimes black despair took hold and threatened to break her spirit. On those days, she had to give way to it and allow herself to sob it out.

She waited for a few minutes and then checked her phone. No response yet. Who knew how long he'd make her wait? He would sometimes go silent for hours when she had angered him in some way.

She noticed her message was sent at 11:11. Of course. Sylvia had explained to her that there were many numeric indicators and signs of a Twin Flame connection. 11:11 was a significant number. It cropped up repeatedly in their communication.

It's easy to behave well when the person you're in love with isn't with someone else. Only a fool would sign up for this.

She sighed and then shoved her phone into the pocket of her jeans as she went to greet Daniel's children with a bright, fake smile. Cara wished she was meeting George for coffee.

Three hours later and still nothing. She stared at her phone, willing him to respond. No message came. Her heart was heavy, and her eyes ached from holding back the unshed tears.

Cara, who was usually kind and compassionate, was shocked by the violent feelings provoked by the intensity of her relationship with George. Had she hurt him too much by going to Daniel? Was he gone forever?

Nice, present day

'Jo. Jojo!'

'Over here,' an olive-skinned, athletic-looking man in his mid-thirties waved to attract Joanna's attention.

'Ah, hi! Great timing, I almost missed you,' she said.

There was something about Alex which made her feel carefree and young. She giggled a lot when she was with him.

'I feel better already, just seeing you,' she said.

'Then I've fulfilled my reason for being,' he said, taking a mock bow. His smile revealed a cheeky dimple in his chiselled chin and a set of perfect Hollywood style, white teeth.

Joanna touched his boyish face and ran her glossy pink nails through his dark hair before she leaned in to kiss him.

This is my prize for being a well behaved, loyal wife and mother for so long. At last, it's my turn to have some fun.

Joanna could taste her new-found freedom. She was giddy and exhilarated and surprised to not feel guilty. She'd felt cold and dead inside for so long; she thought that anything must be preferable to chugging along in the depressing fog of her empty marriage. To feel alive again was worth taking any risk.

'Where are we going?'

'Let me surprise you,' said Alex, flashing her a mischievous grin.

'Great! It's nice not to have to plan everything for a change. You do remember I have important meetings tomorrow in St. Tropez?'

'Sure, no problem. I'll drive you there in the morning. But today I've got you all to myself. . .'

'Yes, I'm all yours!'

Alex slid his arm around her waist, and they sauntered off to his car. They looked like two lovers without a care. And that's what they were for today. Until Joanna returned to York. Until her soul draining routine resumed. She decided she wouldn't think about that now.

George was a good man. She'd loved him since she was a teenager. But gradually, over the years, he withdrew his tenderness, and the deep feelings she'd had for him slowly shrivelled. It was painful to want someone who didn't want you. In the end, she'd closed her heart in an effort to protect herself from his wordless rejection. A sense of obligation replaced the love she used to feel for him, and it saddened her that she could barely recall the happiness they must have shared in the early days. She knew she had loved him, but now, looking back on their youth, she realised George hadn't adored her in the way she'd dreamed of when imagining her future husband. He was a catch: handsome, charming, intelligent and funny, and so she'd let herself believe he felt the same. And he had loved her. Just not enough; not enough to last a lifetime. He was a devoted father and a kind, dutiful husband, but she was stifled by his lack of passion. She didn't want kindness; she wanted him to take her in his arms and make love to her as if he couldn't live without her. But they hadn't had sex for several years, and even then, it had usually been initiated by her. They hadn't made love and meant it for longer than she could remember. She accepted that he only stayed with her out of duty.

Joanna knew him well after twenty years of living together. He didn't want to have to deal with the unpleasantness of ending their marriage. He didn't want to be that guy who might be judged as selfish and uncaring. He loved to be admired and respected. They both paid a high price to retain the romantic couple image they'd projected for so many years. Even their closest friends and family had no idea they weren't the ideal couple they pretended to be.

But Joanna knew something had changed recently. It was sudden. They'd been distant with each other before, but now he was distracted and especially impatient. He was always popping out. It wasn't just the long business trips anymore. She'd also observed he'd begun guarding his phone as if he would be court marshalled if anyone got their hands on it.

Was he having an affair?

She didn't feel anything. She'd stopped feeling years ago. It was time to stop acting out this charade. She'd come to the conclusion she'd rather be alone than feel lonely in this sham of a marriage.

'Jo? Jo? A penny for your thoughts. Where have you gone?' Alex waved one hand in front of her face, laughing, as he drove.

'Oh sorry, I was thinking about my meetings tomorrow.' She touched his arm and tried to pay attention.

The hire car rolled along the winding roads, and she peered around the bends over the steep cliff edge at the choppy blue waves below. It reminded her of her life; she was liable to crash at any moment.

Alex steered the car into the circular drive of a sumptuous chateau-style hotel, typical of the French Riviera. Palm trees rustled in the light sea breeze as if to welcome them.

'Here we are. Like it?'

'Oh, I love it!' And she did. She threw her arms around his neck and hugged him. She was determined to make the most of her brief window of freedom. She was grateful for Alex.

'Let's get changed and order cocktails by the pool. The weather's perfect for it.'

The entered the hotel and went to check-in.

'Mr and Mrs Andrews?'

'Yes, thank you, that's us,' said Alex.

He took the key card, and they stepped into the elevator. Outside their room, he picked her up effortlessly and swept her inside, over the threshold. The door closed with a loud thud behind them.

York, 1536

Cara heard the beat of hooves outside the window and a loud rap at the front door. She shivered with a mixture of cold and fear.

'Let's hope that's good news from George. It seems like weeks with no word.'

'It's only been a few days, my lady, try not to fret. The journey is a long one; I'm sure we'll hear something soon even if not today.' Edward said.

There was a tap at the door.

'Yes?' she called. 'Please enter.'

Sir John Locke burst into the room, holding out an envelope to Cara. 'This is for you, my dear. I think it must be word from George although there's no marking. Pray open it and let us know the news. He's been in my prayers.'

'Thank you, Sir John. I can't express how grateful we are to you for your hospitality.'

Cara broke the seal; her heart hammered at an alarming pace. She scanned the note. Edward and Sir John saw her shoulders relax. She released a sigh, appeared to read the note again and then looked up. Her expression was joyful.

'Thank God. He's arrived safely. He is under the protection of James V's special envoy while they await word from the king as to whether he will grant us full asylum.'

Cara read George's words again when she was alone, in an attempt to bring him closer.

'*My beloved wife*

I am arrived and very pleased about it. I've been given safe harbour whilst we await word. Give my love to our little ones and know you have been in my thoughts every minute of every day. I will get word to you as soon as I have news. Please stay where you are until then. Take care, my darling.

Your devoted husband (IAS).'

IAS was one of their secret codes. It meant, 'I am safe.' He and Cara exchanged hundreds of private notes when he was away on missions for King Henry. Over the years they had gradually developed a lexicon of codes so they could exchange vital information in their love letters. They were counterparts — a fearless team in all things.

Cara pressed the note to her lips, and then with regret, she cast it into the roaring flames in the fireplace. She would have liked to keep the note under her pillow on the hard floor of the basement. It would have helped her to feel close to George as she tried to sleep. But sentimentality had no place in dangerous times. She knew she must follow their standard protocol which was to burn all notes and not be tempted to keep them as tokens of love.

In Berwick-upon-Tweed, George waited for the reappearance of the special envoy. He'd been informed that word had arrived from King James V and his fate, and that of his family depended on the contents of the letter.

CHAPTER 16

York, present day

'Hello, how are you?' said Cara.

'Okay. You?'

'I've missed you.' Her voice was low, almost a whisper.

'So why didn't you answer your phone when I called you then?' said George, his tone was light, but she detected a note of anguish. She knew him well after five hundred years.

'Because I was upset. I mean, I am upset. You don't want to see me, but you won't let me go either. I don't understand what you want from me.' Her voice rose as her words gathered momentum.

'I want to talk to you every day. I thought I'd explained.'

'I feel as though I can't be with you and can't be without you. I don't know what to do,' she said.

'Why do we have to do anything? Can't we just enjoy things as they are for a while?'

Cara paused as she tried to quell her emotions. 'It's horrible not seeing you. It's been weeks.'

'I know. It's not easy for me either.'

'So why can't we at least see each other? As soon as we get close, you push me away. We go round and round in the same old pattern. I don't know how you expect me to deal with it.'

'What we have is more important than sex. You mean more to me than that,' he said.

His words stung. Her throat constricted and tears welled in her eyes.

'Oh I see, so we won't bother having sex again?' she said. 'I've never been rejected by anyone who supposedly loves me, as much as I have by you. I don't get it. Don't you want to be with me?'

'Of course, I do. You know, I do. That's the problem.'

'What do you mean? I wish you would just say what you mean, for once. You talk in riddles, George. Trying to figure out what you mean and what you want is exhausting.'

A tense silence hung between them.

'Pining for you is too hard,' he said after a long pause. 'That's what happens when we see each other as we did before. I can't do it. I will want you every day and won't be able to have you.'

Cara closed her eyes. Intense, raw pain ripped through her heart; she feared it would consume her. She wished they were together in Tudorville; or anywhere but here in this dreadful limbo.

She tried to calm herself and said, 'But you can have me. Don't you find it even harder, us not seeing each other? It's not just the sex. It's being close to one another. I miss you.'

It was too much. Cara lost control and began to cry silently.

'Could we just be friends for a while without seeing each other?' he said, relentless.

His words seared her soul. After they met in the bookshop, he had been demonstrative and loving, like her husband from Tudorville, but now he had sealed his heart again. He had made up his mind, and she knew nothing would move him. Cara was gripped by white-hot anger, the type she had never experienced before.

Why must he insist on being so stubborn? I could shake him.

'After what we've shared, it's beyond me how you think that's possible. Do you really think what we have is only friendship?'

'No. I didn't say that. But I think it's the best we can have now, in the circumstances. I'd rather have that than nothing. I want you in my life.' His voice was hard and flat, devoid of the customary lilt she loved so much.

Cara swallowed, her throat thick with tears.

'I've got lots of friends. You're deluded if you think this is friendship. Is this how you feel about your other friends? Do you call them every chance you get to talk for hours? Do you have sex with your other friends?' Her rage spilt forth, and she struggled to process what he said. She almost screamed with frustration. 'This is crazy. I can't do this friends thing you keep talking about.'

'Cara, please slow down. Try to understand.'

'You didn't want to slow down in Seville, did you?'

'I'm sorry. Things have moved on since then.'

'How? How have they moved on? We're both still here, hanging on the phone, wanting each other. What the hell has changed?'

'It's difficult to say. Maybe things will be different in the future, but right now, I need some time to figure things out.'

'Great, you need time. I'll give you all of the time you need. Get in touch when you want to see me again.'

'Right. Okay, I see. Got it.'

The hurt in his voice was too much for her to stand. The tears slid down her cheeks, and the salty liquid splashed on to her lips.

'Don't you see? I can't live in the grey like this. It's too difficult. How am I supposed to do this if we're together but not really together?'

George's voice softened, 'I'm sorry. I'm doing everything I can not to hurt you. I've put you in an impossible situation. I know that. It's not your fault.'

'Other people leave their marriages when they fall in love with someone else. There's no reason why you can't, other than you don't really want to. You want to have us both. I don't blame you. It's the perfect arrangement for you.'

Her words sprang out like sharp arrows, but even as they hit their target, she was sorry. She hated hurting him, but it was too much for her to handle. This time it was finally over. Let him be with his bloody Joanna in this life if that's what he wanted. She was done waiting for him: she would walk away for good now. He had been her husband five hundred years ago; that would have to do. In Tudorville he was still hers as long as she could save him from the gallows.

'I can't do this anymore. I have to go now,' she said, wishing she could run away and hide like a wounded animal.

'No, Car, wait. Don't go like that.'

'I'm sorry. I can't do this anymore.' She pressed the end call button on her phone and stood sobbing in the same spot for a long time. She had no spark left in her.

Later that night, Cara lay on her bed, mentally exhausted, staring into space, unseeing. She had replayed their conversation in her head, repeatedly, until she'd worn herself out.

It was no good. He obviously wasn't that bothered

because she hadn't heard from him again. This time it was truly over. Usually, he pushed her away and then pulled her straight back again. It had been like that ever since the day they met in the bookshop. They each had the knack of tugging at one another's heartstrings.

She switched the light off and drew the quilt up to her chin for comfort, like a child. She wished she could sleep and turn her thoughts off as instantly as she did the lamp. She was desperate for sleep. None came.

Finally, she drifted into a restless doze. At three in the morning, she awoke to a black wave of loss and dread. What had she done? Why was she so headstrong and impulsive? She didn't want to be without him. A future without him was inconceivable. She tasted the panic in her mouth; the heaviness crushed her chest and made it difficult to breathe.

She checked her phone—still no word from George. The past few months had a nightmarish quality. She tried to stop thinking by forcing herself back to sleep. Sleep eventually came, and she forgot everything for a merciful few hours.

The alarm sounded, and she reached to hit the snooze button on her phone. Another wave of despair hit her as consciousness seeped in. There were some messages. Her spirits soared. He did care.

'Please don't do this. We will find a way. What I wanted to say came out all wrong yesterday. I'm sorry. Can we talk today?'

She was lost in a maze with no way out. But she didn't want a way out; she loved him. Each time she decided to end it, he said or did something which made her love him even more. She reasoned, if he didn't want her as much as she wanted him, surely he wouldn't keep pulling her back. This wasn't the easy option for either of them. It was like being spun in a washing machine on a manic, never-ending cycle. They were locked in and couldn't open the door.

Cara's heart soared for the first time in days as she closed her eyes, exhausted from all of the conflicting emotions. He was like a drug. She sank into a blissful sleep as relief washed over her. She hadn't lost him. When they were at peace, all was right in her world. None of this made any logical sense, but she had no strength left to fight these powerful feelings.

York, 1536

A young servant girl rushed down to the basement, letter in hand. She had been sworn to secrecy about the mysterious residents who were below stairs, as was the entire household. Any news was exciting for the bowels of the earth inhabitants, but Cara leapt off the chair with anticipation and had to stop herself from snatching the letter from the girl's hand. It must be from George. It was as though she'd been waiting months to hear from him again, but it had only been five days since the previous letter; five agonising days.

It was difficult being cooped up in the basement, keeping the children occupied. They were used to spending a lot of time outdoors on the Willow Manor estate. May missed Nutmeg and kept begging to return home in-between bouts of tears.

'Come along children, it's time for today's lessons,' said Edward. 'Let's give your mother some peace and quiet. Just because we're not in the schoolroom, doesn't mean you're excused from your studies, you know.'

'But we too want to hear news of Father,' May complained.

'You'll hear soon enough, come now, you'll see your mother again after we've done a bit of French.'

May sighed and grumbled before she settled down on a

blanket on the floor next to Thomas. Rays of sun streamed in from the one high window, casting a warm pool of light on the children's shiny heads.

Please let him be well, prayed Cara.

She tore the letter open and scanned the words on the thick, heavy parchment. The sight of George's bold, black handwriting immediately soothed her frightened soul.

'There is good news, my darling. My request has been granted. I know you will wish to set out immediately, but I ask you to wait a little longer. You must have patience. I've been informed it's a dangerous season to travel. I'll send a letter or get word to you again somehow as soon as it's clear. In the meantime, rest, and prepare yourselves for a long and arduous journey. Please don't take any risks because the timing is critical.

As always, your loving husband (IAS).'

He knew her well. She was impatient and disappointed that they couldn't already be on their way. The note implied they would be given safe haven at one of King James V's homes. She imagined it might be Stirling Castle in Scotland. That would explain the reference to the long journey. She sought out Sir John Locke.

'Sir John, I've had a letter from my husband. He alludes to the roads being more dangerous than normal and bids me wait until we hear from him again before setting out to join him. The good news is King James has granted us asylum.'

Oh, that's wonderful news indeed, my dear, Lady Cara. I'm sure you and your family can't wait to escape from my dreadful basement. I'm only sorry we can't offer you more comfortable accommodation in the main house.'

'Your hospitality is most generous, and we are not unaware of the great risk you incur by hosting us in this way. Please don't apologise. You have been more than generous. There is one thing, Sir John.'

'Yes? Anything I can help you with, simply ask.'

'Do you have any idea as to why it's more dangerous to travel to Berwick-Upon-Tweed now, as opposed to at other times?

'Strange you should ask today because I had word only this morning that King Henry and a small band of courtiers are on early summer progress. It's not the full court, but a sizeable group nonetheless. I imagine George has heard the news and doesn't want to take any chances that you'll bump into them on your way.'

'I see, yes that makes perfect sense. Thank you. It looks as though we'll be on your hands for a few more days yet until we get a sign that it's safe to leave.'

York, present day

Sylvia embraced Cara in a warm hug. 'How are you? I've been wondering when you'd come and see me again.'

'Thank you, Sylvia. I've meant to book in with you for a while as you're the only person I can talk to about this craziness.'

'Wasn't Professor Eddie Makepeace helpful?'

'Oh no, I mean, oh, yes. He's a wonder. Thank you so much for introducing me to him. He's a great help, and he's already taught me so much about time travel. It turns out we were close friends back in Tudorville. Sounds unbelievable, I know. But I haven't confided in him about my relationship with George. It's all too emotional and delicate. I haven't discussed the Twin Flame stuff with anyone but you. Not even George.'

'Yes, I can't imagine the Professor being all that useful in matters of the heart. He's probably more interested in his experiments.'

'Exactly. He's asked me to assist him in his research. He wants to catapult me to the future so we can save the world. Nothing too major! As if I don't have enough to deal with!' Cara laughed.

Sylvia smiled and raised her eyes heavenwards.

'The thing is, I just don't know what to do about George. Everything is wonderful between us back then, but in the present, we fluctuate between heaven and hell. One minute he can't get enough of me, and the next he's distant and won't even see me.'

'Sounds pretty run of the mill behaviour for Twin Flames.'

'Really? I haven't known anything like it before. I get angry and hurt every time he does it. Just as I think I understand him, he withdraws, and I go ballistic. I've never behaved so erratically.'

'Nothing surprises me with Twin Souls. It's typically hot, emotional and very messy. . .but beautiful too, which is, of course, what makes it impossible to walk away. You won't experience that type of intensity with anyone else, now or in the future. He is the one for you. I found it infuriating with my husband too, at times.'

'Infuriating, yes, that's exactly it!' said Cara

'Shall we pull some cards for you, my dear?'

'Oh yes please, that would be good.'

Sylvia beckoned for Cara to take a seat as she busied herself shuffling her decks.

'I'm using my favourite Tarot Deck and Angel Oracle Cards.'

Cara crossed and uncrossed her legs as she shifted about on the plush, green chair. What if she didn't like what she heard? What were angel oracle cards? They sounded a bit woo-woo.

Hmmm, like my whole life isn't completely woo-woo. . .

'What specific question would you like to ask of the cards?' said Sylvia.

Cara focused with difficulty. 'It's a little embarrassing, but I'm just going to say it because it's been on my mind so much lately. I'd like to know if he really loves me; I mean in the present day. I know he loved me five hundred years ago, but I'm uncertain how he feels about me here and now.'

'Okay. Right. Well, I can promise you he loves you deeply, without looking at the cards, based on your past reading, but let's see what the cards reveal to us today. Please tell me when to stop.'

Cara allowed several seconds to pass as she watched Sylvia shuffle the glossy coloured cards before placing each one face down on the table, in a pile.

'Now,' said Cara.

'And tell me when to stop again,' said Sylvia.

They repeated the process until there were three cards, face down, in a row.

Sylvia turned them over, one by one.

'So we've got Temperance, Five Of Cups and True Love.

'This is an interesting combination. I love this spread for you.'

Cara smiled. 'Is it good? I do hope so—it feels as though I've been in turmoil for months.'

'Temperance, from the Tarot, indicates this is a time that requires great patience. Your higher self is now coming into play, be guided and take your time. What you dream of will be realised when you exercise self-control.'

'What does it mean for George and me do you think?'

'The Twin Flame journey is about both of you having spiritual lessons to learn before you reach your next level of consciousness. This is the sole purpose for you being reunited in this life. The more you struggle, the more you push away your inevitable union. I read Temperance as a sign to accept that you are counterparts and that you must trust your union will come to pass.'

Cara nodded. Yes, it made sense. Not for the first time, she resolved to be more patient with George. . .and with herself. She wished he would be more patient with her too. He could be tough.

Five of Cups is a fascinating one. It means you've suffered a loss or disappointment which certainly seems to be true, given what you've told me. The message is to not focus on disappointment; it will only deepen the loss. Moderate your actions with self-control, and by not allowing disappointments to dampen your spirit, you'll move forward with greater ease.

As for your question about whether George loves you now, Five Of Cups symbolises a broken marriage. You did say he is married?'

Cara nodded.

Sylvia's words didn't shock her. It had been evident to her all along that his marriage to Joanna wasn't sustainable, no matter how he clung to the status quo. He was supposed to be married to her in this life too, like in Tudorville. It was a dreadful mix up, like picking up the wrong grocery bag and taking it home by mistake.

'The True Love card also verifies what you already know. This is the romance of a lifetime, or in the case of you and George, the romance of multiple lifetimes. Stop doubting his feelings for you. He's involved in an internal battle which although you think is all about your relationship, actually isn't. That battle is already over.'

'It doesn't feel like it,' said Cara.

'There was never any doubt how it would end. He already knows on a soul level, you are meant for each other, but he obviously doesn't remember your past life as you do. He's now involved in a battle where he's fighting with his idea of who he is and what people will think of him if he dares to follow his heart. In this type of intense partnership, the outcome is inevitable. There's nothing either of you can do to stop your feelings for one another. The less you try to control circumstances, the easier it will be. George must learn his lesson, his way, as you are learning yours.

'Okay,' said Cara.

Her head was spinning.

'Have you got any more questions?'

'Yes, I'd like to know what will happen if I end it with him. It feels as though there's a hole where my heart should be when we're not connected. Sometimes the pain is so intense I'd rather die than feel it. But I struggle to be in touch with him when it seems like there's no future and he won't see me. And then I hurt him as well as myself.'

'That would be a brilliant question if you were in charge of ending it. It's difficult to understand when we try to plan our relationships logically,' said Sylvia with a knowing smile.

'I'm not sure I understand what you mean,' said Cara, puzzled.

Temperance and True Romance cards highlighted the need for you both to let go of trying to control circumstances. Each of you is fighting to gain control of the steering wheel. The reason you keep butting heads is that there is no wheel! Neither of you can control the destiny which you pre-ordained, together, thousands of years ago. You are both light-workers, here to raise the consciousness of the planet as counterparts. Once you let go of the controls and get out of the way, events will unfold as they are supposed to. It will work out in a way that you probably can't even imagine now. You will be together. There's no other outcome.'

'I wish I could be as certain as you sound,' said Cara.

'One final thing,' said Sylvia.

'Yes?'

'Either of you can try to end it as many times as you like, but it won't work. It's impossible to end a Twin Flame connection. That's why you haven't been able to do it. It's nothing to do with doing the right thing. You are the right thing. Remember, you've been together for five hundred years. There could be a period where you both try to end it repeatedly. You may manage for a while, but he will be back in your life. That much I can promise you.'

'I'm not sure whether to laugh or cry,' said Cara.

'Be grateful Cara; most people never experience a Twin Flame love. You got the True Love card for a reason.'

As Cara left Sylvia's office, quiet contentment settled upon her like a soft, snug cape and she was soothed for the first time in weeks. She resolved to do her best to take Sylvia's advice and give up trying to finish with him. It was out of her hands.

Surely he must remember soon, and he would see how ridiculous it was for them to not be together.

CHAPTER 17

York, six months later, present day

'If we use my new TT system, we should be able to catapult you into any timeline we choose. Do you see the potential we have at our fingertips? It's incredible!' said Professor Eddie Makepeace.

Cara looked at him, wide-eyed. 'So, hold on, let me get this straight a minute. You've come all this way to see me because you want to use me as a guinea pig for your new. . .what—system?'

'TT: for time travel. It sounds dangerous, but it's not that bad, I calculated it has a seventy-five per cent success rate.'

'Wow! seventy-five per cent?'

'Yes. Isn't it amazing?'

'Er. . .what about the other twenty-five per cent? What if I fall into those stats?'

'Let's not focus on the negative. The chances are good

that you'll arrive in exactly the time for which we programme you. Think of the discoveries we'll make if we send you into the future.'

'The future? Gosh, I hadn't even thought about the possibility of going to the future. Who else has tested this wonderful TT system?'

'Um, well, no one yet. You'll be a pioneer. That's why it's so exciting.'

'I've told you before, Eddie, much as I'd love to help you out with your experiments, I just don't think it sounds like a sensible idea. It's so hit and miss. I mean, how would I get home?'

'We'll work out all of those little details once you agree to take part. It's a special system. My team and I have made considerable progress since we talked about it last time.'

'No, Eddie, absolutely not. I don't recall the specifics, but I've got an uncomfortable feeling that I've been your guinea pig in the past. And I don't think it ended well. Am I right?'

'I can't remember.' Eddie avoided her eyes and shuffled the paperwork in his briefcase. 'We've been through a lot together over the centuries. But you're here, aren't you? It can't have been that bad!' He ran his long fingers through his messy hair and shot her a boyish, 'please don't spoil my fun,' look.

'Interesting how your memory fails you at this crucial moment.' Cara laughed, always charmed by his innocent enthusiasm.

'Will you promise me you'll consider it, Lady Cara?'

'Please don't call me Lady Cara, Eddie, it sounds ridiculous! I'm just an ordinary woman now.'

'Okay, I'll try, but you'll never be ordinary. How about Countess?'

Cara rolled her eyes, and Eddie laughed. They shared the easy affinity of old friends.

'Purely out of interest, what timeline would you like to catapult me into?'

'Well, I'm curious to see what we can learn from the citizens of 2100. Technology will be so advanced by then; there'll be quantum leaps which we can apply now if we know what to look for. I'll be able to lead my team of scientists at the university to replicate your findings.'

'But is that not tinkering with the future, Eddie? What about the danger of unforeseen repercussions? It's like a potential apocalypse movie.'

'You'd report what you discover, and I'd only use what is safe to use.'

'I see,' Cara said. 'It sounds absolutely terrifying. But because it's you, I promise to think about it. Please don't get your hopes up though as I have a lot of reservations. I don't know if I can muster the courage, for one.'

'You are worrying unnecessarily. I've never known a more courageous woman. You saved me from the hangman's noose in Tudorville.'

'One more thing,' she said, touched by his affectionate words.

'Yes?'

'I'm confused. Why don't you go yourself and then you would see it all firsthand?'

'I wondered when you'd ask that. I'm afraid there's one small problem.'

'There always is, Eddie! What is it this time?'

'I have already been to the future. I gathered fascinating data which is why we must continue the experiment. If in the very unlikely scenario you don't come back as planned, I know how to come and get you. But if I go again and don't come back, no one, including you, because you're too inexperienced in time travel, would know how to reach me. Aside from the fact that I rather like my life here, me not returning would mean the end of the research. No one else on the team has the ability to time travel. This is why it's so important for you to go. I wouldn't ask you if it wasn't vital. I've gone as far as I can using myself as a prototype which is why your timing is absolutely perfect.

It's no exaggeration to say that what you discover, combined with our ability to analyse it, could save the planet from extinction. If we know what they know in 2100, we will be able to unpack the data and use it to set a different course. As crazy as it sounds, I think we will be able to save the world from a catastrophic end.'

Cara sighed. 'Somehow I don't feel any better after hearing that.'

York, the next day

Cara sipped her tea at the kitchen table and hummed to the radio. Energised after a good night's sleep, she was enjoying a few peaceful hours of solitude. She had been spending a lot of time with George lately; their relationship was about as wonderful as it could be, given the precarious circumstances. After Sylvia's reading, Cara had resolved to stop trying to control the situation and to accept it, for now, and then a couple of days later, as if by magic, George's embargo on them seeing each other had lifted and the impasse between them dissolved.

The newspaper thudded on to the doormat and interrupted her reflection. She scooped up *The Press* and leafed through the pages, as she wondered what to have for dinner.

What the hell? No. . .

But there it was; a coloured photo of George, her George, slammed into her face. Her spirits plummeted as his dark eyes met hers. Handsome and relaxed, his arm cradled Joanna's waist. The perfect couple. Cara's senses reeled, her familiar insecurities resurfaced and slashed at the wounds in her tender heart.

Here we go again. I can't take anymore.

Her thoughts raced as she read the article. There was a bit of back story about their life together, followed by a brief account of the history of the Tudor Kings' Manuscript. The programme would air the following week.

As if on cue, her phone rang. It was George.

For a couple of seconds, she contemplated not answering.

'Hello?' she said after a few rings, her voice unsteady.

'Morning. You okay? You sound a bit odd.'

The anger fuse lit deep within her like a firework spark before it exploded with a loud bang. 'Oh, yes! You could say that. I'm odd, alright. Even odder than I realised, it seems. A gullible fool, some might say.'

'What are you talking about Car? You've lost me.'

'Have you read *The Press* today?'

'No, why?'

'You're in it!'

There was a long silence before he said, 'Ah, that.'

'Yes, that.'

'I can't believe you didn't tell me.'

'Tell you what? It was just a routine piece of publicity the BBC asked me to do because the show will air soon.'

'Oh, I see. Sounds like you had nothing to do with it. That makes me feel much better. Thank you for that.'

George was silent. Her words hit their mark with the precision of a champion boxer; fast, quick and painful. He'd been caught off guard. He thought the feature was going to be out the following week and had planned to mention it at some point. He knew she wouldn't like it and had unconsciously put off telling her.

'Do you remember the photos being taken?' She prodded him, in the way one pokes a sore, swollen gum. She knew she shouldn't do it, it was going to hurt, but she couldn't stop herself.

'Um, yes, of course. It was a few weeks ago.' His words were clipped, his tone transmuted to ice.

'Aha. So, you had a media photo shoot in your house, as well as at the workshop? It must have been quite a production, but it slipped your mind. You couldn't mention it to me?'

If there was such a thing as seeing red, Cara saw it now.

'Well, when you say it like that, it doesn't put me in a very favourable light.'

He reverted to his trusted tool; self-deprecating humour, but it failed to entertain Cara this time.

She fumed. 'I'm the one in the dark, George. Not you, obviously. Here I am, stupid me, trying to be understanding about your situation and wanting to believe you love me. Meanwhile, you're posing for the whole city with your wife. You're splashed all over the Saturday paper as the model husband.'

'It's only an article; please be reasonable. Let me explain how it happened because it's not what you think. I didn't plan it. I couldn't say no when the coordinator invited Joanna to take part. It was agreed by her and my personal assistant before I heard anything about it.'

'There's nothing like opening the newspaper to read all about the incredible life the man you love shares with someone else. I particularly liked the bit where Joanna says how close you are because of your shared passion for the arts.'

'Cara, will you please calm down? You're blowing this way out of proportion. It's just a business thing. Joanna agreed to take part because the media guy said it would be more interesting that way and they gave her art dealership a plug too.'

'Oh, a win-win for the brilliant Cavendish couple. How fantastic. Well, I've had enough of this nonsense. Enjoy the publicity. I hope it keeps you warm in your cold marriage. Goodbye.'

'Please don't leave it like this,' he said.

She heard his voice crack.

'I have to go.' Cara could barely speak. She was furious; her hand shook as she ended the call.

That he should try and pretend it was nothing, and she was being unreasonable, infuriated her more than him not having the courtesy, or the balls, to warn her about the article.

She was aware that he withheld information, with the intention of protecting her, but she was reeling from this latest episode. He was a master at changing the subject so that the focus was on her reaction rather than on his behaviour. Enough was enough. She was in love with him. There didn't seem to be anything she could do to stop it, lord knows, she'd tried repeatedly, but she couldn't handle any more of this insanity. Living a double life didn't seem to bother him; he took it in his stride. She worried that perhaps he even enjoyed it. What man's ego wouldn't be stoked by the attention of two attractive, intelligent women?

He rang again. This time she didn't answer. If she spoke to him, she knew she would say something she'd regret so she shoved the phone into the kitchen drawer.

Cara was too angry to cry. Her chest felt sore and tight. The tears would come later when her anger subsided, and she was left with the miserable prospect of long, empty days without him. In the months since they'd fallen in love, she'd shed more tears than ever before.

What is it about him that I find so irresistible? If it was anyone else, I would have been long gone.

Thoughts of Sylvia's Twin Flame prophecy, whirled inside her head. She had explained to Cara that no matter how much she resisted the karmic connection, it was ultimately pointless because her and George's life's mission was to love one another unconditionally. She said that their souls had planned the reunion thousands of years ago. They must reunite as one soul, and in so doing, they would raise the consciousness of the planet. They were chosen.

It's completely ridiculous. If this is being chosen, I'll do without it.

Flashes of their life together in Tudorville pirouetted through her mind. It was the most confusing situation; no matter how she rationalised or reframed events, she couldn't seem to achieve clarity. Each time she thought she'd got a grip on their relationship, it shifted, and she lost her footing.

She wished she could be normal again; not a time traveller with a karmic mission, flitting back and forth over five hundred years, in love with a guy who made her crazy.

Cara pulled her jacket on. She'd go and see Daniel. He was delightfully uncomplicated and appreciative of her presence. Even after all of this time, he still loved her and didn't have another woman on the scene. Maybe she'd go back to him; to the sensible passionless life, she'd resigned herself to before she met George. Surely, eventually, the pain would stop if she stayed away from George long enough.

Wouldn't it?

Retrieving her phone, she saw there were two missed calls from George. How could she speak to him now? She slammed the front door behind her and the car wheels sliced through the gravel, leaving a dusty cloud in her wake as she raced out of the driveway. She needed some time alone. After checking in on Daniel who had recovered well from his heart attack, she'd go away for a couple of days. She'd tried to break it off with George numerous times when she felt deceived. But somehow, he usually managed to build a reasonable case which left her feeling like she'd blown the situation out of proportion.

On the occasions when she felt justified in her reaction, she couldn't bring herself to end it because she didn't want to be without him. It was a continuous rollercoaster of emotions with her head at war with her heart. Her logic said she should end it; the situation was clear cut. It didn't matter how much he loved her if he wasn't free. She dreaded a future of pining for him whilst he went off with Joanna. She'd never experienced jealously like this before. Her heart was as though ripped from her chest; the pain was uncontrollable, and she invariably lashed out and temporarily withdrew from him.

But she couldn't handle this latest slap in the face. She'd thought he had stopped hiding things from her, and they were closer than ever before. Seeing the article was soul-destroying.

George phoned intermittently throughout the day.

Finally, she relented and messaged, 'I'm giving us some space. It's for the best.'

'I don't want space. I want to talk to you every day,' he replied.

Her heart lurched. Pushing him away was the hardest thing she'd ever had to do. She wanted to be close to him. Always.

'I can't do this any longer. I'm going to go away for a while.'

'Where?'

'I don't know yet. I'll figure it out. I think we need a break.'

'How long for?'

'I'm not sure,' she replied.

'Will you be in touch?'

'That wouldn't be a break.'

'True. But I don't want a break!'

'I get that. And I love you. I don't want it either, but I don't know what else to do.'

He called again immediately. 'Will you please at least let me know where you are and that you're okay?'

'Yes, yes, of course. I will. I have to go now. Take care.'

The tears spilt down her cheeks. She mustn't fall apart now, or another day would be lost in a foggy, tearful haze. She needed to be practical; she must make plans.

Where could she go to get away?

The phone rang again. 'Hi, Cara. How you doing?'

'Morning Eddie. Yeah great,' she said through her silent tears.

'Did you think about my suggestion?' he asked.

'Yes, of course,' she fibbed. 'I'll do it.'

'What? You will? Brilliant! You won't be sorry. We're going to discover amazing things together.'

'Fabulous. I'm guessing I don't need my passport. Where shall I meet you?'

Cara busied herself, getting ready to meet Eddie. She would rather be anywhere than where she was now, with this agonising pain ripping her chest apart.

The solution was under her nose. She'd turn her Twin Flame, time-travelling curse into a superpower and go to the future where she wouldn't bump into George at all. He really would be out of her life. Yes, the future would be the perfect place to be.

George sat staring at his computer screen, seeing nothing but Cara's face. He couldn't get anything done when they were at odds. They were fine yesterday. They'd talked and laughed for hours on the phone. He couldn't remember what they talked about most of the time, but they never ran out of things to say.

He turned over recent events in his mind. He wished he'd told her about the article and handled it differently. But even if he'd warned her, he knew she would have been hurt. It was a no-win game. Had he lost her completely this time?

Less than a year had passed since they'd met, but it was as if he'd known her forever. It was the strangest feeling.

For the umpteenth time, he considered ending his marriage. He'd wanted to walk away many times over the years, before meeting Cara. Since meeting her, the possibility continuously popped in and out of his thoughts. He'd known the relationship with Joanna wasn't what he'd imagined not long after the wedding. But soon after, Jane was born, life chugged on, and he couldn't bring himself to leave. He hoped that with time he'd settle down and it would be enough. He hadn't. It wasn't.

What would Joanna do if he left? He feared she would fall apart. And then there was his beautiful Jane. He'd had the same fruitless conversation with himself countless times. The idea of disappointing his family was intolerable to him. He was a Cavendish. Cavendish men didn't walk out on their obligations. He thought of his father and mother. They were more like business partners than lovers, managing their considerable estate, the family business and assets. They'd stuck together until the end. They'd lived an honourable, sensible life. What they lacked in passion, they made up for in duty. That was the Cavendish way.

York, present day

191

'Why don't we ever go on holiday like normal families?'

George lowered the newspaper and removed his glasses; he held them loosely as he peered at Jane, his daughter over the breakfast table.

'Whatever do you mean? We've been on plenty of family holidays.'

'When?' Jane challenged him without missing a beat.

'Well, let me see. . .how about when we went to Jersey?'

'Dad, I was a little girl then. I can't even remember it. I mean more recent holidays.'

'We took you to the Cheltenham races not long ago. And we stayed the weekend in Bath for your cousin John's wedding last year.'

Jane flicked her long hair off her face and rolled her eyes at him. 'I mean a proper holiday. You know—like a two-week holiday somewhere hot. To another country like my friends do with their parents. You guys only ever travel separately. Don't you like spending time together?'

'I don't know what you're talking about. Of course, we do. We just both have a lot of travel commitments for work, so then we like to be at home sometimes. You'll see what it's like when you have a career. Anyway, what about Seville? We've been there on holiday numerous times.'

'Yes, exactly, I want to go somewhere new where you won't work when you get there. I hope I never have a career that stops me going on holiday with my family. What's the point of working if you don't do fun things together?'

George sipped his tea and watched his daughter let off steam. He tried to concentrate and follow what she was saying. The words came at him, but he couldn't process them properly. Since Cara had disappeared, he'd been unable to focus on anything. Every nerve in his body was raw with pain. Not usually anxious, he worried he was on the edge of losing his grip on reality. Cara was all he could think about. He snapped himself back to the present moment with Jane.

'Work can be fun,' he said. He pondered how to diffuse her attack without making a commitment he wouldn't keep. The last thing he wished to do was to be holed up in a hotel for two weeks with Joanna. But he couldn't argue with his daughter's logic.

'You're a workaholic; it's the only thing you like to do. And Mum's not much better. She's always off on some business trip or other.'

'Can we go to America? Gemma has just come back from California, and she had an incredible time. I told Mum about it, and she said she'd talk to you.'

'Did she? Well, she hasn't said anything to me about it yet. No doubt, you two will be plotting together, and I won't know what's hit me.'

George's attempt at a laugh sounded hollow to his own ears. The pretence that all was well was wearing him out. He hadn't slept properly for days.

Jane laughed and put her breakfast plate into the sink before she circled back to kiss George on the cheek. 'Come on, Dad, cheer up, you know you want to take me to California. 'I'm off to school. See you later.'

Like most fathers, he found it impossible to resist his daughter.

He wondered who he thought he was kidding. Even Jane could see through her parents' happy marriage facade. He tried to pull himself together, ready to face what promised to be a busy morning at the workshop. He dreaded another day with uncontrollable, anxious thoughts racing around his mind. His future now looked bleak; the sunshine had disappeared with Cara when she left.

Where did she go? Would she be in touch soon?

He was giving her the space she'd asked for, but no

message had arrived. He wondered whether he should call again to check if she was okay. She'd dropped out of his world and how he despised the world without her. His worst fear had been realised; she'd cut him off from any contact, and he had no idea when or if she'd be back. His days had lost their spark; the work he used to love was now dull and meaningless. His thoughts suffocated him like a gloomy shroud. He felt trapped in what had become his miserable existence as he went over and over their recent conversations. Was she lost to him because of his stubborn refusal to take action?

He left the house wondering who she was with and what she was doing now.

CHAPTER 18

Y ork, present day

Eddie jumped up from the leather sofa in the hotel lobby, and wrapped his arms around Cara before carefully tilting her backwards so he could examine her face.

'You look tired,' he said. 'Are you okay?'

She noticed dark circles beneath his eyes.

'Yes, thanks. Have you not been sleeping well, either?' she laughed.

'I confess I was a tiny bit worried you might change your mind. I know it's no small thing I'm asking of you.'

Cara hadn't slept more than a couple of hours. She'd felt anxious and alone in the dark hours of the night. She was angry at George. Why had he forced her into this impossible corner with no way out? She had no choice but to leave him.

'I won't pretend not to be terrified, Eddie. I thought of backing out, but the truth is I don't want to be here right now, so I'm all yours. I'm officially your guinea pig to catapult as you wish. . .'

'Dear Cara, I promise I'll take good care of you. Shall we go over the plan?'

'Yes, please. We better had as I haven't a clue what to expect in the future.'

Cara's heart was heavy; she feared the unknown. What if she couldn't handle what awaited her there? More frightening to her still was the prospect of a life without George.

'It will be strange to time travel and not meet George,' she said, wanting to talk about him one last time with someone who knew him.

'Why are you so sure you won't meet him?' asked the professor.

'Well, if I'm going to the future. . .he's only here or in Tudorville, isn't he?' Eddie noticed the light in her eyes when she spoke about him. He may be a physics geek, but he knew how deep the love was between his master and mistress of five hundred years. Is something wrong between you?' he asked, his voice gentle.

'Yes, you could say that. Something is very wrong.' Tears sprung into Cara's eyes. Eddie's kindness was killing her. She had to be tough now so she would have the strength to go. She must leave her old self behind. There was nothing for her with George anymore.

'There is a slim chance you'll meet him in the future. I have no way of knowing which other lives you share. You are time travelling partners, or you wouldn't be in two timelines together. You're obviously soul mates, so it's very possible that you, me, and George have been in other timelines together which we're yet to learn about.'

'I hadn't thought of that, but it makes sense.' said Cara.

There was a flicker of hope, followed by a sharp sense of dread. Would they be together again like in Tudorville?

Or would the future replicate the painful tangle of the present? She prayed she wouldn't meet him in another impossible scenario. She'd rather live without him than attempt to plough through this quicksand of pain. Like Moses, she could see the promised land but wasn't destined to enter.

'Before we run through the details of the experiment, would you like to be in touch with anyone?'

'If I've understood correctly, my father won't even know I'm gone. It will be as if I'm still here?'

'Yes, that's how it usually works, but we can't be certain. I don't think he'll notice anything untoward. At least I hope not. There are no guarantees, though.'

'It's so weird, isn't it? I'm here but not fully here.'

'Yes, it's difficult to explain. One version of you should be here in the present day; then another will experience 2100 and report back to me upon your return.'

'I need to get away from George—our relationship needs to end, so I'm counting on it that the other Cara will stay out of his way too.'

Eddie ran his fingers across the patchy stubble on his chin. 'I must say, I feel disloyal to the earl.'

'Do you? Oh, yes, of course, you've not met George in this life yet, have you? How silly of me.' Cara patted Eddie's arm. 'Don't worry Eddie; he's a different person in the present day. He's not the man you adore and serve in Tudorville. I'm afraid he never will be. That's why I must leave.'

'I'm sorry to hear that. I can see you're troubled. What can I do to help? I'm certain George would wish me to continue to take care of you, no matter what's going on between you. He charged me with that sacred duty many times in the past.'

'Thank you, Eddie. You are very kind, but there's nothing you can do about George. And I'm too upset to talk to my father. If he hears my voice, he'll immediately know something's wrong. I don't want to risk agitating him, so I'll just go and hope I'm back soon.'

'Sounds sensible. Anyone else you want to notify before you go? Just in case. . .'

'Yes. I'll write a letter to George to say it's over. I don't want to speak to him, and a text message would be cruel. Could you arrange for my letter to be delivered by hand to his workshop?'

'Of course, no problem. I'll take it myself as soon as you've gone.'

'Are you sure you're ready to do that?' he asked, searching her face for signs of uncertainty.

'Yes, it's the only way. It may seem harsh to cut him off, but there's no future for us in this lifetime. I've fought for him; I've done all I know how to do, but it's not to be. It will be easier for both of us to forget and move on if we don't see each other, and aren't in touch.'

'Okay,' he said. 'I'll do whatever you want. It's the least I can do to thank you for embarking on this dangerous mission. It's no exaggeration to say that future generations are at stake and what you discover has the power to save the world from disaster.'

Cara ordered a coffee and settled down on the shiny leather sofa in the lobby to write a letter to George using the hotel notepaper. She couldn't bear to continue hurting him, and she couldn't stand the pain in her heart. This was the only way she could see to save them both from the continuous turmoil they'd been suffering for months.

'I'm ready now,' she said. She handed the sealed, addressed envelope to Eddie. 'I don't want him to worry about me; I promised I'd be in touch to let him know I'm safe.'

Eddie put the envelope into his shabby brown briefcase.

'When I say it's time, I'll need you to think about the

future; specifically the year 2100. With a time travel ability as powerful as yours, I believe you're capable of travelling to any timeline. It's important that you focus on exactly where we want you to go so you don't end up in the wrong year,' he said.

'Yes, that makes sense; it seems easy enough. But where do we want me to go? The year 2100, but where?'

'Good question. Go to London.'

'What do you want me to find out when I'm there? Oh, and how will I get back?'

Eddie walked Cara through details of what he wanted her to do. Finally, he said, 'I want you to go to Royal Holloway; to the Quantum Physics department, to be specific. Tell them as little as you need to, to get an appointment with the lead researcher or head professor. Tell him it's vital he shares his latest data on their calculations of how long the planet will exist, based on current climate conditions. Tell him your father worked with me or make something up to get his attention. You're persuasive; I'm sure you'll come up with something.'

'As for returning home, you simply focus on being here. That's how it works. You'll likely get to the place you think about. There were a few minor hiccups in my experiments as it was only me doing the focusing. I suspect for best results, it takes two aligned minds to increase the chances of arriving in a specific time and place. But I think it should be simple to get home because you know exactly what it's like. This is the TT system I've been refining over the past several months.'

'You only *think* it will work?' asked Cara.

'Well, as I said when we discussed it, the system has a seventy-five per cent success rate. But if you don't get back with your report in the next six months, I promise I'll find you and bring you home. Don't worry. It'll all work out fine.'

'What if I end up in the wrong time?'

'I doubt that will happen if we're both focused on 2100 but if you do travel to another time and place, put your attention on the present day, come back, and we'll try again. Think about George, or your father. That will maximise your power because you'll subconsciously want to travel home.'

They went up in the elevator to Eddie's hotel room.

'Concentrate,' he said. 'Stay calm.'

Cara tried to focus on arriving in 2100, but all she could think of was George. She imagined him in his workshop trying to decipher the critical points of a manuscript, squinting without his glasses. Was he missing her or was it business as usual?

Focus, Cara, focus. 2100, here you come.

Her thoughts flitted about. It was impossible to control her unruly mind. Next, she imagined George in Tudorville. Was he still in the safe house? He'd be on edge, waiting for news of her and the children.

Then the icy chill enveloped her, Eddie's face became a blur, and she felt herself slip away. A shorter period was required in the vortex each time she went.

York, 1536

Cara was jostled from side to side on the cold hard seat, as the carriage bumped about on the uneven track. Where was she? This didn't seem like 2100.

Blustery, freezing winds hit her face, and her hair blew into her eyes as she stuck her head out of the window and called, 'Driver, where are we?'

'We're still on the outskirts of York, my lady. These back-roads are treacherous after the heavy rains. We'll be lucky if the wheels don't get stuck in the mud.'

'Oh, Lord,' she said, looking at Eddie whose head rolled about, bouncing on and off his chest as he dozed. The children slept on either side of him.

'You're here with me!'

'What? Oh, I must have fallen asleep.'

'I didn't expect to see you now. I'm supposed to be in 2100.'

'Of course, I'm here with you. Whatever do you mean?'

'You sent me on an experimental time travel mission for you: Eddie Makepeace, esteemed Quantum Physics Professor from the twenty-first century.'

'Oh, dear, I see. Yes, it's coming to me now. The TT System must have been slightly off-kilter.'

Fortunately, she could talk to Eddie about their other life because unlike George, he knew what was going on.

'*Slightly off-kilter?* I'd say it's about six hundred years off and also in completely the wrong direction!'

'What were you thinking about when you left the hotel?' he asked.

'That must be where I went wrong. The more I tried to stop thinking about George, the more I couldn't get his face out of my mind. I wasn't even thinking about London. Sorry, I've messed it up.'

'Don't worry. We'll have to reroute you later. Better not try with the children here.'

'But hold on. What day is it, Eddie? Please tell me we received word from George saying it was safe for us to set out? We were supposed to wait for the all-clear. He said on no account to leave without hearing from him. He was most insistent.'

'I don't recall,' said Eddie. 'I woke up and found myself here. This is more confusing than when I travel alone.'

'You can say that again,' said Cara.

They trundled along in the carriage for a couple of hours.

Cara worried they'd left too early; she was unable to relax. Neither of them had any recollection of what had happened before the journey. Typically, she remembered snippets from Tudorville and then later the memories would flood in, and the timeline would slot into place. The timelines of recent events were muddled in her head. It was like watching the middle of a movie but missing the beginning. Living in two parallel realities was a tricky business.

An ominous dread swept over her like a dark curtain. She was supposed to be in 2100, not racing to George in daylight while the king's army searched for them.

She sensed something had gone terribly wrong.

'Stop! Stop!' A loud voice thundered from behind the carriage. A soldier on a black stallion, wearing King Henry VIII's livery, drew up alongside and hammered on the small windowpane. Another soldier pulled up, and the two of them peered in at her as she pushed the drapes aside.

Cara panicked. These soldiers must be on progress with the king's party that George had warned her about in the letter.

'Alight from the carriage immediately,' boomed a voice.

The children stretched and rubbed their red eyes. 'Mother what's going on?' said Thomas.

She patted his head. 'Shh. Stay quiet, don't move; wait here with May, please. If anyone asks your name, pretend to be too frightened to speak. Don't say your real names, whatever happens.'

She turned to Edward. 'Please stay here with the children, and I'll see what these soldiers want. It may be pure coincidence. I'll be back as soon as possible. Don't worry.'

'What's the meaning of this?' said Cara as she opened the door and stood on the carriage steps, her voice stern and commanding. Her heart galloped, but her countenance was steady. Life at court had prepared her to handle the unpredictable.

'What's your name, ma'am?' said the first soldier.

'Before I tell you anything, I'd like to know who dares stop my carriage in this cavalier manner. Please identify yourselves immediately.'

The first man squared his shoulders and stood to attention. 'We are the King's soldiers, Smith and Cartwright; our orders are to find escaped prisoners wanted for treason and witchcraft. We've been informed by these here bounty hunters that you are the Countess Cavendish.'

The two scruffy men who'd been on their trail since they fled London, emerged from the trees looking sheepish.

'Do you confirm this is the Countess Cavendish?' Smith directed his question to the bounty hunters.

'Yes,' they chimed in unison. 'The earl should be with her too. We want a reward for the pair of them.'

Cara thought she recognised them from the brothel tavern.

'No. You are quite mistaken,' said Cara. 'I'm Lady Sarah Bravenger of Manchester. I'm a widow, on the way to visit my kin in Scotland, with my two children and their tutor.'

Smith barked an order to Cartwright who then pulled Cara roughly off the steps and onto the ground, pushing her in the direction of Smith. Smith captured her arms and tied a piece of rope around her wrists.

She kicked and shouted, 'You oaf, what do you think you're doing? I'm Lady Sarah Bravenger. You're making a dreadful mistake.'

'I'm going to search for the earl. King Henry wants em both.' Cartwright barged into the carriage.

Three pairs of frightened eyes stared up at him.

CHAPTER 19

T he Great North Road, 1536

Edward scratched his head. He was angry at his lack of foresight.

'I could kick myself,' he whispered to Cara.

They were pitched from side to side as the carriage bumped over potholes on The Great North Road. The rain hammered relentlessly on the roof, and Cara peered out at the ominous rolling clouds in the dull, white sky.

The king's soldiers were under orders to escort them to London. Cara had been arrested again; this time on charges of treason, witchcraft and breaking out of prison.

She squeezed Eddie's arm. 'It's not your fault. You weren't to know this would happen.'

'That's true, I suppose. Time travel is unpredictable. My intentions were good, but I feel as though in my ambitious overreaching, I've managed to sign our death warrants instead of save the world.'

'It's not over yet. Let's stay calm. We must keep our wits about us,' she said.

Thomas and May leaned into her on either side as they slept. She stroked their heads and thought of George.

'What are the chances of Swifty making it to Berwick-Upon-Tweed, undetected, do you think?'

'It's hard to say. It's a long shot, but he's a wily young lad. If anyone can evade the army and travel unseen, he can. He's been living on the streets for years. He knows how to blend in, and he's certainly as speedy as his name.'

'If we can alert George, he might at least escape to Scotland. That way there'd be a chance he could return later and save the children. I can't bear the thought of him waiting for us, not knowing we've been caught. I can just imagine his face when he realises we left without getting the all-clear from him. He specifically warned me to wait and be patient.'

'Don't be hard on yourself, my dear. You weren't impatient. He doesn't know about your time travel, here or in the future, correct?'

'I've wanted to tell him in present day, but it's never been the right time. How do you tell the man you love that he was married to you, five hundred years earlier when you were both charged with treason by King Henry VIII? Oh; and incidentally you also had two children together. Far fetched doesn't even begin to cover it.'

'Quite! I do see your point,' said Eddie, with a wry smile. 'I've not confided in anyone other than you about my own travel. One of the chaps on my research team suspects there's more to my research than meets the eye, but that's about it.'

'It's odd how Sylvia knew to connect us up, don't you think?' said Cara.

'Yes, and no. There's a glorious serendipity to all of this.

As much as it feels wildly out of control, I do believe it's unfolding just as it should.'

'It's good that you're philosophical. I begin to panic when I think about what will happen to the children if I'm executed—and to George, of course. Which reminds me. . .goodness knows how poor little Princess Elizabeth is faring at court after losing her mother, Queen Anne.'

'You won't be executed. The future version of you is alive, so I don't see how you can have been.'

'But is it not possible that could change? If I were to die now, wouldn't that simply wipe out all trace of me in the future?'

'I suppose it might.' Eddie paused, trying to understand the implications. 'Honestly, I don't know. We don't know enough about how it works in these specific situations. This is another reason why it's so valuable for my research; to observe and document what happens when you travel. It's possible that by arriving back here at the worst time, it could wipe out the future you. . .but it's unlikely, I think. I doubt you'd have lived in the present day at all if that were the case. The fact that the three of us are alive in the future, and what's more, we're connected, bodes well for us all.'

'Except for Thomas and May. We don't know what happens to them.' Cara's voice trembled. Her maternal instinct was rich in Tudorville, which was such a different experience to that of her future self.

'King Henry is capricious, but I don't think he'll take it out on the children. We'll get them to safety somehow,' whispered Edward.

'If you could get them back to Willow Manor that would be the best. At least that way they'd be in the custody of George's parents.'

'Yes, and the earl would most likely go to them at the first opportunity. No doubt, the tides of fortune will soon turn at court. They always do. If he's able to stay out of sight for a while, he may be back in favour with the king again before too long,' he said.

'I have a horrible feeling that with my botched time travel, I've messed up the future. I mean, we were on the road to Berwick-Upon-Tweed too early, weren't we? We left before George said it was safe. If we'd waited, it seems likely we wouldn't have been caught at all.'

'You were supposed to be on your way to 2100. We couldn't have known you'd arrive back here, en route to the border, so it's out of our hands. There's no point worrying about that now. Let's hope Swifty alerts George, and they formulate a plan.'

She was grateful to have Eddie's support. Goodness knows how she'd handle all of this without him at her side. Not for the first time, she silently thanked Sylvia.

'You may be accused of treason, but you both have loyal connections in London and the north.'

Cara agreed. George inspired loyalty in all who knew him. He was respected and admired by the tenants of Willow Manor and his network of influential peers held him in high esteem. Just as Sir John Locke had offered them protection, many of the great northern lords were George's close friends and allies. They'd grown up together, fought together and served at court together.

He looked at her, with kind eyes, 'Also, I can't imagine the earl heading off to Scotland without you. I'd wager he'll find a way to rescue you.'

Cara rested her head against the carriage seat and prayed for a miracle. It seemed the only thing that could save them now. The stakes were high; if George tried to save them, he would then also put himself in grave danger. She didn't know what to hope for. Every scenario was fraught with jeopardy.

Had she risked the lives of everyone she loved with one

critical error? She blamed herself for trying to run away from George. Now they would be lost to one another forever, and endanger everyone dear to them. She closed her eyes and fell into an uneasy doze.

Berwick-Upon-Tweed, 1536

George paced back and forth in front of the roaring fire. The cold floor creaked beneath his feet. He'd been confined to this house ever since his arrival in the border town. He'd exchanged one prison for another and was restless. How he wished he'd been able to give Cara the go-ahead to come to him; he ached to have her close, and he missed the children, but it was too risky.

He continued to pace back and forth for much of the afternoon, occasionally lingering by the fire to rub his hands in the warmth of the orange flames.

His heart was heavy. He'd woken with a sense of foreboding which he couldn't shake as the day wore on. Something wasn't right with Cara. He knew it; he felt it in his gut; he always did.

George watched Swifty as he gulped steaming potage from a bowl. He was impatient to hear news of Cara, but the boy almost passed out on arrival, so weak was he from the arduous journey.

'Are you feeling better?'

'Yes, thank you, my lord. I hadn't eaten for days.'

'I'm glad to see the colour creeping back into your cheeks, drink up and then pray tell me all you know.'

'My lady, the children and Tutor Edward were all captured on their way here.'

George cursed under his breath.

He knew it. He'd warned Cara not to set out until he sent the all-clear. What the blazes was she doing?

'Did something occur to make her leave so suddenly?'

'I'm not sure, my lord. It all happened so fast. I was in the kitchen when I got word to ready myself for the trip. Sir John lent us one of his plain carriages, and we were headed on our way to you.'

'Yes, and then? Tell me exactly what happened.'

'It seemed to be okay; the rain was coming down hard; we were on the road for hours, but then we heard soldiers shouting and giving chase. On one of the breaks, Tutor Edward had instructed me to run like the wind to find you, if anyone stopped us. I was sitting up top with the driver, so when the soldiers checked the carriage, I slipped away.'

'I see, so he thought it likely that soldiers would be on the road. Well, that was good thinking so thank heavens for that. Why they didn't wait, I don't know! And then?' said George.

'I managed to get away, and I hid in the bushes. I saw them arrest my lady, and then they made them turn the carriage around and escorted them back in the direction we'd come.'

'Did you hear anything more, Swifty? Think carefully, please. We must save them, but I need to know everything. Is there anything else?'

'It was hard to hear exactly what they were saying, but I heard them talking about taking them to London.'

'Yes, that makes sense. I imagine they'll be taking the countess to the Tower. We must hurry. I need your help again, I'm afraid. Knowing how efficiently Cromwell operates, I fear they'll rush her into a makeshift trial before any of the lords have time to intervene on my behalf. We must hasten. Ready yourself to leave in ten minutes, and we'll make our plan on the road.'

Swifty nodded, and George went immediately to inform

King James's envoy of the latest news and to ask if he may borrow some horses.

They rode hard in the driving rain without stopping. Every second counted if George was to save Cara.

They arrived exhausted at Madame Alicia's. George was grateful for his network of loyal friends.

She ushered them in via the back entrance of her establishment, and they huddled in the warmth of her cosy parlour.

'Madame Alicia, my good lady, have you paper and ink to spare? I must write to the king forthwith; his soldiers are on the way to London with the countess. I must intervene and propose a bargain before it is too late.'

George took another gulp of red wine to steady his nerves and commenced writing the most important letter of his life.

Once satisfied, he handed Swifty some coins.

'Pray, go as fast as you may, my boy. Seek out the Post Master and reward him royally to arrange for the letter to be delivered to the king at Hampton Court Palace. It must be today!' George called after Swifty's disappearing back.

The Tower of London, 1536

Cromwell read George's freshly delivered correspondence aloud to King Henry.

'Your Majesty,

I humbly write to explain the unfortunate misunderstanding that has arisen between us and to dispute the false charges made against us. There has been a dreadful mistake. My wife and I never have and never would be disloyal to you. You are our one true King, and as such we obey you in all things.

This sorry day, I beseech you to have mercy upon my wife and children.

For the past five years, you have trusted me as your special advisor, and I have never betrayed you. I respectfully remind you that you recently bestowed the title of earl upon me, in recognition of my service to you and as a reward for The Tudor Kings' Manuscript.

I beg you, your Grace, not to take out any misgivings or suspicions you have against me, on my family. My wife has been a loyal servant in your household for the past two years, as you bade her, and is not guilty of treason or witchcraft. She is a God-fearing soul. My children are merely innocents caught up in these difficult times.

I, your envoy and special advisor on countless diplomatic missions, perhaps more than any other who has served at your side, have uncovered treasonous plots aplenty. I fear this is simply the latest ploy to destabilise your throne.

I humbly beg you consider my request which I ask not for myself but for the sake of my family.

Please release my wife, children and their tutor. They are blameless, and I know you to be a fair King of the highest honour. I trust you would not have them take the blame for a crime for which you believe me to be guilty.

You have my word as a gentleman of honour, and as your loyal servant, I will then turn myself in, to face any charges, your court wishes to levy against me.

I await your reply and trust that in the benevolence for which you are renowned, you will allow my wife and children to be released in exchange for me.

As ever, your most humble servant
George Cavendish.'

Cromwell handed the letter to the king who scanned it briefly before tossing it on to the table.

'Curse that damned Cavendish! I trusted him with my life. I thought he was my friend. And all this time he and his lady wife were cooking up schemes behind my back, and in my palace no less. I've seen Anne's head roll, but still, her spider's web continues to unravel sinister horrors.'

'You trusted him, Your Majesty. It seems he betrayed you as did the Boleyn woman.' Cromwell gauged the king's reaction; satisfied, he continued to press on.

'I do wonder though, whether, as trying as it may seem, if it would be more prudent to take the long view; to play him at his own game as it were.'

'How so, Thomas? He and his wife were both charged with treason, as well as numerous other evils your councillors dug up with your meticulous investigation. I shall have both of their heads on a pike. Better yet, they'll be boiled and covered in cumin first—damn traitors. I won't lie though; my heart bleeds at the loss of another dear friend. It seems there's no one left for me to trust in this court of devilish rogues.' The spittle flew from the king's mouth as he annunciated each word, his face flushed.

'Please be assured, your Majesty. I am your loyal servant and shall remain so until my dying breath. However, in my endeavour to protect you and the Crown, I must speak the truth, no matter how distasteful. I fear that if we dismiss Cavendish's offer, he will disappear into hiding, never to be seen again. He'll have no reason to show himself. They'll be no bargaining chip for him to play if he believes his wife and children are already lost.'

'What exactly do you suggest? To let him have his way, just so? I will be a laughing stock.'

'That is exactly what I propose, to prevent that very thing. But rather, this way he turns himself in, and we avoid the embarrassment of looking like fools because of his escape. Few will care what becomes of the Cavendish woman. The people are bound to applaud your clemency if she is released with her children. We will ensure the news gets out and spreads across the country. This is no small thing considering recent events at court. It would go some measure towards rebuilding the people's trust. The Cavendish family are well-loved, especially in the North.'

'What say you? Are you in agreement, your Grace?'

King Henry, stared out of the window, his countenance grim.

Cromwell held his breath and waited.

'Your plan is a cunning one, Thomas. As ever, you are several tricks ahead of everyone else. You're like a conjurer with that sharp mind of yours. Yes, okay. You have my permission to make the exchange. . .but only on the condition that I have words with the earl before he's executed. I will hear his account of events, as much as it will pain me. He was my dear friend for many a year.'

Cromwell inclined his head. 'Very well, Your Grace. And so it shall be. Thank you. Your judgement, as always, is wise.'

In the courtyard below, Cara, Edward and the children were escorted into the Tower, pushed roughly up the stone steps and imprisoned in a cell. May fell on to the freezing, hard floor and began to whimper.

'Hush, my love. By the grace of God, we won't be here for long. Your father will come for us. You'll see.'

CHAPTER 20

The Tower of London, 1536

Cara noticed the familiar signs. The air in the cell was freezing, but when she was about to time travel, there was a distinct edge to the cold. The atmosphere whirled with icy crispness. It was time again—the vortex beckoned.

This was the perfect way to escape. She would disappear into the ethers. If she could teach others to time travel, she'd be the most popular woman in prison. But her power was bittersweet. She wanted to stay in Tudorville. How could she leave Thomas and May? And she couldn't bear to abandon George. She must know what happened to him. She felt the familiar wrench of loss. How would she be able to make sure they were all safe if she went now?

'Edward?'

The tutor was trying to distract the children by tracing letters on the dusty floor. It was working. They threw themselves into the guessing game with gusto, oblivious to their dreadful surroundings.

'Yes, my lady?' He raised his head.

'I'm sorry.' She mouthed the words in a low tone, hoping the children wouldn't hear. 'I think I'm about to slip away. Please do whatever you can to petition the officials to send you all to Willow Manor. They have no interest in you; there's no reason to hold you here after routine questioning. You know what to do. I'll be back as soon as I can.'

She was gone before she heard his reply.

When Thomas looked up a few minutes later, he smiled at the version of his mother who remained behind. She was unconscious of her ability to move between timelines.

London, present day

Eddie's tall, lanky frame bobbed about with excitement, unable to stay still when Cara appeared.

'Here you are! Back so soon. I didn't know what to expect.' He hugged her. 'How did it go? Let's have a cup of tea, and you can tell me all of your news.'

'I'm afraid I've let you down, Eddie.'

'That's quite impossible. I was so worried about you; it's such a relief to have you back in one piece; you could never let me down. I've been wondering whether the risks were too high and perhaps I shouldn't have pressed you to go. Me and my lofty ambitions.' He grimaced and shook his head.

Cara smiled. 'How odd, you said something similar in Tudorville.'

'Really? At least I'm consistent then, if nothing else. Five hundred years of dogged determination to get my own way. I do hope you'll forgive me if I've caused you distress.'

He noticed her eyes welling up. She tried to hold back the tears, but they seeped from beneath her lashes as the emotion rumbled deep within her chest.

Cara was like a volcano about to erupt, but she was determined to keep herself together. There was too much to do to allow herself to fall apart now.'

'What's the matter, my dear. Whatever it is, remember we always get another chance. That's the beauty of having the ability to live in quantum time.'

Eddie went through the comforting motions of making tea in the tiny kitchen which was more like a cupboard, in his office at Royal Holloway.

'There, there, sit here and take a moment. There's no rush. I'm sorry to push you so. I can be a real bully when it comes to my experiments.'

He put a steaming cup of tea on the table, and she embraced the hot, blue china with her cold hands.

'Thank you. How are you?'

'Um. I'm fine. . .had trouble sleeping though cause I was worried about you.

'Bless you. How long have I been gone?'

'It's been a couple of days, at least. Let me check my notes. I lose track of the days when I'm working.'

'He rummaged in the desk; extracted a clipboard and a crumpled sheet of paper wedged on to it.'

'Don't you keep your notes on your computer, Eddie? I would have thought a Quantum Physics Professor would be more hi-tech than that,' laughter interrupted her misery. There was something about Eddie which always lifted her spirits. His goodness was palpable. She felt safe with him despite the chaos in her life.

'You can't beat good old-fashioned pen and paper. I love the feel of the ink pen between my fingers as the nib scratches the paper. Let me see.'

He pulled his phone out of the pocket of his tweed waistcoat to check the calendar and then referred to his sheet.

'Okay, you've been gone one hundred and forty-four hours and twenty-two minutes precisely.'

'Wow. I have no sense of time whatsoever when I come and go.'

He reached over and patted her hand. 'Can you tell me what went on? I can barely wait to hear!'

Cara didn't know if it was the hot tea or being in Eddie's soothing presence, but she already felt better. The sense of dread had lessened its grip; she was steady enough to reveal what had happened. She filled him in on the details of how she'd arrived in Tudorville instead of in 2100 as they'd planned.

'I've already explained this to the 1536 version of you. We were arrested together in the carriage on the road to Berwick-upon-Tweed.'

'Oh, how frustrating, it will catch up with me soon, no doubt. It seems to take a little while for me to update; the memory transfer is wildly unpredictable. I'll probably need to travel again to be able to get it all. I recall some things about the past in great detail, and others seem to elude me altogether. I can't get the measure of it; it's most annoying for a scientist.'

They sat on wooden university chairs, a quiet cama-raderie connecting them as they sipped their tea and pondered the situation.

'I'm not sure what the best thing to do is, so when that's the case I usually come to the conclusion that when we don't know what to do, it's a good idea to do absolutely nothing. Let's wait until an idea comes to us,' he said.

'Yes, I think you're right. I'm dying to dash back to try and fix things, but I think I'd better hold on or I may make it worse. I've done enough damage. My impulsive behaviour doesn't help matters.'

Eddie chuckled.

'I must rectify things with George. I will find him today and apologise for disappearing like that. I had this dreadful premonition in Tudorville that I've messed everything up.'

'Try not to worry. He'll be waiting for you.' He shook his head. 'Who would choose to fall in love? Not me, I can tell you.'

'Have you never been in love, Eddie? I can't remember a lady in your life, but then I only meet you in the same period when you're tutoring Thomas and May at Willow Manor.'

Eddie sighed. 'I've been in love, alright. But I shan't be doing it again if I have any say in the matter. Horrible, painful ordeal it was. Would rather have a tooth extracted with a pair of pliers than go through that again! At least you know toothache will stop with a dose of medication.'

Cara laughed and almost spat out a mouthful of tea. 'Oh, you are a delight, Eddie. It certainly feels like hell on earth sometimes. But when it's good, there's no other feeling like it in all of the world. That's why we love to be in love. Although I don't think we choose it. It just comes at us out of nowhere.'

'You and the earl are two sides of the same coin. I haven't found my soul mate. I thought I had, but it wasn't to be. I'd rather be alone than suffer like that. Not everyone has the good fortune to meet their one true love. Most of us fumble about for several lifetimes, trying to talk ourselves into believing that the wrong person is the right one.'

'That's sad, but I do think perhaps you're right. I'd never experienced a connection like this until George, even though I believed myself to be madly in love when I was younger. Then—with my fiancé, Daniel, I was pretending we were right for each other because it was convenient and I didn't want to risk being hurt again.'

Eddie could feel Cara's pain. If only he could do something to make things better between her and George. Not for the first time he wished he had a magic wand. He blamed himself for sending her off on the mission.

'Sylvia says when you meet your counterpart, they are your Twin Flame; the missing half of your soul that Plato refers to in Greek Mythology,' said Cara.

'Maybe in my next life, I'll meet my Twin Flame. I'm gay, Cara. One man, in particular, caused me a lot of heartache.'

Cara hugged him. 'Thanks for telling me, Eddie. Even these days it must be tough. I'm sorry. I should have known.'

'Oh, you do know. You don't remember yet, that's all. It can be tough but not as tough as it was in Tudorville.'

Speaking of Twin Flames, I'm such a fool. I let my pride hijack my intuition. If I hadn't run away in a rage, we wouldn't have been arrested. I can only hope Swifty made it to the border to warn George. By the way, did you manage to get my letter to him?'

'Yes, I popped it through the workshop door, just as you instructed.'

'You didn't see him?'

'No. I rang the bell and peered through the window, hoping to see how he was doing, but there was no-one there. The place looked different, but I'm not sure why.'

'I wonder where he was. Thank you. What would I do without you? I'll head back to York to find him shortly, and I'll call you tomorrow.'

'Okay, my dear. Try and get a good night's sleep. A flash of inspiration will come to us soon. It always does.'

York, present day

Cara approached George's workshop; her heart drummed so fast she couldn't think clearly. She longed to see him but was embarrassed to tell him how she felt. What if he didn't want her anymore? What if she'd hurt him irreparably and he'd decided it was for the best to let her go?

No matter how embarrassing, she must now tell him she regretted running off as she did. It had been a mistake. The letter would have wounded him. It seemed stupid and cruel now. Why had she thought it was her only choice? Her heart was raw, and she'd been punishing him because she was angry about the piece in the newspaper.

She now understood it was pointless to try and break it off. Whenever she did, they were soon back in the same painful on-off cycle because they were destined to be together. They were both in so deep there was no turning back. If he still wanted her, she would allow him to be however he wanted. She couldn't bear the thought of life without him.

Sylvia had tried to explain at the beginning, but Cara hadn't been able to grasp the truth about the inevitability of their union. She was so used to making things happen; to pushing things along. No more. Now, she would let go. There was no strength left in her to push. She would surrender to unconditional love, and trust that things would work out for them as they were meant to. A sense of relief washed over her, and she was calm for the first time in days.

No. 20 The Shambles loomed before her. Despite her foggy mental haze, it struck her that the front door was a pale blue rather than the usual rich, glossy black. There was something different about the window too. The blinds were new, and there was a tall cactus plant in a blue pot, next to the doorway, which definitely wasn't there on her last visit.

There was no *Cavendish Fine Manuscripts* sign either, but Cara hadn't noticed that yet. It's one of life's truths that people walk around not registering what's under their nose. The thought flashed through her mind that George was obviously getting on with his life remarkably well without her. A dull, ache settled in her chest. The weight of it trapped her breath, and she gasped for air. She paused a moment to pull herself together, drew her shoulders back and raised her hand to the brass knocker on the pale blue door.

Hold on; even the brass knocker looked unfamiliar.

A petite woman appeared in the doorway.

'Yes?' She smoothed her hands across her pleated skirt as if she didn't know what else to do with them. Then she looked expectantly at Cara, a tight smile stretched across her lips.

'Hello.' Cara coughed. 'I'm looking for George. Is he around? I'm sorry. . .I don't know your name. Are you his assistant?'

'Assistant? George?' She looked confused. 'No, I'm not an assistant, although my father may think otherwise.' She let out a stifled, self-deprecating sound. There's no George here. This is a private residence. It's my father's house actually.' She leaned closer to Cara as if to share a secret of great importance. 'He's not so good lately. I've come to stay with him for a week or two. Do my bit, you know.'

'Right, yes, quite. I see.'

Cara did not see, but she had no idea what else to do or say. She seemed to be awake in her worst nightmare.

'Thank you. I'll be on my way. I must have got the address mixed up.'

'Are you okay? You look a little pale.'

'Um, yes I'm fine. Thanks again.'

Cara gripped the door frame to prevent herself from toppling backwards off the step; her legs like jelly.

'One more thing, please. How long has your father lived here? If you don't mind me asking.'

'Oh, let me think.' The woman stared into space and then counted on her fingers.

Cara had the urge to scream at the woman's slow movements, but she managed to maintain the fake smile pasted on her face. She thought she might die if she had to keep it going much longer, such was the panic which gripped her.

'We lived here as children. I think my parents bought this house shortly after they were married. Let me see. . .another show of counting—it must be close to forty years. Does that help at all?'

'Oh, thank you, yes.' Cara's words barely made it through her dry lips; she squeezed each one out as if it cost a fortune. 'You've been very helpful. I must go. Thanks again, and sorry for bothering you.'

Cara stumbled away. She was reeling. Her worst fear had been confirmed. George wasn't here. She'd ruined it all. She'd killed him with her vain, reckless behaviour.

She threw herself on to a wooden bench and stared ahead. Groups of people buzzed around, going about their lives. People who knew nothing of George. They marched by as if nothing of any significance had happened; as if her whole world hadn't collapsed with one innocuous conversation. She didn't want to see anyone or anything. She wanted to disappear with George.

He must never have existed in this new version of the timeline.

A violent rage burned through her and she began to sob; loud, desperate sobs which poured out of her and shook her entire being. She couldn't stop. She didn't want to stop. She sat there wailing long enough to cry out all the tears she'd been choking back for months, and until her throat was as parched as a teetotaller's kitchen cabinet.

When she could cry no more, she stood up and walked home in a daze, not feeling anything but her own pain-filled heart. She thought this must be what dying was like. She pulled herself along, but her spirit had deserted her.

To lose your one true love is dreadful in any circumstances. To have your true love die is to be grief-stricken, but to be confronted with the reality that the man she had loved for five hundred years no longer existed, struck terror into Cara's heart.

George wasn't alive. She'd known it the minute they were arrested; when she realised her timing for making the trip was off. But she prayed she had imagined it. George often teased her about her superstitious tendencies. That was one thing she'd brought with her from her old life. In Tudorville, everyone was superstitious. Superstition was the norm.

She caught sight of her puffed, tear-stained eyes in the car mirror as she drove in the direction of George's townhouse. Even though she knew the truth in her bones, she was compelled to go there and see for herself. There was still a tiny flicker of hope that she'd made it all up and she was wrong.

She found a parking space a couple of houses over from George's front door, blew her nose and settled down to wait. It had only been about ten minutes when the door opened, and a man appeared. He was roughly the same height and build as George, with similar hair colour. Her spirits rose. But then she caught sight of his profile; it wasn't him. She would know George anywhere. A woman stood in the doorway, to see him off, but Cara couldn't make out her appearance. The man kissed her before he turned to leave the house. Cara and the woman watched him walk along the path and turn towards town.

What had she done? Where was George? When was George?

CHAPTER 21

York, present day

Cara sat in her car outside George's house. Late morning turned to early afternoon. She was frozen to the spot. She couldn't get her head around what had happened—how could he just disappear?

Irrationally she considered whether he might have done it to spite her. When she was upset, he liked to remind her that nothing he did was to hurt her. And she believed him; most of the time. She knew he didn't consciously mean to hurt her, but sometimes when she pushed him too far, his anger was steel-edged and he pushed back; hard. He was only human, no matter how much she idolised him.

Cara's anger evaporated when he allowed her a glimpse of the vulnerability beneath his confident veneer. If anything, it made her feel more loved. It was one method by which she gauged the depth of his feelings. If he weren't madly in love with her, he wouldn't be so affected.

But she'd run from him. Now, perhaps he was running from her. Could it be so? She'd read about the cycles of Twin Flames on a popular blog, following one of her visits to Sylvia. Thousands of distraught couples were caught in love limbo, in search of the other half of their soul. Many of them didn't understand what it was they were searching for. They just intuitively knew something was missing from their life. The classic Twin Flame dance moved to a seductive rhythm. Cara was disorientated from spinning. Lately, their relationship was more of a tragic tango than a love affair. It would require both of them to be courageous to make the changes to be together, with minimum collateral damage. She didn't know exactly how, but she sensed a resolution was possible with some willingness to be uncomfortable for a while. But he wasn't willing.

Cara would do anything to turn back time and bring George back. Such was her despair; at that moment, she would be relieved even if he stayed with Joanna.

Please God let everything reset to how it was, and I will tinker no more. Just let him be alive.

As she sat in the car, praying for a miracle, it occurred to her that this must be true unconditional love. It certainly felt better than being the jealous bitch from hell. She laughed aloud at her craziness. At least something positive was emerging from this nightmare.

Cara raised her head as she heard a sudden noise and saw the front door open. George's wife exited the house. So, it had been Joanna standing in the doorway kissing the George lookalike. Cara watched as she flung her handbag over her shoulder and bounced down the path, laughing with a teenage girl who resembled George's daughter. They jumped into a white Range Rover, and Cara watched them pull away. Her head ached.

Had she just witnessed her first alternative reality?

Joanna must have married the man she was destined to be with if George wasn't in the picture. If only Joanna had been married to this other guy all along, none of this mess would have happened. George would have been free when she met him, and they would have avoided this disaster. Or would they? She had no way of knowing. She wondered whether there was some way to change their circumstances while keeping George alive. That would be the perfect solution to all of their problems.

Cara turned the key in the ignition and steered the car down the bumpy road in the direction of her office.

She hated to admit it, but without George, everything was meaningless. Her spark had vanished and now he was gone forever. She blamed herself.

Cara closed her office door behind her, heart racing as she stabbed at Eddie's number on her phone. He answered after a couple of rings.

'Eddie, you won't believe it!'

'Hi. Are you okay?'

'Seriously, you won't believe it. I have to talk to you or I won't believe it either.'

'What the devil's going on?'

'I've just seen a man who looks like George leave his house.'

'Right, okay. . .and?'

'He's not George, but he kissed Joanna; George's wife. And then a girl came out who looked like his daughter but I'm certain wasn't. It was so bizarre. George isn't alive, Eddie. It's as I feared. He's been deleted from this timeline.'

Her voice shook, and her hysteria echoed back at her

through the phone. 'His phone is dead too. It's like he never existed.'

'Take a deep breath, my dear. Try and calm down. It's tricky for me to understand what you're saying. What else has happened? Is that it? Couldn't the lookalike be her brother or a relative?'

'No. I went to George's workshop first. It's a private residence belonging to a family who has lived there for forty years. No wonder it looked different. Remember you said something was off when you delivered the letter?'

'Ah yes, the building did seem different, but I couldn't put my finger on it. My mother used to say that I walk around with my eyes closed, so for me to notice something odd, it must have been striking.'

'Could George be a time traveller too do you think?' Cara interrupted his musings.

'George, a time traveller? I hadn't considered it. I suppose he could be. Practically, of course, we know it's possible. I don't remember anything of significance from Tudorville though, do you?'

'No, since Sylvia told me about Twin Flames I've assumed he's the other half of my soul, reincarnated in the form of his direct descendant who bears the same name. They are identical to look at, but then that's not at all unusual in families, is it?'

'Um, no, I suppose not. Let's try and think this through clearly before we rush into action. There must be a lot going on that we're unaware of. . .that we just don't know yet.'

'Agreed. There would seem to be two possible scenarios. The first is that I've messed up the timeline by travelling back too early, getting caught, and interrupting the natural order of events. If he's dead, he must have been captured and executed at Tower Green, like Queen Anne. We do know that Henry is in his season of killing.'

'Okay, yes, that's possible. Although any number of things could have happened after you returned; not necessarily his execution.'

'True, but as much as I hate to think it, if he's not alive in the here and now, the chances are high that he was killed in 1536.'

Eddie looked into the video camera and saw her pale face and grey, haunted eyes. 'You look dreadful, my dear. It's going to be alright. We'll figure this out together.'

Cara gulped back the emotion and made a stoic effort not to cry. She knew this was a critical time to be strong. If she gave in to the urge to think about her feelings she'd sink into a pool of despair. Their whole future hung in the balance.

'Thank you. You're a dear friend. I'll fall apart and be no good to anyone if I don't do something to save George now. The waiting is killing me.'

'What's the other scenario?' Eddie probed gently, wishing he had the power to alleviate her distress. He still blamed himself for sending her on the fatal mission which had quite possibly cost George his life.

'I'm wondering what the implications of George also being a time traveller could be. Is it possible that him not being alive now is pure coincidence and could have happened anyway?'

'Um, it's hard to say,' replied Eddie.

'There's no time to waste. Let's assume I messed up the timeline by returning too early. We either try to turn back time so George is still alive in present day, or we must save him from the Tower in Tudorville before they execute him. There may still be a chance. I'm terrified they caught him and he died at the Tower like the queen. The king has turned into a ruthless tyrant. All he cares for is satisfying his lustful vengeance.'

'In quantum terms, it's true. If George doesn't exist now,

then it would seem as though he died. Although it doesn't necessarily mean it happened in Tudorville. Just to complicate matters, it could have been any time in-between, or if he is indeed a time traveller, then the number of other possibilities increases tenfold.'

'This is terribly confusing. What do you think gives us the best chance of saving him? At this point, I'll do anything to bring him back, even though we'll be living separate lives. If I can go back far enough in time to before we met and fell in love in Tudorville, I think it should reset the timeline to how it was before our experiment, and he should be alive today.'

'Is that what you want?' asked Eddie.

'No. Of course not. But anything is better than him being dead. I can't bear it. I'd rather he's dead to me but living his life.'

'Okay, well we can't know if George is a time traveller, and ironically there's no time to find out. There are too many unknowns. I think you're right. It does seem as though he's not alive now because of our meddling,' said Eddie.

They talked through various options and began to formulate a plan. Cara would attempt to leave for Tudorville today. It was a blood moon eclipse; a perfect day to slip through the gateway and attempt to turn back time to save George.

The Tower of London, 1536

Cara, the children and Edward were released first, in accordance with George's terms. The Tower guard pushed them one by one through the tall wrought iron gates.

Swifty and George watched them stumble out into the gloomy London morning. Heavy clouds hovered on the low, murky skyline, and the threat of rainfall loomed.

George couldn't take the chance that the children would recognise him, so he had disguised himself in a sailor's uniform and a blond wig which he'd appropriated from Madame Alicia's costume chest. He would try to catch Cara's eye; it could be the last time they would see each other.

The pre-wedding hustle and bustle on the streets around the Tower made it easy to avert his face as his family passed. A few members of the crowd jeered. The atmosphere was charged with anticipation; they were spoiling for another execution.

King Henry was to marry Jane Seymour, his next queen, on the 30th of May. Impromptu street parties had broken out all over the city, despite the uncertainty and tension in the air. The people had not loved Anne Boleyn, so most weren't sorry she was gone. Katherine of Aragon had been their true queen, but they recognised that the old order had changed.

Even in these humiliating circumstances, Cara walked like a noblewoman, shoulders back, head high. She knew, especially in these circumstances, it was critical not to show any sign of weakness. She'd been raised to be proud and strong, and this was the behaviour she modelled for her children.

As she reached out to touch May's shoulder, a pair of familiar dark eyes caught hers. She turned to search the crowd. Was he an apparition or was George watching them? She hadn't eaten more than a crust of bread for days, and she barely trusted her senses. The tiny portions of food they'd received weren't enough to feed the children. She needed to ready Thomas and May for their next ordeal. They wouldn't like being parted from her again, but she must send them to Willow Manor, to their grandparents. The agreement with the king was that she would retire with her children to a quiet life at their country home and never attend court again.

It was dangerous to flout King Henry's orders, but she couldn't go to York while George was on the run. She must find him. Together they could get through anything, separate they were weak.

Thank God, she'd arrived back again so soon; she'd only been gone a couple of hours in Tudorville. She had tried to turn back time by focusing on travelling back to the day before she met George for the first time, but once again she'd failed in her audacious attempt to navigate time on demand. Perhaps it was only possible to travel back and forth in a linear fashion. But if that was so, how had she deleted George's timeline?

She'd tried to do what she thought must be the right thing by sacrificing their shared history, but she hadn't pulled it off despite her best intentions. Now she was relieved to be back in a time when her one true love lived. She would go full force into making sure George wasn't executed. She'd do whatever it took to save him; to save them. Staying in London and disregarding the king's rules was a risk she was willing to take, made slightly lighter by knowing that in the event of neither of them surviving, the children would be cared for by George's parents. Cara and George had lost their newly bestowed titles and lands, but they still had their family home. Cara would gladly give it all up to live a quiet life, but not without her husband.

George stared longingly at Cara's back as she walked away; perhaps forever. He couldn't take the chance that the king's men would see them together, but he'd had to have a glimpse of her. The risk of his family being caught and thrown back into the Tower was too high. That would serve no one. He must keep them safe, no matter how much his heart ached at being so close and unable to reach out to touch her one last time. He watched until they were out of sight, then turned and nodded farewell to Swifty before walking towards the Tower gates to turn himself him.

George sat on a hard, wooden chair near the window overlooking the spot where Anne Boleyn had lost her life. He reflected on how low Henry's favourites had fallen in such a short period. It was over. What more could be done? He would try to go to his death with honour and be grateful that it was him, not Cara who would face the executioner. If he knew she was okay, he could handle anything. His eyes lit on the dusty floor and flooded with unexpected tears as he saw Thomas and May's names etched into the dust. As he'd suspected, he'd been thrown into the cell they had occupied immediately before him. Thank God, they were safe and on the way home to his dear parents. He knew he could rely on them to take care of Cara and the children.

The following morning the cell door was flung open, and a gaoler called, 'The king has come, and he requires your presence immediately.'

George rubbed his gritty eyes and leapt to his feet. Somehow, he'd managed to sleep for a few hours despite the hard, lumpy mattress and the freezing cold air. He'd tried not to dwell on what was ahead of him so he could sleep; not spin in his hopeless grief. This was his chance to appeal to the king who had been his companion and friend for many years, not just his master. Perhaps he would have mercy when he realised George was still his loyal servant.

George entered the audience chamber where Henry sat on one of his many thrones, fell to his knees and kissed King Henry's hand. The king's cluster of rings shone against the backdrop of the dim room.

'Your Grace, I'm overjoyed to see you again, but I'm distraught to find myself in such dire circumstances.'

'Rise, rise, Cavendish.' I'm heartsick at these charges brought against you and the countess. We released her at your request and for the sake of your children and the friendship we shared, but this profound treachery deeply wounds me. What have you to say for yourself?'

Sire, I beg you to please reconsider. I would never do anything to endanger you or your crown. My life has been dedicated to serving you.' George's head remained bowed.

'It seems you and your lady wife were more loyal to your former queen than to your king. I was informed that you hatched plans to double-cross me in league with the northern lords. And you! The one and only northern lord whom I trusted. I would have granted you anything. How could you do it?' Spittle flew from the king's lips, and he flushed an angry pink as he ran his hand through his faded red hair.

'I swear I didn't do anything other than be your trusted advisor as I have always been since you appointed me these many years past. And my wife served the former queen at your bequest. We held no special affiliation to her. The charges against us are cooked up by one of your enemies in order to turn you against us. Please believe me, Your Grace.'

Henry sat down heavily. He was weary of the web of deceit that surrounded him.

'It is with great sadness, George, that I must condemn you to remain in the Tower to await sentence from the Council. They will meet within the week and decide your fate. I pray that you will not be executed like so many of my dear friends, but it's out of my hands. It's for Cromwell and his men to evaluate the evidence to see what the charges must be.'

There was nothing more George could say. He knew the king well enough to know he was washing his hands of the situation because he didn't wish to offer him a reprieve.

'I hope you're grateful for the release of your lady wife and children. I'm a benevolent king, but I'm unable to show mercy in the face of such double-dealing and treachery. Your title has been revoked. For the sake of your father, who served my father with an unblemished record, your family will remain untouched at their home in York. Of that, you have my word so you may face your fate in peace.'

CHAPTER 22

Y ork, a few days earlier, present day

For perhaps the hundredth time that day, George wondered where Cara had gone. She wasn't at home when he popped by on two consecutive days. She wasn't reading text messages or returning his calls. It was as if she'd dropped off the edge of the earth. She'd frozen him out of her world, wherever she was. A chill ripped through him as he contemplated this grim realisation.

After a couple of days consumed by worry, he decided to call her work number, but his call was diverted to an automated message which said she was away on business, and her office was closed indefinitely.

Right-ho, Cara. The message was clear. He wouldn't bother her anymore—he would leave it up to her.

It was a first for her not to be in touch with him at all when he was trying to make contact. Even when he'd done something unforgivable she would at least respond by message to let him know she was okay. He was restless night and day. There was a dull ache in his chest, and he hurt all over.

He argued inwardly that perhaps it was better this way. He did everything he could to convince himself it was so. But it was no good; he concluded that even if it was for the best, he hated it. He wanted her, he yearned to hear her voice, and now he regretted his mulish behaviour. He could kick himself; her disappearance was obviously a result of something he'd done. He'd given up trying to figure out exactly what triggered their separations, but she had been so angry about the newspaper article, and he had brushed it off as if it wasn't a big deal.

Cara could be unpredictable, and as much as it drove him crazy, it was also one of her qualities which bewitched him. He could no longer ignore that his marriage wreaked havoc upon their lives.

It was a wonder she'd waited for him this long. He nursed his lukewarm cup of black tea. Hunger pangs clawed at his belly, but he had neither the desire to prepare food nor the appetite to eat. Everything seemed pointless, and yet time continued to tick by as he stared at the mahogany grandfather clock in the workshop. Unable to concentrate on anything for more than a couple of minutes, work was increasingly a challenge. Clients, friends and colleagues buzzed in and out, and it was an effort to rally himself to engage in mundane conversation. He knew it was unkind, but their concerns seemed banal. His usually optimistic and bouncy personality was buried beneath a weight of gloom.

Life at home had a nightmarish quality. Joanna kept catching him when he was zoned out, and she remarked several times on his vacant stare. Worse still, he could barely muster a decent excuse. He'd lost the will do so.

'I'm feeling under the weather,' was the best he could do. 'A bit tired.'

He realised that for the first time, he couldn't make himself care enough about whether she found out what was going on, to come up with a plausible excuse. He'd lost interest in everything since Cara disappeared.

Joanna looked at him as if he was an alien species she no longer knew or understood, and the chasm between them grew as the black void in his heart deepened. He was physically unwell and emotionally bereft.

George pondered on his recent meeting with Queen Victoria and Prince Albert. He admired the royal couple; they were impressive beyond their titles and pomp. No wonder they were still so celebrated, almost two centuries later. All he could remember from his last time travel sojourn was that Queen Victoria had charged him with visiting Spain under diplomatic pretence so he might be her eyes on the ground.

Like many monarchs before her, Queen Victoria was eager to learn what the Spanish were up to and she had nominated George, one of her favourites, to carry out the secret mission. As if all of this heartache in his present-day life wasn't enough to deal with. He never knew from one minute to the next when he'd be drawn back to Victorian times. He never knew how long he'd be gone, or what was happening in his normal life when he hurtled back to the past. He pondered his strange situation. The Spanish goose chase could be a long one because in those days it could take months to travel across Europe. Not that it was any indication of how long he'd be there. He'd managed to work out, through conversations in both timelines that when he flitted back and forth, no one else seemed aware that anything had changed. His physical presence remained. He didn't understand how it worked; only that it did.

He found it bizarre, yet fascinating. It meant there was something about his consciousness that travelled with him, but he remained physically present in both timelines continuously. He'd love to talk to someone who understood time travel, but so far he'd had no success. He couldn't risk telling the wrong person. It sounded mad, and he wouldn't blame anyone for thinking he'd lost his mind if he told them his version of events. Was he the only time traveller in history? It was a lonely and frightening thought.

Hopefully, Cara would forgive him, and reappear soon so he would be lifted out of this dreadful slump. He knew from experience that his dark mood would dissipate in an instant when he was with her. If only he could tell her what was happening. But would she even believe him?

He was at a loss as to how to sort out the mess that his life had become, but he knew he couldn't be without her any longer. If she made contact, he resolved he would figure something out so they could be together. He would stop pushing her away. She only ever asked to see him; to spend time with him. It didn't seem unreasonable now that she had gone. He was consumed with remorse. If he stopped resisting the inevitable, he hoped she'd be less inclined to keep breaking it off.

He oscillated between feelings of anger at her for deserting him, and empathy because of what she had endured due to his refusal to end his marriage. He'd previously concluded that if he was in her position, he would cope better. He pulled a face. Now he wasn't so sure. He had chastised her in the past for her erratic behaviour, but as the empty hours turned into dull days and endless, lonely nights, his understanding deepened and regret crushed his soul.

If only he had revealed that they were married to one

another a couple of centuries earlier and that no matter how pig-headed she thought him, she was the only woman he had ever loved. It was just going to take him some time to work things out. Things would be so much easier if she knew there was no need to be jealous. If she returned, he would wait for the right time to tell her. For now, he had no choice but to keep their Victorian life to himself.

Over the years he'd grown accustomed to keeping his emotions buttoned up. It was a form of self-defence. If he revealed his true feelings to Joanna, it would be impossible to keep up the charade. Their relationship only hung together if they both played their part. He pretended he was in love with her, and other than the occasional comment, she pretended she didn't know he wasn't. Their marriage would have imploded years earlier if either of them had been honest about their feelings. Joanna yearned for what he couldn't give her, and so he gave her friendship, dressed up as a romantic partnership. They had played Oscar-winning performances, but now he'd run out of lines.

Perhaps there would come a day when he would live with Cara openly as they did in Victoriana. He barely dared to allow himself to hope it would come to pass. He didn't manage disappointment well. It frightened him.

If he told Cara about their previous life together, who knew what she'd make of it. He had almost told her when he'd experienced deja-vu at Hampton Court Palace. There was something familiar about the Tudor apartments. It was as though they'd been there together before. It was the same feeling he had when he went back to Victorian times and met Cara for the first time. They'd been introduced at a dinner at Windsor Castle in the Summer of 1840. The festivities at the castle were merry, following the royal wedding, earlier that year.

One look at Cara and he was bewitched. It was exactly

like when he'd met her in the bookshop. Love at first sight. Miraculous but real. Neither of them could bear to be apart for more than a few hours. After years of ducking out of matchmaking attempts by his mother, one week later he proposed and he and Cara were married before Christmas. When you know, you know. And he knew now too, but he was locked into a situation and couldn't find the key to exit.

How could he explain they were married two hundred years earlier but he was sorry he wasn't free now? No, he shook his head. He didn't understand the connection between them, which transcended hundreds of years, but their bond was unbreakable. No matter how many times he retreated or she broke off their relationship, they were drawn together again like magnets. George decided the only plausible explanation was that they were soul mates. He used to think the idea of soul mates was a load of romantic nonsense but not anymore. And besides, thinking they were destined to be together gave him a slither of comfort when his sadness threatened to smother and choke him in a black curtain of depression. There were days where he felt her loss so keenly that he could barely catch his breath.

Ever since their lives collided in the bookshop, he'd experienced the indescribable ability to navigate between present-day and the Victorian era.

Nothing like it had ever happened to him before. One minute he was a workaholic, preoccupied with the business of rare manuscripts, and the next, well. . .he'd read *The Time Machine* at school and thought it was a marvellous work of science-fiction.

And to think that now he was a bona fide time traveller. He didn't know how to get his head around it. Meeting Cara in another time was disorientating. They were involved in two parallel lives, and sometimes it was more than he could process. Yet he couldn't deny it.

They were celebrated as a perfect match in Victorian circles, but here their relationship was tumultuous. If he could go back on demand, he'd leave York immediately and buy a ticket to join her. Anywhere. If only it were that easy; he'd leave this impossible situation behind.

But he didn't know how to travel back whenever he wanted. He didn't even know if it was possible. Time travel on demand wasn't in his box of tricks. He had no control whatsoever over when he went or returned.

He was optimistic Queen Victoria would permit Cara to accompany him if the proposed trip to Spain went ahead. Looking back, he could see the links between their two lives. It was no wonder he'd loved Spain as soon as he visited as a young man on a business trip. There had been an inexplicable pull. Now it was obvious why—he'd probably spent time there in his past life.

Whether Cara had been with him wasn't yet clear, but he suspected she had. He hoped so; he couldn't stand the idea of them being wrenched apart there too.

London, 1536

'Cara, welcome back. How is it going in the future?' Eddie asked once they'd left the Tower and had a chance to whisper as they walked side by side along the cobbled street.

'Terrible. It's going terribly, Edward.' Cara naturally called him by his formal name in Tudorville.

'Why, what's happening?'

'Well, George isn't even alive for one thing! His wife is married to another man who resembles him but most definitely is not him. Of course, that would be the answer to my prayers if only he were alive. It's what I've wished for. I still can't understand how he married her. It's not right.' Cara shook her head. Thinking about it made her melancholy.

'Oh, my lord. That's a major hiccup indeed,' said Eddie, scratching his head. 'So what can we do?'

'Well, you and I decided we'd have a Plan B in case Plan A didn't work, which it obviously didn't.'

'How do you know?'

'Because I'm here with you again! Plan A was for me to travel back to disrupt the timeline so that George and I never met. That way we wouldn't have married, he wouldn't die at the Tower, and we'd avoid all of this heartache in the present day.'

'Is that what you want?' said Edward.

'No, of course not.' Cara shook her head again. 'That's exactly what you asked in present-day!'

'Oh, dear. Well, I'm sorry my lady, but it's tricky to know what I've said as my future Professor self! Please bear with me because I'm an earlier model. What do you want exactly? I'm confused.'

'Sometimes, I don't even know what I want. Anyway, Plan A is obviously a no go so we're moving on to Plan B. It's our only option.'

'Which is?'

'It really is infuriating that you don't remember your own plans, Edward!'

'It'll come to me soon, but if you want my help now, you're going to have to update me,' he laughed.

Cara rolled her eyes. 'Plan B is that we find a way to rescue George from the Tower before he's executed.'

'Okay, well that makes sense. Good plan. Then he'll presumably be alive in the future unless something else happens to disrupt the timeline.'

'Yes. I suppose something else could happen, but I can't

put my energy into thinking about that. There are too many variables.'

'Hold on a minute though,' said Edward.

'What?'

'How on earth do you know for sure that George is in the Tower?'

'I saw him in the crowd as we were released. He was watching us. I doubted my eyes for a moment because I see him everywhere, but now I'm sure it was him. The heroic fool has gone and done a typical George thing.'

'And what would that be?'

'He's exchanged himself for us and escorted us to our freedom. That's why we were released from the Tower. He's my Twin Flame. He protects me.'

'Ah, yes. That does make sense. It is a typical earl-like thing to do. So how does Plan B work? How do we break him out?' said Edward.

'Um, well there's good news and bad news,' said Cara.

'Why am I not surprised? Give me the good news first to soften the blow.'

'The good news is we're in place to implement Plan B.'

'Right, and? What do we do?'

'That's the bad news. I've no idea yet. We didn't get that far in our plan formulation. We thought we'd figure it out as we go.'

'So, he is locked in the Tower of London, and we're supposed to come up with a way to break him out and then get us all to safety while we're being hunted down?'

'That's about the gist of it. You've always been razor-sharp, Edward. That's why you're so good with the children.'

'Thank you. Although you employed me as a tutor, not a prison vigilante.'

'Life is never simple in the Cavendish household. You

must know that by now! Let's think about what we're going to do,' said Cara.

London, 1840

George trailed his fingers down the exposed flesh at the back of Cara's corset. She quivered at his touch, and he leaned forward to plant soft kisses on her neck. The feel of his lips on her skin electrified her senses, and she experienced a jolt between her legs. She was weak with desire.

He pressed against her, and the familiar fierce current passed between them. The extent of her lust for him still took her by surprise. Nothing had prepared her for this degree of sexual intensity.

'How is it that I'm the luckiest woman in the world and get to be your wife and make love to you whenever I want?'

He pulled her into his arms; she lost her balance and sank back into him. She'd never felt more alive. Each morning she looked at him lying next to her in their huge four-poster bed and offered up a prayer of gratitude.

He dropped more light kisses on to her neck and then slowly spun her around to face him. His hand tilted her chin upwards, and he gazed into her eyes, laughing as he said, 'I don't know Mrs Cavendish, but it's definitely time for you to perform your wifely duty.'

Cara looked coyly up at him as she raised a dark eyebrow and then curtsied with mock deference. 'Why, of course. What do you have in mind? How may I serve you, my lord?'

He placed her hand on the growing mound beneath the flap in his britches. Then he reached over to remove a cushion from the chaise-longue and placed it on the floor.

Cara took his cue, dropped to her knees on the cushion

and caressed him. She unbuttoned the flap and his manhood pressed against the soft material, crying out for her attention. Impatient, he pulled his suspenders off, and his britches fell to his ankles. She slid his drawers down his muscular thighs, and his cock sprang up to meet her. Her hands were warm as she moved them firmly along the length of him.

A virgin before their marriage, she had sensed how to please him from the first sexual encounter. Their desire was mutual and even though she hadn't been schooled in the ways of pleasuring a man, pleasing her husband came as naturally to her as breathing. It was as if they'd always been together. They were a perfect fit, both physically and intellectually. Making love to George was effortless, just as she had known it would be. Such was their blaze of passion, delighting him gave her an immense thrill.

He was a sensual lover, and he guided her to erotic heights she'd never imagined existed. They barely slept on their wedding night; such was the build-up of craving for each other's touch since they'd met. Months of secret touching and chaperoned visits had them both in a fevered frenzy.

George groaned as she touched him. He thought he would die of bliss as she rolled her tongue around his cock. But then he began to slip away. He could feel the ebb of energy whirling around him. The air grew cold; the vortex was drawing him towards present-day York.

'Not now, please, God, not now. Don't take me now,' he whispered.

Cara raised her head to look at him. 'What?'

But then he was gone.

She made love to him, oblivious that a part of him had left.

York, present day

He woke up in bed a little after six. He turned to see Joanna asleep next to him. A bitter taste of bile rose in his throat and threatened to choke him. So wretched were his feelings of loss, he had to stop himself from crying out like a wounded animal.

He turned over and clamped his eyes shut in an effort to go back to sleep and blot out the pain. It was no good. Images of Cara and pangs of desire shot through every inch of him. He wanted her. They'd been together, she'd been making love to him, and now he was back here again. His marital sheets were warm, but his heart rebelled.

He couldn't do this anymore. It wasn't working. He couldn't keep up this hollow pretence any longer. His chest hammered as he contemplated his life; his lives. What the hell was he going to do? Where was Cara? When would she come back or when would he return to Victoriana? It was torture; having the sweetness of her ripped away without warning. He was weak with longing. He pined for a normal life with Cara. What was wrong with him? He'd never asked for any of this.

He went into the bathroom and peered at his face. He looked ghastly as though he hadn't slept for days—his eyes were bloodshot. His complexion was a sickly yellow beneath his tan. He was frustrated by Joanna's presence, and resentment bubbled below the surface. He knew it wasn't her fault, but that didn't help him to manage his disappointment in the same way it once had. He used to be able to box up his feelings and get on with things. Not anymore. Before Cara tumbled at his feet in the bookshop, he'd been proficient at controlling his emotions and had resigned himself to a mediocre marriage. Now, his carefully constructed tower had come tumbling down. He was powerless to stop it. He didn't even want to.

He showered, dressed for work, and left the house before his wife stirred for the day. He didn't want to be there anymore.

Joanna opened her eyes as the bedroom door clicked shut behind him. She'd been awake for some time but hadn't wanted to face the awkwardness between them.

Before she turned over and drifted into a light doze, she wondered what was going on with him. She sensed it had gone too far; he was absent even when at home. Whatever he had planned, it clearly didn't involve her. Their life together was over. She knew it must be just a matter of time, but she dreaded hurting her daughter. How did you tell your child their parents didn't want to be together anymore?

CHAPTER 23

L ondon, 1536

'What are you thinking, my lady? You've got that look on your face. I can see you're cooking something up,' said Edward.

'I'm running through some possible ways of breaking George out of the Tower.'

'Oh, I see. Just another of the everyday little challenges we've been up against lately then!'

'Yes, that's about it,' Cara smiled.

'So, what are the options?'

'Well, no one has ever broken out of the Tower as far as I'm aware. But we won't let that stop us.'

'No, quite; go on, although it would appear to be an impossible task.'

'There's always a first time. And the first time is going to be George.' Cara's face was set. Not much could deter her when her mind was made up.

'I do admire your fearlessness. But aren't you at all afraid, my lady?'

'Afraid? Of course, I am. I'm petrified. But I'm more afraid of losing George forever. That makes it simple. We can't not rescue him. There's no alternative.'

Edward nodded. 'You can count on me to do anything I can to help. I feel wholly responsible for this mess.'

'It's not your fault, and there's no point thinking that way even if it was. Although I was rather hoping you'd say you would help. Thank you. I can't do this without you.'

'What do we know so far?' he asked.

'Swifty brought me word that George is being held in Cradle Tower. If my memory serves me correctly, that tower is close to the outside wall, overlooking the moat. That's probably the best possible place he could be for an escape.'

'Is it? However will we get him out of there?'

'There's a wharf below. If George uses a rope to climb across the moat, he can get down to the wharf. We will be waiting for him in a boat ready for a quick getaway.'

Edward's eyes widened. 'Where are we getting-away to if I dare ask?'

'I don't know yet. Let's figure out if this is a workable plan first and then we will decide.'

'It could work, but how will we give him instructions if we can't see him?'

'He's been allowed to keep Swifty as his servant. Swifty is permitted to come and go so we could get him to deliver a message to George. But that might be too risky.'

'What other way is there?'

'Do you remember when you told me you'd considered the priesthood, Edward?'

'Um, yes.' I don't care for that glint in your eye though.

What on earth has my failed vocation got to do with anything?'

'Perhaps there is a way for us to see him. I have an idea. You probably won't like it, but it might work. It may be our only hope of preparing George adequately, so we have a real chance of rescuing him.'

'Tell me more. What do you propose?'

Cara beckoned Edward closer. They sat at a table in a tavern on the Great North Road, pretending they were making their way to Willow Manor in case they were still under surveillance. They awaited word from George's father to whom Cara had sent a letter and requested that he organise an escort home for the children.

Cara and Edward must remain in London. Cara couldn't break George out alone. She needed Edward and Swifty on the team. She whispered in Edward's ear as she outlined her plan.

Several minutes later, Edward took a long draught of his small ale and leaned back against the wooden bench as he contemplated what his mistress had asked of him.

'It could be the noose for us all. There's no guarantee we'll succeed. It's the most foolhardy, dangerous thing we've ever done.'

'Yes, I know all that. But more importantly, will you do it?'

Edward nodded, 'How can I not do it? I can no more leave the earl to rot in the Tower than I could leave you. You are like family to me. The only family I've ever had that's worth saving.'

Cara's eyes glistened. She hadn't known Edward had a troubled upbringing. She'd presumed he had a loving family waiting for his return. On reflection, he'd never mentioned anyone special or requested leave to visit family or friends.

He was a man of secrets, but he was a good man. Of that, she was certain.

She squeezed his hand. 'You're like a member of the family for us too. The children adore you, and George is always singing your praises. Thank you, Edward. I can't thank you enough for the trust you place in me. This is our only chance to save George from disappearing; both now, and in the future.'

They continued to discuss the details late into the night as the children slept upstairs, exhausted from their ordeal. They would spend the night in the tavern, waiting for George's father and then begin to execute the great escape.

Cara struggled to sleep. Gloomy thoughts of George alone in Cradle Tower plagued her. It was after three in the morning when she finally fell into a heavy slumber. A couple of hours later, she was awakened by a tap at the door.

'Scuse me, ma'am. Sorry to wake you. There's an urgent letter arrived for your attention.'

She leapt out of bed and ran to open the door; her loose wavy hair tumbled down over her shoulders. A young servant girl waited, letter in hand. Cara was relieved to see her father-in-law's seal.

'My dearest Cara.

I'm shocked to hear the news of George in the Tower of London. I shall hasten to make contact with the northern lords and enlist their support in petitioning for clemency for George from the king. In the meantime, in accordance with your wishes, expect to see my steward, Hancock. He is about to set out in a carriage to bring the children home to us. He should have covered a considerable distance by the time you read this letter. You and our beloved son are in our thoughts, and we pray for your safe return. Do whatever you may for George, and never fear; the children will be in good hands. Godspeed. Your father, George.'

Cara held the letter for longer than necessary; she took comfort in the familiar scent of the thick notepaper. Her thoughts drifted back to idyllic days at Willow Manor when she would sit at her writing desk, without a care in the world.

She dismissed the servant girl and dressed quickly. There was no time to waste. As soon as the children were on their way to Willow Manor, she and Edward would leave for the Tower. The rescue operation must begin.

York, present day

Cara tried to lose herself in her work, taking on more projects than she could handle in an attempt to fill every waking hour. Not that she was sleeping much. But she didn't want any time to think. All she wanted was to see George again; to know he was safe. But she had to learn to live without him now. She was trying to come to terms with the new world order, but her soul rebelled against the stark reality which faced her each morning as she dragged herself out of bed.

She yearned to be back in Tudorville to see whether they had rescued George from the Tower. She longed for the cold vortex to transport her back in time. The feeling of helplessness overwhelmed her. Trying to summon the vortex was futile. Thinking about Tudorville had no effect other than to exacerbate her loneliness. Cara had fallen into a bottomless pit of despondence and couldn't find a way out.

She consoled herself that at least things with Daniel had worked out better in this version of the timeline. Their relationship had ended surprisingly. The disruption had not only wiped George out of existence but had changed the course of Daniel's life. There had been no heart attack. Once she'd had a chance to digest the latest events, Cara had dropped by his house. Everything was a bit of a haze, and she wanted to ascertain precisely what the current situation was.

Always used to a warm reception she was in a rush and didn't bother to message first. Later she regretted it. A blonde, dishevelled looking woman had answered the door. When Cara introduced herself, the woman smiled shyly, shook her hand and then asked her to come in while she called Daniel.

The woman bustled off into the other room, and Daniel gave Cara a warm squeeze when he saw her. 'Cara, my dear. What brings you by? I didn't expect to see you after how things ended between us. . .' His words trailed away.

'How things ended?'

'Yes, you know. I was angry. I said some things I regret. I have been meaning to get in touch to apologise but the weeks have sped by. I realise now it was inevitable. I know you didn't mean to hurt me. There was no excuse for such surly behaviour on my part.'

His words were measured as if he'd been practising a script.

'Oh, yes, right. Thank you. I'm sorry too.' She looked around the room, taking in the intimate scene.

'You're in good health?'

'Yes, never better.'

'Alright, brilliant. Well, I just wanted to check-in and make sure you're okay. It looks like you're enjoying some company.'

'Ah, yes.' Daniel shifted from one foot to the other,

looking down at his shiny black shoes, before he raised his eyes to meet hers.

'It's been a while since you and I—I was so angry. I went on a dating site and, well. . .it was amazing really. We connected and hit it off so fast. I was reeling when you ended our engagement; it was such a shock. At first, it was a rebound reaction. I decided life's too short to sit around moping. But then we clicked. I'm relocating to the office in Manchester, and Sarah has agreed to accompany me.'

Cara stared at him as the revelations crossed his lips.

'You know I'm not one for being alone. I hate it.' His tone was apologetic, and she could see he was nervous.

'How wonderful. I'm happy for you. Truly. Now you'll be near your kids again. That's what you always wanted. So, it's all turned out for the best.'

Cara felt not even a smidgeon of jealousy. Not for the first time since they split up, she marvelled that she'd ever agreed to marry him.

'Thank you for understanding. It means a lot. I want us to part on good terms.'

He leaned over to give her a gentle kiss on the cheek and then walked her to the door, his hand rested gently on her arm.

'Daniel? Will you do something for me?'

'Yes, of course. Anything.'

'Please take care. Would you go and have an examination to be sure you're in tiptop shape?'

Daniel looked startled, 'Any particular reason?'

'It sounds silly, and I'm probably just fussing over nothing, but I had a dream you were unwell. It would make me feel better if you go and have a check-up. Promise?'

'You always fussed over my health. Okay. You know I'd do anything for you. Take care, my love. Be happy.'

Cara noticed his eyes shone. She felt a profound sense of

gratitude that he was okay, and immense relief that they were no longer together. Even in this new formation of time, they were finished. She'd been prepared to call off their engagement all over again, if necessary. With or without George, she was now certain she wasn't supposed to marry Daniel. Thank goodness, she didn't have to go through all of that again. He was doing great without her.

In finding the courage to free herself, she'd freed him too. She had hoped, but not really believed, that breaking it off would work out for the best for him also. She shook her head. It wouldn't be the first time she'd overestimated her own importance.

The heavy feelings of guilt she'd carried with her since their break up, evaporated. She was filled with optimism for the first time in weeks.

As she climbed into her car, she realised Daniel hadn't even asked how she was doing.

London, 1840

George was shown in for an audience with Queen Victoria. The daily red box lay open on the table for her urgent attention, and she studiously sat writing as he entered.

'Good morning, Your Majesty.' George bowed as the queen beckoned him to sit.

'Thank you for coming so quickly, Lord Cavendish.' She rang for tea and then got straight to the point.

'As we feared, Maria Christina has been superseded as Regent by General Espartero. It's a dangerous time in Spain, and we need somebody behind the scenes to report back to us. May we count on you, my lord?' The queen sought Prince Albert's eyes across the exquisitely decorated drawing-room.

He bestowed a warm smile on his beloved wife. A smile that said all she needed to know.

'Yes, Your Majesty. I will leave as soon as I can make travel plans if that is your wish.'

'Am I to be based in Madrid or where would you like me to reside?'

'We've received word that there may be a counter-revolution brewing in Seville. It makes sense for you to go first to Madrid to see what you can learn of the new Regent's intentions. We had good relations with Maria Christina, which means we won't be held in high esteem by the General. Conditions permitting we'd like you to then continue to Seville and settle there for a while to see what you can glean of the situation.'

'I will travel under cover of being commissioned to locate an important manuscript.'

'Yes, that's a splendid idea. We British will be under suspicion after we've supported Maria Christina through the Carlist wars. We don't want to wave any more red flags. It will be perfectly normal for you to be there working; in search of a rare manuscript.'

'I have one request your majesty if I may be so bold.'

'Of course, whatever I can do to assist you on your mission is yours. No question. What do you require?'

'I believe it would strengthen my cover if I were to have my wife accompany me on the trip. As you know, we've only recently married and I believe it would appear strange to outsiders for me to leave her to her own devices so soon after our nuptials.'

'Yes, indeed, my lord. Strange, and also no doubt extremely unappealing for you newly wedded lovebirds.' She laughed, and her eyes twinkled. 'I am altogether sympathetic. Goodness knows it's rare to witness a couple marry for love and not social advancement. You have my blessing. I too couldn't bear to be parted from my dear husband so soon after our marriage. I hope never to be parted from him.' She looked at the prince with a flirtatious glint in her eye.

George excused himself. The queen raised her gown above her ankles, to reveal dainty feet encased in silk slippers. She glided across the room to sit beside the prince who perused a leather-bound book. The royal couple were beautifully matched both in wit and countenance. But most of all, they complemented one another with their natural affinity. It was evident to all who entered their realm that theirs was no marriage of convenience, despite being a favourable blending of blue blood.

George was excused and then hurried to his nearby Windsor house to find Cara and tell her the exciting news. They would make their first trip abroad as husband and wife. He was lightheaded such was his relief that they were not to be separated. The thought of living without her in Spain for weeks, or even months, had filled him with a sense of foreboding. Sensing she would feel the same, he had been reluctant to mention a word to her about the impending trip. Now he'd grown accustomed to having her always by his side; he couldn't bear to contemplate not being in her company every day. He'd been blessed to be united with the love of his life, and he had no intention of wasting precious time. A day without her was a tedious affair. He wasn't a devout man, but he frequently thanked God for his good fortune.

'Cara, Cara,' he called, as he placed his hat on the stand in the entrance hall. 'Where are you? I have tremendous news.'

He ran up the stairs, two at a time, and burst into the bedroom. Cara sat on a velvet stool at the dressing table, wearing only a creme silk undergarment as she arranged her gleaming chestnut hair into a loose bun.

'What's going on? Whatever is all of the excitement so

early in the morning, my darling? You were quite sober when you left for your meeting. I presumed it was to be a dull gathering.'

'We are going to Spain! To be more precise, we're going first to Madrid and then to Seville. Remember we talked about how wonderful it would be to visit Seville together?'

'Oh, yes. The delights of a Mediterranean climate and streets strewn with juicy oranges.'

She dropped her hairbrush on to the table, moved quickly across the room and threw herself into George's arms. He lifted her off her feet, and she kissed the tip of his nose and then his forehead.

'How delightful. Are we to travel on business or what is the reason for this most fortuitous trip?'

He sat down, pulled her on to his knee and proceeded to recount the details of his audience with the queen.

'Why didn't you tell me this was brewing? You usually tell me your plans for the day.'

'Because I didn't want you to worry. I thought the queen would ask me to undertake the trip to Spain, but I was concerned she wouldn't permit you to accompany me. I suspected she might come up with some nonsense about you remaining here as one of her ladies. She's taken quite a shine to you, and you know how she likes to have her favourites nearby.'

'But she gave us her blessing so readily?'

'Absolutely. She was most understanding. Being a new bride agrees with her and has worked in our favour. As you know, she adores the prince. She seems to be in love with the very idea of love. In truth, it matters to me not why she said yes, but simply that she did. I couldn't contemplate making the trip without you. I planned to make up a plausible excuse to extricate myself if you weren't to accompany me.'

'And what would that have been may I ask?'

'I've no idea. I was hoping something would occur to me as and when the need arose.'

'Well knowing you, I've no doubt you'd have come up with something genius, but it's so much better that we're to make the trip together. I won't have you falling into the bad graces of her royal highness on my account. That would be an awful blemish on the Cavendish family name.'

'True. Aside from when my ancestor, George, was accused of treason by Henry VIII and thrown in the Tower, our family has served the monarchy with honours as far back as we can find records.'

'That's fascinating. What happened to him?'

'What happened to who?'

'To your ancestor, George.'

There was a loud knock on the door. 'I'll see what they want,' said George. 'You finish getting dressed and let's meet downstairs. Be quick, my darling. We must make plans to depart for Madrid as soon as possible. Let us leave before the queen has pause for thought.'

CHAPTER 24

H ampton Court Palace, 1536

The king had returned to his favourite palace with his new bride, Jane Seymour. He shifted his cumbersome weight in his seat. His swollen leg throbbed and made it difficult for him to settle. Sweat glistened on his brow, and he mopped the drops away with a silk handkerchief.

'Cromwell. Where are you?' he shouted. 'Must I wait all day for you to honour me with thy presence?'

Cromwell sauntered into the room where he spent most of his waking hours, governing England behind the scenes. Officially he was supposed to assist the king, but King Henry had little patience for the minutiae of daily kingship, so he handed more and more of his affairs over to his chief minister. Cromwell hurried for no man; not even his king.

'Yes, your majesty. I trust you and Queen Jane are recovered from the festivities. That was indeed the wedding of the century. You will be the envy of the whole of Christendom once word spreads.'

He stopped talking abruptly as he noticed the king's irritation, etched into the folds of his ruddy face. He knew every mannerism and was sensitive to the ebb and flow of his master's volatile nature. A touch of flattery typically fluffed the king's ego and restored his good cheer, but it didn't hit the spot today. 'What can I do for you, sire? I see you are troubled.'

'Ah, Thomas. You know me better than I know myself. Thank God I have you as my right hand. I have an urgent matter for you to attend to.'

'Oh? Pray tell, Your Majesty, and I'll take care of it post-haste.'

'George Cavendish must be pardoned.'

Cromwell cleared his throat. 'You have had a change of heart. We agreed he would face the privy council. The evidence gathered against him is so compelling that he is undoubtedly for the hangman. May I humbly ask why you are no longer in favour of the execution, my lord?'

'I've changed my mind.'

'Yes, but is there any particular reason, Your Majesty?'

'I can't put my finger on it. As much as my pretty bride makes me merry, I find myself cross and melancholy this morning. I slept little last night.'

'There, there, sire. Does your leg pain you?'

'Yes, Thomas, it's like having my skin plunged into a burning cauldron. It's so painful, at times I wonder what I have done to deserve this purgatory. I barely endure the agony.'

Cromwell made sympathetic noises and passed the king a glass of wine. He waited for the alcohol to kick in. He knew it would soothe his nerves and go some way to alleviate his pain and perhaps improve his mood.

'It's a beautiful day. It would appear that the beginning of summer is upon us. Would you like me to request entertainment; perhaps a masque in the gardens? I'm sure your lady, the queen, would appreciate the merriment.'

The king tutted and shook his head. 'I have no patience for more nonsense, Thomas. I appreciate you trying to distract me, but it is not necessary.'

Cromwell coughed. 'I must advise against pardoning Cavendish. We will look lily-livered by reneging on the charges and taking such a weak-bellied stance.'

'Are you calling your king, weak-bellied, Thomas? Is a king not allowed to change his mind?'

'It is not for me to tell you what you must or must not do, sire; but it is my duty to advise you, and I do so with great care.'

'I know you mean well, Thomas.' The king took another big gulp of his wine. 'I had the most terrible nightmare about Anne. I'm convinced she will haunt me from her grave forevermore with her brazen ways. I must do right by George. They were friends, you know. George's wife was Anne's favourite. My conscience does not rest happily at Anne's execution. I should have sent her to a nunnery, not have her death blemishing my poor innocent soul. I am plagued by guilt after acting in such haste.'

'Your Majesty, she was found guilty before the council. It was out of your hands. The evidence clearly pointed to her incrimination. Treason, witchcraft, adultery and incest are no inconsequential charges for anyone, never mind the Queen of England.'

'Yes, yes, I know all that. I know we had good reasons. But I feel a foreboding grabbing me by the throat and suffocating

eager to hear more. She thought herself truly blessed to have the best job in the world.

Cara filled Sylvia in on the situation with George, how his life was at stake in Tudorville and how she'd returned to find he had disappeared from the present-day timeline.

The psychic's eyes widened. Cara was the most fascinating client who had walked through her door in the twenty-five years she'd been in the business.

'So you see, I'm desperate for any guidance you can give me. I need to save George from execution so he won't be deleted from the future. What I'd like to know is if you can see anything that I'm missing. It's all so confusing; I'm sure I do not see everything. I woke up this morning thinking about you, wondering if there's anything you can tell me that will help me to save us all from disaster.'

'Let's do a reading and see what the cards tell us. This situation is way beyond my tiny mind. We need all angels on deck.'

Cara nodded. As ridiculous as calling on angels seemed, she was grateful for any divine assistance they could summon.

Sylvia shuffled the cards. 'I'm using a blend of decks.'

Cara clasped her hands together. She was becoming quite familiar with the cards, and a sense of peace descended on her as she watched Sylvia's hypnotic hand movements.

Since meeting George she'd begun to accept that divine assistance was always available and it wasn't down to her to make everything happen. It was a new worldview, and it gave her comfort.

'Angel Gabriel is present with us today. He has something to tell you,' said Sylvia as she laid out the cards one by one on to the shiny, wooden desk between them.

Cara's chest tightened as she tried to breathe normally. She waited, her heart pounding.

'It's a warning. This card indicates that all is not as it seems.'

'You can say that again,' said Cara. She took a deep breath and giggled. 'Sorry I'm nervous. Please go on.'

'I'm getting the message loud and clear that you must tread lightly and go slowly. You believe one thing is the case, but it's untrue. By taking the wrong action, you will cause irreparable damage.'

Cara pondered the card, unsure what to make of it. Their whole future depended on her not messing this up. She would either save George or leave him for dead if her plan wasn't successful. What other option could there possibly be? What was she not seeing?

'This next card indicates the depth of your Twin Flame connection. But there's more. I can't decipher the exact meaning, but the spread would seem to indicate that you and George are more than uni-level Twin Flames. But. . .' Sylvia paused, her eyes closed again as she swayed gently and surrendered herself to the experience.

Cara could feel the energy swirling around them, and she felt herself slip into a light trance. The air was warm, not freezing, like when she entered the vortex.

'I'm receiving a message that you are multi-generational Twin Flames. This is a rare phenomenon. I've never heard of it before, but it makes sense given your two shared timelines.'

'I see,' said Cara. Not really seeing at all but hoping to make sense of the jumble of Sylvia's insights.

'What about saving George? Do you see it is possible to restore him to the present day?'

Sylvia's skin glowed, and her face wore an ecstatic expression. 'George is not lost. He will be saved. It's out of your hands.' And then her eyes flickered open, and it was over.

'Was that helpful? I don't even know what I said. All I

know is it was channelled through me more strongly than ever before,' said Sylvia, visibly shaken.

Cara thanked her, paid and rushed back to her car, more confused than when she went in. If it wasn't up to her, then what was she to do? Did the message from the Angel Gabriel mean that as she wasn't in Tudorville, she must trust her 1536 self to break George out? She had set the plan in motion so it could be continuing, regardless of her being unaware of it. But she couldn't know for sure without going back. Frustration mounted as helplessness gripped her. This wasn't the time to give in to overwhelm. She must find a way to save George, but what was the meaning of the mysterious warning?

Cara drove home, numb. She dragged her weary frame out of the car and into the cottage, flicked on the lights and the radio to distract herself as she prepared a light supper of scrambled eggs on toast. After only a couple of mouthfuls, she pushed the plate away, feeling nauseous. She went upstairs and drew a hot, bubble bath, to try and relax but lay there agitated and pulled the plug out five minutes later. She would go to sleep and forget about everything. As much as she wrestled with the idea, it seemed there was nothing she could do for George at this point, except wait. Sleep would help to pass the hours until the vortex called her back in time. Then she'd know what to do.

Twisting and turning in bed, she found it difficult to get comfortable. She was mentally and physically exhausted but couldn't fall asleep. For a brief moment, she longed for the days before she'd met George. Her life had been peaceful then; dull but calm. And now he was gone, and she would face a future without him unless she could find a way to bring him back to life in this timeline.

'Cara. Cara. Please come back to me.'

She awoke to the rich timbre of George's voice and began

to weep; such was her yearning for him. His beautiful voice was tormented. Checking her phone, she saw it was three in the morning. It had been so vivid. Disappointment filled her senses as reality flooded back, and she realised it was just a dream. They were still separated by time. And then the vortex enveloped her, and in a moment she was gone.

Cradle Tower, London, 1536

George lay shivering on the lumpy mattress in his cell. Such was the sudden wave of despair that engulfed him; he called out, 'Cara. Cara. Please come back to me.' He rarely shed tears, but he was powerless to stop them spilling down his cold cheeks. The pain in his chest was intense. It wasn't Cara's fault, but he felt as though she'd abandoned him. He couldn't bear another empty day in this cell, awaiting his death, knowing he'd never see her or his children again. He was hopeless. There was nothing left to live for.

Cara and Edward had secured lodging near to the Tower of London. It was the middle of the night, but she was unable to sleep. She could feel George's pain as if it were her own. Sylvia had told her that Twin Flames share a telepathic bond and can feel and hear each other even when separated. She knew he needed her now, but she couldn't go to him. She'd be arrested, so she did the next best thing. Cara threw her cloak over her long white nightgown and headed towards the Tower. She must be near him. If there was any chance he might be able to sense she was near, she was willing to take the risk.

A couple of guards snoozed by the Tower gates, and all was eerily quiet. The full moon glowed high in the sky and cast a golden hue over the ancient castle walls. Cara was overcome with emotion and fell to her knees, grazing them on the hard cobbles, as she clutched the necklace George had given to her as a gift upon their engagement. She feared she couldn't take much more, but she must be strong for him. He had sacrificed himself for her and the children; she must not let him down.

'George. George.'

She stood up, silently crying out to him as she leaned against the thick stone wall. A veil of tears streamed down her face. She mustn't alert the guards; she'd be no use locked up in the Tower alongside George, even though she was tempted to throw herself on their mercy in the hope of catching a glimpse of him. Standing there in the dark velvety night with the moon dancing above the towers, she felt strangely closer to him than she had in weeks. Was it possible he could feel her presence? She was comforted and didn't know how long she stood, chained to the spot, her heart heavy. She prayed for God's mercy. Had he forsaken them?

Some hours later, first light crept over London, and she drew her cloak tightly around her shoulders and slipped back to her lodgings before the Tower inhabitants began to stir.

London, 1840

George whistled as he busied himself with preparations for leaving for Madrid. Always a happy fellow, there was a new bounce to his step at the delightful prospect of spending months or possibly longer, with Cara in Spain. He hoped they would have more time alone together than they managed to have here near the court. His royal post was demanding, and he was frequently away on business. Cara wasn't able to join him as it would not have been fitting, so the trip promised to be a wonderful interlude for them.

He wrote a letter to his good friend, Carlos, asking him to look for a suitable villa for them in Seville. Madrid would be a temporary stop, but it would be sensible to have their own place in Seville.

CHAPTER 25

L ondon, 1536

Cara awoke in bed, at her modest London tavern lodgings. It was as if she'd not left. Except for one thing: an ominous warning echoed in the chambers of her mind.

Sylvia had said that the Angel Gabriel warned her that all was not as it seemed. Or could it have been only a dream on this occasion? Perhaps she hadn't time travelled at all. She pulled her legs up towards her chest and curled up into a ball as she willed herself back to sleep. She wanted to shut out reality. Her mind was foggy, and she couldn't think clearly. Sleep wasn't to be. A few minutes later, there was a gentle tap on the door.

'Yes, who's there?'

'Lady Cara, it's me, Edward. I must speak with you.'

'Yes, of course. Please enter.'

Cara shot up in bed and pulled the sheet over her nightdress.

'Good morning Edward. Is everything alright? Judging by the light, it's barely dawn.'

'Yes, it's not much more, my lady. But I thought I should come and tell you the news immediately I heard it.'

'Heard what? Whatever did you hear?'

'Swifty brought me word just a few moments ago that yesterday evening they began building a new scaffold on Tower Green. He couldn't get away last night. He said he overheard that it's similar to the one they used for poor Queen Anne. The lad's terrified; white as a ghoul. Raced here to warn us.'

'Oh my God,' said Cara. A tremor shot through her body, and she began to shake. 'We're running out of time. We must put our plan into motion today. There's no time to waste.'

'But surely they must allow George to be heard by the Privy Council to sentence him before they take such action?'

'Well, you know how quickly that can happen. It was merely a formality for the queen. They'd decided on the verdict before she had a chance to speak up in her own defence.'

'Yes, I see,' said Edward, His brow was furrowed and he looked as though he'd had a long night. 'What do we need to do to execute the plan?'

'We must get word to George, so he's ready to escape. Is it possible for Swifty to pass on a secret message?'

'It's possible to give him a message but whether it will remain secret depends on how closely George is watched. The boy is downstairs in the kitchen being fattened up like a yuletide goose, by the cook, who's taken a shine to him. She says the waif looks like he hasn't eaten a good meal in weeks. He's filling his face as fast as she fills his bowl.'

'Oh, thank goodness. That is fortunate. We must catch him before he leaves.'

She talked Edward through precisely what they would need to do, and he rushed to the kitchen to give Swifty instructions.

Cara dressed and pondered over how she and Edward used modern expressions. She would guess that 'filling his face' wasn't an expression used in 1536. They would have to watch their tongues or people would become suspicious.

She hurried down to the parlour to meet Edward and the children. Who knew when she'd see them again?

'Are we all set?' she asked Edward.

He nodded and gave her a thumbs up. The children laughed and mimicked the movement with their small thumbs.

When they were alone, she would need to warn him to try to keep his language and behaviour appropriate for the times.

She glanced out of the window, not tasting a morsel of her breakfast. Her stomach was tight with nerves. First light pushed through the dark, rain-filled sky and she wondered what this new day would bring.

'One of your grandfather's men will arrive shortly, and he'll escort you both home in the carriage. Please do your best to stay out of mischief and do what he tells you. It's for your own safety.'

Cara's business-like manner was met by May's teary eyes. Cara softened, unable to steel herself against her daughter's anguish. She relented, pulled her on to her lap and stroked the little girl's hair, which seemed to have the desired calming effect.

'Can't we stay here with you, Mother? Please? We don't want to go home alone. We'll be quiet as little mice if you let

us stay here in our room. We promise, don't we Thomas?'
She looked up at Cara, her face appealing.

A small smile played over Thomas's mouth as he
shrugged his shoulders in a helpless gesture. He'd long since
stopped trying to tell May what to do. His sister had been
strong-willed since birth. He knew she was more likely to
comply with his mother's wishes when he didn't interfere.
Thomas didn't know exactly what was at stake, but he sensed
his parents were in terrible danger. He feared for his father's
life and didn't wish to make things worse.

'No, I'm afraid not May. All I can say is that it's critical
that you return to Willow Manor with as little fuss as possible, please,' added Cara.

'What about Father? When will you both come home to
Willow Manor?' asked May, her deep brown eyes, so remi-
niscent of George's, plucked at Cara's heartstrings.

'You need to trust that I know best and not ask any more
questions. I promise I'll explain everything when we return
home. In the meantime, please be on your best behaviour for
your grandparents. And stay close to your brother.'

'Will Nutmeg be there when we get home?' May bright-
ened at the mention of her beloved pony.

'Yes, of course. I will miss my little girl terribly, but
Nutmeg will be overjoyed at your return.'

May nodded. Cara breathed a sigh of relief. For everyone's safety, she didn't want to tell the children more than
they needed to know.

She'd made a habit of talking to them freely about the
realities of life. But this was one of those occasions when the
less said, the better.

Cara longed to return to York with her family and to live
a peaceful life in the country. She'd had enough drama to last
her a lifetime and wouldn't mind if she never saw London
again. But the drama wasn't over yet. She must be strong.

They heard noises in the courtyard as they finished eating, and Cara dashed outside.

'How wonderful that you made it. I can't thank you enough,' said Cara.

'My lady,' Hancock, the steward from Willow Manor, bowed his head. 'I'm under orders to escort the children home, and I'd like for us to be on our way without delay.'

Ten minutes later, Cara stopped waving as the carriage disappeared from view, and she could no longer glimpse her children's faces.

'Right, let's make haste, 'she said, turning to Edward.

'We must go to the nearest church. I have no idea what the protocol is for borrowing a priest's garb, but we're about to find out. We must not dally.'

York, present day

Cara had lost her bearings; recently, she was flitting back and forth, daily, between present-day and Tudorville. She struggled to keep track of time as she careered between her two lives. Surely this couldn't go on indefinitely. It was becoming impossible to act appropriately and not give herself away. Five hundred years of cultural change was a great deal to have missed. She was well-schooled in the Tudor and modern eras, but large chunks of the years in-between were a blank.

Visions of George in the Tower terrorised her thoughts, and she found it increasingly difficult to focus. What was happening back then? Had Swifty succeeded in returning to Cradle Tower to ready George for their plan? Her body was here, but her head was consumed by the past.

'Cara, Cara. Are you with me? I was asking what you think.'

'Oh, yes. My apologies, please excuse me while I grab a glass of water and I'll be back with you in a moment. Would you like one?'

She had a client meeting this morning and must try to be present, or she'd soon have no business left. She opened the kitchen door and stuck her head out for a blast of fresh air.

She'd been surprised to see that the new lawyer representing one of her client's agencies, looked almost identical to Sir John in Tudorville. It was uncanny. She wondered how many doppelgangers lived double lives and were liable to pop up at any moment to startle her. Returning to wrap up the meeting, she escorted the doppelganger to the door, turned the key in the lock behind him and breathed a sigh of relief.

The hardest thing about her double life was pretending everything was normal and that she was like everyone else. The only person she could fully relax with now that George was held captive, was Eddie, and even he gave her blank stares when he lost track of what was going on. Her existence had become a tangled web of lies, and she didn't like it.

A seed of an idea had been niggling at her. The Angel Gabriel warning had reactivated the thought. What if George was alive after all? What if in the same way she'd disrupted the timeline sufficiently to change the trajectory of her life with Daniel, something similar had occurred with George?

Sitting at her desk, she typed George Cavendish into the search bar of her computer. A plethora of results flicked up. His was a common name, so it was no surprise. She began to click on the links and follow some of the threads. It was a Pandora's box, and she was about to give up when an image caught her eye. She enlarged the photo, and there he was: George. Her George. Or he looked like George. The image wasn't clear. Maybe she was mistaken. There was something slightly different about him; he was a little heavier in the face. But no. His brown eyes were the same. She would know them anywhere. Her breath caught in her throat and she felt giddy.

Could it really be him or was this man simply another lookalike? Was it possible that George didn't die at the Tower even if they hadn't intervened and saved him? Was he perfectly okay, living another life in Seville, oblivious to the life he had missed? Was she about to risk messing things up yet again, by insisting on rescuing him? Perhaps he didn't need rescuing at all. One question led to another, and her head began to spin.

'Perhaps he doesn't need rescuing at all.' The revelation hung in the air as she said the words aloud. She could barely believe it herself. The implications were huge. If he was living a different life, perhaps he was single. If he was single, they could be together without any of the conflict. If they rescued him, they would reset things to the old timeline.

She'd searched for George online soon after they'd first met, but he wasn't much of a one for social media, and apart from the standard business listings, there wasn't much to see. There were a couple of articles about his business background and a mention of his marital status, but that had been about it.

When she'd returned to find he wasn't in the same house with Joanna, she'd jumped to the conclusion he must have died in 1536, and that unless they saved him, it was the end of his lineage. But now it seemed possible she was mistaken.

Her researcher's analytical brain processed the data in her mental fog. She needed to remove herself from the emotional whirlpool so she could think clearly.

The questions competed for attention in her head. She scanned the newspaper article that accompanied the photo.

George Cavendish was on the board of directors of an import-export company, and he had several homes but was said to spend most of his time in Seville, Spain. There was no mention of a wife, although that didn't mean he wasn't married. She cautioned herself to slow down and not get her hopes up.

He was alive. It was incredible. She would get the first flight out there and go and see him for herself. It was the only way she could know for sure.

'Eddie, Eddie?' She drummed her fingers on the desk with one hand as she hit his name on her phone with the other.

'Hi. You sound a bit frantic. What's going on?'

'I am frantic. I've discovered George is alive! We mustn't save him from the Tower. We would risk messing things up again. He's alive Eddie!'

'I see. So we mustn't save him from the Tower. . .because?'

Don't you see? The timeline has recalibrated itself without our interference. We didn't have to do anything to make it happen. In Tudorville the scene is set for George to be executed, which is why I thought he wasn't alive in the present day unless we save him. But now we know he is alive even before we've saved him, we risk losing him all over again if we meddle. If our rescue attempt doesn't work and we're caught, or if it works, but the future compound effect is one we can't possibly understand now, we could do more harm than good. Do you see?' Cara ran out of steam as her words rushed out.

'Steady on. I don't think we can know for sure, based on what you've said. It's all supposition. I'd say it's sixty-seven to thirty-three percent in favour of us messing it up if we rescue him,' said Eddie.

'How on earth did you calculate that?' asked Cara. 'It seems rather exact.'

'I am exact, my dear. I'm a Quantum Physicist. They pay me to be exact.'

'Ah, yes. Haha. That's true.'

'The real question is, are you willing to take a chance on the thirty-three percent? It could quite well be that in another time formation, he's still only alive today because we did save him from execution. Have you considered the consequences of not saving him?'

'Yes I have, but I can't take the chance of losing him again when he's alive, and he may even be free. Eddie, please try and get back to Tudorville to stop the rescue going ahead. At least until I get in touch and tell you otherwise.'

'But you know we have no control over our comings and goings. That's the reason we got into this mess in the first place.'

'Please Eddie, please. Remember your certainty about when you think of the place and time you want to travel to; you will get there? Please try again. Try for me, for George, for Thomas and May. We need to delay the rescue and reevaluate once I've been to Seville and met this version of George. We can still implement our plan at the last minute if we need to. It's too much of a coincidence to ignore, and I didn't tell you that I had a warning from Angel Gabriel when I went to Sylvia for a reading.'

She imagined Eddie rolling his eyes. He was sceptical of anything that he couldn't at least attempt to prove with the power of numbers.

Eddie coughed. 'Okay, okay. I'll have a go, but I'm not promising anything.'

He shook his head. He found it impossible to say no to Cara.

'Thank you. You're the best.'

Seville, present day

Cara emerged into the arrivals hall which was flooded with Spanish sunshine. She blinked and fished around in her handbag for her tortoiseshell sunglasses.

Making her way outside, she joined the queue to wait for a taxi. Before leaving, she had looked up the address of the villa which had belonged to George on her last trip. It was unlisted, and she couldn't confirm who lived in the house now, but she had a strong hunch it was a good place to begin her search for the new George.

There was a pattern in her two simultaneous lives so she thought it as good a punt as any that the villa might lead her to him, or at least provide a clue. The same places cropped up repeatedly in her time travel.

As the taxi wound around the bends of the steep rolling hills, Cara experienced a feeling of deja-vu that was more intense than just a memory of her last visit. The sense of having been there many times before was akin to what she'd experienced with George at Hampton Court Palace. They'd visited together for his interview and wandered around the apartment they'd shared in Tudorville, and even he had commented on feeling as though he'd been there before. That was strange in itself. How had he experienced that when he hadn't been in the apartment before? It must have been a karmic thing.

The taxi pulled up outside a set of majestic gates, and Cara used her rudimentary Spanish to request that the driver wait for her when she went to knock on the door. As she walked towards the grand entrance, she was accosted by memories of her time with George. They'd eaten lunch on the verandah and made love many times during that first perfect night. A wave of desire rippled through her. It had been too long.

She heard the sound of a woman's laughter and looked up.

Cara raised her hand and rapped hard on the imposing wooden door. The villa looked the same as she remembered. Several seconds later, a maid appeared.

Cara smiled and said, 'Ingles?'

'Good day. Yes, I speak English. How can I help you?'

'Thank you. I'm wondering whether this is the Cavendish residence. I'm looking for George.'

The maid smiled and nodded as she stood aside and beckoned Cara to enter. 'I'll get him for you. Your name, please?'

Cara stood in the marble entrance hall and began to panic. She hadn't thought this through at all. The last thing she'd expected was to find George immediately. She'd thought he would be out or away on business even if he lived there. She hadn't truly believed he'd live there! It was too much of a coincidence.

'Cara Bailey,' she stammered. 'I'm here on business.'

A few minutes later, George bounded down the winding staircase and headed towards her, smiling.

'Hello. Lovely to meet you,' he said, hand outstretched. 'I feel at a slight disadvantage because I don't recognise your name. You do look so very familiar though. But I can't place you just yet. Don't tell me, Cara; I'll get it soon.'

Her heart lurched. He was as charming as ever. That didn't seem to change no matter the era. His smile was contagious, and he pushed his dark floppy hair away from his eyes.

Cara was giddy. This was all too weird. Seeing him like this, almost identical, and saying he recognised her.

'You look a bit pale. How rude of me, may I get you a glass of water? Or you know what, even better - come up to the verandah and join us. We're having a small luncheon, nothing fancy but come and have a drink. It's scorching this time of day.'

She smiled and followed him, not knowing what else to do.

'Wherever have you been darling?' said a stunning brunette in a red dress which accentuated her slender figure. Cara guessed she must be in her late thirties. The woman touched George's hand as she reached his side, and he rested his arm lightly across her shoulders.

They were close. Cara regretted showing up like this. It was too much to take. She feared her heart might explode out of her chest. What had she been thinking? Of course, he would be involved. She couldn't just drop out of the sky and expect him to be waiting. It was no different to last time.

'Kate, meet Cara.'

'Oh, how lovely. You must be one of the few friends of George's I haven't met. Are you over on holiday or do you live in Seville?'

Cara wished the vortex would magically whisk her away now. As if things could get any worse, the woman; Kate, seemed genuinely nice.

Kill me now.

'What will you have to drink, Cara?' asked George.

'Water would be great, thank you.'

'Can't I tempt you with a Pimms? It's refreshing with the fruit and ice.'

'Just a small one then. How kind of you. I've only just flown in, and I'm a little tired, so I'd better not drink much,' she garbled, barely knowing which words spilt out of her mouth.

'Of course. You said you were here on some kind of business? How may I help? I'll just grab our drinks, and then we can talk. Kate, take good care of Cara, introduce her to everyone, my love.'

The endearment pierced Cara to the core. George returned with the drinks, Kate reached for hers, their fingers touched, and her slender hand encircled the glass. Cara noticed she wore both an engagement and wedding ring. They were married. Obviously, they were. She must have been insane to come here like this. Not for the first time, she cursed her impetuous nature. Why couldn't she be slow and sensible? Cara looked at George's hands. They were suntanned, his fingers bare. But these days that meant nothing. Men often didn't wear wedding rings.

She had to get away from here. She shouldn't have come. Cara took a sip of the Pimms and tried to be nonchalant but felt as though she was drowning.

'May I use the bathroom, please?' she said, desperately thinking of a way to excuse herself.

She went to the bathroom, splashed cold water on to her hot cheeks and tried to calm down. She had to get out of here. It would be rude to leave now, but she couldn't face George and Kate again. She'd come to find the truth, and she had. It was all the more devastating because she'd allowed herself to hope.

Closing the bathroom door quietly behind her, she rushed down the steps, made a dash for the front door and slipped outside into the bright sunshine. There was no reason to stay.

CHAPTER 26

M adrid, 1840

After a long and arduous voyage, Cara and George arrived in Madrid.

The air was unseasonably humid for this time of year, remarked George's old friend, Sebastian. He was the issue of a Spanish mother and an English father and did his utmost to capitalise on his unique heritage.

A couple of days after their arrival, over a late supper, Sebastian filled them in on political events.

'I don't believe we've seen the end of the civil wars,' he said.

George was surprised how well-informed Queen Victoria was; he hadn't yet gleaned anything new.

The Carlist victory had elevated General Espartero to power. The former Regent, Maria Cristina; Isabella, the child queen's mother, had been forced to name the general as president of the government. The pendulum had swung again, and the repercussions could prove fatal for those who fell on the wrong side. They must be cautious, Sebastian warned.

Madrid was a vibrant and exhilarating place, but the tension was palpable. Cara sensed that people viewed them with suspicion, and it took the fun out of exploring the beautiful city. Sebastian had warned them upon arrival that it was unlikely they'd be received warmly by the general after Her Majesty's government had openly backed the regent.

Maria Cristina had fled, and as Sebastian predicted, George's request for an audience with the general was rebuffed with no apology. The general was apparently detained on urgent business for the foreseeable future, and the official word was that no audiences were to be granted. Spain was still in a state of war.

'Britannia may well rule the waves, but she doesn't rule Spain, old boy. My advice to you is to keep a low profile while you're in Madrid, and then continue on to Seville as soon as possible, without attracting undue attention. You'll have more freedom to come and go as you please; it's a different mentality. In Madrid, we are watched. I have a love-hate relationship with this city.'

'Why don't you come back to England? You'd be able to live a peaceful life in London without all of this subterfuge. You have a residence there, do you not?'

'Yes, I do indeed, and I will visit again soon. But Spain is my home. I will not forsake her. England is like a dull, predictable wife, and Spain my exotic mistress. She's the love of my life and knows how to hold me effortlessly.'

'You old Spanish romantic, you. I can't say that Madrid has seduced me, but I have great hopes of falling in love with Seville. Perhaps I'll find my exotic mistress there,' laughed George.

'I'll believe that when I see it,' said Sebastian. 'I've never known a man more besotted than you are with your new wife.'

'Ah, yes. It's true. I won't deny it. I'm a lucky man indeed. She's the only woman I want. Like you and your fierce loyalty to Spain, my dear fellow.'

'I envy your steadfastness in love. Us Spaniards are, too. . .how do they say in England - flighty?'

'Yes, you are a fickle lover Sebastian. I've lost count of all the women you've been ready to die for in the time we've known each other.'

George and his old friend sat and reminisced over a couple of glasses of wine after Cara retired to bed.

Later that evening when Cara and George were finally alone together in their rooms, Cara said, 'When may we leave for Seville, George? How long must we stay in this feverish city? I do like Sebastian, and it is kind of him to accommodate us, but I'd rather be on our way soon.'

'I like it here no more than you, my love, but I'm keen to gather information for the queen, and I am cautious to not draw attention to us with such a swift departure. Visitors tend to stay a while when they travel as far as this. We must bide our time and act like the dullards we are not. We're supposed to be here on business, so I must at least pretend to be conducting some.'

'I understand. Yes, I confess I'd forgotten about the business cover. I do hope we can leave shortly, though. You should see how the women stare at me. I don't think we'll ever blend in here, were we to stay two hundred years. There's something about this city, no matter its magnificence, that makes me nervous. They don't trust the English.'

'They don't trust anyone; least of all each other. The country has been ripped apart by the bloodshed of civil wars for too many years. Aside from that, my darling, please don't let standing out concern you. Let me assure you now; you're never going to blend in anywhere. Personally, I'll be keeping a watchful eye on the Spanish rogues, not their stout, envious wives who must surely look at you and weep! I can't say I blame them.'

Cara smiled and giggled as she brushed her hair and met her husband's dancing eyes in the mirror.

'You really do say the most ridiculous things. I must be cautious not to take your lavish compliments too seriously, or I shall become quite insufferable.'

'Nonsense, my darling. Every word I utter is God's own truth.'

She rose from the stool, reached up to drape her arms around George's neck, and leaned into him.

'You are the most marvellous man, and I adore you.' She kissed his lips, and then each of his hands.

Cara dimmed the lights and climbed into bed. George was about to join her when there was a sharp knock at the door.

'Whoever can it be at this late hour?' asked Cara.

'I've no idea.'

'Yes?' called George. 'Coming.'

He opened the door, and Cara heard a muttered exchange as George exited the room.

Several minutes later, he returned, waving a letter, and said, 'You won't believe it.'

'Try me; I wager I will.'

George laughed as he rearranged a stray lock of glossy hair across her shoulder.

'Alright then, if you're so bold, let's see if you can guess.'

'Let me see. Hmm, it's a letter from Queen Victoria ordering us to leave for Seville at first light.'

'Um, no. That's not it although it's a fair try. It would, however, be physically impossible for a letter to have made it here so quickly unless it had travelled in our luggage!'

'Oh,' said Cara. 'Good point.'

'In that case, let's try something more local. It's an invitation from the child queen, Isabella, appointing you as her English ambassador. In fact, no, I've got something better. She wishes you to be the new regent until she's of age to reign.'

'Er, no. That's not it either. I have to say; you do look incredibly pleased with yourself for someone so wrong! I'll take it that you have run out of sensible answers,' George laughed.

Cara loved nothing more in the world than to hear her husband laugh.

'Oh well, come on then, I'm weary at this late hour. Pray, tell me and let's end the Spanish suspense. I've run out of patience not answers if the truth be known. You know I'm very poor at waiting.'

'Yes, you're probably the most impatient woman in Spain.'

He climbed into bed, turned her face towards his and kissed her, before relinquishing the letter into her eager hand.

'Oh, my goodness,' said Cara, a few seconds later. 'I wasn't all that far off, after all! Will we leave for Seville tomorrow?'

Seville, present day

Cara wandered around the nave of the cathedral, unseeing. Panic rose within her and crushed her chest like an iron fist. She had trouble breathing. The all too familiar dreadful feelings threatened to engulf her. Again. It was happening again.

Cheerful, carefree tourists smiled at her. She couldn't face happy people today. Could they not see that her world had ended?

Perhaps that was why they smiled. They witnessed her pain and tried in their own small way to offer comfort. People were kind, but they didn't move her today. She wished she were dead. If only someone would shoot her; put her down like an injured animal who couldn't bear any more pain.

The thought of killing herself crossed her mind. She was thinking the unthinkable. She was thinking the thing that well-balanced people were supposed never to think. You were expected to be strong; to pick yourself up after heart-break and just carry on.

She had no one and nothing to live for. If she ended it now, it wouldn't affect the Tudorville timeline, and if George managed to escape, they'd be together anyway, she reasoned. She had nothing more to lose. Whatever was supposed to happen in 1536 had already happened.

She'd done her best in the present day to rearrange circumstances, and it seemed that George was no worse off. He was better off because he looked happy with Kate. The disruption of the timeline had set him free from his unful-filling marriage to Joanna. He and Kate had a wonderful life together. Joanna seemed happy with her family, so all was well. No harm had been done. The players were oblivious to the time travel musical chairs which had decided their fate.

George wasn't in love with her in this formation of events, so he was spared the never-ending heart wrench. She loved him enough to be grateful for that. There was no point in them both suffering. Only her life was a disaster, and she felt sorry for herself today.

She must give him up once and for all. Him being with Kate was a clear message. She wasn't religious, but since she'd begun time travelling, and through her conversations with Sylvia, she'd come to believe there was a universal power behind the scenes. The Twin Flame journey had shown her that things were rarely as they seemed. But Twin Flames or not, she couldn't reunite their souls alone.

She must let George go this time. It was not to be. She must accept it was time to call it quits and not be any more of a lovesick fool than she'd already been. Her heart ached at the thought of what would surely be the most daunting challenge yet. She didn't feel up to it. Death was an alluring alternative to living what must be a bleak forty-years alone, without any hope of his voice, without his presence.

She knew from past attempts that it was no small thing to let him go. She'd lost count of how many times she'd steeled herself to give him up. Her logical mind dictated she should cut him out of her life, but her soul wouldn't permit it. Her heart had remained open to him no matter what. Each time he'd hurt her, she'd thought it must surely be the final blow. How could she take any more of this agony?

Inevitably she would lash out at him, and they'd spiral into a nightmarish dark pit of heartache and mental anguish.

And then a strange thing happened. They would wake up to the beauty of their unconditional love. She'd see that he never meant to hurt her. She forgave him. He forgave her. It happened simultaneously, as if by magic. And the slate was wiped clean.

Whenever she tried to break it off because it seemed the right thing to do, she'd been unable. Being apart was intolerable for them both. It wasn't sustainable, so how could it be the right thing? It was an insoluble conundrum. They always found a way back to each other, their bleeding hearts in tatters after the agony of separation.

What would surely have broken another pair of lovers, only served to deepen their connection. Each separation forced them to confront their deepest fear of not being good enough. It was a peeling away of the false layers of ego. Once their disconnected souls were stripped bare, their true nature revealed pure, transcendent love. And they became one, just as they had been in the beginning.

Who could exist without pure love, once tasted? The ordinary would never suffice.

Such was the power of Twin Flames. Cara didn't understand it, but there was nowhere to run. He was her, and she was him. Killing herself wasn't the answer. She would pull herself together.

At this moment, she had no desire to live, but she couldn't hurt her father, and besides, she knew she would only be postponing the inevitable cycle.

She would go back to Tudorville and try to save George, as initially planned. The thought of a future life without him was too much for her to contemplate. The present-day would now be different. He wouldn't be the George who couldn't live without her. He didn't even know her. He wouldn't fight to keep her. It must surely be easier to resist him this time.

Somehow, she would have to make a new life for herself. She had never felt so alone. How could he abandon her? If what Sylvia said was true, George's soul hadn't fully awakened, or they would already be together. A flaming rage consumed her, and she blamed him.

She would never love again. He was the only one for her.

Cara stumbled away from what was arguably the most impressive Cathedral in Europe, oblivious to its beauty, as she suffocated beneath a heavy wave of panic. The pain sucked the breath out of her lungs. She collapsed on to a wooden bench, and sobbed, oblivious to the lovers who passed by, hand in hand, their faces aglow in the glorious afternoon sunshine.

Her phone rang. She retrieved it from her handbag and through the haze of tears, saw the call was from an unknown number. She tossed the phone back into her bag. Less than a minute later it rang again. And then again.

'Hello? Who's calling please?' Her tone was clipped. She only answered in case it was an emergency. Misery clawed at her soul, and she had no desire to talk to anyone ever again.

'Cara? Cara Bailey?'

'Yes, this is Cara. Who's speaking?'

And yet even as she said the words, she recognised his voice.

Why was he calling? She mustn't be drawn in. He had no idea what he was doing. She couldn't let it happen again, for both of their sakes.

'This is George. George Cavendish.'

'George, right. Hello, yes.'

'You looked unwell, and we noticed you disappeared. I wanted to call and make sure you're okay. Kate tells me I can be a bit dense about this kind of thing, but she doesn't miss a trick. Are you alright?'

'Yes, I'm fine. I'm sorry I left without saying goodbye,' she lied. 'It was rude, but I had an urgent message from the office and had to get back.'

She needed to end the call. Hearing him talk affectionately about Kate was too much to bear.

'Oh dear, sorry to hear that. Nothing too terrible, I hope.'

'Just an unexpected hiccup with a client which I must attend to. I'll get the first flight out in the morning.'

'I see.'

George sounded disappointed.

'Would you like to get together for a quick drink this evening and we can discuss the business you wanted to see me about? I'm intrigued. Will you give me a clue?'

Cara's heart somersaulted. This was unfair. This was bloody unfair. How was she supposed to resist him? She couldn't manage to avoid him, even when he didn't know who she was!

Tears clogged her throat, and her head ached from sobbing. He mustn't know she was falling apart or he would suspect something. And what the hell was he coming on to her for when he was married to gorgeous Kate? Maybe she'd been wrong all along, and he was just an incorrigible cheat. Maybe what they had wasn't special at all.

'It's nothing terribly exciting, I'm afraid. I recently came across a manuscript which belonged to your family and dates back to the Tudor period.' Somehow, she managed to annunciate the words.

'Oh yes, of course. I should have realised by your business card. The manuscript is the pride of the family. Not that I know much about it but I'd be happy to help you in any way I can. Kate knows a lot about our family history, but I'm afraid she had to leave for Madrid after the party.'

'Oh, too bad. Unfortunately, I'll need to take a rain check as I have a conference call this evening and have to be up early for the flight.'

What a deceitful toad. Kate had only just turned her back, and here he was asking her out for drinks. She was beginning to think she'd had a lucky escape in this timeline.

'Oh, what a shame. Okay well, no problem. I know how rushed these business trips can be. I have a breakfast meeting at the airport tomorrow so how about I pick you up from your hotel and that way we get to chat in the car? It's the least I can do. What time is your flight?'

It sounded like a bad idea, but she couldn't think straight, and a coherent refusal wouldn't form on her lips. She mumbled her flight time, and she heard him making plans to pick her up at the hotel. It felt as though she was underwater and couldn't come up for air. Finally, she heard herself say, 'Okay, great, I'll see you then.'

Oh my God, what had she done? Was she completely insane? It was as though she'd had no control over her words. She stood up, brushed the leaves off her jeans and wiped her eyes with a tissue. She must look a right state. All of this was beyond her.

She would see him tomorrow; one last time. There was a renewed bounce to her step as she walked back to the hotel in the gentle evening sunshine. Joy flickered in her sore heart. She could breathe again.

George said goodbye, grateful he'd managed to arrange to see her again. Honestly, he wasn't interested in the manuscript but he'd not been able to stop thinking about the slim, vivacious brunette who'd disappeared so suddenly that afternoon.

There was something about her which made him feel alive.

The Tower Of London, 1536

At first light, Cara and Swifty huddled against the chill wind in the bottom of the small rowing boat. The dark water of the River Thames lapped gently against the stone walls of the Tower. Cara could hardly draw breath, such was the suspense.

'Can you see any sign of them with your sharp eyes, Swifty?'

'No, my lady. Nothing stirs at Cradle Tower.

Cara sighed. They should be leaving by now. Every second they delayed increased the risk of them being spotted.

'I don't understand. Edward was supposed to exit the

window with George immediately. Whatever can be holding them up?'

She could just make out Swifty's forlorn expression. His face held no answers.

'Are you absolutely sure you secured the rope in place so they would be able to grab it as they opened the window?' said Cara.

'Yes, I did exactly as you and Edward bid. The rope is ready. I can see it being blown about by the wind, from here.'

'Well, all that is left to us is to wait a bit more. If they're not out soon, we'll need to leave, or we'll be arrested in vain.'

They sat in sombre silence. The plan had seemed foolproof, but something must have gone awry. Cara was frightened that Edward had fallen under suspicion. It was awful enough they hadn't broken George out, but now it looked as though Edward would be captured too. He'd entered the Tower under the disguise of a priest from York who at George's request would prepare him to make peace with his impending death. The Tower official had permitted him to send Swifty to bring the priest who waited nearby in the city.

'Look, look,' said Swifty, pointing up at the Cradle Tower. 'Do you see?'

'No. What?' asked Cara.

'Someone is waving the white cloth at the window as you instructed.'

Cara's spirits dipped yet further. That was it then—it was over. She saw the flash of white material.

'We must leave without them. Swifty, push us off from the wall to get us going. Let's take it in turns to row; I'll go first.'

She rowed as fast as she could, but at times it seemed as though they made barely any progress. Voices echoed from a distance around the eerie, dark river banks. It wouldn't be long before the sun rose high in the sky and the place buzzed with morning activity.

Cara concentrated on moving the oars to block out her gloomy thoughts. She didn't want to leave George and Edward behind, but if they too were caught, none of them would have any chance of escape.

May's sweet face beseeched her to come home and spurred her on as exhaustion mounted until they had put a fair distance between themselves and King Henry VIII.

'Swifty, you take over for a bit. I thought we'd be rowing out to meet the trawler, to head for France, but now we must remain in London. Look out for the next spot where we can moor the boat. We may still use it.'

Swifty nodded, eager to please. He would row around the world for his mistress.

Cara leaned against the side of the boat to recover her strength. Their only hope of freeing George was if the tower guards suspected nothing. If that was the case, they might get a second chance.

She must learn what had become of Edward.

CHAPTER 27

L ondon, 1536

The dreadful stench instantly alerted Cara to her arrival in Tudorville. Her years of study at York University hadn't adequately prepared her for the reality of Tudor filth. The smell of acrid urine was rank. It was a normal part of the daily routine for Londoners to toss the contents of their chamber pots out of the windows. It was pure luck if a pedestrian escaped being doused in urine as they navigated the cobbled streets.

Ew. She wrinkled her nose in an attempt to block the odour. It took her sensitive nostrils a few minutes to adjust before her senses settled and the urge to heave, abated.

Cara spotted Edward waiting on the corner. As he turned and walked towards her, his smile lit up his pensive features, and he reached out to hold her in a warm embrace.

'Thank goodness, here you are,' he said. 'I've been willing

you to turn up. It's difficult to make any progress with the other Cara. She hasn't a clue what's going on.'

'How did you know it was me?'

'I'm not sure. I had a feeling you would be back today. I just knew.'

'Talking of which, where the heck were you the other day? What on earth happened when we were waiting on the river to rescue you and George from the Tower? I've been dying to find out. I was so agitated to have to travel and not know what was going on.'

'We couldn't get out. We were chaperoned from the second I was admitted.'

'Were they suspicious?'

'I don't think so. They're just accustomed to observing closely when a new visitor arrives, that's all. Unfortunately, we couldn't move. I wanted to talk it through with you, but of course, you'd disappeared.'

'Sorry about that. I know it's tricky as hell when you go off on one. What's she like then? Is she very slow?'

'Who, Cara?' Edward laughed and shook his head.

'Slow? No, of course she's not slow. She's you. But she has no idea of the implications of her past or future actions, so it's of no use to discuss our plans beyond the immediate time. It only confuses the present. She's got enough to deal with. I can't unload our calculations and deliberations on to her; it would blow her 16th-century mind.'

'I do envy her. How wonderful to be a simple wife, living a simple life,' Cara sighed.

'Well, I think you forget the reality of it. Life is not exactly simple. George is under threat of execution, remember?'

'That's true. How could I forget? How's she coping with George being locked in the Tower, by the way?'

'Not well. When I came out, I told her what I'll tell you;

he's in a low state of mind. We can't leave him there much longer. The Tower is a hellhole, as you know.'

Cara's eyes welled up, and a wave of emotion blocked her throat. She swallowed. 'I must go to him.'

'Yes, that's exactly what she said.'

'That's good. I couldn't bear it if she didn't adore him as I do.'

'Oh, you need have no fear on that score. They're crazy about one another.'

'Edward, you're not helping.'

'Oh, I thought I was. You said it was good.'

'I know what I said. Don't you know that a woman sometimes says things she doesn't actually mean?'

'Um, oh dear, I'm on shaky ground. I'm not very up on the ways of the fairer sex.'

'Scientists!' Cara rolled her eyes.

'It's as though he's with another woman. It's not as gut-wrenching as him being married to Joanna or even Kate, but it's still horrid.'

'Trust me; she is just like you! He's not fallen for another woman. But who the hell is Kate?'

'I'll tell you later. I can't believe I'm jealous of myself. How absolutely ridiculous! Let's talk about something else, or I'll go mad. What's been happening since the morning of the aborted rescue?'

'If we plan another rescue I think we'll be better to have Swifty in the Tower with my lord, and me down below with you. They're used to the boy. He blends in, and as long as we get word to George via Swifty, he'll know when we'll be waiting.'

'Yes. Makes sense. That way we won't alert them to anything out of the ordinary.'

'There's something else, though. Don't get your hopes up too high as it could be complete nonsense, but Swifty heard a rumour from a guard, who heard it from a courtier, who heard it from someone at the Tower, that the king is going to pardon George.'

Cara stopped. 'Good lord. Why didn't you tell me earlier?'

'You weren't here! Anyway, it's only a rumour. We can't rely on it being true until we get some kind of solid indication it's really happening. You know the palaces are always awash with whispers, and most of it never comes to anything. The servants love to gossip.'

Cara hardly dared to hope it might be true.

'I still want to see him as soon as possible. It feels like forever since I've seen his face.'

'Okay. What do you propose?'

'I've given this some thought. It's all I had to focus on in the present day to keep myself from going around the bend. You won't believe what's happening now, by the way. The alternate George is a complete arse.'

'Oh, dear. Is this something to do with the Kate you mentioned? Could there be some misunderstanding? It wouldn't be the first time you two have tripped over your crossed wires. The earl is a good man; surely even in an alternate timeline, he couldn't be a wrong-un.'

'Trust me. It's just as well he's married to someone else, and I won't make the same mistake again. It must be the time travel lucky dip; sometimes you get a bad egg in the gene pool.'

'Goodness. So he has married again?'

'Yes, indeed. How many times must that romantic fool marry? He'll be giving the king a run for his money at this rate,' Cara ranted. There was a note of hysteria in her voice. 'In fairness, he doesn't even know what happened. He's unconsciously trying to repeat our whole story, and this time it's even worse. He's with this fantastic woman, but he still propositioned me. At least when he was married to Joanna, I had some compassion for his situation. This time he's just an out and out philanderer.'

Eddie shook his head, doubtful. He knew better than to say any more, but secretly he bet there was more to it. His mistress wasn't in a benevolent mood, so the less said, the better. He might not understand the fairer sex, but he knew when to shut up.

'How will you get in to see George?' Edward deftly changed the subject.

'I'll disguise myself as his mother, and petition to see him before his death. It's perfectly reasonable for his mother to be desperate to see him one last time. It's harsh that they banished his wife and children. I think in the circumstances, even Cromwell, may show mercy.'

'Yes, I hope you're right. What about the rescue? Shall we wait and see what happens - in case the pardon isn't a rumour?'

'I think we better had. I keep remembering the warning from Angel Gabriel about things not being as they seem, and the risk of doing irreparable damage by taking the wrong action. If the rescue were to succeed and Henry had planned to pardon George, he would be furious. He hates being outwitted. That's when he's at his most dangerous. I saw it with Anne. She knew how to play him like a fiddle until she lost his trust. He's like a child; he detests being thwarted. We must let him be in control, or George will die. The king loves to be admired as the benevolent king so let's play him at his own game.'

'Yes, agreed. Although we still have the sixty-seven to thirty-three per cent ratio to consider. If we don't rescue him, we have no way of knowing what the ultimate compound effect will be. Just because George is alive now, as someone else, doesn't mean he would be if we hadn't rescued him.'

'The whole thing makes my head throb. I've thought about nothing else. I go back and forth on the pros and cons and can't decide whether it's best to rescue him or not. I think given the possibility of a pardon, combined with Angel Gabriel's warning, and your prediction of a thirty-three per cent chance of a bigger mess, we'd better wait.'

'If in doubt, do nowt,' said Edward.

'Yes, absolutely. It's the best way. When we know, we'll know, and we won't take action to break him out until then, no matter how tempting it may be. It's a gamble, but we'll take it until we have reason to do otherwise.'

'Yes, my lady.'

'Edward?'

'Yes, my lady.'

'Please stop yes, my ladying me.'

'Yes, my lady.'

She raised her eyebrow. They giggled. The humour touched Cara's sore heart as they made their way to the London lodgings.

'You know the king well. Holding off makes sense, but I also think if we haven't heard anything positive about a pardon in a couple of days, we should reevaluate. We need to get George out of the Tower,' said Edward.

'Yes, of course. I can't wait to get away from the city but is there something you've not told me?'

'Only that Henry's council is hunting down all who could be suspected of any remote sign of allegiance to the pope. It's like a reverse inquisition. Meanwhile, the priests inform me that all hell is breaking out on the continent.'

'Oh, my God. Of course. How dense of me to not have thought of the trouble brewing. Sometimes I forget we're witnessing history and we already know how it turns out. It's May 1536. The Spanish inquisition is about to hit Portugal. Pope Paul authorises the inquisition to root out the thousands of Jews who settled there, following their expulsion from Spain when they refused to convert to Christianity in 1492,' said Cara.

'Yes. And the people here are resentful,' Edward nodded.

'They don't know who or what to believe in anymore. They've lost two queens in such a short period, the monasteries are being dissolved, and they can no longer pray to their effigies. There's a sickness at the heart of the nation, and his name is Henry. He's more power-hungry each day that passes without a newborn son in the nursery,' said Cara.

'I want to see us safely away from the city before the unrest kicks off. London is like a powder keg waiting to be lit, and I don't want us still here when it explodes.' Edward spoke his treasonous words in a whisper, looking about him as he talked.

'Don't you have Jewish blood?'

'Yes, my grandmother was Jewish, which makes me officially Jewish, but we keep it quiet. I was raised a Catholic, and in Henry's new England, we became Protestant like everyone else. What he and Anne did was a scandal, and all just to arrange an annulment so they could marry and remove queen Katherine. Mind you, Katherine of Aragon was the fruit of evil parents, Isabella and Ferdinand. They instigated the Spanish Inquisition and have thousands of innocents' blood on their hands. What goes around comes around. But still, the king tossed Katherine aside like an old shoe, and poor Anne fared even worse.'

'What happens to Jane Seymour? I know I should remember, but I'm afraid I don't, and as I haven't any internet access right now, I can't pretend otherwise just to impress you. He still has three more wives to get through, so I do know it's not a happy ending,' said Edward.

'Poor Jane Seymour dies next year, after giving birth to a son: Edward.'

'It's coming back to me now. But as I say, I want to get us away as quickly as possible. When there's unrest, the Jews are the first to be targeted. I'm surprised they didn't dredge that up to add to the list of charges against you.'

'I expect they know that charges of treason and witch-craft are enough to warrant burning me at the stake, should they so desire. Don't worry Edward. We'll be safe in the city for a while longer.'

'How can you be so sure?'

'For the same reason, you knew how to calculate the sixty-seven to thirty-three per cent odds. I'm a historian and a bloody good one.'

Seville, 1840

'Isn't this Cathedral breathtaking?' said George, as they wandered hand in hand through the nave. The afternoon sunshine infused the beautiful old building with light, and a sense of peace washed over Cara.

'I'm relieved we were able to leave Madrid so quickly. I didn't like it there at all,' she said.

'If someone was watching our movements since we arrived, there's nothing to arouse suspicion. I made it known that the purpose of our visit was primarily to research the whereabouts of a British manuscript, so it's fortunate indeed that Carlos was able to get us a lead so quickly,' said George.

'Yes, I wonder how he managed that.'

'Turns out he has a close friend who specialises in that kind of thing so as soon as he mentioned it, the friend knew exactly who to ask.'

'When will we meet this brilliant friend?'

'I'm not sure. The Spanish clock is notoriously unreliable,

so we need to go with the flow and see what happens. It can be quite frustrating—the Spaniards are in no rush.'

'What about the villa? Shall we go and see it before we move in?'

'No, Carlos accepted it on our behalf. He said it's a splendid place and if he hadn't taken it immediately, someone else would have snapped it up. I do hope you like it, though.'

'I'm certain it will be perfect. How could it possibly not be? You and me, together in a villa in the Sevillian sunshine, doing just as we please, whenever we please, however, we please. It sounds splendid, indeed.'

'Yes, it's a rare treat for us to be able to spend all of our time together. It's a relief to be away from the routine and the rain of London for a while.' George squeezed Cara's hand.

'I'm looking forward to having a break from the dreary ladies' society functions. You have no idea how dull it is listening to them droning on and on about the latest fashions and gossip.'

'I can only imagine. Although the men's conversation over brandy and cigars isn't particularly scintillating.'

'I suppose so, but I find it immensely irritating that we women must always be excluded. You're privileged as a man, so you don't understand what it's like. It would be nice to be given the option to join you gentlemen once in a while. Society's rules make me feel quite rebellious.'

George laughed. 'The old-fashioned rules are stifling. It is a wonder that women put up with them for so long.'

Cara studied George's face, curious to learn more. 'Whatever do you mean, old fashioned?'

'Oh, you know. Things change. Anyway, we'll be back in London soon enough so let's make hay while the sun shines — it's certainly shining here.'

'When will we move into the villa? I can't wait to see it. It will be fun to be at your side for your business affairs too.' Cara bubbled at the possibilities of her newfound freedom.

'I do love it when you bob up and down with excitement. It's most adorable.' George kissed the top of her head.

'Well, women should be allowed more freedom. It's positively dreadful how we're cast aside while you men have all of the adventures.'

'I couldn't agree more, my love. You're ahead of your time. I have a feeling women will have their day too.'

'Do you really think so, or are you just trying to make me feel better?' Her eyes met his, searching, wanting to believe what he predicted would come to pass.

'Well, you know I always like to try to make you feel better, but I'm also sure it won't always be this way. Women will be able to go out unchaperoned and even do business independently in the future.'

'I'd like to see that! You're such a visionary,' said Cara, in awe of her husband's foresight.

'Us visionaries pay a high price, my darling,' he said in a self-deprecating tone as if he was the most carefree man in Seville. Inwardly he rued the high price he paid for the dangerous gift of seeing into the future.

He hadn't travelled to the present day in a while, and he liked it best that way because he was with Cara all of the time here. It was difficult when he kept going back and forth. He didn't want to think about what was happening with Joanna; last time he was there, the atmosphere was awful.

He did his best to enjoy every precious moment in Victoriana. Still, he noticed he often slipped into a state of anxiety at the prospect of being pulled into the vortex without warning. He had no control over it. The feeling of helplessness winded him.

After a couple of hours of admiring the Cathedral and

exploring the neighbouring streets, they set out in the direction of Carlos's house.

A young woman sobbed on a low stone wall near the Cathedral, as they passed by. Cara smiled, attempting to offer some small solace, grateful for her own bliss. The woman looked away, unable to meet her eyes. She was envious of the carefree lovers.

Carlos said, 'Edward, these are my very good friends, Cara and George Cavendish. They're on business from London and will be staying locally for a while.'

'Cara and George, please meet Edward, my dear friend who managed to pick up the trail of the manuscript you're so interested in.'

They greeted one another and became better acquainted over drinks. The conversation soon turned to the manuscript, and it was agreed that the next day, Edward would introduce them to the dealer who had more information of its whereabouts.

'It's lovely to meet you, Cara. I've heard so much about you that I feel as though I've met you before.'

Cara looked at Edward and wondered if he was flirting with her. Always an astute judge of character she concluded that he wasn't.

'What do you make of that Edward fellow?' she whispered to George, later, when they were alone. He acted as though he knew me. It was rather odd.'

'I thought he seemed like a fine fellow. It looks as though we may not have very far to go to find this manuscript, after all.'

'That's good news. I can't wait to hear more about it. I'm fascinated by history. Did you say it was a Tudor manuscript?'

'Yes, that's right. It used to belong to my family. My ancestor, George Cavendish, commissioned it in honour of Henry VIII and before the birth of his long-anticipated first-born son. It's called *The Tudor Kings' Manuscript.* Unfortunately, Henry's only legitimate son, Edward, died young and was the end of the male line.

The manuscript was tossed aside, but Queen Victoria recently read about it in the Tudor archives, and it piqued her interest. She wants us to locate it while we're here on our mission, and bring it home.'

'How very romantic. You're so lucky to have such an impressive family tree. It must give you a wonderful sense of pride to know you carry the name of your ancestors, and you've served the royal family for hundreds of years. I wish I had such a claim to fame.'

'Funny you should say that, but by some strange coincidence, my ancestor George's wife was also named Cara. Cara Cavendish, so you see, you also have a royal lineage.'

'That is rather lovely, although she's not my blood, so it's not really the same, but thank you.' Cara kissed George's cheek.

'What's mine is yours. Anyway, I told you about her before.'

'No, you didn't.'

'I'm certain I did.'

'I'm sure I'd remember if you had.'

'Alright, you win. I won't argue with your freakish memory! I've lost before I begin.'

George had a vivid recollection of telling her. It must have been in the present day. It was easy to get confused; he must be more careful. Just as well she was accustomed to his unreliable memory, or she'd be interrogating him at every turn. He had no answers for the bizarre circumstances he found himself in, so it was better he continue to keep his secret for now.

Edward bid Cara and George goodnight and began to meander home, his spirits high on one too many glasses of sherry. He pondered on what was surely about to happen now that his long time travel buddies had joined him in Victoriana. How exciting.

Neither of them seemed to recognise him, which was a bit of a disappointment. For a minute he'd thought Cara showed a glimmer of recognition, but it quickly faded. It was lonely without a confidant. Carlos was his lover, but Edward didn't share any of the strangeness of time travel with him.

CHAPTER 28

S eville, present day

George reversed his soft top jeep into a visitors' spot in the car park. It was a glorious, sunny Seville morning, and there was a bounce to his step as he dashed through the hotel's revolving doors.

He was excited; it wasn't his usual style to ask a woman out immediately, but this was Cara! He'd been uncharacteristically pushy with his impromptu invitation to drive her to the airport. When she had declined his offer of a drink, he panicked. There was little chance they would meet again if he didn't pursue her in this new Seville life.

Since the moment she'd stumbled into his villa, he'd felt the spark, and the memories had come flooding in.

He didn't understand exactly what was happening, but he knew he must see her again.

'How may I help you, sir?' the receptionist flashed him a bright smile.

'Thank you. I'm here to collect one of your guests: Cara Bailey. We arranged to meet in the lobby, but I can't see her.'

'Please take a seat, and I'll check.'

George sat down in an opulent leather armchair and drummed his fingers on his thigh. Cara had a flight to catch. He calculated it would be at least another fifteen minutes before they got on the road, and then they would most likely be caught in the thick morning traffic.

The receptionist glanced in his direction, and he sensed something was wrong. He rose and approached the reception desk.

'I'm sorry, sir. . .I only just realised that Ms Bailey already checked out.' A light blush stole across her neck, and she shifted her weight from one side to the other, not able to meet his eyes. 'I'm not sure how I missed her,' she mumbled.

'Oh, I see. No problem. You can't know what everyone's up to.' He smiled to reassure the nervous young woman.

'We probably crossed wires about where to meet. I'll give her a quick call. No harm done. Thank you.'

'Well, that's the thing, sir.' Her blush deepened.

'My colleague said she ordered a taxi, and Ms Bailey left for the airport over an hour ago.'

'Oh, right.' George felt winded as he stared at the rosy-cheeked receptionist.

He tried to gather his whirring thoughts.

'Did she leave any message?'

He had to ask. Surely, she wouldn't just leave without letting him know. There must be some misunderstanding, some explanation.

'Give me a moment, please. I'll go and check for messages.'

He wouldn't get to see her after all. What a strange turn

of events. Perhaps she'd had second thoughts. Or, maybe he hadn't allowed her a way to refuse politely, and so she made up an excuse to avoid seeing him. Thoughts bounced around his head. He'd made a fool of himself. It wasn't like him to have his defences so low.

'May I ask your name, sir?'

'Cavendish. George Cavendish.'

'Ms Bailey left a note for you with my colleague.' She pressed an envelope, embossed with the hotel insignia, into his hand.

'Apologies, once again, for not realising Ms Bailey had already checked out.'

He took the envelope and thanked the receptionist, a bemused expression on his face. He tore it open; his heart beat fast as he raced out of the hotel lobby. He jumped into the jeep and read the note.

'Dear George

I'm so sorry I missed you. I had to dash for an earlier flight and didn't want to disturb you by calling at the crack of dawn.

Have a good breakfast meeting and perhaps we'll see each other again.

Kind regards

Cara

p.s Please give my best wishes to Kate.'

George stared at the note. *Kind regards.*

His stomach lurched. She was so formal. Had he completely misread the signals? Why hadn't she messaged him to say she was getting an earlier flight? None of it made any sense—unless she didn't want to see him.

But a little voice in his head said he hadn't imagined the

attraction between them even though she didn't recognise him.

He pulled out into the heavy morning traffic towards the airport. Maybe, there was still a chance of seeing her. He decided he would message her when he arrived; on the off chance she was delayed.

George wasn't a man used to being brushed aside by women. His ego was wounded, but it was more than that. He was devastated, and most confusing of all, he had no idea what had happened to his old life—and now she had no desire to see him. By the sounds of it, she'd taken more of a shine to Kate. Not that he didn't appreciate Kate's charm; she was extremely likeable. Perhaps if he'd said his sister would join them, Cara would have been more at ease to meet them for drinks.

She would be gone soon. He drove as fast as the traffic permitted. A depressing fog settled upon him and he turned on the radio in an attempt to distract himself. He shook his head and wondered what to do for the best. He was agitated and didn't like it one bit.

He pulled in to the airport and decided to call her. He must hear her voice. Perhaps she'd really had to go early. No answer. He had only ever clicked with Cara in this way.

He didn't want to let her go without giving it his best shot. If she wasn't interested, then there was nothing more he could do. He felt a haunting sense of loss.

Cara buckled her seatbelt and stared out of the window at the rays of sun glinting on the smooth, sharp lines of the runway. It was a beautiful day, and the flight was on schedule.

Cara was uneasy about lying to George. She hoped she'd done the right thing. But it didn't feel right. She hadn't known what else to do. She'd fretted late into the night and barely slept. There was no way her conscience would allow her to repeat the same mistake with him, no matter how much she longed to see him. The fall out on both sides would be too great. He didn't know what he was getting into. She must protect them both.

It had been unkind to let him come to the hotel to pick her up. She hated being cruel; especially to him. She couldn't face listening to him talking about his life with Kate, or even worse, flirting as if he was a free agent. She knew she was assuming the worst; it was possible he was genuinely interested in the manuscript and wanted to help. But she couldn't take the chance. If that's all she was to him, then she couldn't bear to face that scenario. However she turned it over in her mind; it was a lose-lose. What a mess she was in. Again.

'Please turn off all electronic devices.'

She fished her phone out of the side pocket of her bag and saw a notification. There was a missed call and a new message—both from George. Of course. No matter what timeline they were in, she recognised his familiar traits. He didn't give up easily.

She read the message:

'Morning. I tried to catch you before your flight for a quick word. Sorry to have missed you. Have a safe journey home. Maybe we can have a drink when I'm next over.'

The pain clawed at her chest. She slumped into her seat, unable to contain her tangle of emotions. She closed her eyes, willing herself to sleep so she could turn off the incessant thoughts.

She must let him go. She must begin a new life without him and leave him to his life with Kate. They simply weren't meant to be together in this timeline.

A thick black wave of depression engulfed her. Not that Tudorville was any better; it looked like she was about to lose him there too. If only she knew what to do for the best.

The cabin crew readied the plane for take-off. She

clamped her eyes shut, fell into a troubled doze, and dreamed about a new scaffold on Tower Green.

Seville, 1840

George and Cara settled into the villa with remarkable speed.

'I feel as though we've lived here for ages. There's something about this place that feels like home,' said Cara.

'Yes, isn't it beautiful? I could see us living here. Let's hope the queen doesn't summon us home any time soon, and we can find sufficient occupation to maintain a good cover.'

'This villa is breathtaking. Carlos is a gem,' said Cara.

'Indeed. I forgot to mention I invited him and Edward over for a drink this evening. We'll have a chance to discuss the manuscript and get a feel for what's going on in Seville, so we have something to report.'

Later that evening George made arrangements with Edward to meet with his contact who had custody of the Tudor Kings' Manuscript. He would commence negotiations to reacquire the three-hundred-year-old document. He was warned it might take some time because Edward thought the collector was reluctant to sell.

Once they had completed their business, Edward said, 'I was wondering—are you by any chance related to a Joanna Cavendish of York?'

George spluttered and almost choked on a mouthful of red wine. That was the last question he'd expected.

'Joanna? That's an unusual name. I can't say I've heard it before. Is there someone, in particular, you're looking for?'

'Yes, she's a friend of mine, and I've lost touch with her. It's been difficult to get word to England with all of the unrest here. With your surname and links with York, I thought you may be related.'

'I'm sorry, no. The name Joanna doesn't ring any bells. Cavendish is a popular name in those parts.'

George excused himself. He was shaken. Why would Edward ask about Joanna who lived two centuries into the future? It seemed too strange to be a coincidence, but what else could it be?

Recently he'd returned to present day and found himself living in this exact villa in Seville. There was no sign of Joanna and no Cara either. For the brief time that he was conscious of what was happening; he'd appeared to be single and living alone. He'd set out to discover what had happened to his life in York, but the vortex had swept him back to Victoriana without any answers. And now this mysterious Edward had arrived on the scene.

He made up his mind to talk to him alone and find out what he knew about Joanna.

Tower of London, 1536

Cara was relieved to be back. She wore a blue and white high-necked gown and a navy headdress trimmed with tiny jewels. The headdress cast a shadow over her pale face and served to obscure her features. She had used cosmetics to etch deep lines on to her face in an attempt to look older than her years. George's mother dressed modestly but in a style which befitted her position as a lady.

She'd obtained permission to visit George, and she had to consciously slow her step to avoid attracting attention. She wanted to run to him, but that wouldn't do. George's mother was a sedate, mature woman, and everything depended on

Cara being cautious. Her heart ticked at an alarming rate as she approached the entrance to Cradle Tower. If she was caught disregarding the king's ruling, who knew what would happen?

The guard escorted her towards the heavy cell door and pushed it open to reveal George, pacing back and forth near the narrow window. He was expecting his mother. Cara hadn't dared risk a message to say she would be coming. She wanted to brighten his morning, and this way her cover was in place should his mail be read.

His eyes widened as he scanned her face, and his chiselled lips broke into a joyous smile. His beard was long, and his once white shirt was now filthy and in tatters. No one would guess he had been one of the king's inner circle.

'My son,' she said, moving towards George, her arms outstretched, smiling.

The guard coughed and stepped back abruptly. He was uncomfortable with emotional scenes.

'Ten minutes. I'll be outside if you need me, ma'am.'

'Thank you,' said Cara.

The door slammed. George appeared welded to the spot.

'Is it truly you?'

Cara raced to him and threw herself into his arms. They held each other in silence. Neither of them moved, not wanting the embrace to end.

He held her at arm's length and examined her face. 'I feared I'd never see you again. How clever of you to come disguised as my mother,' he whispered. 'I should have guessed.'

'You're so thin, my darling. I brought you something to eat.'

George pulled her back into his arms and squeezed her as if he didn't believe she was real.

'I can't breathe,' she laughed but didn't pull away. It was

the most beautiful feeling in the world to be in his arms again.

'I don't think I can eat. You get used to not eating much after a while. I've no appetite.'

Cara broke off a small piece of the hunk of bread and cheese and handed it to him. 'Please try and eat. You must keep your strength up.'

He nibbled the bread and looked at Cara. Her presence lifted his spirits more than any food.

Cara tried to hold back her tears as she looked at his tired face. His eyes were haunted, and his skin sallow. The sight of him plucked at her heartstrings. She thought it must be the most awful thing in the world to love someone more than you love yourself, but be powerless to save them.

The hard bread stuck in his throat, and he began coughing.

'How are Thomas and May?' he managed to wheeze, conscious that the minutes were passing.

'They're fine. Hancock collected them and took them home to Willow Manor. They both sent you their love. They will be safe there.'

'That's good. Well done.' He paused and then said, 'I saw you when you were released, you know.'

'Yes, I saw you too. I knew you were watching over us. My guardian angel.' She squeezed his hand.

He lowered his voice to a whisper. 'But weren't you supposed to go too? Swifty told me the agreement with the king was that you all return to York.'

'Yes, that's right. Hence, my disguise. I thought even Cromwell wouldn't be so cold-hearted as to refuse your mother access, after banishing your wife.'

'You must be careful. If you're recognised by Henry's spies, who knows what he'll do to you? He is irascible when crossed.'

'Don't worry. I'm staying in lodgings with Edward where no one has any idea who we are.'

'That's good. I do worry. There's not much to do in here but think, which inevitably turns to worry.'

'I worry about you too. I think of you all the time. You're the one locked in this godforsaken tower. I wish I were in here with you. I had a vivid dream the other night; it was as though you were calling to me. I walked over here in the middle of the night to be near you.'

George looked startled. 'I did call out your name the other night. It was the strangest thing; I could feel your presence soothing me. I can't remember exactly when it was—the days blend into one another. Perhaps it was the same night.'

Tears spilt down Cara's cheeks. George pulled her close and buried his face in her soft, scented hair. She mustn't see him cry.

'I will have to go soon, my darling. Our ten minutes must be almost up.'

'Yes, I know.' He increased the pressure as he held her small hand in his large one, wishing they could stay like that forever.

She leaned in towards his ear. 'We think there's a high chance of you being pardoned by the king. I don't want to risk breaking you out now, in case it's true. It would only make matters worse if we don't succeed. What do you think? If you want us to break you out, we will put the plan in motion immediately. Just tell me what you want me to do. You know the king's mind better than I.'

They heard the guard shuffling outside the door.

Cara stared at George, beseeching him for an answer. She needed his guidance. He shook his head, unsure what to say.

They held each other tightly for one last moment.

'I'll think it over and get word to you via Swifty. Try and

get some rest. You look exhausted. I'm okay. It'll all be okay, I promise.'

'Alright, my darling. I hate to leave you,' she said.

The guard threw the door open, stuck his face over the threshold and gestured to Cara that it was time to leave. Then he waited outside, leaving them alone.

'I love you,' she said quietly. 'We'll get you out of here and be together again soon. Just let me know.' She ran her fingers down his beloved, gaunt face and kissed him gently on the mouth. As she drew away, he pressed his lips to her hand. He turned abruptly so she wouldn't see the gut-wrenching pain on his face. At the door, she blew him a kiss, tears streamed down her face. 'Goodbye, my love. See you soon.'

He steadied himself and managed to muster a bright smile. He couldn't let her go like this. It could be the last time she saw him, and he didn't want her to remember him as a broken man.

The heavy iron door slammed behind her and George was left alone in the freezing, dank cell, with his dark thoughts. His spirits had been cheered by her brief visit, but the pain of separation now tore at his heart. Being without her was brutal. He didn't know how to bear the loneliness. If it weren't for Cara and the children he would wish himself dead.

Would Henry pardon him? He prayed so, or Cara would be forced into a dangerous life on the run if they succeeded to break him out.

CHAPTER 29

Y ork, present day

Cara was exhausted after the trip to Seville. She took the following morning off work and pottered about the cottage. She felt flashes of sadness but mostly cold, all-consuming anger which seared her soul.

Usually, when separated from George, she felt despondent, as if she had lost a vital body part. Missing him formed a dull ache in her chest, omnipresent, even when she tried to distract herself.

Over time she had grown accustomed to the feeling and had become better at bearing it but could still be brought to her knees in a heartbeat. A memory, a smell, or the sight of something which reminded her of him, was all it took.

But this fiery anger took her by surprise.

Why was she so angry at him? In the grand scheme of

things, this time was no worse than the others. He didn't even know what he'd done so being angry was pointless.

And then the answers flooded in. She had thought they had a second chance. She had believed he was free and they could finally be together after all of the heartache and suspense since that first meeting in the bookshop. The disappointment was crushing. For a fleeting period, she had allowed herself to hope that she and George would have a proper life together. A life composed of more than blissful snatched moments - a life she didn't have to hide. Even when she had met Kate and was hit by the new reality, George pursued her, making it yet more difficult for her to let him go again.

Why did he do it? Did he somehow unconsciously sense their connection? Or did he know more than he was letting on? When he had been married to Joanna, and they had grown so close, sometimes she suspected he knew there was more to their relationship.

Like when they were at Hampton Court Palace. How could he not know on some level about their past? It seemed crazy that he would complicate his life with Kate if there wasn't more to their relationship than a fleeting fancy.

Most of all, she was angry at him for the choices he had repeatedly made; the choices which now dictated their destiny. They must both continue to pay for his weakness, and it made her bloody mad.

'I would kill you with my bare hands if you were here now, George.' Saying the words out loud felt good. She'd been trying to control her anger for too long. He had messed up. If she were to believe in the Twin Flame journey, their souls had made a pact before they inhabited their physical bodies.

They were supposed to reunite against any and all odds.

George had failed miserably, and she must give up on him. She couldn't do this anymore.

Cara's moods fluctuated to the extreme. Occasionally the searing anger dissipated and gave way to an intense longing to feel his arms holding her close against his hard chest, but it soon passed, and the anger bubbled back to the surface.

Consciously or not, he had chosen all of this. He was the reason they weren't together. She had ended her engagement immediately after they had fallen in love because it wouldn't have been fair to stay with Daniel. But George resigned himself to leading a double life, despite the havoc it wreaked on them both. He hung on to his life with Joanna to the point where the time travel powers that be had taken it from him. And now he was with Kate.

She was tired of trying to make a life with him when he would make no space for her in his. This must be part of the Twin Flame journey. Perhaps they both had different lessons to learn, which she was yet to understand. It was all too painful—she had been squeezed dry like a lemon. Her heart had never bled like this before. She had no more left to give.

She hoped the anger would last because it wasn't as painful as the familiar heart-wrenching agony which wracked her soul when she let herself give in to her love for him. It was no good. She would have to find a way to exist without him; at least in this timeline.

Listless and weary, she made a cup of tea in an attempt to soothe her soul, and then sat down at the kitchen table. Even the tea reminded her of George. Everything reminded her of him.

She didn't know what was going on in Tudorville, but she hoped it was better than this mess. Surely, they deserved some luck in one of their lives together. Why did it all have to be so difficult?

Her phone rang. She peered at the screen. It was an

unknown number. Hmmm. Who could that be? She didn't want to talk to anyone and so she let it ring until the voicemail took over. That's what voicemail was for, she reasoned. It was probably one of those automated sales calls anyway.

She browsed her emails and mindlessly deleted, filed and responded to the urgent ones, quickly restoring order to her inbox. If only life was as simple to organise.

Later that evening, she checked her phone and saw there were two notifications of new voicemail messages. She pressed the button and listened.

'Hi, Cari. It's Dad. Haven't seen you for ages. Wondering what you're up to. How are things? Missing you. Call me when you have a moment.'

She'd been terrible about keeping in touch with people lately, even her dear father. Leading a double life, unable to tell people what was really going on, was disorientating.

'Well Dad, I'm a time traveller now. I've fallen for this great guy who married me five hundred years ago, but in this life, he's married to someone else. Well, two someone else's actually.'

She imagined the scenario. Yes, exactly. Who would even believe her? No wonder she had withdrawn.

She pressed the number to listen to the next message, trigger happy, ready to delete it in an instant at the first unwanted word. The number of unsolicited sales calls she received was a constant annoyance.

'Hello, Cara. This is Kate. It was lovely to meet you at the villa in Seville the other day. I'm so sorry you were unwell, and we didn't get a chance to talk properly. George explained that you wanted to know more about the Tudor Kings' Manuscript. It's me that usually deals with those family matters, you see.'

Ouch.

'Anyway, I'm back in London and am free this weekend if

you want to give me a call. I'd be happy to help in any way I can. This is the best number to catch me on.'

There was a pause for a few seconds and then as if as an afterthought, Kate said, 'By the way, my brother was most insistent I call you. He's taken rather a shine to you. He always did have good taste. Hope to hear from you soon. Bye.' Kate laughed, and the message clicked off.

Cara's heart thudded. De-dum-de-dum. What? She was his sister! What a fool. And the memories of their meeting raced through her mind. He'd never once said, meet my wife, or let me introduce you to my wife. And Kate had never said anything about him being her husband. She realised now; they had been no more affectionate than any fond siblings.

Duh!

Cara had jumped to conclusions even though she had initially allowed herself to hope he was free. She had grown so used to not being able to be with him that at the first sign, she'd buckled.

Remorse flooded through her and not for the first time where George was concerned; she felt stupid. Things were rarely as they seemed. When would she learn? He had pleaded with her so many times not to jump to conclusions.

She began to laugh like a lunatic. Loud, joyful peals of laughter rocked her body as tears streamed down her face. Was she mad? Could it really be true that not only was he single, but he also had a wonderful sister who was trying to match-make?

Cara sipped her lukewarm tea, stunned. In less than twenty-four hours she had gone from being optimistic, to the depths of despair, and now ecstatic with relief. How was it possible that such a simple misunderstanding could rock her world to the core?

One thing was certain, the Twin Flame mission, whatever it was, had woken her up. She had never lived so fully and experienced such a range of emotions as she had since falling in love with George. A warm glow spread through her body, and she sat transfixed; unable and not wanting to move.

London, 1536

Cara awoke shivering. Her nightgown was damp and was plastered to her clammy skin. Her head was full of vivid images of George walking to the scaffold on Tower Green.

She shook her head and attempted to shake the dreadful vision. It was only a dream. There was no need to panic. They still had time to save him. She lay there dazed before the nightmare began to recede.

Cara's heart pounded as she jumped out of bed. Worrying wasn't going to help. They would break him out today. What were they waiting for? For King Henry to show mercy? That was a fool's game. The king had never been in a more unpredictable state of mind. She would not leave George's fate in his hands for one more day.

If he could give the order to execute his own devoted wife and replace her within a few weeks, why would he spare George?

Henry had made a clean sweep of the ranks, with Cromwell dancing to his tune, producing evidence on-demand to substantiate the hundreds of trumped-up charges against so many former favourites. Henry only had to point to his next target, and Cromwell found a way to make it work. He was like the devil's conjurer. The truth was of no consequence in this evil court. No one dared question Henry, or they'd find themselves next in line to have their head whipped off. He was out of control.

Barely any of the key players from their inner circle were

left. George was one of the last remaining few of the old guard. Anyone who reminded Henry of his life with Anne had better watch their back.

There was a loud thud. She rushed to the door to find Swifty peering up at her.

'Morning, my lady.'

'Hello, you. What's going on?'

Swifty appearing at her door usually heralded bad news.

She ushered him in. It wouldn't do for anyone to over-hear their conversation.

'What's happening? Pray tell.'

'It's my lord.'

'Yes.' Cara couldn't contain her impatience as Swifty pondered how to break the news to her.

'They came for him at first light. He's for the scaffold today. I slipped away saying I'd deliver the news to his mother, but I must get back. They said I can stay at his side.'

My nightmare was a premonition.

Cara began to tremble and sat down on the edge of the bed.

'We're too late. I can't believe this is happening.'

'What should I do, my lady? Will you accompany me as his mother?'

The young lad, mature beyond his years, looked as though he were about to cry. She hugged him, for her own comfort as well as his.

'You are true and loyal to your master. Thank you. Does Edward know?'

He shook his head. 'I couldn't find him. He was not in his chamber when I knocked.'

Not for the first time she wished she had her mobile phone. If only she could bring it with her when she travelled. Not that she would have anyone to phone. The useless thoughts whirled around her mind.

'Please go and look for him while I get dressed. I'll meet you downstairs in the breakfast parlour in a few minutes.'

'Yes, my lady.'

She hurriedly disguised herself once again as George's mother. Her chest was tight, and her eyelids heavy. There was no time for the luxury of emotional outbursts. A steely determination pushed her on.

Edward paced up and down in the parlour and gestured to the food on the table.

'I can't eat,' she said. 'We're too late. I must go to him, Edward.'

'Yes, of course. Do you think it safe?'

'I don't care at this point. I can't not go. We should have broken him out when we had the chance.'

'It's all moved so fast. How could we know?'

'I blame myself. I should have known. Henry is a deadly opponent once he makes up his mind.'

'I'll come with you. I'm as much to blame as anyone in this mess, if not more so. If I hadn't urged you to travel to the future, none of this would have happened.'

Early morning crowds formed outside the Tower. The turrets blended into the backdrop of the cold, grey sky. A light spitting rain settled on the grass. The smell of sweat mixed with boiling broth hung in the air. It was a fitting scene for the most awful day of Cara's life.

The small crowd was buzzing with anticipation. Even a private execution on Tower Green was a day out: a distraction when someone else's misfortune bolstered the mood of the desperate commoners. They consoled themselves that life wasn't that bad; at least they were alive, unlike the wealthy fool who was about to lose his head. His money hadn't saved him. They believed there was a righteousness to it. They'd rather be poor and honourable than rich and depraved like the nobility at court. Their attitude gave them courage. It was a day of celebration unless you were unfortunate enough to care for the accused.

Cara and Edward were admitted to Tower Green. The scaffold was sturdy, and the execution block readied. The executioner hadn't appeared yet, but the tension was palpable in the damp London atmosphere.

'This is barbaric,' said Cara. 'I can't bear to stay, but I can't leave either. Where is he? I don't see him.'

'He's not been brought out yet. He will come through that door over there.' Edward pointed to a small door at the base of the Tower. 'The locals call it Death's Door.'

A strangled sob escaped Cara's raw throat.

'If George wasn't of high rank, the execution would take place on Tower Hill, and there would be thousands watching,' said Edward.

Events merged one into the other as Cara's panic increased. Time stood still, and all she heard was the drumming of her own heart. Despair consumed her every cell. The nightmare had become a reality. This was the end. Her only wish now was that George would see her for a final few seconds before he met his maker. She wanted him to know she was here with him until the end. He must know she had not forsaken him.

She had run first to the Cradle Tower to see if she could catch him and had asked the guard whether it was possible to admit her. The request had been rebuffed with a sharp, 'You were here yesterday. Cavendish has had his last visitor. We're preparing him for execution.'

The words cut through Cara. The last vestige of hope was extinguished. It was all she could do to not fall to her knees and beg for mercy. But she knew the guard was powerless. He was simply a pawn in Henry's killing machine. She almost broke down, but she would not give anyone the satisfaction of seeing her on her knees unless it would save George. To save him, she would do anything. Pride was expendable. But no, it was no use. She would weep forever, but not now. Not now. She must keep it together and be here for him; a symbol of all that had been good about their life together.

She felt a double loss. Now she would be without him in both timelines. Yes, this really was the end. Perhaps her time travel era was over. Once he was gone, the cycle would be complete. She remembered Sylvia holding the Twin Flame card, talking about their Twin Flame mission. Sylvia said their reunion would help to raise the consciousness of the planet.

Well, the mission had failed. It was about to be aborted. Cara was rarely beaten, but a bitter taste of loss filled her mouth. What other misery was in store for her? She had had her fill and wanted no more. She wanted to die with him. What was all of this grand plan for if it was only to end like this?

Her Tudor conditioning reminded her that to wish to die was a sin against her creator. She thought of Thomas and May and how much they needed her. Even the thought of their dear, tender hearts did nothing to restore her desire to live. She didn't want to be in Tudorville without him. Life was too cruel. Despite her best intentions to be stoic, the tears seeped from her eyes and spilt on to her cold cheeks.

Edward nudged her when George stumbled through the door, pushed along by the guard, hood pulled down over his head; wrists bound.

The executioner followed behind, heavy axe in hand. Murmurs rippled through the crowd. Everyone was in place. It would be over in a few minutes. Cara was breathless and feared she would faint. Only the thought of George looking for her kept her on her feet.

Edward encircled her shoulders with his arm, and she leant against him. They were a couple of rows back from the scaffold.

George's hood was removed, and he squinted as his eyes adjusted to the light. He looked up and saw her. Even at a distance, she could feel his love. She made an effort to smile for him, but it was more of a grimace.

He smiled back and mouthed, 'I love you forever.'

Cara blew him a kiss. 'We will meet again, my love. I am with you always,' she called, hoping he would catch her words over the noise of the crowd.

She touched her heart with both hands and gestured towards him. She didn't know if he could see but she thought he looked comforted.

George paid the executioner and officially forgave him for what he was about to do.

The executioner pushed him down towards the block and steered George's head into position.

Cara gasped. This was it. She steeled herself for the final axe-blow. She had recently witnessed her mistress, the queen, being executed, not imagining that her husband would soon follow.

King Henry stood in the vestibule with Cromwell.

'You'd better hurry, sire, or you'll miss it,' said Cromwell.

CHAPTER 30

S eville, 1840

George itched to talk to Edward again, but it proved surprisingly difficult to orchestrate. Over the coming days, they frequently met socially but were never alone long enough for George to broach the subject of Joanna.

He grew more restless by the day. Being in Victoriana with Cara was like a dream come true, but what of his old life in York? He seemed to have gained a sister but lost a wife and daughter. It was disorientating, and he was nervous about what other surprises awaited him on his next trip.

George hadn't been able to get Edward's comment about Joanna out of his mind. There was something familiar about him, but he couldn't figure out what it was.

Could Edward be the missing link between now and then? The more time he spent in Victoriana, the more entangled his memories became.

He'd been to his townhouse and watched from a distance as Joanna arrived home on the arm of another man. He'd waited for Jane, but she didn't appear.

Where was she? He missed her, of course, but in a strange way, it was as though he'd never lived the old life. He wasn't surprised to find he was unmoved by seeing Joanna with another man; he felt no jealousy and no regrets. He was relieved she looked happy and it seemed that as if by magic he was released from their marriage.

He had no idea how or why their lives had switched like this, but he was grateful for a second chance. He was now free to be with Cara. But first, he would need to get her attention. He must win her heart all over again. It occurred to him that she might not be single in this strange, new paradigm where all the players had changed position, like a game of musical chairs. That would be a cruel twist of fate.

He wanted to find Jane, but to do that he needed to learn how time travel worked, and he sensed Edward was the key.

He had been amazed to find that almost two hundred years into the future he lived in the same villa he now shared with Cara in Seville. No wonder he was confused.

How could she have been so in love with him both in Victoriana and York, but in this new version of events, not even be interested in seeing him? She hadn't recognised him when they met, but he was sure there had been a connection. He had begun to fear he might be delusional. What if he had imagined the other lives?

There was so much he didn't understand; there were empty pockets of time where he didn't know what had happened. In present day, he didn't always understand what had been going on, but then suddenly visions and memories would hit him. He hoped Edward could help him to make sense of the chaos. He had no other leads if he was wrong about Edward.

Each time he travelled back to the future, he uncovered a little more of his old life. The most alarming thing was he was deeply in love with a woman who didn't know him. He had been stunned when Cara walked into the Seville villa. Here was his beloved wife from two hundred years ago, but she had no idea who he was. He'd blown it by moving too fast, and she had run away. What an idiot. He didn't know what to do; he was desperate. What if he couldn't find her again?

He wondered whether his sister had managed to speak to her yet. He had been most persistent that Kate call, to the point where she had teased him about having a Cara crush.

He had dismissed the notion in the way only a big brother can and told her not to be such a foolish girl. But he knew he hadn't hoodwinked her.

And then one day that week the stars aligned. Cara was busy being a social butterfly at a ladies' luncheon hosted by a friend of Queen Victoria's. Carlos was called away from home on urgent business shortly after George arrived for an afternoon visit.

'You two relax and have a drink while I attend to this unexpected nonsense. I shall be back in no time at all, and then we'll dine on the terrace,' said Carlos.

He dashed off to ask the cook to postpone lunch.

'Are you happy with the progress we have made so far on acquiring your family's manuscript?' asked Edward.

'Yes, it seems to be moving along nicely. The chap was resistant to the idea of selling at first, but last time we talked he was open to a better offer. I feel sure we can come to an arrangement soon.'

'That's great news. I'm pleased I was able to be of service to you and Her Majesty.'

'I haven't thanked you properly. What a stroke of luck that you were able to introduce me to the collector.'

Edward smiled. He liked George just as much in Victoriana as he did in Tudorville. It was challenging to avoid saying something that might alarm him. He was intrigued to find out whether George had any memory of his other lives, and suspected he did after his strange reaction when he had enquired about Joanna.

'I was thinking about our conversation the other day,' said George. 'You know you asked me about your friend, Joanna?'

'Oh, yes.' Edward coughed and attempted to appear nonchalant.

'I was wondering whether you and I may have met before —in another time,' said George. He looked Edward straight in the eyes, and held his breath.

Edward paused. 'We have indeed,' he said, after a moment, smiling, and returning the direct stare. 'I'm pleased it's coming back to you.'

'Am I right in thinking you are a fellow traveller?' asked George.

'Yes, that's correct. May I ask if you are thinking of a particular destination?' said Edward.

'York. What do you know of my life in York? You mentioned Joanna.'

'Your family has roots going back to before the reign of Henry VIII. There was a George Cavendish who I knew back then in Tudor York. His wife's name was Cara.'

George sat down. 'So, it's true. You also travel. I don't know what to make of it all. If I didn't experience it myself, I would think it too incredible. I have to say it's a great relief to meet you.'

'Likewise. I wanted to talk to you the other day but didn't know what else to say. You didn't respond well to my question about Joanna.'

'I'm sorry about that. I was unprepared. It's so much to take in.'

'It isn't an easy life. But it gets better when you have friends. Before Cara came to ask for my help at the university campus in the future, I had no idea there were others. I thought I was alone in that timeline, as well as this one. It's been tough in Victoriana too, so it was a relief when you and Cara arrived in Seville. I'm sorry if I startled you. I was impatient and wanted to know if you remembered me.'

'Thank goodness you said something or I wouldn't have suspected anything. When did Cara come to see you at the university? What university?'

Edward chuckled. 'It's only to be expected you will have a lot of questions. Cara and I are friends in Tudorville, as well as two hundred years into the future or what we call 'present day'.

'Cara? You mean Cara is aware that she time travels? I thought it was just me.'

'You had better sit down. This will take a while. I will begin at the beginning. At least it will be the beginning, according to what I remember. I have no way of knowing when we all started out together. We could have lived in other timelines and not be aware of them yet. For all I know, we may have been together for millions of years.'

George nodded. 'I knew nothing of any of this until I woke up in a different life. There was no warning; just—bam! Was it the same for you?'

'Yes, we have no idea until we're in a new life. And even then, we don't remember everything. It all depends whether we're conscious of our travel; sometimes we don't know what's happening, as I suspect is the case with Cara in this timeline.'

Edward brought George up to speed on events in Tudorville: George's marriage to Cara, their children, and how they were trying to save him from execution at the Tower of London.

George stared at him. 'Cara and I are married in Tudor times as well as now? How mind-boggling.'

As Edward talked, memories unlocked in George's mind. It was like watching a movie. He saw snippets of his time in Tudorville, including Edward as his children's tutor.

'Over the coming days, you will remember snippets. It's like updating your software. You will understand more as time goes on. One day you'll wake up, and perhaps even be conscious of additional lives,' said Edward. 'Memories flood in, and it all starts to make sense.'

'I'm puzzled about my life in the future. I seem to have lost my old life and now have a new one. I only just met Cara, and she ran away from me!'

'Oh yes, she told me about that. She said you were being an arse.'

'Oh,' said George, looking hurt. 'Why on earth would she say that? All I did was try to help her with the Manuscript and offer to take her to the airport. She was quite cold, which floored me. It isn't like her.'

'She said you're married; this time to a woman called Kate. Oh. . .and that you asked her out. She said she wouldn't put you both through all of that again.'

'Oh, lord. Oh no,' said George, shaking his head. 'If that's what she thinks, no wonder she didn't wait for me at the hotel!' George laughed. Her odd behaviour was beginning to make sense. Thank God for that.

'What?' asked Edward. 'I'm afraid I must be out of the loop on the latest developments.'

'Edward, you know so much more about how this travelling business works. Is it possible for me to go to the future whenever I want? Like, now, I mean? I must see Cara. I need to clear up this misunderstanding about Kate. I can see why she thinks me an arse and couldn't get away from me fast enough. I'm finally single, but she thinks my sister is my wife!'

'What?' repeated Edward. 'I'm so confused. You mean Kate isn't your wife?'

'No, of course not. She's my baby sister. And fortunately, rather a fabulous one.'

Edward beamed. 'Oh, I say, that is excellent news, absolutely wonderful news. There's nothing more tiresome than you two being at loggerheads. Negotiating Brexit would be more peaceful! The countess was in a terrible state about this new marriage business. I did try to tell her that she had probably got the wrong end of the stick, but you know how stubborn she can be. She wouldn't listen.'

'Countess? Is Cara a countess? And what's Brexit? Sounds like a breakfast cereal.'

'It's a long story. Trust me; you're no worse off not knowing. It will all come back to you in good time. We'll fill you in as we go along.'

George looked puzzled. 'Yes, I might have had enough for one day.'

'Never mind. You'll soon get the hang of it. We're only living three simultaneous lives, after all! In answer to your question, unfortunately, we have not yet mastered how to travel to different timelines on demand. It was my meddling, trying to send Cara to the future on a special mission, that disrupted your timeline and overwrote your old life. In the future, I mean.'

'It's so confusing,' said George. 'So, if I've understood correctly, she was only pretending not to know me in Seville?'

'Yes, that's right. She didn't think you would know her. Some people have no clue. Carlos is like that. He's a sleeper traveller; he has absolutely no memory of knowing me in another life. I've given up hoping he will remember. Cara believes you're the reincarnated soul of your ancestor; her husband, from Tudorville—not a time traveller. Mind you, it's all very new to her too. I admit, I thought that was a bit far-fetched, but who's to say?'

'I wish I could go and see Cara now to put things straight in the future. I may even be back in time for lunch. It's not as if I don't want to be here.'

'Quite so, but I'm afraid we have no control over it. I hope to do some more experiments soon, but Tudorville is so fraught with danger, we haven't had the luxury of time to test my latest theories.'

'What have you been up to? I'm starving, let's eat.' Carlos entered the room, and their conversation came to an abrupt halt.

Halfway through lunch, George signalled to Edward that he was about to travel. The vortex had summoned him. Edward smiled as he ate. It would all be sorted out, and the countess would be happy again.

'How was your afternoon?' Edward asked Cara, upon her return.

They made polite chit chat until it was time for Cara and George to return to their villa.

'Goodnight all. See you again soon, I hope,' said Cara. Carlos hurried ahead to escort them out, and George followed. Cara hung back before turning to Edward, 'See you when I see you,' she said.

Edward stared at her. Her eyes twinkled with a mischievous glint. He couldn't help laughing.

'Here you are. I didn't think you knew me,' he said.

'Oh, I'd know you anywhere, Professor.'

She hurried over to him and kissed his cheek. 'Night, night,' let's catch up soon.

Seville was going to be a lot more fun from now on.

London, 1536

'No. You do it,' said the king. I haven't the stomach for any more grand ceremonies. Make the declaration.'

Cromwell hurried out and whispered to the executioner who then moved aside.

Cara struggled to breathe. Something important must be happening. She prayed for a miracle. No one ranked as highly as Cromwell except for the king himself.

The king's chief advisor extracted a note from the pocket of his black cloak, his face solemn.

'I hereby declare George Cavendish, accused and found guilty of treason, is to receive a full pardon, this day, by order of our most merciful king and ruler of The Church of England. New evidence has exonerated him, and he is now free to go.'

There was a cheer for the king. It mattered not one way or another to the crowd whether George lived. All they cared for was the drama.

'Long live the king,' roared his subjects, entertained by the unexpected turn of events.

People all around the Tower broke into animated conversation.

Cara gasped and stumbled on the sodden grass of Tower Green; her foot caught in the hem of her gown, as she strained to see George. Edward stooped to help her up. Tears streamed down both of their faces, and they clutched at each other, not believing their good fortune.

Cara ran to George and flung herself into his arms, kissing his lips and face. His skin was ashen, clammy beads of sweat clung to his upper lip, but she sprang straight into action.

'Let's get you away from here. It won't do to linger.' Cara steered George away from Tower Green, Edward and Swifty followed closely behind.

George paused and said, 'I should quickly go and thank the king or at least Cromwell.'

'No, please, no, George. I beg you let us not delay or take any chance that he may change his mind. Please come away with me now, and we'll gather our wits and leave for Willow Manor. You can write to him from home.'

Cara touched his shoulder, as if uncertain he wasn't merely a figment of her imagination. Her eyes implored him to accompany her. He nodded and clasped her slender fingers in his large, comforting hand. She was home.

Cara sobbed all the way back to their lodgings through the rainy streets of London. He soothed her, but the tears wouldn't stop, and her whole body shook.

'You're in shock, my darling. There, there. It's all over now, my love.'

His filthy shirt was drenched in sweat.

At the lodgings, George washed for the first time in weeks, and they ordered a light meal which they ate beside the roaring fire in their bed-chamber. Their tired eyes glowed in the firelight.

'It feels almost too good to be true,' she said. 'It was so close. I nearly lost you forever.'

George kissed her but he couldn't keep his eyes open, and nodded off.

A few minutes later, Cara roused him from the chair and helped him into bed. He was asleep within seconds.

She removed her heavy blue gown and tucked in beside him, covering them both with the soft bedding. She sank into the mattress and wrapped her arm around him. The emotion and exhaustion had taken its toll.

As she fell asleep, she knew that home was wherever they were together; it mattered not, which timeline, city or country.

They slept undisturbed in each other's arms for hours. Bliss. The were reunited in Tudorville.

CHAPTER 31

L ondon, 1536

Cara was worried the king would summon George to court.

'Let us not tempt fate by staying here longer than necessary,' she said. 'He has pardoned you. It would be just like him to want you back at his side now. He's like a jealous child.'

'Don't fret, darling. I'm confident we're in the clear. The king has a new wife and a court overflowing with sycophants to pander to his every whim. We will travel home to Willow Manor forthwith, and I shall write to thank him from there as you suggest. There's nothing to detain us. We are finished with London, at least for the present.'

'You're still not well. You were confined to that damp cell for weeks. Shall we have a doctor look you over before we set off? It's a long, arduous journey even at this time of year.'

'I'm fine, a little tired that's all,' said George. 'Let us make a start this afternoon and stop at Madame Alicia's for the night. I'd like to thank her again and arrange compensation for her help when we were on the run. We can then wake up after a good night's sleep and make the final leg home in the morning.'

Despite his words, she knew he wasn't in good shape. His ordeal had weakened him, and he was bruised all over. He didn't tell her exactly what they had done to him in the Tower, and she didn't press. They were both keen to put this dark period behind them.

That afternoon George, Cara, Edward and Swifty packed up their meagre possessions and set off for York, via carriage, on The Great North Road. Cara breathed a sigh of relief.

The journey passed without upheaval. This time there were no wanted posters plastered over the trees, no bounty hunters and no soldiers hunting them down. George nodded off to the gentle rumble of the carriage wheels, and she snuggled into him, savouring his closeness.

She had barely any memory of life in Tudorville prior to them being on the run. It would be a new experience to live a normal life, although she imagined it could only ever be as normal a life as a time traveller was able to live. But she would take any life with him. Maybe one day she would confide in him. She would tell him the truth. He would understand. If she could find the right words, there was nothing she couldn't tell him. There had been no chance for her to confide in him before because they had needed all their wits about them just to stay alive. It had been an intense time since the moment she was transported to Tudorville and found herself in Newgate Prison.

Cara gazed out of the carriage window at the passing windblown trees. She longed for the ordinariness of a normal life together. She was certain she would never forget to appreciate what other couples took for granted.

She didn't know for how long she would travel back and forth to Tudorville, but she vowed to make every day count.

How wonderful that they would be together in the future too. It had been so close to being over for them, but after all of the heartache, George was single. She broke into a spontaneous smile, and her heart filled with joy when she recalled the moment Kate casually mentioned she was George's sister.

Cara knew in her soul they would be reunited. He was irresistibly drawn to her even though he didn't understand why. She nestled her head on George's shoulder and fell into a contented doze.

Cara awoke as the carriage came to an abrupt stop and she lurched forward.

'We're here, wake up, George,' she touched his arm to rouse him. She saw Madame Alicia and Edward talking outside as she helped George to his feet.

Madame Alicia greeted them. My lord and lady Cavendish. I'm so relieved to see you safe and sound. I understand you are on your way home.'

'Yes, thank you. By the grace of God, George was pardoned, and we're free. We wish to rest for the night if you have room for us and to thank you once again for your assistance when we were in such difficulties. We owe you our lives.'

'It is an honour. Of course, of course. Come in out of this dreadful weather. I have the perfect room for you.'

That evening they made a merry party. Madame Alicia's table was replete with tasty dishes. They dined, drank and were entertained by a roving band of players who performed a masque about the latest court intrigues. Freedom had never tasted so fine.

As the hour grew late and the flame in the fireplace dwindled to a pale golden glow, George whispered to Cara, 'We'd better go to bed. Let us leave at dawn. I can't wait to see the children's little faces. I sent a note to my father so they will be awaiting us.'

'Yes, let's. That's a splendid plan.' They bid the revellers goodnight, excused themselves and walked hand in hand up the staircase to their room.

George closed the door behind them. Cara was about to ready herself for bed, but George caught her hand and spun her into his arms. He then manoeuvred her against the wall, bent his head and crushed her lips with his. His tongue teased her mouth until they were both breathless with desire. They hadn't made love in weeks.

'Ooh. I thought you wanted an early night,' she said.

'That's exactly what I want.'

He pressed his lean, hard body against hers, his desire building. There wasn't an ounce of fat on him after his sojourn in the Tower.

Cara melted; he knew exactly how to inflame her. She craved him. They were made for each other's touch. She clawed at his shirt and unfastened the buttons, removing the garment and running her hands across his broad chest.

She trailed seductive kisses down the side of his neck, across his shoulder, and down the inside of his arm until her lips reached the tender skin of his wrists, sore from the handcuffs. She pushed herself into him and felt him shiver against her. Then, slowly, she released the firm length of his manhood, which strained against the crotch of his breeches.

Sex was exquisite between them. George had never known such pleasure before. He was no innocent and had enjoyed many a sexual rampage with the king in their younger years. He'd been with some of the most beautiful women in England, but nothing could compare with this. It transcended the act of pure sex. The term lovemaking didn't do it justice either. When they made love, they became one.

She could take him from zero to ten on the desire scale, in seconds. When they came together, it was like the eruption of a volcano.

There was no effort involved. It was an exquisite merging of mind, body and spirit. They knew intuitively what the other needed.

They were connected between timelines and distance by an invisible chord. Even their own ego fuelled folly hadn't succeeded in separating them. Their Twin Flame bond was unbreakable. Theirs was a love that would never die. They lay satiated in each other's arms and fell into a blissful sleep.

The following afternoon, the carriage turned into a long driveway lined with tall willow trees. George and Cara heard high pitched chattering voices in the distance. The children ran as fast as they could down the driveway, Cornelius at their heels, barking and wagging his tail.

The carriage drew up outside Willow Manor. Thomas and May threw themselves at George and Cara as they opened the door. George's parents rushed out to meet them. There were happy tears and hugging all round.

They were home. The ordeal was finally over, and the Cavendish family reunited.

York, present day

George raised his hand to knock on Cara's front door.

Suddenly he regretted his decision and let his hand fall to his side. He turned and hurried out of the driveway, hoping she hadn't spotted him.

A big drawback of instantaneous time travel was that there were no empty pockets of time to plan what to do or say upon arrival at one's destination. He had been in Seville in 1840, and then with the blink of an eye, here he was, almost two centuries later, outside Cara's cottage. He wished for the luxury of a long drive or flight to mull things over.

What if she thought him quite mad? He was worried if he said the wrong thing he would spook her like last time. They barely knew each other in this life.

Coming straight here to discuss their five-hundred-year love affair had seemed like the most brilliant idea, until now —until he arrived. George paced up and down the lane that ran around the back of the cottage. Before they lost their other life, they had walked here together, hand in hand, many times. The crisp evening air hit his face and began to soothe his agitated senses. He walked up and down for twenty minutes, uncertain what to do next.

Cara heard a knock at the door. She wasn't expecting anyone. She moved her bedroom curtain to peek outside, but there was no car in the driveway beside hers.

Curiosity got the better of her, and she bounced down the stairs to open the front door. Her mood had elevated since Kate's message. Life was beautiful again.

'George! What are you doing here? I mean, how did you find me?'

His tall frame towered over the low Tudor doorway; his presence was intoxicating. He was the last person she had expected to see tonight. Appearing suddenly like this was what the old George used to do.

'You didn't return my calls, so I decided that turning up might be the best way to get your attention.' He pushed his dark floppy hair out of his eyes and an appealing smile lit up his face.

'I was going to call you,' said Cara, grateful she had eventually showered and dressed.

She looked at him, barely able to believe he was here. He was irresistible when he turned on the charm. It wasn't a fair game. 'Come in,' she said and stood aside to usher him into the hallway.

'I know this place,' he said. 'I've been here before, haven't I?'

'Yes. Yes, you have. Many times.' She nodded. There was no point pretending otherwise.

'How do you know?'

'I've been talking to our friend Edward.'

'Ah. Well, in that case, you arriving like this makes perfect sense. Do you remember us spending time here together or did he tell you about it? You've been here a lot over the past year or so.'

'Since my talk with Edward, it's beginning to come back to me. It's unbelievable—a bit like watching a movie trailer; I only see snippets. I remember this cottage. And I've even started to remember things about Tudorville. I don't understand how I didn't know any of that before.'

'It's quite a thing to get your head around, that's for sure,' she said. 'It's the same for me and Eddie.'

'Eddie?'

'Yes, Eddie Makepeace. In this timeline, he's a professor in quantum physics at the Royal Holloway University. That's where I met him. I wouldn't understand much about time travel if it weren't for him. Not that I understand all that much even now.'

'He is the link between us, isn't he? I knew it the minute he appeared in Victoriana. But I didn't think you knew anything about it,' said George.

'I've known since that day we met at the bookshop. That's when it all started for me.' Cara smiled. She could sense that beneath his bravado, he was nervous.

'Our meeting unlocked my ability to time travel. Although I wasn't aware of being in Victoriana until Eddie showed up the other day.'

George reached for her hand. 'Come here,' he said. 'It's so good to be able to talk about everything with you like this. I've been going crazy trying to figure it all out alone.'

She moved slowly into his arms, her eyes dewy as their lips brushed.

'I thought you were married to Kate,' she said, in a whisper.

'I know. I mean, I had no idea. I couldn't understand why you fled from the hotel, but then Edward, I mean Eddie, told me. I hear you called me an arse. That was quite shocking for a Victorian lady by the way!'

'Yes, well, you can be a terrible arse. I've lost track of how many times.'

'That's not entirely fair,' he said, laughing. 'I didn't marry my sister. You simply misunderstood.'

'That's true,' she said. 'Kate left me a message earlier. It was only then it made sense. I had begun to reconcile myself to never seeing you again.'

'Thank goodness Kate called.'

'Yes. I'll let you off this time. It was my mistake,' she laughed.

'That's very good of you, Mrs Cavendish.'

'Am I *Mrs Cavendish* here too now?'

'Not officially I suppose although we can easily remedy that, but let's not get bogged down with all of that nonsense. We married five hundred years ago and then again two hundred years ago. What's a couple of hundred years between husband and wife?'

'I do love being married to you,' she said. 'I've got an idea for us to celebrate, married or not.'

'Okay, let's hear it.'

'No, I'll surprise you instead. Grab your bag, and let's go.'

'I don't have a bag.'

'You came all the way from Spain without any luggage? Do you want to pick up a change of clothes? We'll be staying somewhere overnight.'

'I came from Seville in the year 1840. When you move between timelines do you travel with luggage?'

'No, of course not. I forgot you've come from back then. How is Cara by the way? Is she behaving herself?'

'Only as much as she ever does. She's a handful at the best of times,' he said. 'You could put in a good word for me.'

They laughed. 'I'll see what I can do. How about grabbing some things from your house?'

'That would be wonderful if I had any things; or more to the point, if I had a house. As far as I know, I no longer have a house in York, never mind a wardrobe full of clothes. It's part of the collateral damage of the disrupted timeline which, according to Eddie, was a result of you two meddling and trying to turn back time.'

Cara looked sheepish. 'Oh yes, I keep forgetting! Sorry about that. You'll just have to live with me then.'

'I could get used to that,' he said.

'I won't pretend to be sad you're not married to Joanna. It was hell. I've been so angry I could have killed you, especially when I saw you with Kate. I thought we were about to go through the whole nightmare again.'

'I'm sorry, my darling. But I didn't know about our past when I married Joanna. What was I supposed to do?'

'I don't know. Not marry her? Leave her?' she said, pulling a face. Those are just a few suggestions for you in case we ever have a similar scenario in a different timeline.

Lord, I do hope we don't. I must have cried enough tears for ten lifetimes this past year.' She paused. 'Anyway, it's over now. We've survived. Joanna seems fine. I saw her with another guy.'

'Yes, I saw them too. The doppelgänger who's taken over my house!'

'Don't be like that,' said Cara. 'As you said, it isn't your house anyway. You have a beautiful villa in Seville, which, by the way, we first lived in together in Victoriana so it must surely be half mine!'

'That's not strictly true,' he said.

'How so?'

'We were only renting in 1840.'

Cara sighed. 'Wait a few years. You'll see.'

'Oh, that's unfair. What do you know about the future that I don't?'

'A lot! But I don't want to spoil it for you. You've enough to be digesting in the meantime.'

'Spoilsport,' he said.

She locked the cottage door, and they jumped into her vehicle.

'Will you tell me where we're going?'

'No. It's a surprise.'

'Oh, go on. Tell me!'

'No. Be patient. I promise you'll love it.'

'I'm sorry about your daughter by the way. I can't imagine how hard it is. You must miss her terribly.' She squeezed his hand.

'Fortunately, I don't have to.'

'Oh. Why's that then?'

'Jane is still my daughter. She's at university. She's the same; only older. It's remarkable—no idea how it worked out as it did, but people always did remark that she took after me.'

'Wow! I was worried about Jane but wasn't sure how much you'd remember. So were you married to her mother? I'm scared to ask.'

'Yes, until Jane was five years old, and then we split up. Her mother remarried, but I've been close to Jane throughout. I can only remember bits of it so far. Edward said I'll remember more as time goes on.'

Cara nodded. 'That's brilliant news. Thank goodness. I might have guessed there would be another marriage in the mix somewhere,' she teased.

'I seem to be the marrying kind, don't I?'

'Indeed, you do!'

Cara touched his hand and smiled. He could have been married fifty times, but she cared not a jot. He was free now, and they were together. That was all that mattered.

They turned into a long driveway, lined with tall willow trees. Cara slowed down and then stopped next to a sand-blasted sign which read, *Willow Manor*.

She turned to look at George.

'Remember this?'

'This is it! Are we home?' said George. 'Edward told me about Willow Manor. Looks as though I have a house in York, after all.'

'Yes, we're home. For one night, anyway. I'm so happy you remember.'

They parked and entered the lobby of the Tudor style country hotel, holding hands.

'Let's hope they have a room for us for the night.'

'Cara?'

'Yes?'

'I love your surprises.'

'Yay. I love you,' she said, kissing him, and linking her arm through his.

They arrived at the front desk to enquire about a room. A

tall man with dark, glossy hair, turned to them, and smiled. It was a present-day Carlos.

'Welcome to Willow Manor. How may I help you?' he said.

George and Cara looked at each other, stunned.

'That's it. I'm texting Eddie. There's no harm in giving time a little helping shove, is there?' she said, as Carlos organised their check-in.

'Absolutely not,' said George. 'Go for it.'

Carlos handed them a key, and they walked up the old winding staircase.

As they opened the door to their room, a greyhound appeared at their feet, wagging his tail. Cara bent down, delighted. She stroked him, and he rolled over for her to tickle his tummy.

'Look, George, look. It's Cornelius; you gave him to me as a present to celebrate our marriage in Tudorville.'

'Hello, beautiful boy. It's been a while.' He stroked the dog's shiny head. Cornelius barked, excited at all of the fuss.

They entered the room, and Cornelius immediately settled down on the rug at the foot of the bed, snuggled up and fell asleep.

They were home.

THE UPRISING (TWIN FLAMES BOOK 2) YORK, PRESENT DAY, ONE YEAR LATER

I t was a rainy Monday evening, the kind when Cara and George were happy to be home at the cottage. George cooked spaghetti for dinner, while Cara replied to emails at the kitchen table. George's phone rang, interrupting the comfortable silence. He dried his hands on the tea towel.

'Hello?'

Cara looked up from her laptop as she listened to her husband's side of the conversation. The hairs on the back of her neck stood up. The vortex was near—she sensed she was about to time travel for the first time in a year. She wondered who was on the phone.

And then she was gone. . .

Get The Uprising on Amazon.

A NOTE TO MY DEAR READERS

I wrote Twin Flames during an extraordinary period in my life when I lived as a Digital Nomad. On my travels, I stayed in thirty locations, including Richmond, Windsor, Fulham, Chelsea, Cheltenham and Stockholm.

I made numerous research visits to the Tower of London and Hampton Court Palace, to glean a sense of what it was like for Cara and George at the Tudor court.

I hope you loved reading Twin Flames. If you did, please leave a review on your Amazon.

Reviews make such a difference—with your support I can keep writing. Thank you so much!

Please join my newsletter for updates:

www.Rachelhenke.com/subscribe

Love

Rachel

ACKNOWLEDGMENTS

Thank you to Russell Cooper for your patient, skilled editing, and for championing me to write a beautiful time travel love story even when I doubted my ability. Twin Flames wouldn't have made it into print without you.

Thank you to Kim Kaase, for all the hours spent discussing Twin Flames, and for your friendship and unwavering support as I wrote this novel during my Digital Nomad year.

And thank you to my wonderful family, for always encouraging me to follow my inspiration, no matter how bold the dream!

ABOUT THE AUTHOR

Rachel is an avid reader of historical romance and fascinated by all things mystical. Her discovery of the ancient Twin Flame phenomenon, coupled with her love of time travel romance, inspired her to finally write her first novel after years of only dreaming about it.

Soon after, Cara and George popped into her head and began telling their story of star-crossed soul mates, in love for five hundred years.

Rachel is also the author of the Amazon bestselling personal transformation book, Living Fearlessly.

She believes life's too short to be afraid, and lives in Surrey, penning romance novels in the sun—weather permitting.

Get new release updates, and author news by signing up to Rachel's newsletter:

www.Rachelhenke.com/subscribe

ALSO BY RACHEL HENKE

See a complete list of Rachel's books and follow on Amazon:

www.amazon.co.uk/Rachel-Henke/e/B004ZGD4Z8

www.amazon.com/Rachel-Henke/e/B004ZGD4Z8

Printed in Great Britain
by Amazon